her
GLORIOUS
SUNSHINE
AWAITS

Printed in Australia
Cover and internal design by Shawline Publishing Group Pty Ltd

First printing: September 2023

Shawline Publishing Group Pty Ltd
www.shawlinepublishing.com.au

Paperback ISBN 978-1-9229-9363-2
eBook ISBN 978-1-9229-9375-5

Distributed by Shawline Distribution and Lightning Source Global

 A catalogue record for this work is available from the National Library of Australia

More great Shawline titles can be found by scanning the QR code below.
New titles also available through Books@Home Pty Ltd.
Subscribe today at www.booksathome.com.au or scan the QR code below.

her GLORIOUS SUNSHINE AWAITS

TRACEY FRIDAY

Also by Tracey Friday:

Thursday's Child
From Orchards to Outback

To Debbie,

My awesome best friend, as we approach 50 years of fabulous laughter and priceless friendship.

During this time, I have witnessed you in full reader mode by devouring a chunky book in a single sitting, hence my ambitious challenge to write a story that hopefully takes you into a second day.

Deb, please start reading late afternoon to give me a fighting chance!

CHAPTER ONE

SYDNEY 1925

'SILENCE IN COURT!' bellowed the judge, ramming his portly knuckles down onto the pockmarked bench to hoist himself up. Then, in sheer desperation, he picked up three bulky leatherbound ledgers and slammed them down with force. The action caused his expensive fountain pen to roll off the bench onto the wooden floor and he cussed through clenched teeth when he noticed the splash of black ink on his polished boot. He was utterly confounded because the aggressive thud had no effect whatsoever in quieting the unruly crowd.

Alice Johnson slowly squeezed her way across the room. It was no easy task. Her tiny body was being continually pummelled like she was caught in the middle of a herd of cattle that threatened to stampede. The men towered way above her, their sway causing fresh bruises on her already painful feet as each step she took became more difficult than the one before. It was scary, but she was used to the confinement. Managing to stay relatively calm, she fought to plough through the raucous courtroom toward the exit.

'SILENCE I SAY, OR I WILL LOCK YOU ALL UP, SO HELP ME GOD.' The judge placed his pen back on the bench, thankful for small mercies that the nib showed no obvious sign of damage, then he reached under his robes for his pistol. He had no other option; the police were seriously outnumbered and the situation was escalating out of control.

The sleeve of his plush red robe plummeted to his armpit when he aimed the pistol to the ceiling and pulled the trigger out of extreme frustration. He cowered his head, half expecting the ceiling plaster to rain upon him from the thunderous shot but miraculously, it remained intact.

He was at the end of his tether and knew it was unethical but it had the desired effect as silence immediately replaced sonorous.

Alice jumped out of her skin from the booming shot and was on the brink of bursting into tears. It had taken her almost six minutes to work the room, being ever mindful of her father's strict instructions that never altered beyond the need of getting the job done and getting out as fast as she could. She took comfort in knowing that her father was tracking her like a hawk even though he couldn't clearly see her all of the time.

Suddenly, he sprang forward, leaping up onto the bars to feign escape by creating a distraction when his impeccable instincts told him that Alice was seconds away from being sprung. In response, the men roared and surged forward like a human tidal wave. He had taught his daughter well and knew this action created an added opportunity for Alice like she was simply plucking apples from a tree.

The judge peered over his wire-rimmed spectacles at the men in the gallery below penned in like sardines. His round cheeks flushed from his recent exertion and the sheer humidity when he addressed them. 'Last warning. Any more and you will all be fined and locked up for perverting the course of justice.' Then, after he saw the policeman roughly push the accused back to his seat through the bars, he looked toward the foreman of the jury. 'Mr Hargreaves, have you reached your verdict?'

'That we have, Your Honour,' he said, standing to attention, feeling somewhat important when he was instantly bombarded by a barrage of hecklers.

'Q-U-I-E-T!' the judge elongated. Once again, he extended the pistol to the ceiling. 'Do the gentlemen of the jury,' he said more calmly, 'find the defendant, Mr Stanley Johnson, guilty or not guilty of threatening behaviour with a knife and malicious wounding with intent?' Suddenly aware of his own threatening behaviour, he retracted his arm and put the pistol away.

Alice knew she was moments away from serious harm if she didn't get out before the verdict was announced. The crowd silenced yet again waiting for the foreman to speak. In the nick of time, she managed to finally push her way out of the mass and was just within a whisker of the courtroom door when she stumbled and fell heavily on her hands. A stocky man bent down and picked her up then seemed to give her a quick hug before he ran out the door. Alice started to follow but she again tripped over her shoelaces costing her precious time to regain her feet.

'Not guilty.'

The split-second silence reverted to jeers and cheers. The boisterous men then shoved and shuffled their way as one fused form over to the bookie and surrounded him to claim their money on the outcome of the verdict.

'Mr Johnson,' shouted the judge. 'You are free to go. Do not find yourself before my court again or I will personally lock you up. Do I make myself clear?'

The policeman stepped forward and unlocked the holding cell.

'Perfectly clear, Judge.' Stanley Johnson, aka Shiv, bolted out of the cell and roughly forced his way towards his daughter who was cornered by a growing mob of angry men.

'Little thief,' shouted one who was shaking Alice so tightly by the arms that her head rocked uncontrollably back and forth. His strong hands could have easily snapped her bones like a twig. He was snarling inches from her face. 'Give me my wallet or I will take my belt to you.'

Alice's eyes grew wide with fear and tears streamed down her angelic face while she tried her best to recoil from his pungent breath.

'You animals. Get the hell away from my daughter.' Stanley growled, shoving the men away while also grabbing as many as he could by the collar jolting them backwards before the two policemen descended into the throng.

'BREAK IT UP,' shouted one, managing to stand between the men and the child while the other scooped Alice up into his arms.

'What's going on?' the policeman yelled, struggling to hold the men back.

'I see it from back there,' answered Stanley. 'All of a sudden these villains turned on my daughter. What you gonna do about it? She's five years old, for crissake.'

'A thief's a thief no matter what the age. You know that, Shiv. She's your daughter, speaks for itself...' roared one irate man, surging forwards. 'Just shows you, don't it? Her old man on trial and she's working the room. My wallet's been lifted and the little brat done it.'

'She's innocent,' raged Stanley, snatching Alice from the policeman's arms. 'She just came to see her father. Shame on all of you.'

'INNOCENT, MY ARSE. SEARCH HER!' demanded a voice from the back. 'Go on, search her. Come on. Do it.'

The policeman turned to Stanley. 'Look, let's get this done so we can get out of here. Put her down, please,' he ordered.

Again, a quietness descended when the policeman crouched down. He smiled and asked, 'What is your name?'

The men listened, wanting to hear what the child had to say for herself.

'Alice,' she said in a barely audible and shaky voice. Her shoulders heaved up and down when she gasped for breath then she wiped her button nose with her sleeve.

'Righto, Alice. Are you carrying anything at all?'

'A handkerchief in my pocket but I forgot to use it,' she said and started to cry again.

'That's alright. I sometimes forget too. Now, hold out your arms like this'—he demonstrated for her—'and I will pat your sides, back and middle to prove to the gentlemen here that you have nothing to hide. Is that alright?'

Alice looked up at her father who gave a brief nod. After the policeman had conducted his search, the men looked confused at one another as one by one they said that they'd had their wallets stolen.

The policeman's knees cracked in protest when he started to stand back up and said with more than a hint of sarcasm, 'Perish the thought, gentlemen. Who would have guessed that we have a light-fingered pickpocket in this very courtroom? And it isn't this little girl. Looks like she was just trying to get through the crowd to see her father. Now, if any of you wish to take this further, come down to the station and we will take statements. In the meantime, shame on all of you. Now, clear off before we arrest you all for wrongful accusation.'

The men had no choice but to disperse. Both policemen knew that none of the *alleged victims* would have been seen dead stepping into a police station of their own free will.

The irony was that everyone knew that they were all as bent as a nine-bob note and crooked to boot. They started to eye one another suspiciously when they lined up to receive their winnings to make up for their shortfall, hoping to God that the bookie hadn't had *his* pockets lifted as well.

While he could not prove anything, the policeman who had spoken to Alice did have his suspicions. But what could he do without causing a further riot and furthermore, did he want to do anything about it anyway? They were all crooks so he wasn't going to lose any sleep by not investigating as he should. He wasn't sure *how* it had been done but there had to have been a third party or even more. The chance that they were still here was remote and even if they were, they would have to be downright stupid. While nothing surprised him anymore, and based on his gut feeling, he couldn't begin to comprehend that a father would ever manipulate his small child to rob inside the courthouse.

But then, who would suspect the sheer audacity?

*

Stanley arrived home, slammed the front door and tugged at his tie to loosen the grip. 'Rose, you there?' he shouted impatiently up the stairs, annoyed that the knot of his tie wouldn't give way. 'Rose, get down here.' The humidity was getting to him, thus making him more irritable than usual.

Alice and Big Alf had arrived earlier and had sat waiting at the square kitchen table in silence, although the battered chair protested every fidget when Alice swished her legs to and fro. It was unbearably hot and her cheeks flushed a beautiful baby pink that complemented her light blue eyes. The open back door did nothing to alleviate the mugginess or the damn flies buzzing around their heads. Her feet still hurt when she wiggled her toes, and her long golden hair that her mother had plaited for her earlier that morning was beginning to curl from the moisture.

On the verge of getting down to get a drink of water, she changed her mind upon hearing her father's tone. Alice was confident that he would be pleased with her today but decided to remain put until knowing for certain.

She was fascinated that Big Alf appeared to float on air as his raincoat hid the chair and when he placed his heavy forearm on the edge of the table, her attention shifted. The edge was weak, causing it to dip and groan and Alice believed the table would collapse under the strain.

Regardless of the weather, Big Alf wore his trademark dark grey raincoat, tailored from a thinner fabric for the hotter months, over a smart black suit and waistcoat, white shirt, and black tie. He was fairing quite well considering he was in his early sixties despite carrying more weight these days. During his younger years, he had proudly sported a dark bushy moustache but now he was clean-shaven because it better suited his receding hairline. Ironically, his eyebrows grew bushy with age, and they enhanced his menacing brown eyes and intimidating tough image. He was the same height as his boss and some would say, that was where the similarity ended.

Big Alf fanned his perspired face with his fedora but it only intensified the heat. He stopped and threw it into the corner then ran his index finger around his shirt collar, causing the grime and sweat to spread.

The head of the house entered the kitchen and turned the tap, hoping for a cold drink. Stanley did not offer one to anyone else and gulped noisily, hoping to quench his thirst, finding that the water was anything but cold. He slammed the tin cup on the table that was barely big enough to accommodate four people, where Alice eyed the cup and prayed that there was a little left as she was now extremely thirsty. He turned to face Big Alf and his eyes lit up at the stash of wallets, watches, jewellery and a multitude of cutthroat razors that were strewn beside Rose's dog-eared bible.

Stanley was in his mid-thirties. He was of average height and build with dark blue eyes, short dark hair and clean shaven. Ever dapper, he looked quite well-to-do in his dark grey suit, tie and waistcoat with a crisp white shirt underneath a set of black braces. This was his normal garb and not just reserved for court appearances. He was handsome enough but underneath the exterior lay a nasty, vicious and spiteful reprobate. He was a ruthless bruiser who would not bat an eyelid to cut, maim or kill if anyone dared to look at him the wrong way. He was also the type to sell his nearest and dearest, even for a minimal profit or for no profit, depending on what type of mood he was in. He never ventured outside the house without his trusted blade and was known only as Shiv by his associates due to his weapon of choice where he was only addressed as Mr Stanley Johnson on court days.

Rose entered the kitchen carrying a bundle of threadbare bed sheets that were almost transparent in places whereby it was a wonder that they did not completely disintegrate in the wash. She summed up what the haul on her kitchen table meant and could almost envision a bolt of lightning striking the table between the stolen property and her bible. Nonetheless, she smiled and praised her daughter and died a little more on the inside every time she did so. Appeasing her husband was fundamental in not receiving a beating, not only for herself but for Alice as well. Praising meant that she approved when she was oh so far from it.

But what could she do?

After placing the sheets in the sink, she quickly tucked the loose strands of her long golden hair behind her ears that had broken free from her plait. She turned around and pecked Stanley on the cheek who thought that his once beautiful wife looked a little haggard lately. Rose was also in her thirties, slender and a little shorter than her husband and contrary to his thoughts, only needed a few good night's sleep.

Rose felt imprisoned and hated her life and husband for what he was doing to their daughter. Alice was too young to understand that what she was doing was not only wrong but that her father was subjecting her to extreme danger.

Above all else, her greatest fear was that Alice would turn out to be exactly like her father and there wasn't a single thing on this earth that she could do about it if they were to remain alive. Rose was trapped and she despised herself for being too damn frightened and afraid.

Over the last five years, Stanley had gradually drained the lifeblood out of his wife drip by precious drip, making her defenceless and above all, compliant. What made it crueller was knowing that he thrived on it.

The kitchen table frequently held piles of money while they lived in downright poverty and that was the bare bones that Rose just could not fathom. Stanley had the wealth, albeit dishonest, to easily afford a nicer place to live in on the better and safer side of town. He explained to her once that he did not want to draw attention to himself so they would remain put. He and Alice were always well-presented and suitably dressed when they went off to work, yet she had to beg for money for the upkeep of the house and to clothe herself. He always kept a sharp eye on all their outgoings by making damn sure that she was fully dependent on him without a single coin to her name.

Rose used to love Stanley with every beat of her heart. But that had instantly changed after her arduous labour when the midwife stepped out of the bedroom to fetch more water from the kitchen. She had noticed Mr Johnson knocking back the whisky when she wiped her hands on her apron and, in passing, congratulated him that he had a daughter then proceeded downstairs.

Stanley had walked into the bedroom still clutching the bottle and with a gentle click, closed the door behind him. Rose instantly noticed that he never acknowledged the barest of glances in the baby's direction, who the midwife had wrapped in a blanket and placed in the middle drawer of the dresser for a makeshift cot.

Like a cyclone, his rage erupted from the pit of his stomach when he snarled and looked down at his wife's sweat-drenched brow in disgust. Quick as a viper, he slapped Rose hard across the face just minutes after she had given birth to Alice on October 1, 1920.

In complete denial, Stanley was confused. Why didn't he have a son? He had looked after Rose extremely well during her pregnancy and he could not understand her nerve in repaying him with a worthless daughter. *That* was the day Rose Johnson's life had dramatically changed for the worse.

Stanley convinced himself that he would be a laughingstock for not producing a son, and therefore, perceived as being half a man where he had mistreated and rated his wife and child insignificant from that moment on.

The midwife was barely down the stairs when the torrent exploded. 'YOU STUPID, INCAPABLE AND WORTHLESS BITCH!' he ranted within an inch from her face. 'What the hell are you playing at? Are you going out of your way to make a fool of me?'

Rose couldn't believe her ears. She was overcome with fear and shock because he had never struck her or used foul language in front of or aimed at her. Ever. The smell of whisky on his breath was overpowering. From the time he had slapped her, to now, he had knocked back several huge gulps. Her face was still stinging and she did not recognise that the violent man before her was the same gentleman whom she had married. Rose began to edge away by subtly shuffling backwards on her bottom, but it was not easy. She was extremely sore down below due to the midwife being rough in her haste to stitch her up.

Without anaesthetic, Rose endured eight stitches, tensing herself each time the midwife plunged the needle through her already delicate, torn and bloodied flesh. But the worst pain was when she yanked the thread through, causing a burning sensation as she clenched the edges of her pillow so tightly; she believed her tendons would pop. Most of all, she tried her hardest not to scream and frighten her baby and turned her head to cry out into the pillow. She tried again to recoil from him and felt a long trickle of blood ooze between her legs where the headboard prevented her from moving any further backwards.

'I'M WAITING!' he shouted, expecting her to come up with a miracle. Rose was still stunned at his sudden turn of behaviour and foolishly put it down to him being drunk and that he would return to normal when the effects wore off.

'She's a beautiful baby, Stanley.' Rose smiled in the hope of bringing him around. 'I know we had Alan in mind for a name, but how about Alice? I think it suits her.'

'Call *it* what you damn well like,' he said despondently, glancing in the baby's direction. He then turned back to his wife. 'I still can't believe what you've done to me, woman. Have you *any* idea?' He started to pace like a caged animal while running his fingers through his otherwise well-groomed hair.

After a few tense moments, he said, 'I'm off to the pub to drown my sorrows.'

'But Stanley, I need help with the baby and I'm still bleeding.' Her pleas fell onto deaf ears. 'Stanley, please!'

He approached the doorway. 'Rose, I really don't care or give a damn. Perhaps someone at the pub knows of a boy we can swap with...' And with that bright idea, he ran down the stairs and slammed the front door behind him.

'YOU BASTARD!' Rose screamed with all her might, causing Alice to wail. To prevent losing another surge of blood, she gingerly reached over the side of the bed and picked up her boot. Then, in quick succession, she used it to pummel the wall over her head to alert her neighbour for help as tears of despair flowed down her cheeks.

CHAPTER TWO

Rose snapped back to the present when her husband shouted, 'Don't just sit there like a fat lump. Count it,' ordering Big Alf to sift through the hoard. Alice now desperately wanted the dunny but knew it was best to stay put and tried to wriggle discretely to make the urge go away.

Stanley couldn't believe his eyes. He stepped nearer to the table and picked up a distinctive dark brown leather wallet with a small diamond embedded in the top corner. He turned it over and over in wonder and looked at his daughter. 'You lift this one?' he asked.

Clutching the sides of the chair, she gave a small nod bracing herself for fear of the wrong answer and for what may be coming her way.

'You know who this belonged to?' He waved it in front of Big Alf.

He looked up and shook his head. 'No idea, Shiv,' he said and was annoyed that he had forgotten the tally and began a recount.

'I never spotted him,' replied Stanley in wonder. 'Too busy answering damn questions and keeping an eye on Alice. I do believe this once belonged to P W Jones.' He waited for the big man to respond, who did a few seconds later when his brain caught up with the wit and broke into one of his almighty belly laughs.

As the men laughed, Rose and Alice looked at one another, not understanding what was going on. After a while, Stanley enlightened and said, 'P W Jones is notorious. He is *the* pickpocket master. Your daughter, Rose, has pickpocketed the pickpocket.' And with that, he again burst into rapturous laughter.

She was a little confused and amazed because he rarely told her anything about his business. 'But he wasn't today?'

'Are you completely obtuse, woman? He would be an absolute imbecile to chance or even think about lifting in a court right under the noses of the law. Out of his stupid tiny mind. Instant jail and throw away the key.'

The question had to be asked. 'So why risk it, Stanley?'

'Why not? I was damn inconvenienced; I lost money today by not earning. It was only right that I be paid for the morning's entertainment that I so graciously and generously provided to one and all.'

'But the risk was enough to deter P W Jones, yet it was good enough for...' She looked at Alice and stopped in her tracks because the atmosphere immediately flipped to the negative.

Big Alf shifted in his chair, sensing danger.

'You were saying...?' Stanley sided up and stood nose to

nose with his wife, daring her to move as much as an eyelid or utter another syllable. 'Daring to cross the line, Rose?' he whispered; his intimidating eyes bored into her.

'No, I...'

'No, I... what?'

'Come on, Shiv, she didn't mean anything by it. Come and help me tally this lot. Rose, bring us a whisky to celebrate our good earner today.' The old man was slow on a lot of things but was quick enough to deflect, knowing full well that she didn't have an easy time with the boss.

Rose appreciated what Big Alf had just done and stepped away from her husband, giving her saviour a quick grateful nod before turning to reach down the glasses and whisky bottle from the dresser.

Stanley, through a kind heart, decided not to pursue an unpleasant scene in front of Alice as she had worked well that morning. 'Yes, a whisky to celebrate,' he conceded by sitting down, not caring for the woman's opinion anyway.

He knew all too well that Alice's innocence would be short-lived. And that in the not-too-distant future, perhaps in three or four years' time, she would try and question the dangers of lifting in the courthouse. When he noticed that change in her, he would nip it in the bud and bring her back in line.

But, for the time being, he believed it would be wasteful and immoral of him not to exploit her innocence.

During the past year, he had come around to having a daughter, now believing that it wasn't too bad after all. He even went as far to believe that Alice could even be an asset to the business as girls appeared more innocent over boys.

When she was three years old, he began to teach her the art of picking pockets. And in a rare proud acknowledgement, he knew that they would make a formidable pair one day because she was even better than he had been at her age. When the time came, Big Alf would become an expendable commodity; Stanley had already planned his sudden demise when the time was right for Alice to step into his shoes.

Rose poured the men their whisky and when she noticed her daughter wriggling, she excused her for the dunny. Stanley purposely kept his wife in the dark regarding the business, but if truth be told, she knew more than he thought she did. Upon surveying the pile of wallets and feeling somewhat safer with Big Alf around, she asked out of intrigue, 'How did Alice manage all this on her own?'

Stanley rolled his eyes and left the explanation to his associate.

'Alice wore this, we've been trying it out.' He held up what looked like a large apron pocket with a long material strap attached across the top edge. 'We tied this around her waist with the open pocket placed around the back of her, so her cardigan covered the pocket completely. If you looked at her from the front, you would only see what appeared to be a small belt around her dress. Then when she weaved in and out collecting valuables on her way, she placed them in the pocket behind her. She managed three batches and I was by the door each time and emptied twice, but on the final run, I untied and took the whole thing away. That was why when she was searched, nothing was found and I disappeared with the loot. Mind you, my heart skipped a beat when I realised she was still inside, but good that I had the stash.'

'But why...'

'Enough questions,' snapped Stanley, downing his whisky in one swig then picking up a pound note and waving it in front of Rose's eyes. 'Lock it all away, Alf, and I will see you at the usual place at nine. Don't be late. See yourself out. Hey, Alice,' he shouted over his shoulder, 'go play with the other kids.' He then scrunched up the pound note and in front of the big man, he shoved it down Rose's blouse, squeezing her left breast as he did so. Then turning her around, he steered her out of the kitchen and up the stairs. 'Time to earn your housekeeping money.' He slapped her hard on the backside as the stair boards creaked under their weight.

'It's a lot of money because I'm feeling extremely generous.' He kicked the bedroom door shut and started to take off his suit. It wasn't that he particularly enjoyed undressing for sex with Rose; it was more about the practicality of keeping his clothing neat and tidy. 'You'd better make it worth my while, Rosie,' he ordered, following the contours of her face with his blade, the razor-sharp edge barely touched her flawless skin. 'Let's give that nosey witch next door something to complain about.'

Rose knew he was euphoric from the day's earnings and that she wasn't in too much danger. She also knew that when he was like this, it would be rough but above all, it would be quick, and for that she was thankful. He spun her around and she braced herself when he flung her face down onto the lumpy mattress.

*

Just before eight that evening, Stanley stood in front of Rose's dressing table mirror and checked over his appearance. He put on his jacket and walked down to the kitchen to find her getting Alice ready for bed. 'Come with me, Alice, your father is going to buy you dinner.'

Rose stopped brushing Alice's hair. 'It's late, Stanley, and it's her bedtime. She had something to eat earlier.'

'NOT that I ever need your permission, but if I want to take my daughter out for something to eat then I will bloody well take my daughter out for something to eat. Clear?'

'Where will you go? How long will you be?'

'You are turning out to be one big nag, do you know that, Rose? Come on, Alice, get your cardigan and shoes on.'

It was still humid but already dark when she watched them walk down the road heading toward town. After a few paces, Alice turned back to her mother, wishing she were allowed to stay behind. Powerless to do anything, Rose continued to clutch the hairbrush to her chest and remained on the doorstep until they were out of sight.

Around fifteen minutes later, Stanley walked into the pub still holding Alice's hand and approached the bar.

'Evening, Shiv. The usual?' asked the bartender. 'Hello, Alice, how are you?'

'Yeah, yeah, she's good. Go sit over there.' He pointed to an empty table. 'Bring out a pie for us and I'll have my usual and a water.'

They ate in silence. It was very late and she was more sleepy than hungry and knew that she could only manage a few mouthfuls. The pie did look very tasty though when the bartender put the plate in front of her. She picked up the spoon where it appeared that the person before, or even before that, had either very cracked lips or a bristly moustache because vertical grooves of dried food lined the shallow bowl of the utensil.

Alice mistakenly took a big mouthful.

As her tongue darted around, sifting out the crust and gravy, it discovered a chunk that consisted of far more gristle than actual meat. It was chewy and disgustingly stringy, and as much as she had wanted to, she knew she couldn't spit it out. Each time her jaw closed, she could feel small bits of gristle and fat ooze between her infant teeth. She made the decision to quickly swallow it whole or else she knew she would be sick. She counted to three and on three she closed her eyes and attempted to swallow. But she couldn't. She counted to three again, more slowly this time, then swallowed hard and her whole being involuntarily shuddered as the gristly chunk slid down her throat. She grasped for her glass of water and gulped.

'What's wrong with you? Pulling a face like that,' he reprimanded. 'Finish up.'

'Sorry, Father, I am full up,' she whispered and again reached for her water to wash it further down before it decided to come back up. Stanley wasn't impressed after all the money he had spent on the dinner. He polished it off with another beer and by the time they finished the pub was getting busier. At nine, Big Alf joined them, surprised to see Alice there.

'Just a little celebration,' said Stanley while she yawned. 'You know where you are, don't you?' he asked while helping her on with her cardigan and led her outside. 'Righto, off you go. Straight home and don't talk to no one. I'll see you in the morning. We have a job.' He didn't even bother to wait for her reply before re-entering the noisy pub where the doors slammed behind him.

Alice sidestepped the busy doorway, not wanting to be knocked over, and stared out into the scary night. She was a very tired five-year-old making her way back home in the dark in the dangerous part of town, trying her best not to be frightened for the second time that day.

The further she walked, the more spooked she became. Large rats scurried in the gutters and she heard terrifying screaming and grunting noises whenever she passed dark alleyways. Her heart pounded when someone behind her started to run, their steps echoing louder and louder. Alice's tears streamed as she bolted, pushing herself even harder in a bid to get away.

'Alice!' cried the familiar voice when Rose caught up and embraced her daughter before they both ran back home safely together.

CHAPTER THREE

'Make it a quick breakfast. We've got to go,' ordered Stanley when he entered the kitchen to drink his cup of tea.

'Where are you going today?' Rose asked, giving Alice a cup of water and a slice of bread and jam.

'Bank. She'll wear a light blue hair ribbon and the blue dress with the white daisies. The last time I think as it's getting a little tight. You're growing up too fast.' He smiled. 'This afternoon, you'll go into town'—he turned to face Rose—'and buy her a new blue dress and black shoes.' He placed some money on the table. 'This is plenty and...'

'Yes, you want receipts and the change. I know,' Rose said quietly, feeling deflated that she was not even trusted to do this simple task.

'Good. Finish up, Alice, Big Alf will be there soon. And remember, your name is Polly because—'

'We never use our real names.'

'Good girl.'

As usual, Rose watched them walk down the road. Both

were immaculately dressed and they wouldn't have looked out of place as patrons at a fancy restaurant or theatre while she herself looked frightfully drab. She used to have nice things but as a punishment after Alice's birth, she wasn't allowed to buy anything new for herself. She did her very best to make the most out of what she owned relying on Stanley's generosity to buy her second-hand clothing, although they were always way past their prime.

Rose's beauty was her greatest asset and the way she styled her hair only accentuated her features. Having seen posters of movie stars at the picture houses, she had wanted a fashionable bob haircut but Stanley had threatened her with violence if she dared to disobey him. And so, day by day, she dreamed of a new life, a better life, where her husband adored her and everything was right with the world. And when she had bad days, which were frequent, she would turn to her bible for comfort and pray with all her heart to gain enough strength to forgive her husband.

In the beginning, Stanley had loved and cherished his beautiful wife. But the moment Alice was born, he felt that he had lost everything.

The love he once had for Rose instantly tarnished and became unrepairable. Deep down, he knew he treated her despicably, but he could not help it. It was as if someone had flipped a switch. The greatest tragedy of all was when he finally accepted his daughter but still felt the same way about his wife.

Rose deserved so much better; he knew that as much as he knew he would never let her go alive. Even if another man had wanted her, he wouldn't think twice in killing them both. She was dead to him either way. This suppositious scenario enraged him every time he thought about Rose being with another man. These dark thoughts often led him to the whisky bottle where after a few shots the liquor cast troubled doubts over his already poor judgment. This was when he stared at his trusted knife that taunted him positioned against the bottle, goading him to act upon his overzealous imagination.

Stanley's character was the complete opposite to Rose's. He was obstinate in many ways but in his sole opinion was big enough to admit whenever he was wrong. Everyone who knew him would reject this statement because he could easily cause an affray in an empty room. Since Alice's birth, his clouded oversight hadn't looked at the so-called problem objectively until he worked out the positivity of having a daughter in the business. In his profession, he was always looking for new ways to relieve unsuspecting marks of their money because who on Earth would suspect that a beautiful well-dressed little girl could do such terrible things? He had managed to turn this once misfortune into an advantage as his initial plan of swapping Alice for a boy had thankfully failed. At one point, he had even considered snatching a newborn but no opportunity had arisen. So, he had committed to teaching Alice the tricks of the trade where she was already proving to be an asset.

*

That morning, the plan was in place when Stanley and Alice positioned themselves across the road from the bank. To any passer-by, they were just an ordinary father and daughter enjoying their time together. He clutched a folded newspaper under his arm and leaned against the wall, talking to Alice who was enjoying throwing her small teddy bear up in the air and catching it. After a few minutes, she stopped and began to mimic a hopscotch game while he pretended to read his newspaper but was really observing the doorway to the bank. They were passing the time of day and drew no attention.

Alice then stood beside him and when the coast was clear, he said, 'It's all about patience, Alice. Patience. You must learn to stay calm. There may be times when the day is wasted and you have to walk away. If something doesn't feel right, let it go. Cut your losses and start again the next day. It's better than ending up in prison. What do I always tell you?'

'To trust my instinct. If something doesn't feel right, get away quickly but don't draw attention.'

'That's good, Alice. Good,' he praised, keeping an eye on the doorway. Before he could continue, a well-dressed man walked out of the bank, followed a few seconds later by Big Alf who, in one fluid movement, took off his fedora and tapped it over his left breast pocket.

'Here we go. Left side,' Stanley said, patting Alice's left shoulder then he folded up his newspaper and handed it to her. When it was safe to do so, they walked across the road and remained a few steps behind Big Alf who was walking a few steps behind the mark.

'Hey, Polly,' shouted Stanley joyfully when they ran and overtook Big Alf and preceded to run past the well-dressed man. 'Come back here, you rascal, that's my newspaper!'

Polly ran back and forth, dodging her father, causing the man to walk next to the wall hence giving the little girl more room to play on the narrow pavement.

'I've got it, Daddy, I've got it,' cheered Polly, waving the newspaper up in the air as Stanley playfully tried to retrieve it.

The man was distracted watching the pair and was not aware of Big Alf closing in. Suddenly, and with perfect timing while still looking ahead, Alice darted backwards, instigating the man to halt abruptly. It was a knock-on effect as Big Alf bumped into the man, lifting his wallet and immediately handing it to Stanley to alleviate an accusation in case the man suspected what was going on.

'I am dreadfully sorry,' apologised Big Alf, lifting his hat in acknowledgement and stepping away from the man.

'No, it is our fault. We should not have been playing around like that,' said Stanley, taking the newspaper. 'What do you say, Polly?'

'Sorry, sir,' she said, looking up at the man with her beautiful blue eyes.

'No harm done,' said the man, smiling down at Alice. Stanley and Polly held hands and continued walking ahead then turned down the next side street. Big Alf crossed over the road and also turned into a side street. The whole repertoire took no more than a couple of minutes and earned them fifty pounds from the recent bank withdrawal. It was an absolute fortune.

They were all back at the house within forty minutes and very pleased with the morning's work.

'You did well, Alice,' said her father, handing her a glass of water.

'Thank you, Daddy.'

'Good plan. It worked well,' Stanley praised Big Alf. 'By tapping your left breast pocket, both of us knew which side to work on and it saved a precious few seconds by getting on your correct side to collect. See, Alice, you can always improve a plan. Saving only a few seconds could mean the difference between being sprung or getting away with the loot.'

'Well done, Big Alf.'

'Thanks, Polly.' He smiled back.

*

That afternoon, Alice and her mother walked into town to Buckingham's Department Store. Alice loved going there; it was one of the biggest buildings that she had ever seen. She enjoyed looking at the fancy window displays and lovely dresses and shoes and couldn't wait to be grown up, so she could wear them all.

'Let's go inside,' she pleaded, dragging her mother through the door.

It was the opposite for Rose who hated it because she felt like a fraud and a pauper in her pitiful clothing. But, despite that, she admired the counter displays and fashionable clothes. She loved the newness and the newness smell and ached to own a new dress of her own again. As always, Rose felt conspicuous to the point of nausea from the snide snobbish side glances and looks of disapproval from staff and customers alike, while Alice was oblivious.

As they had shopped there numerous times, Rose tried her utmost to usher the young girl through to the children's section as quickly as she could. 'Can't we stay here for a little while longer to look around?' she always asked.

'Sorry, Alice. We need to get back. I have jobs to do before your father comes home,' Rose always replied.

Once again, she sensed brutal scrutiny by the sales staff and tried her best to fight back stinging tears and overwrought feelings of intimidation and humiliation. Their slow upward and downward glances deemed her worthless while they took pleasure in dissecting her bit by bit.

'May I help you?' asked a snooty middle-aged woman who wore too much lipstick and overpowering perfume.

'Thank you,' said Rose, trying to sound confident, maintaining eye contact. 'We would like a dress for Alice, in blue please and some black shoes.'

The woman gave a slight nod. 'Come this way, Miss,' she addressed the child and led her over to the rack taking much delight that she had dismissed the pitiful woman. She caught the eyes of her colleagues who gave subtle smirks but they weren't subtle enough as Rose had caught each and every one of them. She was overcome with the need to put these bullies in their place for treating her this way.

Alice had selected a dress and shoes she liked. 'Would you

like to try them on?' asked the lipstick woman and when the child nodded, the woman then asked as an afterthought. 'Perhaps your nanny would like to come too?'

'I'm her mother,' Rose said, taking Alice's hand and following the woman through to the changing room.

'Oh, I see. My apologies,' she said before adding a begrudging, 'Madam,' through almost gritted teeth, knowing that her colleagues would tease her about it later.

After a few minutes, mother and daughter stood at the counter ready to pay when the lipstick woman snatched the money from Rose's hand. Despite the sales assistants bullying her for pure entertainment, she was grateful that Alice hadn't witnessed any of it. She was now looking at all the pretty jewellery in the next glass cabinet and marvelling at the sparkles that reflected in the light.

'Thank you,' said Rose, holding out her hand for her change and receipt. Then as some customers walked by, she looked at the woman who was then walking around the counter with her purchase and said rather loudly, 'That shade of lipstick is really for someone much, much younger,' and took the bag.

The woman's eyes opened wide with a mix of shock and embarrassment, looking like a rabbit caught in headlights not knowing quite how to react. She had never believed that this woeful woman would have had the mettle to fight back. Her colleagues were shocked even though they initially sniggered, and therefore, agreed with their customer's remark.

The lipstick woman was still trying to recover from the shock and as Rose turned to leave, she purposely dropped her change on the floor, causing the coins to scatter and roll in all directions. The two other women ran to assist and after a while, she thanked them all then she and Alice made their way out of the department, quickly heading for the exit.

Alice skipped along the pavement all the way home, swinging the bag and feeling delighted with her new things. Rose was skipping inside too as she brightened up from how she had been treated. She gently stroked the expensive gold bracelet with her fingertips as it lay inside her cardigan pocket, having liberated it from the cluster of bracelets that the lipstick woman had worn when they were retrieving her change.

How clumsy of me, she thought. *Still, old skills never die.*

CHAPTER FOUR

As soon as P W Jones walked into the pub, Stanley's hackles were up.

'Shiv. My friend!' He delighted in saying, knowing full well that it would irritate his archrival. And today, he intended to cause immense irritation when he walked up to the bar and ordered a whisky.

Shiv stayed silent, leaning against the bar and carried on reading his newspaper hoping the message would get through that he was not interested in conversation. P W guessed as much but ignored it all the same.

'Whisky? I'm buying,' he said, fumbling about in his breast pocket for a pound note and throwing it on the bar. The barman finished pouring and reached for another glass.

'What do you want?' he snapped before noticing the huge bruise on the man's temple. If Shiv weren't mistaken, P W looked a little shaky. He downed his whisky in one and ordered another.

'I'll bring them over,' the barman announced, not wishing

to be involved in anything these villains were up to but comforted that his trusted metal pipe was nestled under the bar in case of trouble. P W walked toward an empty booth.

'Fine,' said Shiv in an irksome way and sat opposite but not before catching Big Alf's attention in case he needed some backup.

'You never come in here.' Shiv crossed his arms and leant forward, narrowing the gap between them. The ploy enabled him to touch the tip of the blade with his right index finger for reassurance as the knife nestled inside his left jacket pocket. He felt like a coiled snake and stared with indignation into his adversary's eyes. The barman placed the alcohol on the table, feeling the tension and ready to disband if any trouble ensued.

'Thought it about time,' he replied, sitting back against the back of the booth widening the distance again. He looked around the bar with disgust then back to Shiv. 'Wanted to see how the other half lived in the rougher side of town,' he said before necking his second whisky.

'From the decoration on your face, looks like you came from the rougher side of town. What's the real reason? Spit it out and stop wasting my time. I've business.'

'You always have such a fine way with words.' And when there was no response, he continued. 'This is a friendly visit with a friendly warning...'

'How are warnings ever friendly?' His instincts were on high alert trying to read the situation.

'The rule is that you stay out of my jurisdiction and I stay out of yours.'

'So, what the hell are you doing in my pub?'

'Didn't know you owned a pub, Shiv. Very impressive,' P W mocked.

'That whisky has turned your head simple or perhaps it's all the coke you're snorting instead of shifting,' he taunted.

P W took offence but tried not to show it. 'I'm clean, you know that,' he said, adjusting his expensive tailored lapel then brushed his finger across his dark moustache. 'You're venturing into my jurisdiction. Randwick Racecourse is mine.' His eyes turned from friendly to hard cold steel.

'Didn't know you owned a racecourse, P W,' Shiv said where the flippancy was ignored. 'It's a big place. More than enough pickings for both of us and some.' He returned the icy stare.

'It can hold thousands of punters with deep pockets, you know that. So, what's the problem? You have a bigger group of pickpockets than I do, hence you have a bigger take. You must be raking in an absolute bleeding fortune. So why come all this way personally to worry about little old me?'

'Like I said, a friendly warning. I know you use your little girl and I don't wanna see her hurt. Such a pretty little thing...'

'Why do you feel so threatened?' Shiv smiled, trying to deflect when all he wanted was to cut the smug bastard and watch him bleed out.

'It's about respect and control.' P W now leaned in closer. 'You have stepped over the line and have been disrespectful, plus you have something that belongs to me and I want it back.' He stared for some kind of recognition.

'You've lost me.' Shiv held his nerve, now knowing the true reason for the visit.

'Don't play stupid games. My wallet. I want it back and it's not all about the diamond detail. Call it... sentimental.'

'I don't know what you're referring to. You've had a wasted journey. And not that it's any business of yours, but I will continue to do Randwick. I've as much right as anyone to earn an honest quid.' They shared a mutual smile knowing that the pickpocketing business was as far from honest as you could get.

'You are treading on very thin ice. Mark my words. I know you have the wallet because of that reckless act you played in the courtroom.'

'That's horseshit and you know it...'

P W smiled again, appreciating the racecourse quip. 'Very good. Now, hand it over,' he said more sternly.

'You need your eyes tested. I was in the dock, if you'd forgotten, or perhaps that bruise on your head has got your wires mixed up. Everyone in the courtroom, including the judge and police, knew the whole damn room was full to the brim with thieves. So why are you messing your pants desperate to pin it on me? You have nothing to go on, absolutely nothing.'

'Last chance.'

'Or what? You throw me outta town?' Shiv laughed. 'You've seen one too many gangster movies. Perhaps you lost it. Buy another, end your worry.'

'I'm ashamed to say that despite everything. We are alike. And I bet my last coin that you have the wallet. Keep the contents, just hand over the wallet.'

'Bit difficult to bet your last penny when you don't have your wallet to get it from.' Shiv made his way back to the bar where Big Alf was standing.

'You've a smart mouth and a stupid brain, you know that?' P W stood up. He knew he wouldn't get the answer he wanted or the wallet. 'Bottom line, we both know full well you're lying. And for that, you had better watch your back, my friend.' He tilted his fedora and turned to leave.

'And you'd better start watching your front or start walking backwards, so you don't get any more bruises.' The men laughed as P W shook his head in bewilderment and exited the pub.

'I need a piss,' Shiv said to Big Alf and headed for the pub's back door. 'Get me a whisky, I'll be right back.'

He closed the outer door behind him and started to undo his fly while walking the short way across the dark backyard that always smelled strongly of stale beer and vomit. As usual, he did not bother with the dunny, opting to relieve himself against the wall instead, because it was closer. Suddenly, a figure pounced out of the shadows and slammed Shiv into the far wall. The impact winded him and before he knew what was happening a powerful hand grabbed him by the throat and squeezed tighter and tighter until he saw sporadic stars dancing before him.

He knew the assailant long before he felt the moustache bristles touch his ear.

'You lying piece of filth.' Then he loosened his grip and watched Shiv double over and splatter for a few moments before regaining his breath.

'Your whore's perfume gave you away,' Shiv whispered hoarsely. He stood upright and rubbed his neck while his other hand immediately poised the knife to within a hairsbreadth of piercing P Ws' stomach. For a few euphoric seconds, he fought hard against the temptation to plunge, twist and work the blade deeper into bloodied flesh while Big Alf crept up and dragged the attacker away. The big man then executed a well-landed rabbit punch, causing P W's legs to give way beneath him.

'Just not your night, is it?' Big Alf laughed as P W slumped to the ground.

'No, it isn't,' agreed his boss and roughly flipped the man over with his boot. He then bent down and hovered the knife tip within the man's limited line of vision in the darkness, knowing that his only thought would be to wonder what type of cut would be dealt. Shiv's ominous reputation and capabilities were common knowledge, and this was not the time for provocation. P W knew that even a slight movement could mean the difference between ending up scarred, crippled or a corpse; therefore, he had no option but to remain deathly still.

P W almost smiled at the satire where the thought of dying became far less important than giving Shiv the satisfaction of seeing him flail about and fought desperately to control the overpowering urge to move. He was now mesmerised by the tip of the blade where it looked like it had the ability to make the air bleed and doubted that he would even feel the incision.

Shiv flicked his wrist and by the moonlight's sheen, he watched what appeared to be a fat glistening black worm weaving down the left side of P W's face. He stood back up, opened his fly and pissed all over his arch-rival's tailored jacket. 'See you at Randwick... friend.' He and Big Alf then laughed their way back inside the pub.

P W smiled with relief. 'Scarred,' he whispered and silently thanked his lucky stars.

CHAPTER FIVE

During the next few days, Rose had panicked, wondering what she should do with the gold bracelet that she had lifted. Her main concern was where she could hide it because if Stanley found it, there would be serious repercussions. In the early days, he had taught her the art of pickpocketing and they were amazed at just how good she was. Her controlled lighter-than-a-feather touch meant that she had a better aptitude lifting straight from a moving wrist. It was a rare skill and one that came naturally to her. Rose had been eager to try it out for real but Stanley was dead against it, dreading the thought of her being arrested, knowing that she wouldn't be able to handle being sent to prison. It was just for fun he had told her and to be practised strictly between themselves.

Being true to her promise, Rose hadn't pickpocketed outside of the house until she was in the department store with Alice the other day. Her head had been consumed with voluminous voices telling her to do it. The spiteful woman deserved to be taught a lesson for making her feel even more damn worthless than she knew she was.

Stanley could always read her like a book when there was a strong chance that her face would give her away until a permanent safe place could be found to hide the bracelet. She had already moved it five times in the past hour and knew she had to calm down and think rationally. Then, until such a time, a temporary solution came to her.

It was simple but still dangerous. Rose wedged and manoeuvred the bracelet until it was concealed down the central binding of her bible. Surprisingly, due to the vast number of pages, it was not visible even when the pages were opened and turned. Although it would be the last place on Earth that Stanley would ever dream of looking despite being right under his nose, it was therefore the safest place in the house.

Relaxing a little, Rose now allowed herself to wonder if she would be able to do it again or was it just potluck and opportunistic? Nonetheless, this was the most alive she had felt since Alice was born and she began to wonder, *What's good for the goose is good for the gander.*

Her mind jolted from hibernation and a plot was beginning to hatch. It would take time, years even, but it did not matter. At last, there was a beaming light beckoning at the end of the tunnel where until today there was not even a tunnel.

She allowed herself to believe that she had finally found a way to get her and Alice away from Stanley.

Forever.

Rose decided that she would only steal from those she felt truly deserved or could well afford it and she already had a few people in mind. Pawning the bracelet was one option but that was ruled out because Stanley had his ear too close to the ground where it was highly probable that someone would grass her up.

She needed a trusted confidante and despite still being risky, she knew just the person.

At long last, she had glorious and beautiful hope.

*

'Well, well, well.' Mrs Vera Peabody smiled. 'Who would have thought that Mrs Stanley Johnson would come knocking on my door.' She gestured Rose inside her humble brothel disguised as a respectable boarding house and led her down the hallway and into the bijou parlour.

'Hello, Aunty.' Rose beamed back.

'Ah, at least you remember that. Long time, no see,' said the short stout woman who was in her mid-sixties. She had a kindly face, sparkling blue eyes and ample laughter lines and by her attire, she would not have looked out of place within a Dickensian novel as they embraced. 'How are you and Alice? Cup of tea?'

'We're fine thank you and yes, tea sounds lovely.' Rose sat at the small round table that was covered with a light cotton tablecloth decorated with small, embroidered wildflowers. Apart from the pile of expensive-looking lingerie and stockings, the parlour looked more suited to a vicarage as opposed to a knocking shop and a house of confidence tricksters. Plus, she tried to ignore the almost inaudible cries of pleasure and the intermittent swaying of the ceiling lamp that sent a gentle sway of shadows across the room, while Vera poured them a fresh brew.

'How's business?' enquired Rose, glancing at the ceiling.

'Can't complain, love. Can't complain,' she replied, observing notable changes in her niece since the last time she had visited, which had been quite a while ago. 'I've three working girls now and four cons each with their own unique talent for acquiring cash and the like. They obey the house rules by minding their own business and keeping trouble, and mores to the point, the police, away from the door. As long as rent is paid on time, then all is fine. We help each other and do what we can in these tough times.

'You've lost weight.' Vera's small talk ended when she passed Rose a piping hot cup of tea. 'And what on Earth are you wearing? Looks worse than last time. What's going on, love?' she asked with concern.

'Don't. Please,' she pleaded, placing the cup and saucer on the table. 'I'm fine, honestly. It's just that...'

Suddenly, the door almost erupted off its hinges as a bare-breasted scantily clad woman, who appeared to be in her late teens and dressed in a flimsy silk wrap, high heels, stockings and suspenders, burst into the room. 'Vera, I need... Oh, sorry, didn't know you had a guest.' She attempted to cover her modesty while eyeing Rose suspiciously as potential competition.

'W-H-A-T did I tell you about knocking on the door, Dulcie?' Vera admonished by thumping her fist on the table in frustration making the teaspoons rattle in the saucers.

'Sorry...! New girl, Vera?' She pursed her scarlet lips and sized Rose up.

'None of your dammed business. *What* do you need?'

'I need a pot of jam. And don't ask. Mister, whatever his name is, demands jam as an added extra. I hate to think what he has in mind. Jeez, I'm going to get very sticky. Have we got some?'

Rose bit her lip, trying her hardest not to laugh as Dulcie looked daggers at her while Vera searched the pantry.

'Don't know why I'm smiling,' she said, holding out the jar. 'I'm the poor sod who'll have to wash the damn sheets.'

As a parting shot, Dulcie re-opened her silk wrap, exposing her ample breasts and jiggled them wildly in Rose's direction. 'You can't work here, darling. Your tits are too small.' Then she turned around to her employer, snatched the jar of jam and left the parlour where the women burst into rapturous laughter.

'Oh, that was priceless... You were saying?' asked Vera, recovering from laughing when she closed the door.

'The reason I'm here.' Rose produced the gold bracelet from her handbag and placed it on the table. 'Could you sell it for me?'

'Are you in trouble?' Vera looked concerned, then temptation took over when she took and held the bracelet to the light then she bit into the gold. 'Nice little number, this is. You lifting? He won't like it.'

'It just happened. First time in years. Can you sell it?'

'Yes, I can sell it. I'll pay you five pounds for it now. That's a fair price.'

'Thank you. Although I didn't think my cut would be worth that much. Is that a true value or a family price?'

'Business is business. It's worth a whole lot more, believe me. But five is the best I can give and that is for anyone, not just you.'

Rose was thrilled. 'Then I'll take it.' She sipped her tea and when Vera went to put another kettle on to boil, she felt guilty that she may have inadvertently stolen a family heirloom from the lipstick woman. The intention was to teach her a lesson, not to rob her blind. But reasoning prevailed that the woman was stupid to have worn such an expensive commodity to work in the first place. Perhaps she was showing off to her colleagues? *Serves her right. If she hadn't been so horrid, then she would still have her precious bracelet.*

*

From then on, Aunt Vera became a business partner of sorts and provided her with all the support and tools for the job that she needed. In the beginning, they had thought long and hard about where to hide the stash until Vera came up with the only safe place she could think of in easy reach. Who would have envisioned that within the brothel's quiet innocent parlour and taking pride of place on the mantlepiece was Rose and Alice's future slowly stacking up all hidden within Vera's dearly departed husband's urn? Rose hadn't dared to ask the whereabouts of her uncle's remains and accepted that some things were best left unsaid.

Timing was crucial and Rose worked only when Stanley,

Big Alf and Alice were themselves out working for the whole day. These events were relatively far and few between, but she accepted that it would take many years to build up a substantial nest egg for her and Alice's future. The main thing was that she was doing something about it which gave her endless hope.

Her aunt had never approved of Stanley but her assumptions were proven correct when Rose often opened up about her life at home while they chatted over tea in the parlour. Vera was an amazing tonic who gave her faith, courage and belief that one day they would be free of him and the miserable life they had to live by.

Life became more tolerable, knowing that she had someone she trusted to confide in. She did have other friends and neighbours but apart from Ettie, she would be putting them in serious danger if Stanley ever found out what she had been doing behind his back. Unless Stanley wanted to end up dead himself, Ettie was untouchable and that made Rose think that perhaps she could also be an ally if it came to it.

Rose also had to consider her daughter who was growing up fast and becoming very knowing. As a loving mother, she was very mindful in not letting anything slip. The last thing she needed was for Alice to innocently say something to her friends or even to her father as Stanley would put two and two together. The risk was too great and not one that she was prepared to take, particularly as she had come so far.

Although her self-esteem had returned, it caused Rose a far bigger problem by trying her hardest to maintain her old persona as she downplayed her excitement for fear of being discovered. Stanley was as sharp as his knife, so she couldn't afford to make any errors. The saving grace was that he was always on a high after a successful day's lifting and therefore his attentions were elsewhere and not on his wife. Often after they had brought Alice back home and the loot had been counted, he and Big Alf would then spend the evening down at the pub or at one of the seedy clubs in town. Sometimes Stanley would stagger back home in the early hours or sometimes he would not return until the following day.

It was on occasions like this that Rose would sit up in Alice's bed and tell her a bedtime story and then they would drift off to sleep together. She did this purposely as she had learned to avoid Stanley in case he came home demanding sex or to pick a fight, or worse, both.

The most dreadful time had been when he had come home blind drunk where the stench of booze and cigarettes was over-powering and suffocating to the point of almost gagging. His eyes were glazed and she studied his face for early signs that he was going to vomit as he lay heavily on top of her. His unsuccessful attempts to penetrate her and the dousing droplets of salty sweat that stung her eyes were torturous enough without his frustration and building rage. She had held her breath every time he belched whisky fumes and Rose knew, that if she could have gotten away with it, she would have killed him with his own knife, as it tormented her within easy reach on the bedside table.

She had to bide her time. She *finally* had some money to

call her own and that made her temporary suffering more bearable. Well, if truth be told, it wasn't exactly *her* money, but then again, neither was Stanley's or Big Alf's or any of the endless pickpockets they associated with.

CHAPTER SIX

Stanley was elated. His whole being came alive whenever he, Big Alf and Alice attended Randwick because the racecourse was his favourite place in the whole world. Not that he had seen much of the world, apart from briefly serving overseas during WW1. But, like most of his counterparts, he preferred not to dwell much on that and focused on the here and now and finding new ways to obtain money by deception.

There was the odd occasion when he and Big Alf talked about the war and each time Stanley gloated about how he had been sent back to Australia without sustaining even a scratch. He had led the doctor deeper and deeper within a card game that left him up to his eyes in debt. The poor physician's only option was to sign the appropriate forms to medically discharge Private Stanley Johnson.

His deplorable arrogance was core deep where he believed that only a mindless idiot would not take advantage of Alice's young age. So, he had meticulously planned accordingly and adapted suitable distractions to fit.

Today was such a day.

They were always dressed according to the surroundings in which they carried out their scams. Today, Alice looked like the daughter of aristocratic parents. Rose had dressed her in an above-the-knee broderie anglaise light pink dress with short sleeves and a collar with rounded edges with a white bow placed in the centre. To complete the outfit, she wore white gloves, polished black shoes and white ankle socks. Rose had also weaved a white ribbon through her exquisite plait where she looked an absolute picture of innocence.

Alice stood near the bookie's stand and sobbed her eyes out on cue in front of a well-to-do elderly gentleman in formal-wear who was starting to walk away with his ample winnings.

'What's the matter?' he asked with concern, crouching down to the child's level.

'I've lost my father,' she replied between sobs.

The gentleman's heart melted by the little girl's plight and the tears that streamed down from her beautiful eyes and over her rosy cheeks.

'Now, now,' the gentleman tried to reassure, 'he will not be too far away. Here, take this and wipe your eyes. We will find him, you'll see.' He smiled and patted Alice on the back when she accepted the white silk handkerchief.

Alice suddenly felt very bad for the caring gentleman. His eyes were kind, unlike her father's.

Never experiencing the feeling of guilt before. She did, however, begin to think that what she was doing was very wrong.

Very wrong indeed.

Instantly, she felt the urge to run away to save the man from being robbed. She was a split second from bolting, when...

'Is everything alright?' asked another kind gentleman as he also crouched down to Alice's level, addressing the other man. This time, the tears were real because she had no choice but to stay.

'A lost child,' the man informed Big Alf who nodded sympathetically and gave a quick glance in Alice's direction, not out of concern, but his expression told Alice that she'd better hurry up.

Without a doubt, Big Alf then knew what Alice had just discovered about herself as he'd seen this look on many a ragamuffin when realisation sank in. He would talk to her about it when it was safe to do so in the next few days. But for now, he made the decision to put Alice out of her misery and when he assisted the gentleman in standing, Big Alf lifted his wallet. The elderly gentleman was distracted and therefore it was easy pickings.

On cue, Stanley came rushing forward. 'There you are,' he said with relief, picking Alice up into his arms and uttering a 'thank you' to both men before he and Big Alf walked off in different directions. Still crying, Alice waved at the nice man who acknowledged her by tilting his top hat and smiling.

*

Big Alf had thought long and hard about what he would say to Alice. Tragically losing his dear wife to the Spanish flu in

1919, they were not blessed with children but he would have liked a daughter and granddaughter to take care of. Ever since he had been working with Shiv, he had come to think of Rose and Alice as part of his family. He knew they didn't have an easy time with the boss and it churned him up inside whenever he dished out punishment, sometimes just for the utter hell of it.

Shiv had previously told him of his plan to deal with Alice when she discovered a guilty conscience but he wanted to talk to her first before the boss got wind of it.

A few days later, he got his chance when he turned up at the house and walked through to the kitchen.

'She's on an errand,' Shiv said, pointing with his pencil toward the kitchen sink without looking up from his journal as he and Alice sat at the table. Big Alf noted that he did not have the decency to refer to Rose by name. 'I need some peace. Take Alice to the Royal Botanic Gardens and practice the park bench scam and be back by noon. Behave yourself, Alice, or I'll take my belt to you.'

She gave a brief nod and held the big man's hand when they left the house.

They drew no attention and were practically invisible to passers-by, looking like a grandfather and granddaughter enjoying the morning sun sitting on the park bench. 'What happened at Randwick, Alice?' he asked gently. 'You know, when that elderly gent stopped to help you... You looked different.'

Alice shrugged. She knew she had been different but had trouble putting it into words and took her time to answer.

'He was nice, and kind and he wanted to help me.' This was all she could think of. But it was a start.

'That's the point.' He smiled. 'We rely on these people to stop and help. That's how it works, you know that. And besides, he wouldn't have stopped if I were the one crying,' he joked and Alice chuckled then became more sombre.

'I felt bad. Because of me, he lost his money.'

'You saw him, Alice. He could well afford to lose it.'

'It *is* wrong, isn't it?' she emphasised and turned to look at the big man in his crumpled mac who was already sweating profusely. She wanted to hear what he had to say because she could never dare ask her father this question. She knew Big Alf was a dangerous man, and that her father worked with lots of dangerous men, but Big Alf was much kinder than her father. Her father got angry and sometimes he would use his fists or his belt. He had no patience at all, particularly with her and her mother, and that was why she let many questions go unasked.

'It's the way it is... it's what we do,' he explained matter-of-factly.

'He believed me. I nearly ran away but then you came.'

'It's normal to feel like this. Most people who do what we do feel this way at the beginning. It's just a feeling, Alice, it will pass. Now, this chat must be our secret between only you and me.' He looked at Alice who nodded her agreement. 'Probably best not to tell your father about this as he will not like it. Don't mention it to your mother either. Carry on as you are and one day you will be free to make your own choices.

'Do you understand, Alice? Now is the time for us to talk about this. And afterwards, only when we are alone.'

'But I don't like it and Mother doesn't like it.'

'We all have to do things we don't like. It's the way the world works.'

'But why?'

'It just is. Think yourself lucky; you are better off than most children. You have a house to live in and a bed to sleep in and you get to go out to nice places and have nice dresses. It isn't too bad, is it?' Big Alf held his breath, hoping to have won reason with the child and to have saved her from her father's displeasure for the time being.

She nodded, agreeing that she was better off than most children and had nice things when she worked. Her hair was always clean and neatly brushed and, if it was wintertime, she often had a new woollen coat. But outside of work, her clothing matched those of her mother where, despite her young age, she could feel her mood alter in line with whatever set of clothes she wore.

Recently she was beginning to realise how her mother must have felt whenever they went to the department store for her new work clothes. She had tried to ask her mother about it but she had shaken her head and said it was untrue, so Alice decided to watch her mother more closely the next time they visited the store.

Alice thought about this and what Alfie had just said and pondered for a while in silence while they sat and watched people stroll through the gardens.

The bit she liked the most was when he said that one

day she would be free to make her own choices. And when that happened, she would definitely choose not to rob nice people.

'Make the most of it, Alice. Keep doing what you are doing. Learn what you are taught and forever be vigilant. The smallest lack of concentration could mean you will end up in jail and you know how much your father has told you all about that.'

'I will try, Alfie,' she said with all sincerity.

Big Alf smiled. He liked it when she called him Alfie.

'Have you been doing this since you were my age or did you have an honest job?' she asked while watching a small boy throwing a ball for his dog as it yapped with excitement.

The question caught him off guard while thinking of all the endless jobs that he had done over the years, trying his hardest to think of one that hadn't involved crime. 'I was once a night-soil man, or mostly known as a dunny man, back in the 1870s,' he answered and from the puzzled look on the child's face, he continued. 'I wasn't much older than you are now. We had a horse and cart and walked up and down the back lanes collecting the dunny waste every night from the houses and took it away while the people were asleep.'

'Ah, poo,' Alice responded, pinching her nostrils together and shaking her head.

Big Alf flung his head back and roared with laughter at her response. 'Exactly, Alice. There was a great deal of poo.'

When she had stopped laughing, she said, 'I don't need to practice the scam. Can we go and see the ducks?'

'Ice cream?'

'Ducks don't like ice cream.' They held hands and laughed their way to the ice cream stand.

*

The races were always a good earner for the Johnsons, although to look at the sparse family home you wouldn't know it. Stanley's behaviour was dictated by his erratic mood and whether he bothered or remembered to give Rose housekeeping money. It didn't matter to him because he ate out often, but none of this was lost on Big Alf who pondered on what he could do about it.

The following day, he walked back into the kitchen on the rouse that he had forgotten his fedora, which he had purposely left behind, and whispered to Rose that page 402 of her bible had an interesting passage. She had looked at him questionably while he retrieved his hat then, before he followed his boss and Alice out of the door, he double-tapped the side of his nose and mouthed discretely 'every week'. Rose was a little bewildered and somewhat intrigued and, even though she was now alone, she waited for a few more minutes just to be sure before she flipped through the pages. When a pound note appeared between pages 402 and 403, she was amazed and thankful, but above all, frightened.

Humbled by Big Alf's thoughtfulness, she knew that it was to buy her and Alice food for when Stanley forgot to provide. They had gotten used to making food last which often meant having meagre portions spread over a few days. While she didn't mean to sound ungrateful, it had caused a further problem. Her mind began to race. *What if Stanley found out? Where could she hide the money and food safely? When would they eat for fear of him returning home at any time?*

They could have eaten safely in the comfort of Vera's parlour but she seldom took Alice there as it wasn't a place for a child. She laughed at the double standard because their way of life wasn't a place for a child either.

Aunt Vera had assured her that no *funny business* would take place whilst they were on the premises but she had declined. Also, her house was practically on the other side of town, so it wasn't viable for a quick meal anyway. Her aunt hadn't been offended; she understood and often gave her niece some concealable food to take with her whenever she visited.

Rose had taken her time to consider whether to involve Ettie or not when she was suddenly struck with a solution. The plan was perfect as Ettie only lived a few doors down. Rose knew that Stanley hated the old sticky beak because she wasn't intimidated by him. Being the aunt of the notorious Noble twins, he wasn't sure if she felt disdain for him or that she knew she was untouchable.

The Noble twins were popular with the ladies because they were ruthless, handsome and everything but noble in every sense and were described by many as being unpredictable and dangerous. They were built like tanks and at nineteen years old, they were powerful bruisers who revelled in mindless vehemence instilling fear and intimidation within their crime network by demanding money with deplorable threats of violence. Many bruisers met violent ends, but the conceited twins went everywhere together and looked out for each other, and this was not an end that they had ever envisioned.

With Ettie's connections and Stanley's abhorrence, thus making him unlikely to visit her house, Rose felt more comfortable in her decision to involve her friend.

'Ettie, can I ask you something that's just between us?' asked Rose while they sipped tea in Ettie's kitchen.

As soon as she replied, 'Sure, love, what's on your mind?' Rose felt safe because her friend's word was her bond.

Ettie's assumptions had been correct. She knew there was something that her neighbour had wanted to ask and she would bet her bottom dollar that it had something to do with that insect husband of hers.

'Not sure how to say it, so I'll just come out with it... Things are a bit *difficult* at the moment and I would appreciate some help...' There was no going back now because Ettie wouldn't let this go if she had changed her mind to reveal all.

'We're friends, Rose. Of course, I'll help.' The woman stood up and walked over to the kitchen drawer and pulled out her purse without hesitation.

'No. Goodness me, no!' Rose shook her head and waved her hands in a dismissive manner. 'Nothing like that. So sorry I gave you the wrong impression.'

Ettie looked puzzled but carried her purse back with her anyway and placed it beside the teapot.

'Sorry,' she repeated. 'It's the other way around actually.' She placed Big Alf's pound note on the table. 'It's a bit embarrassing, but Stanley gets a little *forgetful* sometimes. I would like to ask if you could get some extra food in so Alice and I can come around when he isn't at home? Although, I cannot say when it may be.' She pursed her lips apologetically.

Although Ettie found inconsistencies in the statement, she nonetheless read between the lines. It made her blood boil knowing what he was doing. She had heard rumours. But despite his perception of her, she wasn't a tittle-tattle. Not that she cared in the slightest what he thought of her.

'I understand. No need to say any more, love. You both come around whenever you need to. The door is always open to you, even if it's every day of the week, and if I'm not here, help yourself to whatever you need.' She leaned over and patted Rose's hand.

'Also'—Ettie lowered her voice—'if you ever need the twins to have a word with him, you only need to say...'

Rose smiled, appreciating the gesture. 'Thank you but that won't be necessary.' They finished their tea in comfortable silence.

CHAPTER SEVEN

Alice was now ten years old.

She often thought back to the morning in the Royal Botanic Gardens with Alfie and, although she had been very young at the time, she had listened and applied what he had told her. Even back then she had been savvy enough to conceal her newfound morals from her father and thus giving her and her mother a little easier home life than it would have been otherwise.

But in saying that there had, however, been a few occasions when she believed that a line was being crossed and that their *mark* did not deserve to be robbed. Whenever her father briefed them on a new scam, she began to think of every possible scenario. She played them out in her head repeatedly, so she could act them out seamlessly if need be. Being gifted in deflection and timing, she could cause the plan to fail without bringing blame on herself. But, like any plan, it was not always flawless.

The only time her father exuded exceptional patience

was when it came to selecting a mark. He rarely rushed or made rash decisions and would often follow them for a while, studying for tell-tale signs. One time, he had spent days gathering information before he worked out how to successfully pull the job. To him, it was almost like a sport.

'They always tell you, Alice, without telling you,' he would say, laughing. 'You just need to observe and the loot will come to you.' And his favourite saying of all: 'I could just stand in the middle of the street and yell at the top of my voice *I've been robbed*, and sure as light is day, you watch everyone around pat their pockets to check. Observe, Alice, and you will reap.'

'Green, nine o'clock,' Stanley said in a low voice as Big Alf and Alice both looked discretely left. It was eight-thirty in the morning and Central Station was bustling when her father had observed an interesting woman. She looked very well-to-do wearing her expensive green coat, chatting intently to the gentleman standing beside her on the platform. Her expensive jewellery was remarkably overshadowed by the small satchel she held.

Stanley was riveted.

The woman stuck out like a sore thumb because to him it was very unusual for a woman to carry a legal-looking bag. He was attracted to the *way* in which she held it possessively to her chest. His gut told him that it contained something worth a very pretty penny.

He was almost salivating like it contained a huge steak oozing its juices. But before he got too carried away, he needed Alice to get a closer look at the clasp. There was no denying, even from this distance, that it looked challenging. The idea was to distract and lift the contents while leaving the satchel so as not to cause immediate alarm or attention to themselves. Every pickpocket worth his salt knew that the place was regularly policed, so a silent swift take was required and he had just the team for the job.

'All will be well, Mrs Kelly,' assured the gentleman quietly. 'Try not to worry until you know for sure when we arrive at the office.'

Alice sidled up as much as she dared, already intrigued by the conversation.

'Thank you, Mr Matthews.' Alice detected deep sorrow in her voice. 'I don't know what I would have done without your or the bank's help. It is so kind of you to assist me today.'

'It is our pleasure.' He leaned a little closer and whispered, 'We couldn't let you travel alone with the property deeds.'

Mrs Kelly was grateful. 'Since my husband's death, I have been at somewhat of a loss as you well know, but it was his dying wish that we continue our plan to gift our whole estate to Dr Barnardo's. We were not blessed with children, so we hope the estate will be accepted where it could provide a good safe home for many children. The house is far too big for me, so this is the perfect solution. I am looking forward to living in the cottage on the estate; it has everything I need. I also hope to become involved as much as I can with the home.'

While Mr Matthews admired her outstanding generosity, he couldn't wait for the journey to be over and the deeds handed safely to Mrs Kelly's legal office. The responsibility was immense, particularly when he could lose his job if something went drastically wrong. Plus, it didn't help at all that Mrs Kelly insisted on holding the satchel.

Envisioning someone grabbing them, Mr Matthews tried to glance around for anything or anyone suspicious. His senses were on overload and felt he'd aged within the last hour. Everyone looked suspicious from the little girl near them to the train guard.

Alice had heard more than enough to change her view. It taught her not to judge people too quickly. Everyone had a story and if her deflection failed then she was prepared to take a hiding. By the look on her father, she knew he wanted the contents of the satchel where his gut had been one hundred per cent spot on. She was thinking wildly and had to be quick because she didn't want to draw attention to herself. Normally this kind of check took mere seconds and she was already well past that.

'Well?' he said calmly when she returned. His eyes bored into her, demanding, *What the hell took you so long? Because if you don't tell me right now, I'll beat it out of you.*

'I've never seen a clasp quite like it...'

'Tell me every detail and be quick, the train is coming in.'

'Is he police, do you think?' asked Big Alf.

'NOT important,' snapped Stanley before she could answer. He was focusing entirely on the contents and therefore breaking his own rules about not taking everything into account.

That helped Alice. 'Yes, he's police,' she said, nodding at her father. 'I heard him say that they are a party of five...' she lied very convincingly.

'T-H-E C-L-A-S-P,' her father said, and grabbed her upper arms and squeezed tightly.

Alice looked him straight in the eye and said, 'I can do it.'

'Good, Alice. Good,' he calmed down. He knew they barely had a couple of minutes before the train departed. It was now or never. He slapped Big Alf on the back. 'Ready?'

Both Big Alf and Alice nodded and started to walk toward the woman.

While they were walking, Alice kicked her heel back a little higher, grasped her shoelace and pulled it undone. With perfect timing, just as her father was almost in touching distance of the satchel, Alice tripped and fell, letting out a short scream of surprise. Mrs Kelly immediately turned around and reached out to help but before she could ask if she was alright, Mr Matthews caught Stanley's eye and summed up what was about to happen. The sound of the train guard's whistle made them all jump as Mr Matthews ushered Mrs Kelly to board. Stanley, Big Alf and Alice had no choice but to retreat before the remaining police in the party intervened.

'Home,' he spat, shoving Alice in front of him. 'I'll see you at the pub tonight,' he said to Big Alf, dismissing him when he started to protest knowing that Alice in serious trouble. Shiv stopped and sidled up to him and in a chilling tone, he said, 'Don't even think about it or you'll bleed out right here, right now.'

Big Alf felt a warning sting followed by a slow trickle down his left side courtesy of Shiv's blade.

*

'STANLEY, PLEASE!' There was nothing that Rose could do except pummel on Alice's bedroom door while her daughter bore the impact of Stanley's belt five times over. Alice had cowered in the corner, shielding her face against the wall while she received the lashes. It was hard but she tried her utmost in not showing weakness by crying out because she knew he thrived on that. Deep down, knowing that she had helped many children to have a nice safe home was far greater than any punishment she received.

'Shut your whining mouth, or you're next,' Stanley hissed in Rose's face then pushed her backwards on the landing when he exited the room. 'She cost me an absolute bleeding fortune today, I just know it.'

Rose ran and sat beside her daughter and gently encased her within her arms. They rocked and breathed a sigh of relief when they heard the front door slam.

*

On the flip side, Stanley enjoyed teaching Alice new life skills, but his definition of these skills was not the usual run-of-the-mill that normal fathers taught their children. He trained Alice in how to handle and use all kinds of knives and how to defend herself. The teachings also included advanced pickpocketing as well as reading and accounting skills. He said that reading was necessary and in their line of work, accountancy was essential particularly around the racecourse for calculating the odds and for knowing and recording the value of stolen property.

It was now spring and they attended many race meetings. Alice was on standby awaiting instruction from Alfie, due after the next race when the punters had picked up their winnings. To pass the time, she observed two young gentlemen who were clearly rich and unaccustomed to how betting or the races worked. Approaching closer, it was obvious that they couldn't decide on what horse to back. They were picking the names that appealed as opposed to studying the form. Overhearing their poor choice, she shook her head in disbelief and when they opened their wallets in readiness to place the bet, she politely intervened.

'Excuse me, sir.' She smiled. 'That bet would be no good. You will be throwing your money away.' Alice was trying to be helpful because she knew this statement to be true.

'Pardon, little girl?' queried the first young man. 'You really think we would listen to you?' He laughed dismissively and patted Alice on the head.

'Run along,' urged the second young man, shooing her away.

Undeterred, she continued. 'My father works here at the racecourse. He knows a thing or two about the horses and form, and so do I, because he taught me. I've watched the horse you picked and he's no good racing in dry conditions like today. He much prefers a softer ground, that's when he won the most races. Today he won't even come in third. Personally, I'd pick *Mister Blue* over *Champion's Dream*. But it's your money.'

They looked at Alice more seriously, then, at one another

in question. 'Well, quite the little expert, aren't we?' said the second man, still not totally convinced but his interest was piqued.

'Look, Bertie.' The first man smiled. 'It's a stab in the dark and we haven't a clue anyway. Just for the sheer fun of it, let's go with...' He looked at Alice questionably.

'Polly,' she answered.

'Let's go with Polly.' And with that, he walked over to the bookie and placed one pound on *Mister Blue*. On the nose, to win.

'Stay with us to watch the race,' said Edgar, 'and there'll be no hard feelings if it comes in last. It's good amusement.'

Alice nodded and joined them by the rail to watch.

'And they're off...' announced the commentator over the speaker when the starter dropped the flag.

It was a tense couple of minutes for Alice that allowed her to study Bertie and Edgar more closely. They were in their early twenties and obviously had more money than sense when she raised her eyebrows in mock as opposed to wonder. Their wallets were easy pickings, but she resisted the temptation. They were transfixed on the race particularly when the horses and jockeys literally flew past them, kicking tuffs of turf high up into the air where the earth vibrated for a mere few seconds. The stands were deafening as every punter seemed to be shouting their two pennies worth urging the jockeys to spur on the horses that were galloping towards the finishing post. At the end of the race, the men were dumbfounded. They looked at Polly in amazement as *Mister Blue* romped in at an easy first place while *Champion's Dream* came a lapse fifth.

'Told you!' she said triumphantly.

'Sorry we scoffed, Polly. Thanks to you, we won a fortune. Here, take this as a thank you.' Bertie handed Alice not one, but two crisp pound notes. The gesture meant more to her than the value.

'Thank you very much.' She smiled and took the money and clasped it in her fist out of sight. It was a momentous feeling. She had seen many a vast fortune but this time it was different. Earning this money fair and square without stealing it felt extremely uplifting. It was a huge boost because it was hers and hers legally. She did, however, quickly glance in the direction of Alfie and her father for fear that they had seen the exchange, but she was positive they had not.

'Care to join us for the remainder of the afternoon?' asked Bertie. 'We could seek your father's permission.'

'No, thank you, I must go.' Polly waved them goodbye and watched them make their way over to the bookie to collect their winnings.

Then, she walked over to a large pillar and stood behind it. Carefully folding the notes as small as possible, she crouched down as if to tie up her shoelace and placed one note down each sock then stood up abruptly just as Alfie bellowed...

'I'VE BEEN ROBBED. Ruthless pickpockets have robbed me!' while distressingly patting down his jacket pocket.

The knock-on effect for all in the vicinity was to stop and pat their own jacket pockets, trouser pockets, rims of hats and handbags giving a very prominent display and kind invitation of where their respective fortunes lie. In readiness, Alice and Stanley wove in and out of the cluster, collecting a good day's pay. Big Alf joined them, still patting down his jacket to keep up the rouse as he too relieved fortunes from unsuspecting punters who would not have suspected the victim as being the thief. Keeping to their strict forty-five-second rule, Stanley then let out a short sharp whistle to let his accomplices know that it was time to depart their separate ways and to meet at the assigned destination.

This racing season was different for Alice. She paid extra attention to the betting procedures, odds and the horses' form where she often stood next to the bookies to observe and learn. After a while, she decided it was time to test what she had absorbed and made silent bets to herself. To her amazement and joy, she was very pleased when she won more races than she lost.

Alice also loved the horses and envied the jockeys as they zoomed past, and she could only imagine the total feeling of freedom that they must have felt galloping around the track.

Overhearing someone say that there was a vacancy for a stable girl, Alice decided to ask her parents about working an early morning shift at the racecourse. Her mother would agree purely that it was an honest job. The problem would be with her father who would need clever convincing where perfect timing was always crucial.

'You already work for me.' He surprisingly remained calm while pouring himself another whisky at the kitchen table. 'Why would you want to work for someone else to be covered in shit for pitiful money and harder work?'

Honest, pitiful money is better than no money you offer, thought Rose, busying herself by washing cups that didn't need washing. She needed to stay and hear this through, not daring to leave Alice alone with her father who could turn at the blink of an eye, particularly when he had been drinking.

Alice had thought of all the excuses that her father would come up with alongside her pre-planned answers to work in her favour. 'I can do both,' she offered. 'The stable lads talk, I've caught pieces of conversation when they head back to the stables and by being on the inside, who knows, perhaps it could be very financially rewarding, Father...' She let that linger because he always responded to money.

Stanley considered this and slowly nodded before he spoke. 'Alright, Alice. We'll give it one month. You give me all your wages and I'll give some to your mother for housekeeping and some to you. But, if nothing useful by way of information materialises then you leave. That's the condition. Take it or leave it.' He finished off his glass. 'I'm off to the pub. Big Alf believes there's some business for us. Don't wait up.' He playfully slapped Rose on the bottom and left the house.

Alice's smile lit up the room. 'That was easier than I thought.'

'Yes, it was.' Her mother was equally amazed.

'I do not care about the wages. I'm just looking forward to working with the horses. I'm off to bed. I start at six tomorrow morning...'

'It's a long way to go on your own, Alice. Wait... you only just asked your father.'

'I'll be alright. I know my way around and I am nearly eleven years old. Besides, I knew he'd say yes. I got the job this afternoon. Night night.'

*

Alice loved the horses and felt immense enjoyment working at the stables and that included mucking out, where she felt a sense of pride that she was earning honest money. She had known for five years that what they were doing was wrong and had wrestled with her conscience.

Unlike her father, good strong morals were seeping into her soul.

As she grew older, she purposely missed opportunities when working the crowd at the races by deliberately reducing her daily takings. The only problem was that when her yield was down from her usual baseline, her father had retaliated by instilling fear and intimidation through fear of losing control over his prized asset.

It had been a long day and Alice was tired from her early shift at the stables followed by pickpocketing among the racegoers in the afternoon. As the sun was descending, the mood around the kitchen table was changing and a dying beam of orange sunlight briefly highlighted Alice's golden hair before leaving her in shadow.

Stanley had been stewing ever since he and Big Alf had counted the takings. He couldn't get it out of his head, consumed by anger that she had dared to recoup much less than normal. Even Big Alf picked up on Alice's unusually light haul.

'What's going on?' he asked in a low but threatening voice. The atmosphere teetered on a knife edge as Rose and Big Alf glanced at one another.

'I am sorry. I had a bad day, Father. You said a number of times that you sometimes have bad days...'

'ENOUGH!' He slammed his clenched fist on the table, making everyone jump when his whisper transitioned to an enraged tone. 'Don't insult me, child. It wasn't a bad day. WE lifted plenty'—indicating himself and Big Alf—'I knew this would come, you gaining morals and all, but NOT UNDER MY ROOF. DO YOU HEAR ME, ALICE?'

'Yes, Father.' She bent her head in what appeared to be shame and regret when it was all she could do to appease him and defuse the situation.

'Next time...' He stared at her with cold-steel eyes.

'Next time, I'll do better,' she answered, looking back up at him. While thinking, *No, I bloody well won't.*

Much later in the early hours, Alice was harshly woken from her sleep. Her bedroom door was hurled open with such brusque force that it smashed into the wall it was hinged to. It instantly rebounded back and hit someone's head who was slumped forward in the doorway before swinging back open, but with lesser intensity. Alice was now wide-awake and sat bolt upright, knowing two of the silhouettes had been drinking; she could smell it. She did not know the other man. No one said a word while her father and Big Alf dragged the slumping man further inside the cramped room and released their grip next to her bed. He landed with such an almighty weighty thump that the floorboards shook, causing her bed frame to jump up.

'Who's that?' she asked, clutching her blanket all around her. 'Is he drunk?' Her eyes then grew wide with fear. 'Is he... dead?'

'Too many questions. Get back to sleep,' her father replied, catching his breath from the exertion of hauling the lifeless body upstairs.

'What's going on?' asked Rose sleepily and nearly let out a piercing scream when she noticed the body on the floor.

'What's with all the damn stupid questions? Back to sleep, both of you.' He ushered Rose and Big Alf away from the room and closed the door, leaving his daughter alone with a dead body in pitch darkness.

For what seemed a lifetime, Alice feared to move a muscle. Her brain could not comprehend what had just happened. Was it a dream? But she knew full well it was not. Upon hearing her parents' door slam, she plucked up all her courage and swung her feet over the side of the bed that was positioned in the corner of the small room. With the chest of drawers at the foot of her bedstead, she had no option but to manoeuvre herself slowly alongside the corpse. Swiftly grabbing her meagre blanket and bundling it up into a ball, she then used her big toe and prodded him as a guide, enabling her to shuffle passed without tripping over him. She did contemplate stepping over him, but she wasn't sure if his arm was stretched out where there was the possibility that her foot could get caught, resulting in a noisy tumble. Her imagination ran riot, almost convincing herself that his hand would strike out and grab her ankle, causing her heart to jump out of her chest in anticipation.

Once out of her room, she took deep breaths to calm herself before expertly avoiding all the creaky stairs. Once in the kitchen, she made herself a makeshift bed on the floor; not that she was able to drift back to sleep.

Stanley was up and about unusually early that morning and Rose scurried to make him a cup of tea. 'Who's that upstairs?' she asked bravely.

'Well, it ain't Father Christmas, is it?' he replied sarcastically.

'DAMN IT,' Rose shouted without thinking and turned around to face him while clinging to the sink behind her for support. Even she was surprised at her raised voice when he shot up, flinging the chair out from underneath him at her foolish bravery.

'Damn it, Rose? Damn it?' But then he conceded that a dead man upstairs in the early hours did warrant a small explanation. He wasn't that unfeeling. 'There was a bit of trouble last night, hence our guest. There was no time to get the body to the docks, so we'll keep him here and Big Alf and I will get rid later tonight.'

'What trouble and why here? And...' Rose clutched her hands to her face, barely able to ask but knowing that she must. 'Did you... did you kill him, Stanley?'

Alice sat wide-eyed, gazing at her parents and wondered the very same.

'Nothing else you need know. Either of you. Get ready

for the stables, Alice. I'll walk some of the way with you.' He walked out of the kitchen and looked back at his wife. 'I'll deal with you later.'

CHAPTER EIGHT

During the course of the following week, Alice had discovered her own confidante within Mr Wyatt.

He was a bookie at the racecourse and a kind, decent family man, Pete, the stable lad, had told her. He also said that Mr Wyatt took a keen interest in people and could often be seen walking around the stables talking to the jockeys, trainers, owners, stable lads and girls. He liked to be among the horses too where his calm nature exuded to the horses who seemed to like him as well.

'Mr Wyatt, this is Alice, our new stable girl. And Alice, this is Mr Wyatt,' Pete introduced them then carried on sweeping the yard.

'Nice to meet you, Mr Wyatt.' When they shook hands, Alice felt her cheeks flush and hoped it did not show. Mr Wyatt was the tall middle-aged man wearing a smart black suit and bowler hat that she had been watching closely in which to learn the betting procedures from.

'Likewise, Alice. How are you liking it here?' He gave a

warm fatherly smile. His face and blue eyes looked kind, and he looked to be a gentleman in every sense as per Pete's initial assessment.

'I love the horses.' She beamed, looking with delight toward the training area at a chestnut mare. 'When I've been here a month, the boss said that I can have a ride around the paddock. Just over two weeks to go!'

'You will enjoy that, I can tell. My daughter used to work here as a stable girl too and she loved the rides when the trainers allowed it. That was a long time ago though, she's married now with a little one of her own.'

Alice smiled. She liked him instantly. 'I've seen you working.' She owned up.

'That's it!' he exclaimed as the penny dropped. 'I thought you looked familiar and seemed to take notice on how I worked. Thinking of becoming a bookie,' he said without ridicule.

'No, not a bookie, Mr Wyatt. Just fascinated by how it all works and to improve my arithmetic. I learned so much from you, particularly when you were patient and informing new people to the races how things worked, that I found myself winning most of the races...' She stopped when he looked surprised, no, horrified, that a child was betting. There also an element of a protective look that a bookie should dare to take advantage. 'No!' she said, shaking her head, 'I placed the bets in my head,' and they both burst out laughing.

'That's good. For one moment there, I thought that you were placing bets with another bookie. I was just about to have a word with them for taking bets from a child.'

'No, nothing like that, Mr Wyatt. Just in my head, I promise.'

The following afternoon, she had the opportunity to meet Mrs Wyatt who had stopped by to bring her husband some lunch and they insisted that she join them. Mrs Wyatt was in her mid-fifties and perhaps a foot shorter than her husband. She was of slim build and wore a smart dark brown tweed skirt, matching jacket, a cream silk blouse and dark brown shoes. It was difficult to tell just how long Mrs Wyatt's light brown hair was as it was styled in a neat bun that nestled at the nape of her neck. She had hazel eyes, pleasant features and wore just the right amount of red lipstick. Alice would have given her right arm to have been their daughter when listening to the stories of their children growing up in a safe and loving home. It turned out that they were more or less of an institution at the races as Mr Wyatts' pitch had been passed down the generations.

As the weeks passed, Mr Wyatt, being the total opposite to her father in every way, was gradually becoming a father figure to Alice. He listened to what she had to say and never judged, although she neglected to enlighten him on her father's profession or her own ashamed talents. She found that she could talk to Mr and Mrs Wyatt about most things and trusted them completely.

Mr Wyatt spoke of the Great Depression and how it was deeply affecting Australia, where unemployment continued on a downward decline. He had seen for himself that despite difficult times, people were turning to sport as a means of escape. Unbeknown to him, Alice had related, knowing all too well horse racing's popularity.

'Phar Lap, "The People's Horse",' he said fondly as they finished their sandwiches that Mrs Wyatt had brought one lunchtime. 'He has become the national hero by raising the spirits of the country. For a few precious minutes, the punters believe that they have a good chance of winning a couple of quid and the possibility of eating well for a while.

'And there's nothing like the excitement of seeing a race, is there? From tufts being flung up as the horses gallop by where the distinctive smell of earth and grass increases to the thunderous sound of the hooves and vibration of the ground.'

Alice smiled, enjoying Mr Wyatt's enthusiasm who obviously loved his job.

'Now, the AJC Plate back in April was the best race that I have ever seen in all my days here at the course. Believe me, I've seen hundreds perhaps thousands of races since I was a lad, but 26 April 1930, for me, will always be the best. Phar Lap won by ten lengths nonetheless! Everyone was in awe and the place erupted. You should've heard it, Alice. The race will go down as one of those special moments in Randwick's history, you mark my words. It was a real privilege to see.'

Alice appreciated what he was saying but didn't mention that she had been there to see for herself. Whether you were a racegoer or not, you had to have been stupid not to realise that it was a grand occasion. She, her father and Alfie were working that day and it was easily their most profitable to date.

The place had been packed with excited punters, most of

whom crammed at the rail full of expectation. But, most of all, Alice was thankful that Mr Wyatt had not been one of their unfortunate victims as it was their rule that staff were off limits, therefore eliminating suspicion from their future presence.

The memory took her back to that special day where she was in awe by all the elegant ladies and beautiful dresses and wished that her mother had been there to have seen for herself. The soft hues and different tones of blues, lilacs and florals complemented the rich grass. She also admired how some of the women had styled waves into their bob haircuts, giving them a softer more feminine look, which would also suit her mother.

As to herself, she recalled feeling like a princess and marvelled how clothing had the ability to change her outlook and attitude. The lilac satin dress felt luxurious and cool against her skin. The full skirt flowed toward the hem that sat just above her knee and the white satin sash gave the illusion that it was tied with a bow at the back. Over the years, they had perfected the apron pocket that she wore to hide her pickings that had been adapted to Alice's clothing accordingly where, that day, she wore a bespoke cardigan of quality material to conceal the pocket.

Her father had been on a high because it was an outstanding money day. Being aware of tough times and until they themselves met desperate measures, he instructed Alice and Big Alf to use discretion and steal only from those who looked like they could well afford it. Stanley believed it made sense to liberate from the well-to-do than waste precious time on poorer targets for minimal return. Hence, in his head alone, he was providing a good service to the community.

*

As promised by Mr Sulker, the owner of *Grey Marble*, Alice was allowed her first ride after working at the stables for one month. She arrived early for her shift, eager to get into the saddle and ride like the wind down the racecourse. After mucking out her five allocated stables, she assisted in leading the horses to the exercise yard. Her imagined *ride like the wind* turned out not as she had anticipated when she found out that it would be basic training only.

Mountain Man, who was the jockey, and built more like a feather than a mountain, interlocked his fingers to help boost her up into the saddle. He adjusted the stirrups accordingly by shoving her feet onto the metal bar. It was deceiving. Alice found that she was much higher up than she expected. Grey Marble was a beautiful two-year-old colt and aptly named, resembling grey marble and was silky smooth to touch.

Alice was finally sitting in the saddle and it was the best feeling ever. She could not have imagined a better way in which to spend her eleventh birthday. It would be a happy cherished memory that she would never forget.

Mr Ferris, the trainer, or just Ferris, as he preferred, looked like a retired jockey as his frame resembled as such, held onto the lead rope and shouted instructions. He told her how she should sit, hold the reins, and place her feet as Grey Marble walked around the circumference of the training yard. Usually, these exercises were carried out riderless but with nil experience, Alice had to start somewhere. It took all her concentration to listen and apply Ferris' instructions and she appreciated learning the basics to what would become vital lessons for her future career.

Since that day, Alice had been a stone in Ferris' shoe when she bombarded him to allow her to get back in the saddle. Ferris may have looked like a tough weathered nut on the outside but he was a softie on the inside when someone was willing to put in the hard yards. Through his vast experience, he knew that this young girl had the potential to be a great rider. She had a natural way about her and every horse she rode responded well.

Soon, Ferris allowed her to join the morning canters, gradually progressing to gallops during the three-furlong sprint where Alice finally experienced the feeling of riding like the wind.

*

Like an apprentice, Alice studied the form more concisely under Mr Wyatt's guidance and impressed him time and time again with her near accuracy on picking winners. She had a skill in collating past performance, weather, course conditions and jockey statistics that reaped results. On race days, she would look at the line-up and form and prior to the beginning of the meeting would hand him her list and they would discuss the outcome when she was next at the course.

'You picked three out of five winners on the nose, Alice.

Well done,' he said and handed the list back to her.

'Thank you, Mr Wyatt.' She beamed, pleased because her father rarely praised her at all these days.

He began to say something then stopped while Alice finished mucking out the stable. He was in two minds whether to continue, then he decided *what the hell*. 'Alice, come over here a minute, will you?' he said, moving out of earshot of anyone nearby and walking over to stand at the paddock's rail.

'Everything alright?' she asked, concerned. He looked a little troubled.

He smiled in reassurance. 'Everything is fine. Look, I've something to ask that's got to be strictly between us otherwise I could land in a deep hot water tub of trouble, particularly as you are only a child...' He looked at her for acknowledgement to which she nodded a little sceptically, her guard on alert. 'It's to do with your form reading...'

She was relieved and her tension lifted. Despite her young age, she had seen many unpleasant things and was worried regarding where the conversation was going but now, she felt guilty for thinking the worst of him.

'You have a natural talent for picking out winners and I know money is tight – it's tight for everyone. How do you feel about investing a sixpence or so from your wages to accompany the list you give me and I'll place a bet for you? It's not ethical, which means that it isn't right or proper as you are a child. But that and the risks aside, to which I will take full responsibility, it would be your own work and your money overall.'

Alice's face lit up like a beacon. 'Really, Mr Wyatt? You would do that for me?' She felt quite humbled.

He was pleased that she wasn't offended. 'Yes, I would. Only a very small amount, mind. Every little helps, doesn't it...' He stopped, noticing how her expression went from pure delight to dismay. 'Alice?'

She was embarrassed. She hadn't a penny to her name. Her father took all her wages and contrary to his original statement, her mother hadn't received any of it for housekeeping either. He had even found the money that the two young men had rightfully given her at the races a while back as a thank you when she helped them pick a winner. He had taken his belt to her for her dishonesty.

'My father looks after all my wages,' she said, looking down at the ground and by that, Mr Wyatt knew exactly what that entailed. He had seen Mr Johnson once, summing him up in an instant as a spiteful man. He had that look about him but never suspected for a minute the kind of work that he was in. Which was probably just as well.

'Goodness me, Alice,' he said, looking a little shocked. 'What on Earth was I thinking?' He rummaged in his coat pocket and brought out a florin. 'Here, this is yours.' He smiled. Alice looked stunned as Mr Wyatt explained further. 'I am sorry, I totally forgot. Between the races the other week, I spotted a sixpence on the ground. So, I looked at your list and placed a bet for you on the next race, which stormed home, so this is your winnings. Well done.' The story was a complete fabrication but it broke his heart suspecting what her father had done. What else could he do?

'My winnings?' She beamed.

'Yes. How about that?'

But how could she accept? Knowing full well what would happen. 'Mr Wyatt,' she said, handing it back to him, 'could you please look after this for me? I'm pretty clumsy and would hate to lose it.'

He knew what she was really saying. 'My pleasure. How say I keep a little book to keep a track of your winnings? And the way your lists are going, you will make a fortune one day. It all stacks up, you know. You continue to give me your lists and tell me how much of your winnings you wish to bet and I'll do the rest. But it must remain strictly between us. Sound like a deal?'

'Sounds like a great deal!' And they shook on their arrangement that continued for the next few years.

Whenever Alice's winnings totalled a pound, Mr Wyatt would let her know together with the overall total. He also showed her the perfect hiding spot for her money and told her that if she ever needed it, for whatever reason, she didn't have to ask his permission. It was hers for the taking. The perfect hiding spot turned out to be within a small storage area where he kept his tote board and the old battered wooden box that he stood on to conduct his business. Mr Wyatt was quite protective of this wooden box, not only because it had been passed down the generations, but because inside he had found a way to conceal an old tobacco tin to store her winnings.

CHAPTER NINE

'Don't be so flaming stupid,' her father said when Alice recoiled. 'It doesn't bite.' He waved the razor-sharp blade in front of her face. 'See this?' He indicated the narrow metal point that glistened in the low lighting. 'This will snap if you strike too roughly. I'll teach you precision, skill and how to know its limits to handle this baby correctly.

'It's Italian. A switchblade, or just switch,' he said as he pressed and held the top bolster and guided the blade back within the handle. 'Isn't it beautiful? The top bolsters are a good size and they will prevent your hand from slipping up onto the blade.' He showed her how to release the safety then he pressed the button in the middle of the handle where the blade rapidly appeared clicking into place. 'Very responsive,' he admired. 'It's been well looked after and the spring mechanism is pure craftsmanship.

'The most valued lesson I can give is to learn blind. That's the best way. The last thing you need to worry about if it comes to it is looking away from a serious situation to check whether you're holding it the right way. Those precious seconds could cost you your life.

'Practice and practice. Find the most comfortable place on you and stick to it. Either put it in your pocket or down your boot and see how fast you can retrieve, remove the safety and trigger the blade. If you prefer to keep it in your pocket, make sure that you put nothing else in there, because even a handkerchief could get tangled. Be smart, think ahead and put in hours of practice so it becomes a reflex action.

'Start by closing your eyes and feel the handle. Just by touch, learn which is the dangerous end and get to know the difference between the safety and the release button. You should be able to retrieve and action within the blink of an eye.'

Alice hated the knife, or switch, as her father referred to it, but took it anyway. It was surprisingly heavier than she had expected. It sat comfortably in her small hand where it felt cold and sinister but above all, deadly.

Stanley had liberated it when he and Big Alf were walking through the market. He had spotted the unusual design and knew that it would be the perfect first blade for her. The handle was made of ivory and had a small emerald embedded within the highly polished silver bottom bolster. The top curved bolsters were also silver but had an ornate patterned engraving. It was such a beautiful well-loved piece that Stanley had initially been tempted to pawn it. But on reflection, he thought it would be an ideal birthday present for Alice, despite being over a month late and the only birthday present that he had ever given her.

And so, for a couple of hours a week, he began to teach her the art of using his preferred weapon of choice. By pointing it on himself, he taught her where to find vital organs. Because he knew of a good place to teach, he also showed where to find the organs on pigs, horses and sheep. He gave detailed insight on how to stop a heartbeat with one strike while avoiding the rib cage to prevent damage to the blade.

Because the world was a dangerous place, Stanley felt that it was his fatherly duty to show his daughter the best way to cut a man's ball bags if she was unfortunate enough to be left with no other choice. Alice may have been young but she had seen couples down alleyways. She had heard her parents through the thin walls and by her mother's cries, she had known that she hadn't always liked what her father was doing. So, for that reason, she paid close attention as he explained what she had to do in order to protect herself.

'You've progressed a long way since you started, Alice, and cutting into flesh is the only way to practice,' he said, watching his daughter hover the blade over the pig carcass. 'Gently, gently,' he whispered, following her every move. 'You must exude total control. Position the blade down and feel for the pierce. If you are precise, you will feel a slight pop or burst; it depends on what you are cutting. This pig has much tougher skin than us and therefore you will need to apply more pressure the further the blade goes in.

'Feel your way, Alice. Let the blade talk to you. Go on, go in deeper, feel and remember. It's all to do with the pressure you apply and together with either controlled speed or a slow incision. How you pull the blade back out also determines the outer wound. Go slow for a drain or quick and brutal if you agitate, spin or flick the blade out to make a mess on exit.

'Remember what I said? Anger will dictate your pressure and precision. Try and stay calm to get the cut you want. I will also show you how to leave an unpleasant scar and to make someone bleed out. There's an art to it, Alice. A beautiful, wonderful art.'

Alice hated the thought of cutting the pig even though it was dead and she didn't want to imagine cutting anything living. Under her father's guidance, she felt everything he said she would and after numerous attempts, she was able to distinguish and apply the different cuts that he requested.

'One more time,' he encouraged. 'Cut me a warning.'

She worked the blade on another carcass by positioning the tip of the knife and flicking the blade. Apart from the sounds of slow intermittent blood dripping and the constant buzzing of the flies, it was very quiet in the holding area where the meat was stored after arriving at the docks. Alice had been spooked when her father had first brought her here a few weeks ago. It was eerie with row upon row of headless hanging carcasses, and the smell was so thick and overpowering that she could taste it. He had known the ideal spot in which to break in as she followed him through a loose wooden board that he swung to the side and was where he often came to practice and hone his skill.

'Very good,' he praised. 'Now, give me a bleed out, that you apply here or here,' he said, indicating on himself where she perfected the quick thrust on the carcass. 'Good. Now for a deep scar.' Alice held the blade at a slight angle and implemented a slow controlled quarter-inch cut where the skin sprang apart, exposing the meat underneath.

Stanley was very pleased. 'You've done well, Alice. We'll be on our way now as the night watchman will be along soon. And remember you must always look after your switch. Clean it thoroughly after every use. The worse thing is for it to jam when you really need it because the mechanism is bloody. Did you enjoy it?'

What an odd question, she thought. *Besides, Father, who on Earth would enjoy cutting up dead animals?*

'I have a better understanding of the switch and I could feel everything you said I would,' she said, before adding, 'Thank you, Father,' as she knew he would like it.

*

Rose also hated what Stanley was doing but kept her tongue. She put things into perspective that he was only teaching Alice how to protect herself and that could only be a good thing. It also helped her overall outlook on home life with Stanley, knowing that it wouldn't be too long before she could take Alice away. Her earnings concealed within the urn of Vera's dearly departed was building up nicely.

She often spoke about her escape plans with Vera but also explained that she would never divulge the destination. It was too risky as they both knew what Stanley was capable of because he would not stop in his quest to get them back. Rose was uplifted and, God willing, believed she just needed five more years before there would be enough for her and Alice to get away to start their fresh beginning. She had worked hard for their future, so five more years was tolerable. In the meantime, she was doing her utmost to get by and play by his rules until such a time came when she could be self-dependent. And that was an extremely liberating thought.

Being beautiful and innocent-looking was Rose's perfect camouflage in becoming a master pickpocket, because who would dream of suspecting her? She kept a change of well-to-do clothing at Vera's house that always uplifted her overall stance whenever she wore the quality garments. But above all, she took her time to plan and never made risky or spur-of-the-moment moves. She ventured more within the busy markets and gathering places and only targeted people who could afford it. Even though she planned her work around Stanley's longer jobs, his comings and goings could still be erratic, so she was always prepared with suitable explanations as to where she had been.

On this particular afternoon, she arrived home carrying a basket containing a few potatoes knowing it wouldn't raise any concern. She knew it was a perfect alibi although it had not been necessary because her husband was otherwise occupied.

'DO IT LIKE YOU MEAN IT, GIRL,' he bellowed, trying to fire Alice up at her half-measure attempt to stab him in the chest as they eyed one another in the kitchen. 'The hoodlum who comes at you like a steam train is going to kill you, Alice, not invite you to a bloody teddy bears picnic.'

'Stanley, please,' pleaded Rose.

'DAMMIT. STAY OUT OF IT YOU STUPID, PATHETIC WOMAN! Come on, Alice. One more time.'

She lunged at her father, hating him for the way he treated her mother.

'That's more like it.' His eyes sparked with pure joy when he intercepted the weapon, pushed her hand back, spun her around and placed her on the floor none too gently.

'ALICE!' shrieked Rose, rushing to help her. She was winded but intrigued as to how she got there so fast while gingerly standing back up.

'Break that down. Show me how that was done,' she demanded, swiping her mother's arm away.

'That's my girl.' The lessons continued as he taught her how to defend herself and she became a sponge to his knowledge. He also lovingly told her about his favourite switch. It was called a clip point due to the forward third of the blade looking like it had been clipped off in a smooth downward curve to the point. He had also modified it with serrations on the underside enabling a messier exit to which Alice had shuddered just thinking about it.

The following week Stanley took her back to the meat storage warehouse down at the docks. The idea was so that she could experience the clip-point blade piercing real skin, muscle and bone and learn how much pressure she had to apply. He couldn't promote enough the importance of getting to know every knife that she would possess in her lifetime because as always, her life could depend on it.

Alice wasn't that naïve. She knew that he had murdered

but she hadn't dared to ask how many. Through the lessons, it became apparent to her as to why her father was known as Shiv. He also explained that he always wore a leather strap secreted under his shirt collar whenever he conducted delicate business to prevent his own throat from being cut.

Just before their hour's training was up, they both took advantage of the stinking hole they were in and cut up as much meat as they could conceal on their person to take home. It didn't look or smell too pretty.

'Waste not, want not,' he said. 'Your mother should be able to make a decent pie or two out of this.'

*

'What's this, Mr Wyatt?' Alice whispered, staring at the small, wrapped gift in awe like she was holding the most precious thing in all the world.

'It's a Christmas present. You can either open it now or wait until Christmas morning. It's up to you,' he said and Mrs Wyatt nodded in agreement. They were sitting eating their small picnic in the stands of the racecourse on the hot summer's day.

Alice looked up at them in amazement and what she said next broke their hearts. 'I've never had a Christmas present before.' A tear surfaced, making her look like a delicate and beautiful angel and her long hair caught the sunlight highlighting strands of spun gold.

Deep down, he wasn't at all surprised given what he knew of Alice's home life and it prompted him to say, 'How about you open it now? We won't see you over Christmas as we are visiting our grandson and it would be lovely to know what you think.'

'Please do,' urged Mrs Wyatt.

Alice beamed with a radiant smile and began to unwrap her present. She wanted to savour the moment and wanted every second to last at least an hour. She was on tenterhooks, as were the Wyatt's, when she opened the lid of the box to reveal a small round silver pendant.

'The design is a four-leafed clover,' said Mrs Wyatt. 'Do you like it?'

'It's the most beautiful thing I have ever seen,' Alice replied in truth, holding it in the palm of her hand.

'Supposed to be lucky,' said Mr Wyatt. 'You know, it's considered fortunate to find a real four-leafed one because they really should only have three leaves. There's a small safety pin in the box under the cotton wool, thought you could attach it through the small hoop of the pendant and secure it about your person or keep it somewhere safe...' The Wyatts had thought long and hard about what they could give her that wouldn't be discovered and sold by her father. The small pendant seemed the obvious choice where it could easily be concealed and was why they did not give her the chain to go with it.

'Thank you both SO much.' She beamed. 'I love it and will treasure it forever. I promise,' she said while hugging them both tightly.

'Splendid, well that's good.' Mr Wyatt knew that his wife was just as emotional as he was. 'Perhaps another sandwich?' he said, offering the plate around.

Christmas came and went without much of a mention or celebration in the Johnson household whenever Stanley was present. Although he regularly came home drunk from his own three-week binge that carried over into the New Year. He was often accompanied and aided by Big Alf and they were just as bad as one another. Alice and Rose celebrated alternating between Vera and Ettie whenever Stanley was either at the pub or sleeping off the aftereffects.

The next big event in Sydney's history was the opening of the Sydney Harbour Bridge on 19 March 1932 that was deemed one of the greatest engineering masterpieces of its time. Rose had read from one of Stanley's discarded newspapers that there had been much hype and excitement since construction began on the approaches to the span some nine years prior and now it was complete.

Alice rarely attended school, courtesy of her father believing he could teach her more realistic life skills better than schooling ever could. Plus, time spent in the classroom was unprofitable. She had been disappointed that he hadn't allowed her to attend a special school day when her peers were cordially invited to walk across the bridge in celebration prior to the grand opening. It was a waste of time in her father's opinion, although she deduced the real reason was the unlikeliness that any of the pupils had any monetary value about their person in which to steal.

But today was another matter entirely...

'Everyone knows what to do?' Stanley double-checked, looking from Alice to Big Alf who were dressed in their finest, pleased by their nods. As surely as a water diviner had the ability to locate precious supplies, Stanley's fingers tingled and twitched knowing it would be a good pickpocketing day. Unbeknown to her husband, Rose planned on lifting too, accompanied by Vera who just wanted a grand day out.

Newspaper articles suggested that tens of thousands were expected to turn out for the official opening by the New South Wales Premier, Jack Lang, but that figure had far exceeded expectation. It was also reported the following day that Francis de Groot, who had served in the First World War and was awarded a ceremonial sword, had upstaged the Premier by riding on horseback and used the sword to cut the ribbon. Not surprisingly, he had been subsequently arrested.

CHAPTER TEN

'Go on, in you go,' urged Stanley. 'I'll be here in case anything goes wrong, which it won't. And Big Alf will be inside with you.'

They had headed into the city for a change of business today and for Alice to try out the new scam she had learned. She found it difficult and complicated and had convinced herself that she would get tongue-tied and lose momentum. She had practised and practised, but for the most part, Alfie told her that confidence was all that was needed to pull it off successfully. The butterflies in her stomach told her otherwise.

Alice took a deep breath, held her head up high, planted a sweet *trust me* smile on her face and entered the haberdashery shop. She hadn't been here before and was distracted by the beautiful displays of ribbons and fabrics in every vivid colour and knew that her mother would like it here too. She thought that they could come here the next time they visited Buckingham's Department store, as it was only just around the corner. But then again, perhaps it wouldn't be such a good idea considering.

'May I help you, Miss?' Smiled the prim lady who looked to be the same age as her mother.

'Yes, thank you. I would like to buy four small black buttons, please.' Alice placed a pound note on the highly waxed wooden counter and with her index finger she slid it towards the woman. With raised eyebrows, the lady immediately thought that it was a vast amount of money to be carried around by someone so young. As per the plan, she assured, 'My father will be along shortly; he is on business and has gone into another shop first to save time because we have a train to catch. He asked me to get the buttons.'

The prim lady relaxed and completed the transaction by wrapping the buttons and handing Alice her change. But before she had the chance to close the till, the young girl spoke quite rapidly.

'Oh! I almost forgot. He also asked if we could have some change, please, if you don't mind?' She smiled sweetly and extended a ten-pound note from her pocket. Knowing about the father, the lady wasn't surprised at all by the very large note.

'I'll see if we have some,' she said, taking the note then looking back in the till and giving her customer a five-pound note and five ones.

'Silly me,' said Alice apologetically, while pocketing the five-pound note. 'I got that wrong. We have change. I meant to say can you please change these five ones for a five-pound note?' And she smiled again while bundling up the pound notes, giving them back.

The woman obliged and gave Alice a five-pound note. Then, after a brief moment, she said, 'You've only given me four,' and proceeded to count them as proof. 'One, two, three, four,' placing them down on the counter.

'Oh!' Alice was shocked. 'I am so sorry.' She placed another one on top. 'Now, that's five and I'll give you back this five-pound note making ten and you give me back my ten-pound note, then we are even.'

The woman did exactly that and smiled. Alice picked up the buttons and walked out the shop, closely followed by Big Alf who couldn't have been prouder at the way she conducted the scam. The whole process took seconds while he and Stanley walked shoulder to shoulder shielding Alice from the shop's doorway in case the woman came running out searching for her after figuring out that she had just been conned out of five pounds.

'Great work. She mastered it perfectly, Shiv.'

'Atta girl, Alice,' he praised, playfully tugging her pigtails. 'It's my turn next. Let's go turn that five pounds into fifty.'

*

Alice was approaching her teen years and growing up too fast for Stanley's liking, and it had nothing to do with normal fatherly concern. To him, this meant that he could no longer rely on or exploit the *I've lost my daddy* routine or for Alice to pickpocket in tiny awkward spaces as her recent growth spurt made her just shy of her mother's average height.

He pondered if he should use Alice's beauty to entice drunks into dark alleyways for sexual favours. It would be extremely dangerous, despite he and Big Alf being near to ensure no harm came to her. Stanley couldn't believe that he almost had a conscience about planning this scenario. *I must be getting soft in my old age*, he thought.

While he still considered this possibility, he and the big man headed off to the pub to work on some illegal off-track betting. When the Depression sapped the economy, the now decline of punters at the racecourse meant that Stanley's take was down. But, on the upside, he was delighted that the starting price, or SP, had become very popular due to the recent surge in telephone installation within local pubs. This meant that the average punter could save on their tram fare and entrance money to the racetrack and use the money instead to place their bets with the SP operator. The operator stood strategically by the telephone while having a pint and listening to the race on the radio. This was popular as the SP was determined only when the race had begun thus making the odds in the punter's favour. It was a profitable and easy way to spend an afternoon, but it came with the risk of getting arrested due to the law heavily cutting down on illegal gambling.

To prevent this, the landlord had hired a *cockatoo*, a young man whose job it was to stand outside and to make a noise whenever the police approached. The last one had failed abysmally. So much so, that he was now widely known as the *bright shadow*, making him practically unemployable.

The pub was packed and the new cockatoo was in place.

Beer was flowing and the men were having a good time on this Saturday afternoon. They placed their bets with Big Alf, the alleged SP operator, who talked convincingly on the telephone while receiving very good odds from no one on the other end.

Big Alf had a pocketful of money after collecting vast amounts in bets from the first three races. And what he paid out in winnings; Shiv was recouping in very small amounts as to not cause alarm when he worked the room. The new SP operator offered good odds to gain trust ensuring bigger bets for the following race and Shiv created another good-feel factor by acting a little worse for wear. He announced to the whole pub that the next couple of rounds were on him by slamming five pounds onto the bar. Cheers exploded and the landlord worked hard to keep up with the demand. Little did they know that they were paying for their own drinks.

On the fourth race, Shiv indicated to his associate that it was time to up the stakes and Big Alf announced the SP. Because the punters were getting drunk, particularly after receiving some *free* drinks, they were inclined to bet more money. The race was now well underway and the packed pub tried their hardest to listen to the commentator's voice on the radio, but it was easier said than done. Then, at the final yards, there descended a hush before Shiv staggered over to the SP operator demanding that he wanted to change his bet. Big Alf pushed the drunk man away, who bumped into the radio, moving the dial thus losing the final crucial moments of the race.

A split second before the place erupted with arguments

as to who had won, the cockatoo burst through the door yelling, 'POLICE! Coming up Gibbs Drive,' and was nearly trampled on as the illegal punters rushed out of the door fleeing in the opposite direction. Shiv and Big Alf were the last to leave, where they gave the cockatoo a pound for his trouble, then all three men ran down Gibbs Drive before splitting up in different directions.

*

It was on this same afternoon that Alice approached her mother with an idea. 'Let's go and see a movie.' She beamed at Rose. 'It'll be fun and we haven't gone since I can't remember. We love the movies. What do you say? It will be a special treat.'

Rose was a little taken aback and stared at the sink full of washing. 'Don't think we should. We've lots of work to do here before your father gets home.'

'We'll do it together when we get back. Look, I have money,' she said and emptied her pocket onto the table. 'Let's go, right now. We can see 42nd Street. I've heard so much about it. We can even go for tea and cake afterwards. Yes? Please say yes.'

Alice could see that her mother was very tempted. 'Well...'

'Yes.' Alice kissed her on the cheek. 'How exciting. It's about time we spent a few hours together. I can see you're concerned that I have money. I couldn't resist taking a little for myself. To hell with it...'

'Alice!'

'I know, I know, but what have we got? Nothing. That's what we have got. Nothing and bullying, that's what. He's a total bully...' She was getting worked up and angry.

'He is your father, Alice. Whatever you think. Don't forget that,' Rose said.

'Let's not argue, not today. Come on, we're wasting time.'

Rose tidied her hair and smartened up as much as she could. Even though Alice had some nice clothes, she hadn't wanted to embarrass her mother by dressing up so she matched her outfit, and they left the house linking arms and giggling like a couple of children enjoying each other's company.

They arrived in good time for the start of the movie and sat watching in awe at the production where their heads were full of fashion, glamour, and romance when they departed the theatre.

'I loved it! Thank you, Alice, for prompting this. We had a great time.'

'Yes, I loved it too. Come on, a quick cup of tea and a cake to round the afternoon off.'

'Time is getting on.'

'Just for half an hour and we will still be back before father comes home – if he comes home. He'll probably stay on at the pub. Come on, Mother, this way,' she urged, and they walked down the high street and into the next tea shop where they ordered one pot of tea and a small selection of pastries.

'This is heaven,' beamed Rose, pouring the tea. It was the best afternoon. Ever.

'I loved the movie so much. I'll be singing the songs for ages to come.'

'Not out loud, though. Your father will know where we've been.'

'How will he know? The songs are popular enough, he won't guess. It'll be our little secret. Ah, romance. I can't wait to fall in love and to get married.'

'You've years ahead yet. Take your time, there's no rush.'

'What was father like in the beginning?'

The question caught Rose completely off guard and her heart missed a beat. She shakily replaced the cup in the saucer.

'Sorry, I didn't mean to pry.' But she still wanted the answer and kept quiet by taking another sip of tea hoping her mother would continue, which thankfully, she did.

'We were made for one another, Alice. He was wonderful, attentive and a gentleman.' She briefly remembered a time when Stanley had been her sweetheart and the man who meant the world to her.

Before her mother could continue, Alice blurted, 'Goodness! Father? What happened to make him change?'

Rose knew there was no way on Earth that she would ever divulge what had happened the very second that her daughter was born. It was still hard for her to comprehend let alone to tell her only child that he had changed in a blink of an eye because he desired a son. It would destroy her. Rose knew that Alice was stronger than she would ever be and that she hated her father at times. But, still, she could never tell her the real reason.

'Times change, people change...'

'That's it? Times and people change? Well, I won't let that happen. I don't mean to hurt you, Mother, but that will not happen to me. I will meet a man who will totally love me and I him, and we will live happily ever after.' They both smiled and polished off the last of the pastries.

'I will be so thrilled for you, Alice. For that to happen. He already sounds like the ideal man.' They laughed, then left the table to pay for their refreshment before walking back home.

'You're growing up fast and quite the romantic too. Don't change. We live in tough times and that often makes people tough too. Be true to yourself, but most of all, be happy. The world may often be miserable, but we live in a beautiful country with beautiful weather that we often don't see it as we should. I know your childhood hasn't been what I envisioned for you, but you are your own person. I can see that. You are much stronger, tougher and smarter than I'll ever be, and you will go places. Your handsome husband will take you away from all of this.' Rose turned and hugged her daughter tightly.

'Goodness! That was beautiful.' She returned the hug.

'It's the movie. It has overtaken us and made us all gooey on the inside.' They giggled, appreciating their precious few hours of fun and escape before coming back to harsh reality.

CHAPTER ELEVEN

Alice was becoming an excellent rider as her passion for horses continued to grow. Being quite slender, the jockeys and owners alike used her for the dawn gallops and there was nothing she enjoyed more than the feeling of freedom, speed and the crisp morning air billowing through her hair. It was very exhilarating.

The horses and stables meant more to her than anyone could imagine. They were her sanctuary, hence she never complained about the early starts. The racecourse was a fair way from where they lived, where on a good day it would take her about an hour to walk at a swift pace. Most of the undesirables in their area knew she was Shiv's daughter and left well alone. But there was always some chancer who thought that a young girl out and about on her own at an ungodly hour was easy prey. That was when she had been grateful for her father's lessons.

Overall, by her reckoning, there had been around twenty incidents that she had encountered untoward attention during all her early morning journeys. The worst occasion was when a man tried to drag her into a car while the other stayed behind the wheel for a quick getaway. She had been twelve years old. Adrenaline had kicked in as soon as the man stepped out of the car with the pretence of holding a map to ask her for directions. Being on alert, Alice remained just out of reach and was ready to flee. She remembered her father saying that the distance between outstretched arms from one middle fingertip to the other equalled the persons height and trained her how to judge their reach. But a quick struggle soon entailed when the man lunged and grabbed her coat sleeve.

A split second later, Alice stabbed his hand with one forceful strike, causing him to immediately let go. She then ran for her life to the echoes of 'YOU LITTLE BITCH!' while his venomous spat rebounded off all the tall buildings in the early morning quiet. Nearing the racecourse, Alice slowed her pace feeling much safer due to the people around who were getting the course ready for the new day. The adrenaline was wearing off, causing her to shake and that was when she noticed she was still clutching her switchblade. Sure that no one was watching, she bent down and ran the blade through the dew-covered grass to wipe off the man's blood and upon standing, she swished her foot through the grass to disperse the red as it diluted within the dew.

She never told a soul, not even her father.

*

It was now March 1936; Alice was fifteen and had been working at the stables for four and a half years where every second away from her controlling and bullying father had been bliss.

Her views on things were constantly changing and for years she had known the damn difference between right and wrong. How she hated him for the way he treated both her and her mother. She also loathed what he stood for and ultimately for what he tried to turn her into. Above all, Alice wanted more from her life than to be a pickpocket and was realistic in knowing that it was only a matter of time before she rotted in prison.

Over the years they had gotten away with a tidy fortune where her innocence had shielded the danger. But despite the now disintegrated shield turning to stark realisation, she was still trapped.

It had been an almighty sad day when Alice had put the pieces together knowing that her own father had continually put her in danger every time they went out to work. In all honesty, back then, she hadn't been strong enough to stand up to him. She despised herself for being a coward and continued to do as she was told for fear of herself or her mother copping a severe beating.

*

'Quick, sit down I have something to tell you,' her mother whispered while looking at the ceiling. 'Your father will be down any minute. We have a problem.'

Alice's heart quickened and her stomach flipped as

horrendous speculation bombarded her mind. She tried to swallow but her mouth was dry and when she leaned in closer, she saw sheer terror in her mother's eyes. 'What's wrong?' was all she could manage.

'Ettie came here this morning and it's bad news. The Nobel twins have been arrested for murder and will most likely go to prison for life...' She stopped for a reaction to the implication but after a couple of seconds, she continued. 'This means that Ettie cannot help us anymore because she is no longer protected and is open to the wolves and that includes your father.' Seeing that Alice now understood, she held up her palm to stop a barrage of questions. 'There's no time, we will speak more later when it is safer but for now, we won't mention about the twins, your father will find out soon enough. Ettie is now on her way to Vera's because she knows all that she has done for us and she will be safe there before leaving the city tonight.'

They both heard movement above, prompting them to get up and make a start on breakfast.

'I know Ettie has been good to us by getting our food and letting us go round there, but surely she isn't in that much danger?'

The third step from the bottom creaked making Rose speak concisely and rapidly. 'She knows everything about their business, books and stash and that alone is enough to get her killed...'

'Tea, Stanley?'

The conversation regarding Ettie had affected Alice all day. It was good to help a neighbour because Ettie had greatly helped them. But the crux for Alice was her growing disappointment that her mother was not doing anything to help their own situation as she herself was working towards.

For years, Alice had hoped that her parents would be able to sort out their differences. If they were sorted, then there would have been no need to secretly accumulate enough money to get away. This prompted her to remember the afternoon at the movies. Her mother had said that times and people change to which she had thought long and hard about that. Without a doubt, she knew that if she ever married then it would be totally for love with an even partnership. She would never stand being treated by her husband the way her father treated her mother, and was totally perplexed as to what could have happened to turn her father from a loving husband into a complete swine.

After years of planning and saving, Alice would be leaving home in October when she turned sixteen. Her roll of winnings would be substantial enough to get her and her mother away from this place that was strewn with sewer rats of the humankind. There had been numerous occasions where she had almost told her mother of her plans, but had held back for fear of her father finding out through no fault of her mother.

This was a secret that she had to maintain for just a few more months.

Having pilfered for eleven of her fifteen years, she was uplifted knowing that the Johnson women would finally be free of him to leave this place for good and to start their new life.

Mr and Mrs Wyatt had been a lifeline to her as she confided that she had wanted to venture out into the world. As always, they were very understanding and supportive. Her inbuilt loyalty, and perhaps embarrassment too, determined that she never told them the absolute truth about her family. She had wrestled with her morals over the past few years and thought how very double standard they were. She knew she was a good person underneath the top layers where it hadn't been her fault how her father had brought her up and what he had subjected her to. But soon it would be down to her on how she conducted herself to become a better person by making her own choices, making her think of her conversation with Alfie when she was small.

Her arrangement with Mr Wyatt had continued and her bundle of winnings was amounting into a nice little nest egg. Only once a year at Christmas time had she dibbed into her winnings to buy Mr and Mrs Wyatt a small gift in appreciation for what they had done for her. They insisted that it wasn't necessary, but she held firm that it was what she wanted to do as she gained immense pleasure that came from honest well-earned cash as opposed to dishonest money.

*

If only Alice and Rose knew what the other had been planning and building up these last few years. With this knowledge and absolute faith in the other, they may have been able to make good their escape long ago and thus saving a whole heap of tragedy.

But then, things happen for a reason...

*

Alice arose at 4 a.m. as usual and was on her way out of the house by ten past. On several occasions, she would often see her father on his way in and if he wasn't too drunk, he would accompany her part of the way but she hadn't seen him this morning.

Sticking to the busier streets as much as possible was safer where early morning deliveries always meant there were ample people about. And walking close to dark and sinister alleyways were always avoided when bypassing the slums, regardless of the time of day. Her mother had instilled into her that she should never use the alleyways as a shortcut even if she was running late for work. Over the years, Alice had seen for herself all kinds of activity down cool and dark alleyways and none of them looked or sounded pleasant upon stealing glances when walking by. She had seen drug dealing and taking to poor sods receiving a beating to whores earning pittance for performing all kinds of acts on their clients with the aim of getting the required result as quick as possible.

The alleyways and slums at this time of day may have looked almost innocent with minimal activity, but nonetheless, looked sad, bleak and disheartened, probably like most of the people who lived there. Her family, the Johnsons, were no exception. They were all just ordinary citizens trying to get by and to make ends meet and living each day as it came the best way they could.

Soon the streets would be filled with masses of noisy shouting people and mothers washing and hanging out sheets that were almost transparent in patches. And there would be boisterous play from the little ones with their green runny noses and rosy cheeks, trying their hardest to keep up with the bigger kids who swished by on their billycarts.

Alice stood stock still and listened.

Something sounded familiar, but what was it? For a few seconds, it was deathly quiet and while she knew she should keep moving, her feet seemed glued to the ground.

There it was again.

There were shuffling noises coming from the alleyway just up ahead and from the intermittent sound there was talking as well as punches being thrown.

When the sound came again, it confirmed Alice's familiarity. It was her father! There was no mistake. She knew his groan anywhere. Her head was full of questions: *What should I do? What can I do? Do I really want to do anything anyway?* Seeing no one, she edged nearer to the opening of the alley and listened intently. From the distance of the noise, she judged that they were quite a way down, where it would be possible for her to run and hide if she heard their footsteps running back up, unless they exited from the other side.

The alley provided its own echo and after just a few moments of hearing the argument she was shocked to learn that the other man was none other than P W Jones, her father's oldest rival. They were never the best of acquaintances, and it hadn't helped either when she had lifted the notorious wallet in the courthouse several years back. That was when the feud between them heightened to the point where they wouldn't spit or piss on each other if they were on fire.

'You bastard!' hissed P W, as he again punched then flung Shiv roughly against the wall. The three-foot distance between the alley buildings narrowed the opportunity to do much else during a scuffle.

'You bear one hell of a grudge,' mocked Shiv before spitting blood onto his opponent's crisp white shirt.

'You bastard.'

'You already said that,' he replied, bringing up his fist and slamming a good hook connecting with a jaw, causing his rival's head to rebound off of the wall.

'You bastard.'

'Really?' They both returned and deflected punches. 'All because of a wallet you think I have.'

'I know you have it.' They were nose to nose and breathing hard from the exertion when without warning, P W stabbed Shiv.

'This time you're the bastard.' Shiv retaliated, stabbing him back, staring him in the eye, daring him to look away. P W didn't look away, but his eyes flinched then flickered as gravity yanked him to the cold and damp ground with an almighty heavy thud. Alice heard the sickening sound all too clearly reminding her of when her father and Alfie had dumped the dead man in her room. She still had recurring nightmares of that night.

'And you're right. I do have it.' He again spat out more blood onto P W's body and started to run back up the alley.

Almost forgetting to hide, Alice made it behind a stack

of boxes with only a second to spare before her father came stumbling out. She hadn't been sure at first who had fallen to the ground and initially she wasn't sure if she was pleased or not when her father appeared. He was clearly badly injured. He wiped his bleeding mouth on his sleeve and clutched his side and ran in the direction of home.

Alice couldn't help it. She had to make sure if P W was dead or not and silently crept down the alleyway. There was little moonlight overhead and before her eyes adjusted to the darkness, she could just make out a heap of something much darker a few feet in front of her. Approaching nearer, the subtle light made the puddle of blood gathering on the gritty ground by P W's body appear that he had an oil leak like an old rusty car.

Avoiding the pool while crouching down and looking at his face, she saw no sign of life, even when reaching out to raise one of his eyelids.

'I'm so sorry for what my father has done P W,' she whispered, still hearing the sickening thud from when he had fallen and knew that he was dead. Alice felt remorseful because if she hadn't lifted his wallet then he and her father wouldn't have become such enemies to the extent of wanting to kill each other.

Feeling guilty that she had no option but to leave him there, Alice stood and turned back around and walked a few paces back up the alley when her foot kicked something. It hadn't felt like a rat or anything like that, but something told her to find out what it was. She bent back down and rummaged around with her hands locating what felt like a small book and aimed it at the spot where the faint moonlight shined down.

It was her father's precious journal. There was no mistake. It contained all his private details, accounts, dealings and where he had pawned hundreds of items. Alice knew full well the implication and the significance.

This small book was the key to her father's entire *empire*, and he would be lost without it. More importantly, the book couldn't have been any more incriminating than if he were to stand on top of the court's stairs and shout at the top of his voice every crime that he had committed.

It was hard evidence. It would send him to jail.

For life.

Considering the consequences for only a few seconds, Alice placed the book on P W's chest, then when she was at the top of the alleyway she bolted toward the racecourse.

She began to cry, knowing that she wouldn't see Mr or Mrs Wyatt ever again as she retrieved the key to his storage area and took her wad of winnings. Alice wished that she had a pencil to write him a note but she had to move and move quick before more people started arriving for work or anyone spotted her.

It was imperative to get back to her mother before her father went home even though she was pretty sure that he would first get cleaned up, then stitched up before getting drunk. He wasn't that foolish to bring trouble to his own front door. Because, if he had any sense, he would head straight to the nearest club to get himself an airtight alibi, all within the company of undesirables. He would need something more concrete than being at home sleeping with his wife as a wife would naturally stand by her husband and vouch for anything that she was told. The police would see through that.

Making her way back out of the racecourse, Alice moved as fast as she could without drawing attention to herself. With immense luck on her side, a cab had just dropped someone off and was in the process of turning back to the city. She ran across the road and hailed it down, but the cabbie looked at her dismissively, regarding the kid as a waste of time.

Briefly turning to shield the roll of notes, she plucked a pound note and thrust it through the driver's window and gave him the address for the street over from hers. 'Please, as fast as you can, you can keep the change. It's an emergency,' and that was enough for the cabbie to put his foot down for the biggest tip in quite a while. The streets were quiet and they would be there in no time at all. It was his lucky day.

Alice sprinted up the stairs and woke her mother. 'Alice, what is it, what's happened?' She sat bolt upright, becoming more awake with every second taking in the urgency and her daughter's worried face. Alice sat on the bed and took her mother's hands in hers and explained about what she had seen down the alley.

Then she looked deep into her mother's eyes. 'Father left his journal in the alley...'

'And?' her mother questioned eagerly.

'I left it there.' Alice was unremorseful.

'Good girl. We both know it's for the best. I would have done the same,' said Rose, squeezing Alice's hands, both knowing what it would imply. She bolted out of bed and began to dress. 'We need to go and quickly before he comes home. It's too dangerous to stay here. He'll know his journal is missing by now and we'll be the ones who will pay for it, although he may go back to search for it first. Who knows what he will do.'

Rose looked Alice in the eye. 'I've wanted to tell you for so long that I have been pickpocketing and have built up a stash at Vera's. It's for us. To get away for good. I hadn't meant it to be quite like this but now is the time.'

Alice's jaw dropped, her eyes widening in disbelief; this was the last thing she had expected her mother to say. A heavy weight settled upon her chest. She'd thought that her mother had been doing nothing for them, when it was the complete opposite as she had been planning their escape just as much as she had.

'Mother, I've also earned enough money for us to get away...' They continued to stare at each other in amazement and realisation of what the other had been doing.

'Oh, my goodness, Alice! There is so much to say but we haven't time now. We'll talk later when we are safe on the train. Go pack a few things. Meet me at Central Station. We'll get the early Blue Mountains train. I'll get the money from Vera's and I'll meet you on the platform.' They embraced tightly.

'But, Mother, there's no need to go to Vera's, my money is here. There is more than enough to get us by...' She pulled out the wad from her pocket.

'You're a smart and brave girl, Alice.' Rose looked at her

daughter in admiration. 'Like you, I've worked hard for the money and I'm not leaving it behind. Combining with yours will mean a better future for us.

'I'll be at Central in forty to fifty minutes. It's better we go our separate ways now and meet up at the station. If anything goes wrong and I've been delayed by the time the train departs, then leave. Promise me you will leave, won't you? I need to know that you will be safe.' Alice nodded reluctantly. 'Good. I had planned on us going to Katoomba first. Telephone Vera if there is any problem, she will know what to do. Only talk to Vera. If I'm not on the train, wait for me at Katoomba and hide until you see me get off the following train. You need to be sharp, Alice. Your father has many eyes out there. Do you remember Vera's number?'

Alice again nodded.

'He will be arrested and sent to prison, but now is the most dangerous time for us. There is no way that your father will go to prison leaving us here alone. He cannot have us, so no one else can either and he'll make damn sure of that. You know what I am saying. Now go and pack.'

They embraced for the final time then Rose shoved a few things into a bag then rushed down the stairs and headed straight out to Vera's.

Alice looked around her room, unsure what to pack. She already had her knife, then she knelt beside her bed and inserted her arm up to her shoulder within her thin mattress that had smelled of urine with a faint hint of vomit since the day it was given to her. She rummaged around the coarse hair until she located the silver four-leafed clover pendant from Mr and Mrs Wyatt. Quickly grabbing her coat, thinking that it would be cold in the mountains, she ran downstairs.

Like her mother, Alice hadn't envisioned that their escape would be this fraught either. There was no doubt that her father would be arrested for P W's murder, but in the meantime, there was a possibility for him to burst through the door at any second.

Her mind was driving her crazy. Her father knew people; he would track them down. He and Alfie would find them. Everyone knew who they were; they would be easily spotted on the platform in the early morning. They would have to board the train separately or it would be best if they could tag onto someone else and board with a group of people. *But did lots of people board the first train?* She had to make herself look different, and fast.

Frantically opening the kitchen drawer, she took out the large pair of scissors and before she had time to think it through, she began to hack off her long golden plait at the nape of her neck. After a few moments of working the blunt scissors then her knife, she looked down.

It was heartbreaking.

Her beautiful plait was easily two feet long and trying not to dwell, she rolled it up as small as she could and stuffed it into her coat pocket and hoped to goodness that it was worth it.

Within the next couple of minutes, she also bolted out the front door, her eyes firmly peeled for any sign of her father. She had run like the wind all the way and made it safely to Central Station where the time on the large clock meant that her mother would arrive in around twenty to thirty minutes. She hid for a short while to catch her breath then she bought two train tickets for the first Blue Mountains train that was due to depart in just under an hour. At that time of the morning, a young girl all alone caused the old man selling the tickets to raise an eyebrow, but he didn't ask any questions. His job was to sell tickets, not to ask every passenger their life story. Plus, she had the most uneven bob haircut that he had seen, but then again, he was no fashion expert either.

Alice stood behind a pillar near the platform and waited. Her neck was starting to get cold without her hair as she turned up her collar. She then placed her hands in her pockets for some warmth and found one of them springy from the mass of hair and the other felt the reassuring wad of cash and her knife as she tilted her head down and fought the urge to cry.

CHAPTER TWELVE

Rose was also a fast runner and was pleased that her aunt was up and about at such an early hour. 'By the look of you, I presume it's time.' Vera surmised, ushering her niece inside where the fire was already burning in her parlour to take the edge off the cold morning and poured Rose a cup of tea.

'Yes,' said Rose, quite breathlessly shaking her head, declining the tea. 'Sorry, I haven't time to tell you about it now. I'll be in touch when Alice and I are away and safe. She's on her way now and will wait for me. It happened so fast. If anything happens to me, I've told Alice to telephone you.'

Vera never envisioned that it would be like this either. 'Why would anything happen to you, love?' She couldn't begin to imagine or comprehend what had recently happened for them to leave this suddenly and at this time of day. The elderly woman picked up the urn, took off the lid and shook it upside down until all the notes scattered onto the tablecloth.

Aware of the urgency, she tallied and expertly bundled

the notes together in a tight wad and handed it to Rose. The young woman smiled at her aunt and placed it within a small discreet pocket that she had sewn into the front of her skirt then wrapped her coat around her. 'Three hundred and ten pounds,' Vera said, smiling. 'It's a pretty penny, and more than enough to set you two up for a long while.'

'Thank you, Aunt, it's more than I thought,' she said, hugging the woman who had been her saviour. 'I should go. I'll be in touch and thank you for everything. I don't know what I would have done without you...'

'Hush, child, we're family. Now go. Be safe and I will wait for your call. Can you at least tell me where you plan on heading?'

'I'm not going to put you in danger.' The women hugged again. 'I promise I'll telephone when we are safely away.'

*

Alice was getting more and more anxious.

The minutes seemed to be taking forever as she continuously peeped round the pillar to see if her mother was approaching. She also saw the train guard making his way throughout the carriages, checking for? Well, Alice wasn't totally sure what he was checking for. People still inside, lost property? She didn't know. All she wanted to know was when was her mother going to arrive. People were starting to gather on the platform with all kinds of luggage and it probably wouldn't be too much longer before they were allowed to board as it was scheduled to depart very soon.

Her mother had said that it would take her about forty to fifty minutes. Alice did the math and calculated that it would take around fifteen to get from home to Vera's at a fast run, then perhaps ten minutes at Vera's? Then around twenty from Vera's to Central. That made forty-five in total, so her mother should arrive at any moment.

She told herself to be patient, but it was easier said than done.

*

Stanley was getting weaker, but he managed a cheery, 'Surprise!' timing his attack just so by grabbing Rose from behind as she briskly walked down the street and dragged her roughly down an alleyway. 'And what brings you out and about here at this time of the morning, I wonder?'

He took great pleasure from the horrified look on her face when he spun her around to face him, his breath reeking with booze. 'What makes you come all the way out here? Has to be something...' He flung open her coat and forcibly kicked her feet apart. Even though he was losing strength, his willpower gave him the dominance he needed to grab and pin both her wrists above her head. With all his might, he then pushed them into the rough bricked wall causing her to cry out in agony. She stopped struggling, believing it would alleviate the pain.

She was wrong.

'Let go of me, Stanley. What are you doing?'

'Just answer me, woman.' His whisper was laced with angry undertones as they looked one another in the eye.

'Why were you at Vera's? You turned into a whore, Rose?' he scoffed.

Before she could answer, his other hand darted up her skirt. She tried not to flinch and hoped her face didn't give away her disgust as his fingers crudely probed up to her thighs and as her legs were splayed, he hungrily and tightly cupped her mound while agitating and kneading his fingers.

'NO, STOP IT!' she pleaded.

'A bit of luck me spotting you as I came out of the club.' He ignored her plea then smirked. 'Oh, I can feel that you're enjoying it, Rose.' His eyes sparked with glee as she struggled some more. Her skirt shifted slightly and his eyes widened when he felt something heavy touch the back of his hand.

She knew that she was now in far greater danger than she had been a few moments ago.

'What have we here?' He pawed at her skirt and discovered her roll of cash, let go of her but stood crossways to block her exit. Then as he lifted his hands in the air to get a better look at the money, Rose saw the extent of his injury and knew what it meant.

He pocketed the wad then turned on her like a viper. His hand struck out of the darkness, grabbing her throat and again pinned her hard against the wall. Her head connected badly and she feared for her life.

'Stanley, please...' she begged.

'BITCH!' he snapped, spraying warm alcohol-laden spittle over her face. 'Whoring for Vera or pickpocketing when I told you not to? How DARE you disobey me, Rose. YOU THINK I'M STUPID? This isn't luck. Alice saw me, didn't she? Then you ran like your life depended on it to collect your stash before you both fled.' And by Rose's instant flinch, he knew he was spot on. 'You will NEVER get the privilege to run away from me. NEVER...' He spun her back around and shoved his forearm into the back of her neck to keep her restrained against the wall.

The wound left by P W's knife hurt like the dark depths of hell, but it was nothing compared to her betrayal. His strength was rapidly declining and he felt light-headed, or perhaps it was just the booze? He ignored the feeling and lifted her skirt with his free hand and roughly tugged at her undergarments until he was able to see-saw them down her thighs.

There was nothing physically that she could do. But despite this, she felt a calmness because her only saving grace was knowing that Alice would be safe when she boarded the train where Stanley wouldn't be able to get his hands on her ever again. Alice had money and she would contact Vera who would take care of her.

'Clumsy of you to leave your journal by P W's body,' she taunted to hurt him in the only way she knew how.

He released his grip and patted his pocket, stark realisation kicking in. 'I'm gonna take sheer delight in killing you. Should've done it years ago,' he snapped, flicking out his knife.

Big Alf had heard most of the conversation and knew it was time to intervene. 'Stop right there, Shiv,' he ordered from the entrance to the alley and Rose counted her blessings that she was safe.

'Mind your own business, you fat oaf. She's my wife and I'm entitled to do whatever I want. What're you doing here anyway?' He was getting confused, felt nauseous and his knees were starting to buckle.

'Didn't meet up as arranged, knew something was up. One of the boys saw you coming this way. Let's go, Shiv.' He began to walk down the alley, much to the relief of Rose. 'You're hurt.' He could tell Shiv didn't have long.

'This is none of your damn business!' he hissed, letting go of his wife who immediately pulled up her undergarments and stepped backwards.

'We need to get you seen to before you bleed out,' hoping that Stanley would see sense.

'Too late for that old man, I'm just about done...' Stanley knew he was on the brink of death and swiftly reached out and grabbed Rose's arm and pulled her back towards him with all the remaining strength he had left.

'They were going to leave me. Can you believe that? She'd lifted a whole bunch of cash and was going to leave. I cannot let that happen.'

Rose tried to struggle and get away but his grip was surprisingly strong.

'You know that I cannot let that happen...' he repeated and locked eyes with Big Alf, pursing his lips and inhaling deeply for the last time, feeling the blood flowing down his side as he did so. He then looked at Rose and when his intake was at capacity, he held onto it to give him the extra ounce of strength that he needed to execute his final fatal stab.

As Rose's body slumped to the ground, Big Alf pulled the

handgun from his pocket and fired a rapid double tap, one to Stanley's head and one to his heart. The sound was eardrum-bursting within the confined alleyway.

'YOU EVIL BASTARD! There was no need for that,' Big Alf spat and powerfully kicked the lifeless body of his ex-good-for-nothing boss. There was no point checking on Rose; he knew she was dead as he wiped his prints from the stolen gun and left it by Shiv's body. He then rummaged through Stanley's pocket, taking Rose's money then ran to the alley entrance. He glanced all around then bolted down to the next street to which he then slowed to a normal walking pace and headed straight to Vera's for an alibi.

*

Alice was somewhat relieved when the train guard apologised and announced that there would be a slight delay in the train's departure due to an unforeseen circumstance. The passengers weren't privy as to what that may have been, but what was another half an hour? Alice spotted some of the passengers heading off to the now-opened tearoom, causing her tummy to rumble as she hadn't eaten or had anything to drink for hours.

She saw two old ladies talking to one of the station's staff and it appeared that they were supervising the onboarding of their vast array of luggage and supplies that was being loaded within another section of the train. After a few minutes, they seemed satisfied and trundled off toward the tearoom also. *What I wouldn't give for a hot cup of tea*, Alice thought as she again looked at the clock knowing that her mother should already be here.

It was agonising. *Where is she?*

*

Upon hearing a swift knock on the door, Vera thought that Rose had forgotten something, but when she saw Big Alf standing there so soon after Rose had left, her heart skipped several beats and her knees felt wobbly. Without a doubt, something dreadful had happened.

'Vera.' He nodded solemnly and took off his hat, closed the door and followed her into the parlour.

She couldn't bear to ask as she wanted to keep as much distance as possible between herself and bad news, but found herself blurting, 'For God's sake, spit it out, will you?' and sat and listened, not believing her ears that her precious Rose was dead when she had been in this very room right as rain just a few minutes earlier.

Vera was suddenly drawn to Rose's teacup. She reached out and placed the back of her hand against the china and felt its diminishing warmth. She pondered whether to put the tea cosy over it as if by keeping it warm then Rose would somehow still be alive, but she knew it was absurd and impossible.

'He's always been evil,' she said with disgust, shaking her head. 'I warned her a number of times. Oh, dear God, what a tragedy.' Vera again wiped her eyes and blew her nose and fought the urge to break down completely also chastising herself for not pushing her niece for more details as to where they were meeting and heading to.

Despite being deeply upset, she still had her wits about her.

She didn't totally trust Stanley's associate, initially believing he may have come to her for information as to Alice's whereabouts. But Vera deduced that there simply hadn't been enough time for Big Alf to have gone to the racecourse to look for Alice before coming to her door so quickly. So, she kept her mouth shut and tried to put the child to the back of her mind for the time being, because not knowing where she was, there was nothing she could do until the child telephoned.

'Came to give you this, so it'll be safe.' Big Alf reached into his coat pocket and placed Rose's wad of cash onto the table. 'Recovered it from Shiv before I made my getaway. I heard what he said about Rose lifting, thought it only right it be returned to you for Alice's future, poor kid. It would have been what Rose wanted.'

Vera looked at him in surprise, touched by his teary eyes and the genuine sorrow etched on his face, but mostly by his honest gesture. Coming from an ace conman and professional thief, it was something highly magnanimous.

'Thank you, Big Alf, I'll make sure she gets it. What will you do now?' she said to deflect, indicating him to sit down while she dabbed her eyes with her handkerchief then she stood up to add more hot water to the teapot.

'I'll stick around for a while, so it doesn't look suspicious then I'll head north as I've a brother up there. I've a little put by, so I'll be alright. But for now...' He paused, looking down when she placed a cup of tea in front of him knowing that he was a little embarrassed, particularly knowing the business she was in.

'You'll need an alibi,' Vera surmised. 'I'll vouch that you were here. He deserved to die, in my honest opinion. Here's the key to room two at the top of the stairs. It's empty, so get some rest.'

In that moment, they came to a silent appreciation of the other as he finished his tea and nodded his gratitude.

'Thank you. I'll get a couple of hours then I'll head out to meet Alice from the stables and bring her back here so you both can talk.'

Vera felt guilty knowing that that was pointless but rather than saying anything about it now, she decided to take advantage of the couple of hours that he would be asleep to think on what she should do next.

As he headed upstairs, he could hear heartbreaking sobbing coming from the parlour. The big man felt the loss too. He considered the Johnson ladies as family but was comforted knowing that Vera would take care of Alice.

CHAPTER THIRTEEN

The piercing whistle broke the early morning quiet followed by 'ALL ABOARD!' when the conductor checked his silver fob watch and announced the pending departure. The passengers began to make their way over to their relevant class of carriage defined by their ticket and climbed aboard. There followed the usual opening and closing of doors and shuffling noises as luggage was arranged then re-arranged in the overhead racks. The conductor smiled at the familiar rustle and crackle of crisp newspaper pages being flipped over as his passengers settled in for the journey.

Alice had never been as panicked, frightened or confused as she was now.

Her mother had specifically told her to board the train and to alight at Katoomba, but Alice reasoned that she would be waiting regardless. *So perhaps I should stay at Central and wait for the next train when we can travel together?* The quandary was painful.

For such a young person, Alice was streetwise, having

witnessed many heinous things in her life and deep down she knew that her mother had met with misfortune. So many thoughts were buzzing around in her head that she pushed them away and held onto the hope that her mother had simply been held up at Vera's. She loved her great aunt dearly, but she did have an aptitude for talking.

A few seconds later, Alice made the decision to obey her mother's wishes and with a heavy but realistic heart, she stepped out from behind the pillar. Hoping it was the right decision, she boarded the train.

Unbeknown to Alice, at fifteen years of age, she boarded the train to the Blue Mountains as an orphan.

Seemingly the last passenger to board, the whistle peeled once again and the locomotive burst into life. There were a few shudders and jolts that rippled through the train, and she had to hold onto the backs of chairs for support to prevent herself from stumbling onto anyone. The train was surprisingly busy and there was hardly any room for her as she walked through the carriages, looking for a suitable seat.

There were a few empty seats but looking at her fellow passengers there were obvious reasons as to why they were empty. Gut instinct. Her mother always told her to trust it, so she continued forward.

The next carriage she came to was obviously first class with its long corridor and enclosed six-seater compartments. Not wanting to get into any trouble by being there, she tried to walk through this area as quickly as possible. The problem was that when she came to the far end, there was no other passenger carriage. Dismayed, there was no option but to turn around and choose one of those undesired seats after all.

At the halfway point along the corridor, the train conductor entered the carriage and began walking toward her. Alice stood tall and kept walking knowing that she hadn't broken any law because she had made a genuine mistake.

'Can I help you, Miss?' he asked because he had seen the reluctant way in which she had boarded. This was a good way to see for himself if she was alright but ultimately to check her ticket.

'Sorry.' She smiled. 'Just a little lost, I'm heading back to...'

'May I see your ticket, please?'

He stood crossways blocking her path and held out his hand.

'I have a ticket. I'm just a little lost...' She carefully rummaged in her pocket, wishing that she hadn't put her plait there. The last thing she wanted was to bring out a handful of hair. Now that would rouse suspicion and she reprimanded herself for not getting rid of it before she entered the station.

The conductor had a sceptic look about him that said she was either playing games or she didn't have a ticket because she was taking her time.

'Oh, there you are!' exclaimed a little old lady, rolling back the wooden compartment door. 'We've been wondering where you got to, haven't we, Tish?' she said when she looked behind her.

'Yes,' came a reply as another old lady popped her head

out. Alice recognised them from the station's platform earlier.

'This is our ward, Conductor,' she explained, gently shepherding Alice by the arm inside their compartment and slowly sliding the door closed.

'S-m-i-l-e,' she ordered through clenched teeth as all three of them smiled sweetly at the man who tipped his cap at the ladies and carried on with his rounds. Alice detected a pleasant scent of lavender.

'Well, that was exciting.' Tish laughed. 'Perhaps we all better sit down before we fall down.'

Alice was a little confused. The ladies had kindly rescued her but why? 'Thank you for that.' She smiled genuinely this time liking them instantly. She believed they were probably twins between sixty-five to seventy and noted they were the same height as herself but as she was still growing, Alice thought that they were quite sweet. They were a little round like her aunt Vera and dressed similar to her as well. 'I'll wait a few minutes until he's gone, then I'll make my way.'

'You'll do no such thing, young lady. Stay, keep us company. You'll be doing us a favour; we haven't chatted to any youngsters for quite a while.'

'That's right. Please, stay. I'll introduce us. I'm Pip, short for Philippa and this is my sister, Tish, short for Patricia.'

They all shook hands; the ladies hadn't batted an eyelid to the unusual way it happened.

'It's lovely to meet you both, I'm... Polly,' said Alice. Her heart was pounding for lying and her head was all over the place. Had it only been just a few short hours since her father had murdered P W?

'It's lovely to meet you too, Polly. Please, take a seat. We're alighting at Katoomba. What about you?' asked Tish.

'Yes, me as well. My mother has missed the train, so I'll wait for her there as she'll get the next one. Although I may telephone my aunt Vera first to make sure. Is there a telephone at Katoomba station?'

'Yes, there is,' said Pip, wondering why Polly wasn't waiting for her mother at Central. 'We have so much luggage and supplies to load onto our truck that it will take a while, so we'll wait with you to make sure you will be alright.'

'Thank you but, there's no need.'

'We will talk about it later when we arrive. How about a cup of tea? We filled our flasks back at the station,' said Pip, already pouring Polly a cup and handing it to her to which Polly looked so grateful that her eyes watered at such a generous gesture.

'We have sandwiches too,' said Tish, unwrapping and holding out the selection for Polly to choose.

Pip and Tish conversed through eye communication that Polly was perhaps in some kind of trouble or that she was running away. She had no luggage and just prior to shaking hands, they had seen a glimpse of a plait in her pocket when she wiped her hand down her coat to get rid of some stray golden strands. It was obviously Polly's and it appeared to have been recently cut. But the ladies were tactful and didn't mention for not wanting to cause any embarrassment, distress or for her to flee.

'Thank you. These are really nice.' Polly smiled, finishing her tea and sandwiches, feeling much better.

'That's good, we're glad you liked them.' Tish smiled. 'Where are you staying?'

Polly's bottom lip began to quiver. It was all getting a little overwhelming. The ladies could tell she was upset, so Tish continued, 'We travel into the city twice a year for supplies and the like. That's why we have so much luggage. It's good to stay in the city for a couple of days but we cannot wait until we are home again, can we, dear?'

'Yes, that's right,' said Pip. 'There's nothing quite like living in the Blue Mountains. We have lived in Hartley Vale ever since we were children. Do you know it?'

Polly shook her head. The ladies evoked the image of typical compassionate grandmothers and wished she had a grandmother. Her eyes then moved to the seat opposite where she spotted two pairs of small wire-rimmed spectacles.

'We like to park in Katoomba and to do a little shopping there as well, then we drive home. We have a train station nearer to us, but it gives the truck an extra run out.'

'That's nice.' Polly smiled again and took great delight by looking out of the window as the train made its way out of the city. Pip and Tish could see that she was taken with the scenery, so they left her be for the time being. Alice had so many thoughts racing through her head that she didn't know quite where to start.

She hoped to high heaven that her mother was alright but knowing that she would be able to telephone her aunt once she arrived in Katoomba had put her a little at ease. She also felt sad that she wouldn't see Mr or Mrs Wyatt ever again.

They had been the grandparents she never had and missed them dreadfully already. She decided to tell her mother about the Wyatts once they were safe and settled and that she would write to them. Alice found that just by thinking these things through made her feel a whole lot better.

Perhaps things weren't so bad after all?

*

Vera was worried sick as she paced up and down the hallway, never venturing too far from the telephone.

How she wished that there had been a few more minutes to allow Rose to give her more information realising that those precious few minutes, or even seconds, may have just saved her life. Vera scolded herself again for not asking more questions and why oh why hadn't she insisted on going with her to wherever it was to meet Alice? Damn and bloody damn. *How stupid was I?* she thought when she entered the parlour and pounded the small table with her clenched fist, making the teacups jump and her slice of toast bounce free of the small silver toast rack. *Where on Earth could the child be?*

Vera's only hope was that the child would telephone her once she arrived at goodness knows where. She sat and tried very hard to remember all the conversations with Rose over the years to see if she had unconsciously given away any clues but frustratingly, nothing came to mind.

Even though she desperately needed to know that Alice was alright, she was also dreading the telephone call. She would no doubt ask questions and she would need to be given honest answers. But however Vera said it, there was no way to dress up the fact that her father had murdered her mother and that Big Alf had murdered her father. It was such a tragic horrible mess.

*

The train stopped briefly just before Penrith to fill up with water. Alice was enjoying the trip on the steam train and the smell of the smoke reminded her of the fireworks that were at the opening of the Sydney Harbour Bridge. She had never travelled this far out of the city before. The scenery was breathtaking. 'It's very beautiful here,' she said.

'Yes, it is,' replied Tish. 'We enjoy making the journey, although it's not too pleasant in the wintertime.'

'Gets very cold,' said Pip. 'It seeps into your bones. So, we rug up as much as we can almost to the point where we can't move an inch.'

Alice smiled at the concept.

From the moment Alice had entered the compartment she had instantly felt comfortable with the two women, just like she had with Mr and Mrs Wyatt. It was like she was in the company of strangers who hadn't felt like strangers. It sounded silly, but she couldn't explain it better than that.

After a while, the train slowly pulled into Katoomba Railway Station where the passengers found that the mid-morning sun was delightfully warm when they alighted. Pip, Tish and Polly were almost the last remaining passengers on the platform as the guards from both the train and station offloaded the endless luggage onto a trailer that was pulled by Old Eric, the station's horse. As a prior ongoing arrangement, the two Katoomba guards then assisted the ladies by leading Old Eric towards the ladies' truck and loading it up under their strict supervision while Alice gave Old Eric some carrots for his efforts.

'I wondered why you had a bag of carrots in the carriage.' She laughed, patting and ruffling Old Eric's ears. She missed the horses at the track already.

'He likes you.' Tish smiled then she turned to the men. 'Thank you, Mr Pendry and Mr Mellor.' She handed them both a pound note. 'As always, we appreciate your help.'

'Thank you both,' they said, tilting their caps.

'Before you go,' said Pip, 'please, may we use your telephone? Polly, here, wishes to call her aunt in Sydney,' while she rummaged in her purse for another pound to cover the cost which was more than ample.

'Yes, of course,' said Mr Pendry. 'It's in the office. Only... sorry, company policy states that children aren't allowed to use it.' He shrugged his shoulders apologetically.

'How about Polly tells me the number and I'll make the call then quickly pass her on. No one would know and we won't tell anyone. Would that suffice?' questioned Pip, knowing that the pound would speak for itself.

'Very acceptable,' he said, pocketing the money while they all made their way back to the platform with Old Eric plodding behind, hoping for some more carrots. Mr Pendry and Mr Mellor secured Old Eric by looping his reins to his usual spot on the platform then the men started to prepare for the next train as Pip, Tish and Polly entered the office.

'I call her Aunt Vera,' Alice said to put the record straight. 'But she is really my mother's aunt, making her my great aunt, or was it grand aunt? I cannot quite remember. When I was little, Aunt Vera said that she couldn't be doing with the extra-long title, made her feel old she said, so from then on Aunt Vera was what both mother and I called her. I am rambling, sorry.'

'That's not rambling, Polly,' said Tish who was about to mock her sister. 'Now, Pip is the one who rambles.' Pip tried to look hurt.

'Aunt Vera, it is,' said Pip, placing the call and waiting for Vera to pick up. Alice was like a coiled spring as it seemed forever for her aunt to answer the telephone.

Vera was nervous and reluctant to answer but she knew she had to, and with a heavy heart she picked up the receiver. 'Hello. Mrs Vera Peabody speaking,' she said shakily.

'Good morning, Mrs Peabody,' replied a much older voice that threw her as she was convinced that it would be Alice. 'My name is Miss Philippa Graham but please, call me Pip. I am calling from Katoomba Railway Station with my sister Miss Patricia Graham, Tish for short, on behalf of your niece, Polly.'

Vera was momentarily confused. *Polly?* She thought she'd take a stab in the dark and regretted the bad choice of pun, and deduced that Pip must be referring to Alice?

'Yes, Polly. Thank you. May I speak to her, please?'

Pip handed the phone to Polly then went and sat with Tish. 'Hello, Aunt Vera,' said Alice.

Vera was overwrought with emotion from hearing her

voice and battled to fight back tears.

'Hello, Alice... Polly?' she queried but was relieved that it was her. 'Was wondering where you were. Katoomba, very nice,' she said, trying to keep to small talk for as long as she could, knowing full well that the inevitable loomed.

'Yes, Katoomba...'

'So, who are the two ladies?' She interrupted to which Alice explained on how they met and what they had done for her. Vera summed up that the ladies were in the right place at the right time, assured that Alice was in safe hands.

Having no choice, Vera made the decision to trust the women with what she was about to divulge.

When Alice asked, 'Is Mother with you?' Vera's heart broke and tears streamed down her face as she tried her best not to show the emotion in her voice.

'Just one moment, Alice. I need to check on something first. Can you please put Pip back on the line?'

Alice complied and Vera heard the phone being passed from one to the other.

'Yes, this is Pip...'

'Pip, this is one of those rarer-than-rare moments when complete strangers have to totally trust one another. Please, if it's possible, are you able to get Polly out of the room? We need to talk...'

Pip played along, sensing the crux and urgency and said matter-of-factly, 'Excuse me a moment, Vera. Sorry, Polly, I've just had an awful thought. Would you please ask the guards to check if the large hat box has been loaded onto the truck? I can't remember seeing it and it's very important.

Please, can you go with them? You would be better at spotting it than the men and you can speak to your aunt on your return. Thank you.'

After a few moments, Pip said, 'She's gone, Vera,' and beckoned her sister over so they could both listen. And listen they did without interruption as Vera told them as much as she could before Alice returned.

'And that's about it in a nutshell.' Vera finished and wiped her eyes.

Pip and Tish were overcome too and understood Polly's reasoning in not stating her real name and without them asking the other, they both knew that they would look after Alice for as long as she needed them to. 'Thank you for telling us, Vera. We are so sorry to hear all this and for your loss. Put your mind at rest. We'll look after Alice.

'And yes, we agree that it won't be safe for you to travel here for a while. Best let the dust settle on your end as we all do not want anyone to follow you. We'll make the decision now to telephone you one month from today, at this time, to arrange your visit. Would that be alright with you?'

'That sounds perfect. Thank you, ladies... for everything, and I will see you right for Alice's keep.'

'There's no need for that, Vera. Ah, she's coming back,' said Tish.

'Yes, the hat box is there,' Vera heard Alice say in the background.

'Thank you. Here's your aunt.' With force-induced reluctance, Pip handed Alice the telephone, knowing that the next minute would change her life forever. Then there was silence as the ladies stood shoulder to shoulder and studied Alice's face from the other side of the office.

If there was ever a sound for a heart shattering into a million tiny pieces, this was surely it when Alice let out an anguished and raw 'NOOOOOOOOO' as she dropped the receiver and sobbed her eyes out within the comforting arms of the sisters. Vera was powerless to do anything but listen, as she, too, sobbed her heart out on the other end of the line.

Tish retrieved the receiver and bade Vera farewell then the ladies led Alice outside. It was heartbreaking for them to watch her walk as if in a trance where it seemed the most natural thing in the world for her to go with them without question. Even Old Eric stopped grazing to watch them drive out of the car park.

She remembered Vera telling her that she had informed the ladies of her real name and that she should stay with them for a while, but beyond hearing that her mother was dead, she did not remember anything else.

Alice had had the stuffing knocked out of her. She was shattered, drained and in mourning for her mother. She felt guilty for not giving her the respect that she had deserved while all along she had also been planning and working for years to get them away to safety. At this moment, Alice hated her father even more and inwardly praised Alfie for doing her a huge favour.

So much had happened during the last seven hours that she could hardly contain or process her thoughts. She felt so mentally exhausted that the sway of the truck enabled sleep to overtake her tears as she slumped into the safe arms of Pip. Out of respect and retaining trust by not discussing recent events, just in case Alice wasn't fully asleep, Pip and Tish remained silent for the next hour while they drove through the small towns heading for home.

CHAPTER FOURTEEN

Soon Tish slowed to a snail's pace and turned onto a deep rutted track where the truck bobbed over potholes. The sun was temporarily blocked by the tall trees either side then it reappeared, giving the ladies a warm welcome home when they pulled up outside the largest of the three wooden outbuildings. Pip stroked Alice's arm to rouse her where she marvelled at the most beautiful house that she had ever seen.

Her cheeks cracked ever so slightly caused by dry salty tears when she gave a small smile when she stepped down out of the truck.

'And this is home,' said Pip, extending her arm out in an arc. 'We call it Beech Cottage. Do you like it?'

'It's beautiful.' Alice quickly took in the single-level stone building with two white rocking chairs on the wooden wrap-around verandah. The Georgian window frames and quaint front door were painted in moss green and blended in perfectly within the stonework and surrounding bushland.

'Easiest way to remember, Alice,' said Tish, pointing as

she spoke, 'is we have two parallel corridors spanning the whole width of the cottage. As you walk in the door, the front room is opposite and continues on the left side and on the right of the door is the dining room leading into the kitchen. Then, at the back of the house, the other corridor leads to the bathroom, toilet and three bedrooms that overlook the garden. You will see more clearly once you are inside.'

They walked toward the house and climbed three steps up onto the verandah. Pip unlocked the front door with a wrought iron key that was easily the size of her hand and caught Alice looking at it in wonder.

'So, we don't lose it.' She smiled.

A rush of cold air greeted them when the door opened onto the large front room. It was painted in light cream and had a generous stone fireplace that was already made up and ready to be lit. A pile of logs was neatly stacked on the hearth beside a polished copper scuttle filled to the brim with chunks of coal. Above the fireplace hung an oil painting that looked very old. It depicted bushland scenes and was mounted within a thick wooden ornate frame.

Against the left side wall was an upright piano and against the right was a tall glass cabinet filled with beautiful porcelain ornaments. A dark brown rug nearly covered the entire floor and in the middle of the room, Alice was amazed by the two high-backed cream couches where the seating looked heavenly to sit on. She had never seen such luxurious furniture before in her life.

'I'll put the kettle on if you could light the fire, Tish,' said Pip, closing the front door, then Alice followed her down the open corridor passed the dining room on their way to the kitchen. Before Alice took the two small steps down into the kitchen, she looked back and was able to see the full length of the house and noticed that a wooden curtain rail covered the span. Attached were gleaming brass rings that held full-length moss-green velvet curtains that hung either side of the windows and front door. Alice could well imagine how cosy it would feel on a cold winter's night with all the curtains drawn and the warmth from the roaring fire.

Pip opened the range cooker door and lit the kindle inside then she closed the door before filling the kettle and placing it on top of the range to boil. Alice liked the kitchen and thought that it was easily double the size of the one they had at home. These thoughts threatened to cast fresh tears, so she blinked several times to disperse them and concentrated on taking in all the delights around her. There was a deep stone sink and white painted shelves full of copper pots and pans and an open pantry that contained endless tins and jars of food as she took a seat at the small round table, liking the comfy feel of the red and white checked cushions.

Alice felt like she was in some kind of dream. So much had happened since she had discovered P W to where she was now. It did not feel real, but she knew it was.

'It'll warm up soon enough,' said Tish, entering the kitchen, rubbing her hands together. 'These thick stone walls keep it nice and cool in the summer but until then, we take the edge off by lighting the fire. A couple of years ago we finally got with it and modernised, so if you come with me, I'll show you where the toilet and bathroom is. They used to be outside but we got fed up with trudging outside during wet weather and the harsh winter.'

Alice and Pip followed Tish back through to the dining room. On the far side, was the sideboard. It had three doors and two drawers, each with intricate brass handles and on the top was a silver tray that held a crystal decanter and two upturned glasses. In the middle was the dining room table that could seat four people comfortably and placed in the centre was a tall crystal vase that gave the illusion that it was twice the height due to the highly polished surface. But most of all, Alice was in awe by the impressive bookcase that covered the whole wall between the kitchen and dining room. There were many leatherbound books and encyclopaedias where the ladies had displayed them by the tone of the leather covers.

They walked to the other end of the bookcase and out through a door that led to the corridor at the rear of the house.

'Now you can see how we're set up,' said Tish. 'This leads onto the bedrooms, bathroom and toilet. And if you keep walking to the other end of the corridor it will take you back through to the front room.'

'Tish's room is at the far end,' said Pip, 'and next to it is the bathroom and separate toilet. My room is just here, nearest the dining room. And, this will be your room, Alice, for as long as you wish.' She opened the door halfway along the corridor.

Before her was the most beautiful bedroom that she had ever seen. It was painted white and against the right wall was an oak chest of drawers and matching wardrobe and against the other was a cream rug beside a single brass bedstead and an oak bedside table. The bed looked very inviting with two fluffed-up pillows and a padded floral quilt over a warm blanket and crisp white sheets. It sure was a stark contrast to her bed back home with her thin mattress and blanket that had had countless owners before her.

Alice was speechless as she took it all in; the sisters let her take her time. They remained at the doorway and watched her walk over to peer out of the quaint square window that overlooked the garden. Alice felt like she had stepped into a painting where native gums and early summer flowers bloomed proudly for all to see. There was a double swing seat attached to a sturdy gum branch and a wooden table and chairs that held floral cushions. Faraway kookaburras sang to one another and lorikeets chirped within the bottlebrush shrubs while they pecked at the early onset of the red spiked flowers.

'This is a beautiful house,' she said, then was swept by another wave of emotion. 'Sorry...'

'It's okay, Alice. No need to apologise,' said Pip.

'That's right. Come, we'll have some tea, this way. Are you hungry?' asked Tish when she took Alice's coat and hung it up on the hook on the back of the kitchen door because the house was now warming up nicely.

'Just some tea, please. Thank you.' She brushed away her tears but her eyes filled up again, causing another stream. After finishing her tea, she said, 'Thank you for everything you have done for me today.' She tried to smile. 'I am so very tired; may I go to sleep now?'

'Yes, of course,' said Pip. 'Sleep for as long as you need.'

They all made their way back to Alice's room where Tish found Alice a nightgown. They both gave her a hug and a kiss on the cheek and bade her goodnight.

*

As usual, Tish and Pip were up with the lark and were having a cup of tea in the kitchen.

'I could hear Alice crying into the early hours,' whispered Tish, 'felt powerless to do anything. Broke my heart it did to hear her. I wanted to go to her but I wasn't sure if I should or not. Such a tragic story.'

'Yes, it is,' agreed Pip. 'Nothing we can do except be here for her. It will take time, we know that. Best to carry on as normal and take each day as it comes... shh, here she comes.'

'Good morning,' the ladies said together.

'Morning,' said Alice, who was pale as a sheet and looked like she'd hardly slept a wink.

'Come, sit,' Pip said, ushering her to the table while Tish poured her a cup of milky tea with two sugars.

Pip then placed some freshly buttered toast in front of her, thinking it best to just do it as opposed to offering and being turned down. Alice took several sips of tea, enjoying the warmth of the kitchen, then in almost a daze, she took a bite of toast, much to the ladies' delight. Pip and Tish resumed meaningless chatter as they busied themselves in doing nothing in particular, appearing not to watch or distract their guest, so she would keep on eating. Lost in her thoughts, Alice appreciated the gentle bustle around her and she didn't seem to notice when another slice miraculously appeared on her plate out of nowhere.

Pip smiled. 'How about a bath to freshen up? It will make you feel a little better. Then perhaps later we'll show you around the garden.'

'Thank you.' Alice smiled and felt selfish and guilty. But how could she possibly tell the ladies that she had never had a bath in her life? Twice a week she was allowed to strip wash with a bar of soap, a jug and a basin of cold water in her room.

'I'll run the bath,' said Tish, 'and show you where we keep the fresh towels. Just one other thing. For the meantime, we've put another nightgown in there for you. If you could change into that and the warm dressing gown on the back of the bathroom door, we'll wash and dry your clothes. Is that alright with you? Then we'll get you some new ones when we go back to Katoomba.'

'That's very kind of you both but you have done more than enough for me as it is. After my bath, I'll get going. I won't be a bother...' She turned to leave the kitchen.

'It is our pleasure. You are not a bother at all. We'll talk more after your bath,' said Pip.

'The girl can't go,' whispered Tish.

'Yes, I agree. So much happened yesterday that she probably doesn't remember that Vera is coming here next month. We will explain later. It'll be alright.'

Upon returning to her room, she couldn't help but smile in wonder at the ladies' thoughtfulness. They had made a band out of her plait by wrapping it around the crown of a summer straw hat. It looked really pretty.

It was a bright and warm morning and the ladies enjoyed showing their guest their magnificent garden while her clothes billowed on the washing line. She felt a little strange, walking around the garden wrapped up in a dressing gown although she felt clean and refreshed and knew that the ladies were trying to cheer her up while also being compassionate to her recent loss.

'This is the beautifuliest place I've ever seen. If "beautifuliest" is a word,' she said. 'There aren't any gardens like this where I come from.'

'We're glad you like it,' said Tish. 'Ah, hear that?'

As if on cue, a kookaburra broke into song.

She beamed. 'Where is it?' she asked, craning her neck all around trying to spot the bird. 'Yes, there he is!' She pointed toward the higher branches of the gum. 'My mother and I used to see them when we walked through the park. They were her favourite...' She burst into tears.

'That's alright. Come, we'll sit here and watch them for a while,' said Pip.

Alice dried her eyes and sat at the garden table. There was silence all around, except for the kookaburra and his friends who had come to join in the chorus as if in an attempt to cheer her up.

'We need to tell you, that when you were checking if we had packed the hat box, Vera confided in us. We three joined forces as it were to ensure your safety and wellbeing. Your aunt said that her mind would be at rest if you were to stay here with us until she comes here in one month's time when it should also be safer for her to travel,' said Tish as Alice simultaneously gave a hint of a smile, nod and a brief exhale acknowledging her great aunt's ploy. 'Do you know, it felt like one of those one-off moments where we had all known each other for a long time despite never meeting. And, Alice, we would be delighted if you would stay too...'

'Yes!' said Pip. 'At least until Vera comes up next month. Say you'll stay?'

In unison, the two women leaned forward, placing their elbows on the table with their palms facing upwards, cupping their faces and smiling at her sweetly.

Alice nodded her agreement as there was nothing else to be said or done and couldn't help but laugh at the pair in their delightful and easy way that they had gently persuaded her to stay.

'Thank you both and I love what you did with my plait. I was going to throw it away but the hat is much nicer.'

CHAPTER FIFTEEN

Over the next few weeks, the three began to settle into a comfortable routine at Beech Cottage. Alice understandably had good days and bad while the ladies had an instinct for comforting and for when to leave her alone. Much to the sisters' delight, there had been no more talk of her leaving and it was as though they had lived together for years.

*

Alice was gobsmacked. 'You do what...? Here?' she said, raising her eyebrows and laughing in mock disbelief. 'Really?'

'Unsure why that is so funny!' Pip tried to say seriously but broke into laughter alongside her sister.

'Goodness, I'm laughing for the sake of it,' exclaimed Tish, lifting her glasses up and wiping her eyes with her delicate hankie.

'Yes, but...' said Alice, staring at the women across the kitchen table. 'But... but...'

'We're not goats, Alice. We don't butt,' said Pip. 'Now, let me get this straight, young lady.' She was doing her best not to break into laughter again. 'We would be interested to know why this is all so amusing to you?'

'But you're...' She caught Pip's expression that said no goats. 'You're two lovely older ladies, and...'

'And?' they said together and continued to stare at the youngster who was lost for words.

'Well, that's about it, isn't it, Tish?' said Pip.

'Yes, it is. You think that elderly respectable women shouldn't distil whisky?'

'Well, it's hardly *just* whisky, is it?' Alice gently admonished.

'Alright. It's very *nice* whisky,' said Pip, much to the delight of Tish who had another fit of the giggles.

'You know that wasn't the word I was after.' She looked from one to the other, enjoying the banter.

'I'll give you two words. Would *illegal* or *moonshine* suffice?' asked Pip as the three of them broke into laughter.

'But where? I've been in all of your outbuildings.'

'Ah, we're not as silly as we look.' Tish double-tapped the side of her nose. 'Better not to do it on your own doorstep.'

'Yes,' said Pip. 'That was one thing Daddy taught us...'

'Seems like our fathers taught us all a few things out of the ordinary,' remarked Alice. Pip and Tish nodded, appreciating that she had begun to open up in telling them all about her father.

Then their ward solemnly steered the conversation. 'Whisky nearly killed my uncle,' she said, bowing her head.

'Oh, Alice!' said Pip compassionately.

'We're so sorry and wouldn't have told you about the distillery had we known,' said Tish. Both ladies leaned across and placed their hands onto her hand in comfort.

'It happened one Friday night at the pub. He was already drunk when he leapt up onto the bar to steal a bottle but didn't realise until it was too late that the cellar trapdoor was open on the other side. He fell straight through and could've been killed hadn't he landed on the poor unfortunate publican...' Alice popped her head up and winked and they all roared with laughter.

'Oh, you're funny,' said Pip, topping up Alice's teacup. 'You had us going for a moment.'

'Couldn't resist that. I would love to see your distillery if that is alright with you. Can we go there today?' She looked expectantly at the sisters.

'Good idea,' said Tish. 'We haven't been there for quite a while. We ought to check and see if everything is alright and to clean up. You can help us. Drink up and we'll make tracks.'

'Is it far?' she enquired when they climbed up into the truck.

'We couldn't possibly tell you that,' said Tish.

'Top secret,' replied Pip. 'Should we blindfold her, Tish?'

Alice shot them both a look that said *really*. Then smiled and sat back to enjoy the scenery.

Pip drove and Tish sat in the middle, allowing Alice to sit next to the window. She sat at an angle so her upper body was parallel to the door, enabling her to fold her arms across the window frame and extend her head outside. Closing her eyes, she relished the mountain breeze that engulfed her face while her hair billowed wildly around her.

Along with her newfound freedom came a guilt for laughing and feeling pockets of happiness. *If only Mother could have seen all this, and to have known Pip and Tish,* she thought, *how different things would have been for us.* She had inwardly tortured herself since she had learned of her mother's death where she was consumed with *what ifs* that buzzed inside her head in a never-ending circle. *If only I had insisted that she not go to Vera's, that I had enough money for the pair of us. If only we went straight to Central Station... if, if, if.*

The warm mountain breeze together with the woodland aromas were delightful. The city child inhaled deeply, revelling in her surroundings and lowered her head back inside. There was nothing quite like it. The mountains were stunningly beautiful. Alice had never seen so many trees in one place before as the truck made its way around bends and inclines with so many delights to see. She spotted a kangaroo a few feet into the bush who appeared to be washing his face. His claws – or hands, she wasn't sure what to call them – rubbed his face all over. She found it rather cute, watching him rub behind each ear bending them forward in turn and making her smile when they sprang back. He looked up and the gesture touched her heart. He was an amazing creature.

'So,' she said, 'what do you do with the whisky?'

'We have carried on the same way that our father

conducted business,' answered Tish. 'We have a calendar of pre-arranged pick-up dates and deal with one distributor only. A truck comes by where Pip and I have the consignment ready to go. Two men load up a truck, they give us the money and that's it until the next time.'

'Where does it go?'

'That's where we stop,' said Pip. 'We'd rather not know to whom or where it goes. It's illegal and risky enough as it is. There is a market for it and we supply. It's probably passed from supplier to supplier and each time for a little extra profit but we rather not be a part of that.'

'Keep it simple, is what we were taught,' said Tish.

'So, you don't put your label on it?'

'Goodness, no,' replied Tish. 'Better that way for obvious reasons. Non-traceable. But that doesn't mean that someone doesn't put their own label on it somewhere down the line, does it?'

'No, I suppose not.'

After a short while, Pip began to lower the gears and then turned the steering wheel gently into the bushland where there wasn't a road or even a track it seemed. Suddenly they went from day to night when they drove under the thick canopy. The foliage was heavily intertwined, and Alice was momentarily scared.

'Not too long now,' said Tish when Pip turned the headlights on.

'I wouldn't have known that you could even drive through here.' Her anxiety lessened when she saw gradual light seep way up ahead.

'It's even more dark on a cloudy day,' said Pip. 'We're nearly there.'

'Pip,' said Tish calmly a few seconds later. Alice picked up the underlying tone.

Then, when Pip replied, 'Seen it,' in the same tone, Alice knew that something was very wrong. Her instinct told her to keep quiet and observe. She lightly tilted her right foot and felt the reassuring presence of her switch within her boot.

Pip continued to drive slowly, then cut the engine upon reaching the other side of the canopy. In front of them was an open meadow just big enough to accommodate the wooden building with ample space in which to turn a large vehicle around. To Alice, the size of the single-storey building was on par with the ladies' Beech Cottage. Parked out in front was an open truck loaded up with crates of bottles. Then they spotted that the door to the building was wide open.

'Stay here, Alice,' ordered Pip and stepped down out of the truck followed by Tish, who swiftly slid across the seat to alight from the driver's door and closed it quietly. Alice spun around and saw Tish retrieve a rifle from the back of the truck.

There was no way that Alice was going to stay put. She walked around to the women and before they could protest, she whispered, 'We do this together. You know I've been in dangerous situations; I can handle myself. How did you know someone was here?'

The women knew she was right. There was no time to argue and an extra pair of hands would be handy. 'The trigger we set was broken,' enlightened Tish.

'There was the possibility that it may have been an animal but now we're here, no animal we know of drives a truck,' said Pip as she, too, grabbed a rifle.

Alice had just been about to ask what they would do next when she almost jumped out of her skin. Without warning, Tish fired her rifle into the air. The roaring blast sent flocks of birds catapulting up into the sky in a squawking unison. Then the women aimed their rifles at the open door and walked confidently toward the building shoulder to shoulder as Alice followed.

After a few moments, an old man appeared at the door who did not seem capable of lifting a crate of whisky. He stepped out into the sunshine and held his arms in the air. The sisters remained a safe distance away and relaxed their rifles by pointing the barrels down to the ground.

'What are you doing here?' Tish demanded with authority. 'This is private property.'

Alice's reaction was a millisecond ahead, spinning to her side after hearing a branch snap and seeing a younger version of the old man on their left flank.

'You're in no position to be asking questions.' He pointed his rifle at Tish then jabbed the barrel forward, indicating for them to move closer toward the building.

'What do you want?' asked Pip.

'Good stash you have here,' said the older man. 'Would fetch a pretty penny.'

'Take it and go. You got what you came for,' said Tish as her sister nodded. 'We want no trouble.' Both women now had the responsibility of taking care of Alice and felt that these men were a serious threat.

When they neared the building, the younger man approached their truck. He leaned in and snatched the keys from the ignition and placed them in his jacket pocket. Although this was all happening behind her, Alice was fully aware.

'I'll take those,' he said a few moments later and snatched the rifles. The old man stood aside and the women had no choice but to enter the building. The door was slammed shut behind them.

The room was no bigger than Alice's bedroom back at Beech Cottage and with the five of them inside, it was a little cramped. Instinct kicked in, giving Alice the perfect opportunity to repossess the keys to the truck and place them in her trouser pocket. She detected a yeasty and earthy smell and when her eyes adjusted to the low glow from the gas lamp affixed to the far wall, she could view her surroundings more clearly.

'Go through,' prompted the older man who seemed to be in charge. 'I dare say you know where you are going.'

Tish led the way through another door into the main building where Alice was amazed to see where the production took place. During the journey, the ladies had given her a brief rundown as to how they made the whisky. She had been looking forward to having a good look around but due to the current situation, she only took a quick glance, not wanting to take her eyes off the men for more than a few seconds.

Dominating the room were two vast copper stills that

Tish had described as looking like giant kettles. There was a wood burner and a water tank with numerous pipes that protruded from everywhere it seemed. There were stacks of buckets, tables of bottles and piles of wood and coal. Alice saw around ten large hessian sacks that were bulky and appeared heavy, and she could only guess that they were full of barley, but she couldn't be sure. Pip and Tish said they would give her a guided grand tour but for the moment, that was unfortunately put on hold.

'How did you know this was here?' she asked. 'It isn't obvious from the road.'

'Smart, aintcha,' he said with a gappy grin. 'I knew of this place since I was a young'un. Knew your ol' man.' He looked at Pip and Tish, who looked back at him in surprise. 'He brought me and my father here once, never forgot it. Thought it high time I came back. Knew he was long gone and it looked unused, so...'

'You've bled us dry,' said Tish, cutting him off mid-sentence and trying to keep her temper in check. 'Now go.'

'We're going. We're done anyway,' said the younger man who reeked of whisky, obviously having tasted the contraband already, 'and we'll be taking this one with us.' Believing the young pretty girl was a pushover, he forcibly grabbed her arm but her reflexes kicked in and she yanked her arm back. 'Feisty little thing, aintcha? I like it.'

'LET HER GO!' shouted Pip. The sisters stood defiantly between him and Alice.

He lunged forward at the same time that Alice shouted, 'STOP IT!' where he connected with Pip, shoving her backwards who luckily landed in Alice's arms.

'ENOUGH,' bellowed the old man to his son. 'Stop fooling around, grab the girl and let's get out of here.'

Alice was once again seized by the arm.

'We'll lock you inside,' he addressed the sisters, 'and because you've been such a bother, we'll also take your truck.'

'Won't you need these?' Alice dangled the key before her accoster then threw it to Tish as his conceitedness blocked any warning as to what was coming next.

Alice spun around so rapidly that he lost his grip, then with lightning speed, she jabbed her elbow upwards, causing blood to spurt from his broken nose.

'You'll pay dearly for that...' He spat, just as Alice swept his feet out from under him and he landed heavily on the floor.

'What the hell are you doing?' the old man yelled. 'Get her.'

Pip and Tish were frightened for Alice. It was escalating out of control and there wasn't anything that they could do, then they heard the distinct sound of the safety release and turned to see the older man pointing his rifle at them.

Alice stood still as the bloodied attacker regained his feet, grabbed her again and slapped her hard across the face.

'YOU PIG,' shouted Pip. 'TAKE THE WHISKY AND GO. LEAVE US ALONE.'

'That the best you got?' Alice goaded, showing no sign that the slap had hurt because she was an expert at hiding pain. 'Put down your rifle,' she ordered the old man who did so when he saw her produce the switch. Without looking,

Alice released the safety catch and the men flinched when the blade clicked menacingly into place. Pip and Tish were dumbfounded as they hadn't a clue that she had such a weapon, then they squirmed when she pointed the blade to within a whisker of the man's delicate area.

'You have no idea,' said Alice, 'to the hornets' nest that you've just uncovered. You move as much as an eyelash and I'll rip your ball bags wide open. Don't be fooled by a little girl. My daddy taught me well. In fact, Big Alfie and the whole gang from Sydney will be coming up here in a couple of days and it would be very wise if you don't come here ever again. No one messes with Alfie, but if you did, split ball bags will be the least of your worries.' Alice nicked his inner thigh as a warning. She could almost hear his heart skip a beat. He knew she wasn't bluffing.

The three women watched with great relief from the window when the men speed off through the canopy where the dust cloud remained long after they had gone.

'We should've made them leave the whisky. They've bled you dry.'

But the sisters stared at her knowingly with grins on their faces.

'There are so many questions, we don't know where to begin,' Tish said in admiration.

'The switch was the only thing my father was particular about and his teachings paid off. And that is the only compliment I have for him.'

'We know about Big Alf,' said Pip, 'from what you have told us, and assume he's Big Alfie, but the gang from Sydney?'

'That was a mammoth lie. I don't think those men will risk coming back here.'

'Do you know,' said Pip, 'I think I need a sit-down and a tot of whisky to get over the excitement.'

'Amen, to that,' said Tish. 'We're just a little shaky, Alice. It's been an unusual morning.'

'Yes, it has been unusual but they've taken it all...'

'Ah.' Pip smiled. 'Come with us.'

Alice put her switch away and followed them to the far side of the building where, open-mouthed in utter disbelief, she watched as they effortlessly picked up a hessian sack in each hand and moved them to one side.

'Catch!' Tish flung a sack at her where she was amazed to find that the bulk was scrunched up newspaper.

'Oh, that's genius,' she praised. Underneath the cleared space, a trapdoor was revealed. Tish bent down and lifted it fully open in an arc-like movement, then as Pip flipped a light switch on the wall and the generator kicked in, Alice could see a wooden staircase. Tish preceded to climb down.

'Come on,' said Pip, following her sister. 'Mind how you go, hold onto the side rail.'

For a moment, Alice stood at the bottom of the cavern, impatiently waiting for her eyes to adjust to the soft underground glow. And when they did, she looked around in awe at row upon row upon row of hefty oak barrels neatly lined up on their side within wooden half-moon supports.

'H O L Y S H I T...'

'ALICE!' admonished the sisters before they all burst into laughter.

'In a nutshell,' explained Tish while Alice walked around in a daze, 'this and a few side tunnels that we'll show you is what is left of an old collapsed mineshaft. Our great-grandaddy and his two brothers built the distillery over it to take advantage of the hidden space and storage. We've been robbed a few times over the years, so we only leave out a few gallons worth. The true beauty lies in the depths here.'

'You see,' said Pip, 'what those men took is just the tip of the iceberg. Come through here and we'll show you more.'

Quite mesmerised, she followed them down a small tunnel that led into another cave that held a plethora of barrels.

'Then in the next chamber, we keep the whisky that has been maturing for twenty years.'

'That's the good stuff,' said Pip. 'Potent.'

'I am truly amazed but how do you get it upstairs? It's too heavy, surely?'

'Good question,' said Pip.

'Absolutely,' said Tish. 'We have a system. Come this way and we will show you.' She led the way back to the main chamber beside the staircase.

She watched Pip walk over to a simple wooden cart and picked up its handle to wheel it alongside a barrel. The cart was already loaded with a crate that held twenty clanking bottles. 'We then syphon the whisky from here and cork it upstairs,' said Tish.

'Imagine that the bottles are now full. Pip will go back up the stairs, we'll see her shortly. Come on, this way, Alice, and you will see how we get the bottles up to her.'

Just when Alice had thought she had seen it all, her admiration reached another level when she followed Tish down the final tunnel.

'Ah, there she is,' said Tish when Pip pulled back another overhead hatch and dangled down some rope that her sister expertly tied to the corners of the crate.

'It's a pulley!' exclaimed Alice with delight, watching the crate lift effortlessly and steadily up to the production room. Soon, they were all back upstairs.

'That is just brilliant. No one would ever suspect.' She studied the area and discovered that the hatch within the floor was just a bogus section of floorboards. It had copper pipes affixed and when it was fitted back into place anyone would be hard-pressed to find the join, unless you were specifically looking for it. Alice looked up and the overhead pulley was cleverly hidden among several pulley systems for effect as opposed to functional, where no thief would think twice to question.

Later that evening, Tish cooked them a scrumptious rabbit pie with puff pastry, roast potatoes and fresh vegetables from the garden, topped with mouth-watering gravy.

'Quite a day,' said Pip, setting out the cutlery on the dining room table.

'Yes, it was,' said Alice, helping Tish carry the plates of steaming hot food. She had never eaten so well in her life. She was beginning to feel much healthier, full of energy and was truly thankful to the ladies for looking after her so well.

'Do you know,' said Pip, 'today made me think back to the last time we were robbed blind. Remember it, Tish?'

'Certainly do. It was in 1919. Remember it like yesterday,' she replied, tucking into the dinner. 'The country was still celebrating the end of the war, then the next thing we know, we had the Spanish flu to contend with.'

'That was just awful,' said Pip. 'You were born in 1920, Alice, weren't you?' She nodded. 'Must have been a very worrying time for your parents, particularly with living in the city?'

'I've heard about it. Alfie mentioned it a few times; his wife died by it. But my parents never spoke of it. I suppose because they lived through those tough times that they didn't like to dwell too much on the past. My father did not speak of his younger years either and whenever I asked my mother questions about when she was a girl, she always changed the subject. I think it hurt her too much to look back on happier times, if that makes sense. From the moment I was born, she never had an easy time with my father. I truly believe that if I were a boy, things would have been so very different...'

'He was a damn bloody idiot,' blurted Tish without thinking as Pip and Alice looked at her from the out-of-character burst and when no one argued the statement, it was taken as a given. The sisters not only felt Alice's pain, but her mother's too. They would have been so joyous to have had the opportunity for both to have stayed, like the daughter and granddaughter they never had.

'So...' Alice continued, 'tell me about how you coped out here during the Spanish flu.'

Thankful for the change of direction, Pip answered.

'We were fortunate because we had only recently returned from stocking up our supplies in the city before it started around March. So many poor souls were lost. It struck so fast you see, you could be fine in the morning, then dead by teatime.' She shuddered. 'As you know, we're quite isolated out here and self-sufficient but we still barricaded ourselves away even more so. In the evenings we sat in front of the radio for news. It was very grim.

'But we had to venture out. Just the once, to check on the distillery,' said Tish. 'Even though the usual distributor pickup was temporarily suspended, we had to go. It was quite scary, almost eerie, as we drove there. Not a soul we met on the journey. It was like we were the only ones in the whole world. We're used to passing the odd truck or two, but this time there was no one.

'Had the shock of our lives when we discovered that the distillery had been raided. We knew before we entered the building. Fortunately, the caverns hadn't been discovered so we did a quick look around, did what we had to do then left quick smart back home.'

'That was the only time we dared to venture out,' said Pip, 'and the only time we didn't make our usual second trip into the city. We always enjoy the shopping and taking in an art gallery or two. Lucky for us this time around, eh, Tish?'

'Absolutely! We wouldn't have stumbled on this little one, otherwise.' The women smiled at Alice who smiled back, acknowledging. 'Looking forward to speaking to your aunt tomorrow?'

'Yes, I am,' she replied while the sisters felt a pang,

knowing that they were approaching the beginning of the end. 'You'd like her. She's fun just like you two.'

'Well, that is a compliment coming from a youngster.' Tish smiled. 'We only spoke briefly as you know, but we like her already. We'll make tracks after breakfast and we can look around Katoomba until it's time to telephone.'

'That sounds great, thank you.' Alice finished her dinner. 'Your rabbit pie is so delicious, Tish. I'm fit to bursting.' She laughed.

'Hear, hear,' echoed Pip.

'Thank you, both!'

After a brief but poignant pause, the question had to be asked. 'So...' ventured Pip. Tish held her breath. 'You know that you are more than welcome to stay but do you think you'll go back to Sydney? Your aunt will no doubt have plans for you.'

Alice put down her knife and fork and looked across at the kindest, loving and most caring people that she had had the privilege to meet and smiled. 'Thank you. I appreciate that, but if I am truly honest with you, I'm torn.' Both Pip and Tish skipped a heartbeat. 'You have been extremely kind and generous and there for me when I needed someone the most. But I feel I ought to go back. It's where I belong. I feel I have imposed enough...'

'Oh, Alice, you are like a granddaughter to us! We have loved every minute. It's never been an imposition,' said Tish and Pip nodded.

The youngster teared up. 'That is the loveliest of things to say. You have given me a sense of being wanted and belonging and I will never forget that.'

The ladies didn't want Alice to be upset and knew it was unfair to continue burdening her with such pressure. They had said their bit and knew how they all felt. Now it was time to let things lie and to take its course and besides, it was up to Vera.

It was time to deflect.

'You have given us so much too, Alice,' said Pip. 'We were all in the right place at the right time. Goodness.' She laughed. 'Do you remember the look on the train conductor's face when we ushered you inside the compartment and we three grinned at him like Cheshire cats?'

They all laughed, remembering. 'I had no idea what had happened, and I don't think he did either. It was great timing when Pip said "smile" that we did so on cue.'

'That was comical,' said Tish. 'Now, has anyone got room left for some apple pie?'

*

Later, when Alice was taking her bath, it gave the women the opportunity to talk.

'Torn,' said Pip, 'that's what Alice said. She said she was torn. That's a good thing, isn't it?'

'I say it is,' agreed Tish, pouring them both a sherry. 'Between you and me, I'm hoping that Vera thinks that it's still too risky for her to return.'

'Me too. But that's selfish on our part, isn't it?'

'It is, but Alice is happy here. See how she has bloomed.'

'She has. When we speak to Vera in the morning, we'll

invite her up here right away. It will be a tense visit, but we must be happy for Alice if she decides to go.'

'Yes, we must and you're right. We'll bring Vera back here and insist that she at least stays overnight. We'll arrange a special tea out on the lawn and say our goodbyes. And, if it is goodbye, then I am sure that she will visit us from time to time.'

'Yes, I am sure too. Sydney isn't too far,' said Pip. 'Alice will still be in our lives whatever is decided. Let's have another sherry and put the radio on before we turn in.'

Alice was unable to sleep and tossed and turned all night. She was in a pickle with her thoughts focused on one question. *Should I stay or go?* Then the floodgates opened as she ploughed headfirst into a myriad of quandaries. Yes, she was looking forward to speaking to her aunt and to be seeing her soon, but she didn't know her that well as her mother hadn't liked her spending too much time at her house. For years, Alice had known that it was a brothel and what went on in there despite being told it was a boarding house. She understood all this, yet her aunt was her only living relative. *What should I do?*

CHAPTER SIXTEEN

Vera also tossed and turned her way through the night. During the past month, Alice had dominated her thoughts because she had felt responsible for her. It was what Rose would have wanted, but then again, Rose hadn't known Pip and Tish despite Vera herself only having briefly chatted over the telephone. She trusted her gut instinct and knew deep down that the ladies were kind and genuine and had Alice's best interests at heart. It was almost like Rose had arranged for the sisters to be there for her.

Big Alf had taken a temporary boarding room at Vera's and had been an asset in keeping trouble from her door, including a few undesirables seeking to recuperate some of Stanley's outstanding debts. Of which there had been many. She eventually trusted him with the knowledge that Rose was taking Alice and leaving Stanley. This had explained why Rose had been in the area at such an early hour and why he was unable to locate Alice at the racecourse.

During that awful fateful night, Big Alf had overheard

Rose telling her husband that he had left his journal by P W's body. The big man had counted his lucky stars because he was well aware of its contents. Later, he learned that an anonymous citizen had handed the journal into the police station – that would have made for very interesting reading.

He knew that his and Alice's involvement were never recorded, therefore depicting that Stanley Johnson had committed every crime single-handedly. Allowing a thought, albeit briefly, that Shiv was protecting them, he knew deep down that it was just his boss's selfish arrogance in taking all the credit.

The conclusion was that Rose's murder, at the hand of her husband, had been a very sad and tragic incident. The police investigation found that their neighbours hadn't been backwards in coming forwards informing of the violence that they had heard. This had spoken volumes to the police that Mr Johnson was despised by his own where the usual non-grassing conduct had gone completely out of the window.

Mr Wyatt had been concerned by Alice's sudden departure and knew that something dreadful must have had happened for her not to have been in touch. The police had paid him a visit as part of their investigation asking questions about the Johnson family and was shocked to learn that Alice's parents were deceased. His mind was put at rest knowing that the young girl, whom he and his wife considered a daughter, was safe as the policeman informed him that Alice's aunt had sent her away to stay with family down on the southern coast. Unbeknown to the police, that was a huge lie. But during the tense month that followed Rose's death, it was all that Vera could say to make sure Alice remained safe in case Stanley's cronies came looking for his daughter.

The more Mr Wyatt thought about it, the more he found it a little odd because Alice had never mentioned any other family or any reference to the southern coast. They missed seeing her smiley face but reflected that there was nothing they could do but pray that she was safe and well believing that she would contact them soon when the time was right.

As the month progressed, things started to settle down, somewhat enabling Big Alf to bid Vera farewell as he headed up north to his brother's place. He didn't say exactly where and Vera hadn't asked. They knew that it was better that she wasn't informed of his future whereabouts. Just in case.

But, for now, Vera preferred not to make a rash decision about whether Alice lived with her or stayed with the sisters. She knew the right outcome would present itself soon enough. Throwing back the blankets, she dangled her feet over the side of the bed and swirled them about to locate her slippers, giving up on sleep and trundling downstairs to make a pot of tea.

*

Before they entered Katoomba's station office, Alice had posted Mr Wyatt a long letter. She included an explanation and apology as to why she had left so quickly without speaking to him or even leaving a note and ended that she would write from time to time. Pip and Tish were very supportive and had helped her write the letter, making her feel blessed that she had been cared for by so many good people. Then, they entered the station's office with a mix of excitement and apprehension as Tish placed the telephone call while Mr Pendry and Mr Mellor attended to passengers who had just alighted from the Sydney train.

Vera had been pacing up and down her hallway for the last two hours, waiting for the telephone to ring. But despite that, the shrill bell still made her jump out of her skin and managed to pick up on the first ring.

'Hello, Mrs Vera Peabody speaking,' she said automatically, equally nervous.

'Good morning, Vera, it's Tish. Pip and Alice are here also. How are you?'

'Good morning, Tish and everyone. I am well and hope you are too. How is Alice?' She bit on an already chewed fingernail.

'She is very well. Here, I'll pass her on.'

Alice took the receiver. 'Hello, Aunt Vera. It's lovely to talk to you.'

The sound of Alice's voice melted Vera's heart. How she sounded like her mother.

'Hello, love. It's so lovely to talk to you too. How have you been?' She cursed herself for asking such a damn stupid question.

'Some ups and downs, but Pip and Tish have been looking after me very well and we get on like a house on fire.' Alice knew she was going to cry as each word became a little croakier than the one before. Speaking to Aunt Vera conjured up her mother even more as she was a reminder of *home*. 'Still miss my mother,' she blurted in a higher pitch tone before thrusting the receiver back to Tish and bolting outside to sob on the platform's bench.

'Emotional time for you both,' said Tish, taking a deep breath, feeling for them while Pip followed Alice outside.

'Yes, it is,' she replied, trying to hold it together.

'If you think it safe, Vera, how about coming up on tomorrow morning's train? We'll meet you and we'd be delighted if you would stay a while. It would be good for you and Alice to spend some time together and to talk. Pip and I would like to meet you. What do you think?'

'I think that will be grand. Thank you, Tish. But just overnight if you don't mind as I will need to get back. If that is alright with you all?'

'We understand and look forward to seeing you this time tomorrow.'

'Thank you again for everything and for looking after Alice this past month.'

'Our pleasure. Until tomorrow.'

'Yes, until tomorrow. Goodbye.'

'Goodbye,' said Tish. Vera replaced the receiver and walked through to the parlour and made herself another fresh pot and a slice of toast.

Tish took a deep breath; she and Pip had discussed the previous evening how hard the telephone call would be and had hoped that it did not put Alice back a step. Although they knew that sometimes a step back was needed in which to move forwards.

Walking along the platform, she noticed how pretty the window boxes were looking this year with their colourful blooms and that it was not surprising, under the circumstances, that they had been overlooked the previous month.

'Is everything alright?' Tish sat down and was somewhat relieved to see her sister give a brief nod. 'Vera is coming up tomorrow, Alice. It will be lovely to meet her.'

The ladies took comfort in Alice's smile.

'Sorry,' she said. 'Talking to Aunt Vera in her house where we visited together made it almost seem like Mother was in the parlour having some tea. I could imagine her there, then I knew that was impossible if that makes sense.'

'It's alright,' said Pip. 'We understand and it does make sense. It will be good for you both to see each other. Now, we have some arrangements to make for tomorrow.'

'Yes,' said Tish. 'How about planning a picnic tea out on the lawn for tomorrow afternoon and we'll help with the baking?'

'Thank you. I'd like that very much.' Alice wiped her tears as they walked to the car park.

*

It was a very emotional scene for all when Alice and her aunt cried and embraced on the platform.

'Goodness, me,' said Vera, dabbing her eyes. 'What a pair we are and what's all this?' She tenderly touched Alice's new shorter hair.

'I'll tell you about that later and I'll show you my new hat that will explain some of it.' She managed a smile.

'Hello, Vera,' said Pip and Tish and hugged the woman with whom they had never met but shared a special bond.

'Hello, ladies. There are not enough words to express how grateful I am. It is so lovely to meet you both. Do you know that I haven't been up to the mountains in decades? I'd forgotten just how beautiful they are.'

'Yes, very beautiful,' said Alice, 'but just wait until you see Beech Cottage. It's just as beautiful.' She took her aunt's bag and placed it in the back of the truck before stepping up and in to give the three women ample room in the truck's cab.

*

'Well!' exclaimed Vera, looking at Beech Cottage when Tish pulled up outside. 'How picturesque is this?' Alice climbed down from the back of the truck and helped her aunt alight.

'We're so glad you like it,' said Pip. 'Come, we must get you some tea.'

'Can't explain it better than it feels like we have all known each other for years,' said Tish.

'I agree with that,' said Vera, 'the angels were certainly looking out for Alice that day.'

Everyone nodded.

'Come inside, Aunt, I'll show you around.'

'This is most spectacular,' she exclaimed after finishing the tour that ended in the magnificent garden. Alice had earlier set the table for tea and on top of a crisp white tablecloth, she had arranged bird of paradise blooms as a centrepiece.

After they had eaten their ham sandwiches and jam sponge cake, Pip and Tish left them to talk.

'How have you been, love?' asked Vera, sitting back with her cup of tea to listen to what she had to say.

'Honestly, it's been such a mix of up and down. Pip and Tish are amazing and look after me very well, but there are times when I think back to how things were and I feel so sad. When I wake up in the morning, there is a second when everything is alright but then I know it isn't. Oh, how I wish I could go back and do things differently. For one, I would have insisted that Mother and I go straight to Central without her coming to you. The thing is that I had been building up money for us to get away, just as Mother had for us.'

Vera raised her eyebrows in question.

'It's a long story, but I had been making honest money at the track and had planned on leaving home, with Mother, when I turned sixteen. I had enough for the both of us, but she insisted that she would collect her money from you. We learned this about each other in our precious last few minutes together. We'd both been saving for a better future... and now she's gone.' Alice bowed her head and gave into a fresh bout of tears that overcame her. Vera didn't fuss and let her niece recover in her own time.

'I will never understand why he killed her. Never. And I will never forgive him. I saw him stagger out of that alleyway after he killed P W Jones. I found his journal beside the body and left it to incriminate him, thinking that he would rot in jail.' She raised her head and looked her aunt straight in the eye for some kind of reprimand but Vera just nodded, understanding what she had done and why.

'If it's any consolation, Alice, I would have done exactly the same. It's all so tragic what happened to your mother. We both loved her dearly and she deserved better – you both did. But that is how things are and we need to try and move on. Your mother loved you very much and I honestly believe that she was looking down on you and making you safe with Pip and Tish.'

'They have been so good and understanding and have given me space to grieve. I don't know how to thank them.'

'You already have by just being here, which has given them a new lease of life. I could tell just by speaking to them on the telephone how much they enjoy having you here.

'Now, Alice. We need to discuss this before the ladies return. I am sure we've both given ample thought on what happens next. What do you want to do? I won't order you – you're nearly sixteen and not a small child. You are more than welcome to live with me or I am positive that the ladies would like you to stay here.'

'Aunt Vera, in all honesty, I have been torn. I know Mother would want you to look after me despite her not approving of your *business*.' Alice raised her eyebrows while Vera looked back at her in feigned shock.

'Yes, I know it's a knocking shop,' Alice said and they both burst out laughing, lightening the serious conversation.

'Alice Johnson,' her aunt playfully scolded. 'I'll have you know that it's a very respectable knocking shop.'

And when they laughed again, Pip and Tish became

puzzled watching the pair from the kitchen window as tears turned to laughter.

'It isn't an ideal environment for a young girl, I give you that,' she continued, 'but in all sincerity, I promise that I would make changes to suit you. You know, tidy things up somewhat, making sure that business was more discreet and the like.'

'I appreciate that, Aunt Vera. Really, I do. But, not to hurt your feelings at all, I would prefer to stay here for a while if that's alright with you?'

'You're a sensible young woman. I have tough skin and am not offended at all. To be honest with you, I am relieved as I cannot offer you the great opportunity that you have here. Now that I have met Pip and Tish and have been here in person, my mind is fully at rest. And, I say this with utmost sincerity... your mother would totally approve.'

'Yes, she would.' Alice agreed and they stood and hugged one another staying in their warm embrace for a long time. The ladies returned with a fresh pot of tea and a fruit cake.

'If it is fine with you, and it is fine with Aunt Vera, I would very much like to stay here for a while...'

'Oh, Alice!' exclaimed Tish. 'We would like nothing more.'

'Hear, hear. You know how much we enjoy you being here,' said Pip as she hugged them both.

'Thank you. I am very happy to be here.'

'Then that's sorted,' said Vera, walking back to her chair. 'I insist on paying for my niece's keep.' She dibbed into her handbag and handed Tish an envelope who smiled and shook her head before handing it straight back unopened.

'We appreciate the intention, but we cannot accept. And if the boot were on the other foot, you wouldn't accept either.'

Vera nodded. It was true.

'We have all changed a tragic circumstance into a positivity in the best way we can. We four are family now. Thank you, but it isn't necessary,' added Pip. While Vera fully understood, it did not stop her from thinking of other ways in which to contribute.

'A simple thank you doesn't seem to suffice, but I like us all being family.' After a brief pause, she continued. 'I brought something else. It's not pleasant but it's something I feel you should all know about.' She retrieved a newspaper from her bag. 'Page seven.'

Alice took the newspaper and sat down and opened it while the sisters leaned in behind to read over her shoulder. It was one thing to hear about the tragedy, but to read about it in a newspaper, was a different thing entirely. Pip and Tish grabbed each other's hand and held firm when after they had finished reading, the page was suddenly splattered with a fallen teardrop, causing the area around it to crinkle with a ripple effect.

'It'll dry,' said Pip, gently taking the paper but her good intention to brush the tear away caused the ink to smudge. 'Oh, I am SO sorry,' she said, beside herself. 'Why on Earth did I do that? Silly woman I am!'

'It's alright, Pip. It does not matter and you are far from silly. It's just a piece of paper.' She took the newspaper from Pip and handed it back to Vera.

'Sorry, love,' said Vera.

'No harm done. Honestly.'

'I have something else for you.' Vera handed Alice her mother's bible where she smiled in recognition. 'Not as it seems though. Things have changed somewhat,' she said with an apologetic look on her face and urged her to open it. 'During this past month, I deemed it to be one of the safest places I knew to hide.' Alice looked in amazement as a quarter of the way in, the pages had been cut out in an oblong leaving about an inch deep of clear space, where placed was Rose's earnings within the border. 'What your mother worked years for. Just like you, to get away.

'Make her proud, Alice.' Vera wiped her eyes. 'Make something of your life and remember her always. Just never let on that her precious bible has been subjected to foul play. I am sure the Lord would understand on this occasion. Big Alf helped cut the pages. He was always on your side, you know.'

'Alfie.' Alice smiled fondly. 'Is he...'

'He's fine and he was a big help. He's moved on now to see his brother and sends you his best.'

'Thank you, Aunt Vera.' Alice clutched the bible. 'For everything.'

'I know we'll keep in touch, and you can always write. And if you wish, telephone me whenever you are in Katoomba. Now, let's wipe our tears and enjoy the rest of the afternoon.'

Tish poured fresh cups of tea. 'That was beautiful, Vera. Alice told us that unbeknown to the other, they had both been saving to get away. It will always be a tragedy and even though we did not know Rose personally, we agree with what you said. We assure you that Alice's money, together with her mother's, will be safe in the house for whenever she needs it. Now, can I interest anyone in a delicious slice of Pip's fruit cake?'

CHAPTER SEVENTEEN

'Penny for them.' Tish smiled, noticing that Alice was miles away.

'Just thinking about the horses at the track. How I miss them and the rides. Been thinking of them more so since Aunt Vera returned to Sydney last month.' She caught the *knowing* look the sisters gave each other. 'Alright,' she said, 'I know those expressions. After the surprise with the distillery, don't tell me that you have stables and horses tucked away as well?'

'Well, not quite.' Pip laughed. 'It just so happens that we know a family up here who do.'

Alice cheered up at the prospect of seeing some horses and waited for more information.

'Finch's Equestrian owns quite a chunk of land and have turned most of it into stabling and training facilities. They breed thoroughbreds and have had quite a bit of success in the racing world. Quite up your street,' said Tish.

'Oh, my goodness. The mountains *are* full of surprises.

Please, can we go take a look?'

'I think we can manage that. We'll go in the morning,' replied Pip.

'Good idea,' said Tish. 'We'll bake some tarts this afternoon to take with us.'

*

The view was spectacular on the drive toward the Finch's property. Alice could see paddock after paddock and when they turned into the long driveway, she saw a man in the training yard. He was holding a rope while a beautiful sable horse elegantly ran in circles around him. It reminded her of her very first ride.

She couldn't have been happier.

Tish pulled up in front of a large single-level house and when they alighted, a woman opened the double wooden front door and walked down the verandah steps to greet them.

'Ladies, it's delightful to see you after so long.' She beamed, embracing the women.

'It's good to see you as well, Judy,' said Pip. 'Please, let me introduce you to Alice. She is staying with us for a while. Family, from Sydney.'

'Welcome, Alice.' Judy hugged her as well. 'How lovely to see you.'

'Likewise, Judy. What a magnificent place you have here. I love it already.'

'Well, it keeps us busy. You like horses?'

'Quite an understatement,' said Tish. 'Lives and breathes.'

'Then it's a good job you came. I dare say you would rather be out with the horses, than being inside having tea with us oldies?' Judy seemed like a lot of fun. She had a radiant smile, blue eyes and rosy cheeks. She was slim and around five foot five and wore her almost greying hair in a shoulder-length ponytail, which amused Alice, considering, and her clothing pretty much matched Alice's cotton shirt and dark trousers.

Alice smiled, unsure how to answer while she, without warning, let out a roaring elongated, 'J I M M M M,' to gain the man's attention who was training the sable horse. 'This is Alice, show her around, there's a love.' Jim waved his arm in acknowledgement as she bolted towards him.

'Nice to meet you, Alice,' he said. 'I'm just about done here.' He walked toward the thoroughbred. 'We'll lead Pilgrim back to the stables and after he's been groomed, I will show you around.' He smiled, handing the girl the reins and they headed out of the training ground. The sisters had given Alice a run down on the property during the journey, so she knew that Jim and Judy had built the business from scratch over many years and had gained a solid reputation in the business.

'He's a handsome boy,' she said, patting the thoroughbred.

'He is. It's a privilege to work with such a magnificent animal. You know horses?'

'Yes. I worked as a stable girl at Randwick for just over four years. I enjoyed the early morning runs. Nothing quite like it.'

'Agree with you there. That's a special time of day, isn't it?' He smiled. 'Riding high as dawn breaks, watching the first rays of sun shining through the mist.'

'Absolutely!' She liked Jim who appeared, like his wife, to be in his fifties and obviously loved his work and the horses. He had a tanned weathered face and forearms, which was understandable and was about six feet in height. He wore an Akubra, blue shirt, brown trousers and brown braces. His boots looked like they had walked twice around Australia but were probably extremely comfortable.

'What brings you out here?' he asked. 'Haven't seen you with Pip and Tish before.'

Alice had been proud when Pip had introduced her to Judy saying that she was family, so she continued the flow. 'I'm family, from Sydney and when I heard that you had horses, I asked if we could visit.'

'Well, that's grand. Perhaps you can visit from time to time. You'd be more than welcome. Ah, here we are.' They walked into a large, squared courtyard.

'Thank you, Jim, I would love to visit again. Goodness! This is amazing.' She spun around, doing a tally. 'You have twenty horses?'

'Not at the moment. We did up until last week, but then we farewelled ten. All trained and ready to join the racing circuit or back to their owners. It's always sad to see them go, but that's the nature of our job up here. Some would probably race at Randwick; you may have looked after or ridden horses that started out here. How about that?' He chuckled.

'Yes, indeed.' Alice was amazed at the possible connection that she already had with Finch's Equestrian. 'How many staff do you have?'

'It all depends on how many horses we have at the time. There are up to ten staff when we are at capacity, including Judy and myself, but until the next lorry arrives, we are half that. Beth, a young woman who is just passing through is currently our only boarder and is due to leave shortly. The other two, Louise and Thomas, are local siblings who work part-time shifts.' Jim caught Alice's interested look. 'Dare say you'd like to join us for a shift or two?' And when she nodded wildly, he added, 'When we've finished up here, we'll go to the house for smoko and discuss with Pip and Tish.'

'Thank you, I'd like that very much.'

And so, for the past four months, Pip and Tish had driven Alice out to Finch's Equestrian where she stayed over for two nights a week. Alice enjoyed being with the horses and making new friends with Beth, Louise and Thomas.

Beth was a little older than she, and if Alice could summon her up in a few words, she would say she was an energetic live wire with an infectious laugh. She was very pretty and petite and had the same golden hair as she and they had immediately struck up a friendship. The equestrian's staff accommodation was basic but comfortable and meals were served up at the main house. Alice quickly became an asset to the team due to her experience and natural way with the horses.

*

It was the last day of September and the day before Alice's sixteenth birthday. At the end of the meal, Judy brought out a homemade sponge cake that had oodles of strawberry jam oozing between the layers. Her eyes lit up like a beacon and she grasped her face in shock and felt somewhat overwhelmed as nothing like this had ever happened to her before. Immediately after placing the cake before her, Judy began to sing and Jim and Beth joined in.

'If that's what it takes to keep you quiet, we should throw a party more often. Happy birthday, Alice!' Beth laughed when they had finished singing and began to cheer.

'This is just a m a z i n g, thank you all!'

'You are more than welcome,' said Judy. 'We couldn't let an important occasion like a sixteenth go by uncelebrated.'

'How'd...' Alice started to ask, then said, 'Pip and Tish, of course!'

'Come on, Alice, cut the cake,' urged Jim. 'I'm hoping it tastes as good as it looks.' He smiled, enjoying the playful scolding look from his wife. 'Just kidding, love. Your cakes are always delicious.'

Judy nodded her approval.

*

During the journey home, Alice told Pip and Tish all about her birthday celebrations the previous evening.

'Sounds like we missed a good party!' said Pip.

'Absolutely,' said Tish. 'Happy birthday, Alice!'

'Thank you both.' She was beaming from ear to ear, enjoying the drive through the mountains. 'I've never had a birthday like this before.' And as Alice looked out of the window, Pip and Tish exchanged knowing satisfactory glances...

Alice's eyes widened with disbelief when Tish turned into the driveway to see colourful bunting adorning both sides of the tree-lined driveway.

The ladies had also affixed the bunting across the whole verandah in perfect symmetrical semi-circles. 'Don't ask.' Tish shook her head jokingly when she glanced at Alice's expression that questioned, *How on Earth did you manage all this?'*

'A lot of determination and grit plus the aid of a hook on the end of a very long pole. Our arms ache like you wouldn't believe.' Pip laughed.

Alice leapt out of the truck's door before Tish had the chance to put on the hand brake and ran back to the driveway to get the best panoramic view of the decorated verandah. It was like a beautiful dream.

'It's stunning...'

'You'll catch a lot of flies that way,' joked Pip, seeing that Alice was still agape.

'I don't know quite what to say, except thank you so much. No one has ever done anything like this for me before. I will remember this forever.' So many wonderful people had made her birthday very special.

'Would you like a lemonade in the garden?' asked Pip.

'Yes, please,' she said as the sisters followed her through the front door to the kitchen then out the back door to the garden.

Again, the birthday girl was astonished. If she was agape before, she was now overwhelmed and did not know if she would laugh, cry or burst with pride. The garden had been transformed into a scene that looked like it had stepped out of a whimsical fairy tale. There were new linen cushion covers on the garden bench and chairs in various pastel colours and the garden table had been dressed and decorated to the nines with the ladies' best crisp white tablecloth.

Among the covered plates of food was a tall clear glass vase filled to the brim with an array of freshly cut flowers that complimented the new fabrics as well as bestowing a pleasing mix of aromas. A light pink bow was tied to the top of the vase with the trailing ribbon extending down, where the neatly cut edges touched a scattering of pale pink rose petals. Beyond the table Alice could see an assortment of colourful balloons dancing in the gentle spring breeze suspended by string from the surrounding tree branches.

She was so transfixed by the magical scene that she was unaware when someone silently approached her.

'Did someone mention lemonade? Happy birthday, Alice!'

'AUNT VERA!' She embraced her aunt tightly. 'This day gets better and better!'

'Wouldn't have missed this for the world. How are you, love?'

'Very well thank you and you are looking great.'

'I know and you say all the right things! It was so good of Pip and Tish to have invited me. We've been planning this for a while now.'

'Thank you all SO much.' Alice beamed. 'I will remember this forever!'

They made their way over to the table and Pip poured the lemonade while Alice and Vera sat in the cushioned chairs and Tish uncovered the muslin cloths from the plates of food. As she did so, they hushed in unison, listening to the enchanting sound of the colourful glass beads making gentle therapeutic tinkling sounds as they pleasantly plinked against the china. It was one of those simple but special brief moments that you store away to make you smile whenever you conjure the memory.

Alice knew that her life had changed for the better and was all so determined never to return to her earlier beginnings. She wanted to experience more of these moments, to build up happy memories, and to hold on to them with all her might.

But, without a doubt, she would give it all up in a heartbeat to have had her mother by her side at this moment.

Determined not to spoil her special day with tears, Alice distracted herself and smiled noting that the selection of neatly cut triangle sandwiches consisted of her favourites. There was egg and cress, cucumber with grated cheese and also sliced ham with Tish's homemade pickle and she couldn't resist in taking one of each. She also noticed that Aunt Vera had taken the trouble to bring her antique glass cake stand. Displayed upon it were an assortment of fruit scones and scrumptious cakes that looked mouth-watering to say the very least. Beside the cake stand in readiness for the scones were two small crystal pots and embedded within the homemade strawberry jam and thickened cream were two dainty silver spoons as the ladies tucked in.

The afternoon was just perfect.

They would have all been very happy just to sit and look

at the whole scene for hours and wished that there had been a camera to capture it all.

'What's it like to be sixteen? Does it feel any different?' asked Pip as Alice tried not to laugh aloud at the small splodge of cream on the end of Pip's nose when she bit into her scone, and when she looked, Tish and Vera had the same. It was very cute. Quickly brushing the end of her nose with the tip of her finger indicated to the ladies who giggled and brushed theirs away.

'No, no different. Did you feel different when you were sixteen?'

The ladies had another burst of giggles.

'And that's funny why?'

'Crikey, Alice,' said Vera, quickly putting her glass of lemonade down before she spilt any and tried to compose herself. 'How can we possibly remember that?'

'It was a while ago,' said Tish, as she too put down her glass and sought her handkerchief to dab her eyes from laughing.

'Don't listen to them, Alice,' said Pip with all sincerity. 'I remember it very well. Come on, Tish, you must remember that we celebrated our sixteenth on the First Fleet...' Everyone roared with laughter. 'Now,' continued Pip when she got herself under control, 'onto serious matters... Ladies,' she addressed Tish and Vera who nodded and stood up.

'Stay right there,' Vera ordered, 'and don't move a muscle. We'll be right back.'

In puzzlement, she watched the ladies walk back toward the house.

Alice finished her sandwiches, believing that she was

the luckiest girl alive to have been given a special birthday treat like this and flushed. Her stomach churned. *How can I possibly tell them that I will be leaving early in the New Year?* She thought then reasoned that she had, after all, planned on leaving home anyway once she turned sixteen and they had known that already.

Seeing her Aunt Vera had thrown her because she was planning on telephoning her around Christmas time to tell her. While she had no intention to spoil a great day, she knew that this was the perfect opportunity to tell them all together. *But where were they and what were they doing?*

After a couple of minutes, they returned to the garden looking like three naughty children harbouring a juicy secret by holding their arms behind their backs and displaying mischievous grins on their faces.

'You look like triplets,' she teased.

'I thought between us that we were quads.' Vera winked at her. 'Close your eyes.'

Alice did as she was told but couldn't resist the minutest of peeks behind a barely opened eyelid. Vera took a joking punt, 'Closed does not mean the slightest bit open, Alice Johnson,' and Alice flushed with being caught out and laughed closing her eyes tightly. She then heard shuffling noises. *They're moving about, trying to trick me!*

'Alright, you can open now,' said Tish. Alice opened her eyes to discover that the ladies hadn't shifted places at all. 'Thought we'd add a bit of intrigue!'

'Righto,' said her aunt. 'One of us is holding an amazing gift and the other two hold absolutely nothing and you have to guess the correct one, otherwise you forfeit the gift. There's no need to look so shocked. We believe that's fair.' Pip and Tish nodded.

Whenever a dilemma came up with choosing, her theory was that if ever there was doubt, go with the middle. So, based on nothing better than that, she pointed to Pip who dashed back to the kitchen to fetch the most beautiful, iced cake that she had ever seen. It looked like it had been bought from Buckingham's Department Store in Sydney.

'I did not want to risk holding this behind my back for fear of it sliding off of the plate. Do you like it?'

'It's just beautiful. I cannot believe you have made this for me,' was all she could manage.

'We're quite pleased with it,' said Tish. 'Took us a while, but we enjoyed every second and worked on it while you were at Finch's.'

Accompanying Pip toward the table, Alice rearranged a couple of plates, making room for the cake that looked too good to eat.

'That was some lucky guess. You should always go with the one in the middle...'

'Not quite on this particular occasion,' said Tish as she and Vera moved closer. 'You have two more to choose from... that was a little fib back there. Who do you choose next?'

Alice thought that was hilarious. 'I choose you, Tish, and if you have a goat behind your back, I'll eat my hat.'

'Not a goat. I love my flowers too much for that and it would eat your hat as well!' She handed Alice a book. 'Your very own history of horse racing in Australia. The Finches helped us to get it for you.'

'Thank you, thank you, thank you all. I love it and will enjoy reading,' she said, opening the cover and relishing in the newness smell and unturned pages. After a few moments she noticed Vera stepping forward with her gift, so Alice smiled at Tish and placed the book back in her hands while Vera gave her a small box.

Alice gasped when she opened it upon seeing a delicate silver chain with a small oval locket. Vera's eyes were watering when she prompted her to open up the hinged cover that revealed tiny photographs inserted on each side.

'It belonged to your mother. See, there she is as a child. Goodness, how identical you are, and the other is of your grandparents who you sadly didn't get to meet. Rose gave me this shortly after you were born.' As her aunt was talking, Alice was devouring every detail of the old pictures. They unfortunately bore a couple of creases but thankfully did not detract from her grandparents' features where they had looked as loving as their daughter. It was *finally* good to see a real image as opposed to imagination, of which she never believed would be possible. 'It's only right that it comes to you. It is what she would have wanted and what better than on your sixteenth? It has been years since I've thought of your grandfather, my brother. We originated in Western Australia and when I moved to Sydney, we all simply lost touch.'

Alice's face beamed as a small but huge part of her ancestry fell into place.

'Ah, I'm not all surprised that you didn't know. Rose told

me a few years back that she hadn't told you about them. Your father did not like your mother talking about her side of the family. That included me, and it irked him that I lived nearby knowing that you both visited me on occasions. She gave me this pendant for safe keeping in case he sold it...'

Alice clutched the pendant to her chest, knowing that this symbolic keepsake meant her mother would be with her always. Turning around, she held it over her shoulder while bending her head forward allowing her aunt to fix the clasp around her neck. Each were lost for a moment in their thoughts while the sisters again had nothing but contempt for the despicable Mr Johnson.

'It's beautiful and I shall treasure it always.' Alice was determined not to break into tears. 'May I cut the cake?'

Pip handed her a cake knife and in sheer delight they all watched jam and cream ooze over the layers when she manoeuvred hefty slices onto white china tea plates. The ladies took their plates and cake forks and went and sat down.

'I would like to hear more about my grandparents and everyone on your side of the family.'

'Yes, love, I will be delighted to tell you. Let us make it for the next time I visit as I can bring some more photographs so you can see who I am talking about.'

Alice nodded. 'I will look forward to that.' But she was thinking that it would be a while, particularly for what she would soon be mentioning.

'This is so delicious,' said Vera to the reply of 'mmmmmm' from everyone enjoying the delight. 'So, a special day, Alice. What are your dreams? And remember, dreams are meant to be big. Make an impact.'

'You all know how much I love horses, so one day I would like to own a big property like the Finches and to own many horses. And a goat'—they all laughed—'and to marry a man who totally adores me where we will live happily ever after.'

'Well,' said Pip, 'that is a perfect dream. We know you will achieve it because you are an exceptional young woman and deserve all the very best.'

'Hear, hear!' acknowledged Tish and Vera.

'Thank you, Pip, that's lovely.'

Alice placed her plate on the grass and took a deep breath. 'There will never be a right time to say this...' The ladies looked at her, sensing the serious tone and wondered what was coming. 'I found out yesterday at Finch's that they are transporting a team of horses down to South Australia early in the New Year...' She let that hang for a moment.

'And you'd like to go with them?' concluded Tish. Alice gave a brief nod and held her breath for pending protests but was pleasantly surprised instead. 'Tell us more; we'd like to hear it.'

'Judy told me over a cup of tea that the team they use for relocation will be transporting ten horses. Three of them have now retired from racing and have been bought to be used on a cattle station near Mount Gambier. The other seven are bound for Opal Racecourse. I said that I would be interested in going to the racecourse and Judy said that she would give me a letter stating my abilities so I could get a job there. With your permission, of course. I would like to talk to you about it in more detail first and I was going to telephone you as well Aunt Vera...'

'Thank you, I appreciate that, love. Tell us about the team you would be travelling with. It will be a long journey and we need to know that you will be safe.'

'Judy assured me that she has known the family, who are local, for a number of years and said she totally trusts them to look after me. There's Jock who is the head of the team and his two sons, Arthur and Ralph who both have wives and children.'

'Ah,' said Tish, 'that'll be the Dawsons. We know them too, a good family and that puts our minds at rest.'

'That's good to know,' said Alice. 'And besides, you all know that I can take care of myself. That was the one good thing that my father taught me.'

Vera knew that was true and the sisters had also seen firsthand how she had dealt with the creep back at the distillery and that had put them at ease too.

'Us oldies knew this was coming,' said Pip. 'We've even discussed it, but at least we'll have you for Christmas and that is something to look forward to. You have all our blessings, Alice. We won't hold you back as you get your dream under way.'

'Absolutely! Well said, Pip.' Vera smiled. 'We all love you and want the best for you and there is a big world and many adventures out there. You are a sensible, smart girl. And, more importantly, you know that you will always have somewhere to stay if you need it, whether it be here in the beautiful Blue Mountains or back in Sydney...'

The relief was immense and a weight lifted from her

shoulders as she sprang out of her chair and hugged each in turn. 'I shouldn't have worried so much about telling you. I do not know how to thank you all, really, I don't.'

'A letter from time to time will suffice.' Tish smiled. 'It's only the beginning of October, so we have plenty of time yet. And Vera, I know it's too early really, but we would like nothing more than if you came up and stayed for Christmas. There's no pressure, but we'll only accept a yes. You'll come, won't you?'

'No, I can see that there's no pressure at all.' She laughed. 'Christmas it is, and we'll have a mighty good time. So, to continue the celebrations, you wouldn't happen to have a tot of whisky stashed around by any chance?' She winked as Tish, Pip and Alice practically fell off their chairs laughing.

Vera was perplexed. 'I fail to see what's so funny about that.'

If only she knew…

CHAPTER EIGHTEEN

'Promise you'll write as soon as you get to Adelaide,' said Tish as she and Pip hugged Alice tightly when they arrived at Finch's Equestrian. It had been an unusually quiet journey where, without voicing, they all knew that the special time they had spent these past few months had now come to an end.

'I promise, and I know we said it all at last night's dinner but thank you both for everything that you have done for me. I love you both dearly.'

'We love you too, Alice, and you are more than welcome. It's the beginning of a new exciting chapter and we couldn't be happier for you.'

'Absolutely,' said Pip, taking off her hat to fan her face. 'You've certainly picked a hot day for it and as we discussed we'll make tracks back home, so we won't get under your feet. Judy knows that we're not staying. We will catch up with her another day.'

'Take care of yourself and don't forget about us.' Tish smiled, fighting back tears. The ladies hastily climbed back into the truck where Pip turned the vehicle in a wide circle around Alice before heading back down the long driveway while waving out of the window. Pip watched Alice from the rear-view and Tish from her wing mirror as Alice became smaller and smaller until they drove out of sight. Alice fought the urge to run after them before reasoning told her that she was doing the right thing.

Jim had seen the swift emotional farewell from the training yard. Knowing that it was tough on them all, he had held back until she picked up her bag to head up to the house.

'Good morning, Alice,' he said, running over and taking the bag from her. 'Ready for the trip south?'

'Good morning, Jim. Absolutely and looking forward to meeting the team.' She brushed away a tear.

'That's good. Everyone's up at the house. Come up for a cup of tea. The horses are already loaded up.'

'Morning, Alice,' said Judy while she returned the greeting and shook her head declining tea when it was offered. 'Everyone, this is Alice. Alice, this is Jock, Arthur and Ralph.' She indicated to the men in turn who stood and shook her hand welcoming her to the team.

'Pleased to make your acquaintance, Alice,' said Jock who had the build of a jockey and thinning grey hair. His face bore deep wrinkles around his eyes from perhaps years of squinting from the sun.

'Likewise,' said Ralph. 'Judy said you are more than a dab hand with the horses.'

She returned their firm handshakes. 'They seem to like me,' she replied.

'Hello, Alice,' said Arthur, who, like his brother, was the complete opposite build to their father and Arthur was blond as to Ralph's darker hair. All three men had tanned faces and forearms, just like Jim. 'So you'll be a great help. Ready to get moving?'

'Hello to you all.' Alice smiled, liking her new road family. 'I'm ready to go.' She followed everyone outside.

'There are five horses in each truck,' said Jim, placing her bag behind the passenger seat, 'and the boys will give instructions as they go.'

'Thank you both. I have really enjoyed working here.' She gave them both a hug. 'Bye for now...' Instantaneously, her heart pounded and seemed to miss several beats at the same time.

The feeling was so powerful that it left her quite breathless. It was then that she knew, without a shadow of a doubt, that she would never be coming back to the Blue Mountains ever again.

'Ready, Alice?' asked Ralph, breaking her thought. He started the engine, ready to follow his father and brother who were nearly at the end of the long driveway.

'Yes, of course.' She stepped up and in and slammed the door then she leaned out of the window, waving to Judy and Jim as Ralph drove out of the yard. Right now, along with her grieving, she couldn't deal with the realisation of never seeing Pip, Tish or Aunt Vera ever again and tried her hardest to put it to the back of her mind.

Alice and Ralph remained quiet for a while. It was a comfortable silence, each lost in their own thoughts. Ralph was used to travelling on his own and began ticking off the checklist in his head for the tasks ahead, ensuring there was enough fuel for the trucks and feed, water and straw for the horses and provisions for the team. As well as double-checking the route they would take and hoping that there would be no road closures or harsh weather to contend with. The silence gave Alice a little time to gather her thoughts wondering if the ladies also knew that they wouldn't see her again. She clutched her pendant and blinked away threatening tears knowing that despite the initial upheaval, she was also curiously excited to what destiny had in store for her.

Despite sitting up higher in the truck than she had been in Pip and Tish's, it wasn't a gentler ride by any means. Alice began to feel a little nervous because Ralph drove a lot faster and she kept looking over her shoulder, concerned for the horses.

'They're alright. I've been doing this for many years. We've tied them up in their stalls and we stop and check on them every couple of hours to feed, water and muck out. Gives us drivers a break too. Don't forget they have four legs, and they are good stabilisers.' He laughed.

'Sorry,' she replied. 'I'll get used to them shuffling around. Have you done this journey down to South Australia before?'

'Quite a few times, but this will be the first time that we're delivering to Nerra Creek Station. We're going there first then it's onto Opal Racecourse in Adelaide. We've been there a lot; it's an amazing place.'

'I've heard it is. How long will it take us to get to Nerra Creek Station?' She laughed. 'That is a funny name.'

'Around three days, give or take. Yes, it is funny. Jim told me that it originated back in the old days and aptly named by the then owners because the homestead they built was simply, near a creek!' They both laughed. 'The trip varies,' he continued, 'depends on how the horses are and how many times we need to stop. The weather and the land play a huge part too. Just takes a moment for a rut or pothole to ruin the tyres or muddy wet conditions to cause us to be grounded. Every trip is different. So, you know racecourses?'

'Yes. I worked at Randwick for a few years and really enjoyed the work and loved being with the horses. It was quite an escape...' Alice stopped, clenched her fists and pounded them on her thighs, cross with herself for letting that slip.

Ralph had seen this in his peripheral vision but decided not to question. Instead, he said, 'We wish you luck with getting a job there, not that you'll need it. Judy couldn't sing your praises highly enough and mentioned that she's given you a glowing letter for the manager there.

'We know him and we'll introduce you. Look...' he hesitated. 'I'm a father of two little girls, so take this the right way. I don't want to worry you, but he can be slimy and rude to females. We won't just leave you there either. We will be in town for a day or so in resting up before we head back here.'

'I appreciate the warning, Ralph. A heads-up is always good. With a tough upbringing under my belt, I can take care of myself. I've met that type before. I know I've just met you, but let me introduce you to my best friend.' Quick as lightning, Alice reached into her boot and produced and activated the switch.

'Got it!' He glanced at her, temporarily loosening his grip on the steering wheel. 'Crikey, didn't expect that at all,' he said while he regained control.

'That's the beauty.' Alice detracted and put the switch away and accepted a toffee from the bag that he held out. 'Oh, my favourite. Thank you.'

After a couple of hours, the two trucks pulled over where they lowered the ramps and checked on the horses.

'You'll get used to it, lass.' Jock laughed, noticing Alice rubbing her lower back. 'The truck's suspension can be a little challenging to say the least and we haven't met the really rough roads yet.'

'Thanks, Jock. I'll adapt. Here, I'll do it.' She smiled, picking up the bucket and shovel and headed back into the stalls.

'Just a short break. Time to head off,' said Arthur, finishing his cup of water. 'We'll rotate. Come up with me, Alice. I dare say you've had enough of my charming brother!'

'Well, that's nice, isn't it,' joked Ralph as his father joined him in the cab.

'What's the verdict so far, Alice? Like being out on the road?' asked Arthur.

'Yes, it's good to get out and about and to see more of the country. I am enjoying it and the horses seem happy so far.'

'They're pretty resilient. As long as they get a good feed

and water and overnight rest. Mind you, we had an awful time a while back. There was this ol' mare and boy she was moody, shall we say. She kept kicking the stall and after a few hours, it became extremely irritating. We spent ages calming her down before we could lead her out to graze and then it took a whole heap of tact and tricks to get her back in.'

'Where were you taking her to?'

'Out to a family property who bought her for their young children.'

Alice's eyes opened wide with concern.

'But not to worry, she was a sweetheart once she arrived. She turned out to be the most docile creature who adored the children but just turned into the devil when it came to travel.'

'Guess your passengers determine the journey.' She smiled.

'Probably because she was female,' he jokingly taunted while Alice laughed and threw a toffee at his head for his trouble.

As pre-arranged, they stopped around an hour before nightfall and while Jock met with Mrs Gilbert, who owned the small paddock and stables, Arthur, Ralph and Alice led the horses from the trucks into the paddock. Between them they saddled up and exercised the horses before grooming, feeding, watering and settling them in for the night.

Mrs Gilbert dished up a hearty meal at her kitchen table. 'So, Alice, hope the boys are looking after you?'

'Yes, very well, Mrs Gilbert. Thank you. This is delicious. Didn't realise until we arrived that Finch's Equestrian uses your property for stopovers. I thought we'd be camping out under the stars.'

'Ah,' replied Jock. 'We've been so used to travelling on our own that it never crossed our mind to mention it.' He shrugged.

'It's alright,' she said. 'I'm just grateful you all took me on.'

He smiled, pleased with her politeness.

'Mr Gilbert and I, God rest his soul, have a good arrangement with the Finches – been doing this for years. The horses are valuable stock and need to be cared for. Resting up here overnight is good for them.' Mrs Gilbert winked at Alice. 'In case the boys forgot to say, you will stop at another property tomorrow night.'

'Yes, it'll be a new stopover for us as we haven't been down that way before,' added Ralph. 'I know it's early, Alice, but it's better to finish up here and get some sleep. We'll be up before sunrise for breakfast and ready to be out and load the horses at first light. The sooner we can be off the better.'

'Just about done. That was a lovely meal, Mrs Gilbert.'

'You're welcome. Now, follow me. You're staying in the house and the boys bunker down in the room next to the stables. Good night, gentlemen.'

'Good night, ladies,' they replied, walking out of the door, heading toward their quarters.

Mrs Gilbert carried a jug of water and bowl through to a small room at the back of the house. 'You should be comfortable enough in here,' she said, placing them on top of a chest of drawers alongside a bar of soap and a towel before retrieving a set of sheets and a blanket from the drawer and made the single bed with Alice's help.

'As you see, I'm out in the middle of nowhere and the

dunny is a way from the house. In the corner, I have left you two buckets with some water in, one for now and one for the morning. When you have finished with each, could you please place them in the little area I showed you and I will dispose of them in the morning. I do not like to wander around outside in the pitch dark, so I do not expect guests to either. Lots of nasties around...'

Alice was very grateful and could have hugged her for that. 'Thank you, Mrs Gilbert. But how do...'

'I will knock on your door at five. Good night, love.'

'Good night,' she replied, feeling ready for a good sleep and after a wash. She was out like a light as soon as her head hit the pillow.

Jock handed Mrs Gilbert an envelope with their payment from the Finches and they bade their host farewell. They were on schedule and drove out of her property just after six.

'Do you ever tire of the long journeys, Jock?'

'Nah,' he replied. 'Been doing this since I was a lad. Know the land like the back of my hand and took my boys out as soon as I was able. Lost their mother when they were little, so I sold up and ploughed the money into a truck and away we went. Never looked back.'

'Sorry about your wife, Jock. Must have been hard on all of you.'

'Did what I had to do. It was tough but we got by. Makes me proud that they still want to do this when they have their own families back in the Mountains. What of your family?'

'I'm family of Pip and Tish's who know the Finches,' she said, not wanting to go into her family history and was relieved when she saw him nod. Alice knew that he hadn't just accepted her answer but rather that he was smart enough to know that she hadn't wanted to enlighten. She admired him for that.

The day was turning into an absolute scorcher. The humidity grew thicker than a mud pool, and her canteen that had held cold water wasn't as thirst-quenching the warmer it became.

It was as if every fly under the sun was out to personally annoy by relentlessly buzzed around her. The late afternoon sun caused the horizon to shimmer in its final throws where it would have been easy to fry a dozen eggs on the truck's bonnet. She was getting irritated by the prickling heat and by being constantly bumped around on a road hell-bent on producing potholes every few feet. At this very moment, she would have given her right arm just to throw her head into a bucketful of iced water.

Throughout the day they had to make more frequent stops to check on the horses who were more restless than normal. Each time when climbing down from the cab, she had to prise her shirt away from her back that had clung like a second skin. When she did this, trickles of sweat rolled down her spine and turned a brief tickling sensation into annoying biting itches making her scratch relentlessly thus becoming more annoyed.

It was that kind of a day.

Dusk was petering when they finally pulled into the driveway for their overnight stay. It was still humid as hell and Alice knew it would be tedious offloading the horses.

Man and beast were weary, hungry and thirsty but also thankful when their hosts ran out to greet them and to give them a helping hand.

Jock made the decision on this occasion to lead the horses straight into the stables without exercise. With everyone's help and while the horses tucked into their feed and coolish water, they used sponges to rub them down, hoping that the water provided a little relief. It was better than nothing.

Mr and Mrs Kirby and their three children welcomed Jock and his team into their kitchen for a drink while Alice took the first shower in the outside lean-to attached to the end of their homestead. It was a quick transformation and she felt human again when she walked into the kitchen wearing a fresh set of clothes. While Jock, Ralph and Arthur used their two-minute slot to wash away the day's grime, Alice enjoyed playing with the children.

Mrs Kirby had made them quite a country feast. 'Come on, take a seat,' she said, placing the hefty portions in front of them. 'A hard day. Dare say you need this.' She smiled. 'We hope you will enjoy and there's more if you would like.'

'Thank you, Mrs Kirby, this looks just grand,' Jock spoke for them all.

Mrs Kirby then turned to the children and ushered them toward the stairs. 'I'll be up in a minute to tuck you in. Say goodnight to our guests.'

The adults returned their 'cheerios', wishing them a goodnight.

'A nice family you have there.' Jock smiled, handing Mr Kirby their fee for the stay. 'A magnificent meal, Mrs Kirby.

We're much obliged.'

'Thank you,' he said, pocketing the money. 'We hope that you and the horses will be comfortable here.'

'Yes, very comfortable,' replied Arthur, 'and I'm just about ready for sleep myself. We appreciated your help earlier.'

'The very least we could do. We had been looking out for you since mid-afternoon praying that you didn't get lost,' he said with relief.

'We should have gotten here sooner, but due to the heat, we had a few more stops than normal,' said Ralph. 'Nothing to do with getting lost,' he praised, 'you gave the Finches detailed and accurate directions. We wish everyone did that!'

'Let's have a beer to celebrate the start of a long business arrangement. Alice...'

Both Alice and his wife looked up.

'Ah, I forgot you both have the same name. Isn't that a quirk?' Everyone burst into laughter. 'Wife Alice, I'll fetch a beer for the gentlemen if you get the glasses.'

Mrs Kirby nodded and reached down the glasses from her cabinet and then gave Alice a glass of homemade lemonade.

In the morning, and as promised, Mr Kirby helped Jock, Arthur and Ralph load up the trucks after a hefty breakfast. During this time Mrs Kirby gently knocked on the spare room door and handed Alice her clothing from the previous day.

'Mrs Kirby,' Alice said in gratitude and surprise. 'Thank you so much, that is very kind. How on Earth did you find the time to wash, dry and iron?'

'You're welcome. It didn't take long. I added yours to

the children's wash. But don't tell the men,' she added conspiringly. 'I only had time for yours. It has been lovely meeting another Alice.'

'Likewise!'

'Hope you have a better journey today.'

'Thank you and especially for the horses. Three of them are nearly at their new home, the other seven will have to wait a little longer.'

*

'WAGONS ROLLLLLL,' shouted Jock, leaning across and blasting the horn much to Alice's delight who couldn't help bursting into fits of laughter.

'This isn't the wild west, Jock,' she replied, knowing full well the reason why he had said that when she drove under the mountainous sign that read *Nerra Creek Station*. 'We're here at last.'

Jock blasted the horn again and Ralph responded from the truck behind in unison to celebrate their pending first delivery.

The older man knew early on that they would make better progress today and after a mid-morning break before they headed back on the road, he said that it was high time that Alice learned to drive. He ushered her up into the driver's seat and, leaving the door open, he stood on the ground and began to give instruction.

Alice had been dumbfounded for all of two seconds before getting excited about having a go. But before she was allowed to start the engine, he talked her through all the controls and how to drive relating to certain conditions, particularly when carrying livestock. He was a patient instructor who initially held and controlled her feet. He pressed them down so she could get a sense on how much pressure to apply enabling her to feel the strain in her ankles when hovering over the pedals.

Jock couldn't emphasise enough regarding the brake. He urged her, without looking, to move her foot across accordingly stating that unless it was an absolute emergency not to brake too hard unless she wanted a tonne of horse crashing into the back of her.

'What if I forget which one is the brake and which foot to use?' she panicked.

'Remember, Alice that your right foot controls both pedals.' He moved her right foot to the outer pedal. 'This is the accelerator and is for...'

'Moving.'

'Good.' He moved her foot again. 'And the brake is for...'

'Stopping.'

'That's precisely it. You can't want to move and stop at the same time, it's one or the other.'

'Got it... But no. The brake is in the middle and I still may get confused about which foot to use...' She let out a sudden howl. 'What the damn hell was that?' she spat, swiping his hand away then rubbing the back of her calf.

'Will you remember that?' He looked up at her.

'What?' She asked still rubbing and when he raised his eyebrows, the penny dropped. 'How could I forget?'

'That's your brake and accelerator leg.'

'Got it, Jock. But you still bloody well pinched me!'

'Stop complaining, girl.' He smiled and winked. 'If you think that was bad, Arthur says he still has his bruise!'

He then instructed Alice how to manoeuvre through the gears by pressing down on the clutch to open the gearbox without crunching them. After a little while he turned on the engine and taught her how to feel for the biting point but appreciated that this was quite difficult and reassured her that it would come with practice.

Alice, being aware of her precious cargo and not wanting them to be jolted as expensive injury could easily occur, concentrated with all her might as she rose to the pressure. She did some initial jolts, but as they had driven over multiple bumpy roads during the trip, the horses weren't too alarmed.

'You're a fast learner, lass,' Jock praised after she had covered a few miles. 'You listen and apply, I like that. Although you need to concentrate on not veering too much. Look at the road straight ahead, not glancing down at the bonnet, and trust what your feet and hands are doing. It'll come naturally.'

She smiled. Even though she trusted Jock enough to tell him that in the past she had no option but to be a fast learner to prevent her father's wrath, she knew that she would regret it. So, she kept quiet and concentrated on looking straight ahead as instructed.

The weather had been somewhat cooler than the day before and they had made it to Nerra Creek Station in good time. The men could almost taste a beer in the air as they ploughed further into the property bypassing herds of cattle along the way.

'Time to pull over, Alice,' Jock ordered. 'You are becoming a good driver, but the people here may be concerned if they see a slip of a girl driving their prized and expensive horses into the yard...'

'Understand, Jock. I'm starting to get a little tired anyway.' And with his guidance, she smoothly shifted the gears down and came to a smooth stop, allowing them to change places.

CHAPTER NINETEEN

'Welcome!' shouted a man of medium build who would most likely need to duck a little upon entering a room just as Jock and Ralph pulled up outside the stables. 'I'm Harold Oatley. Call me Harry,' he said, extending his hand.

'Nice to meet you, Harry,' said Jock, alighting from the truck and shaking his hand. 'We're mighty glad to be here. I'm Jock and this is my team, Ralph, Arthur and Alice.'

Everyone shook hands and Alice was amazed at the sheer number of others came out of the surrounding outbuildings and gathered around.

'It is nice to see you all,' said Harry. 'Let me introduce you to Marion, my wife, who cooks all our splendid meals and looks after the homestead alongside my mother-in-law, Dot. Next are our stockmen, Joe, Tank, Bruno, Bill and Ray,' he indicated respectively.

Alice cringed a little for not paying too much attention to Harry's introductions of the stockmen but deduced that as they would be leaving the following morning, it probably didn't matter too much. She thought that Harry and Marion were the same age as her parents and caught her breath, whenever she remembered her mother. The stockmen appeared to vary in ages from Big Alfie's down to around ten years older than herself, but she couldn't remember who was who. Although, she would remember Tank, believing he was aptly named and was inquisitive to know if that referred to a water tank or a military vehicle.

Little did Alice know that her path was about to significantly change.

After an array of 'hello's and 'how are you's, Marion asked, 'Alice, would you like to come with Mother and I and we'll get you a drink? The boys can offload the horses then they'll join us.'

Nodding, she followed the women into the homestead and sensed a comfortable *at home* feeling and at ease with everyone.

'You're very young for being in the team.' Dot smiled, ushering Alice to the large table where the kitchen reminded her of the one at Finch's Equestrian.

'Thank you,' she said, accepting a glass of homemade lemonade and watching Marion fill and place more glasses on the table. 'It's just for this trip. I'm travelling on with the boys to Opal Racecourse where the other seven horses are headed. I hope to work at the stables. I worked at Randwick Racecourse back in Sydney for four years, so hoping that they will take me on.'

'You're a long way from home,' Marion said. 'What about your parents?'

'They died, so I went to live with family in the Blue Mountains. They knew I loved horses and after introducing me to Finch's through one thing or another, here I am.' And that was the most she was prepared to give.

'We're sorry to hear about your parents,' Marion said with compassion. She reminded Alice of a younger Aunt Vera. 'So, you're good with horses?' she raised her eyebrows after a pause then looked toward her mother.

'This is good.' Alice held up her glass of lemonade, pleased that she hadn't been pressed any further. 'Horses seem to like me and I certainly love them.'

'Enough to stay on and help out here?' Dot smiled, sitting down opposite. Alice liked the older lady, who seemed to have an air of mischievousness about her, but there was something else that she could not quite put her finger on. 'We could do with an extra pair of hands.'

'Mother, don't put pressure on our guest. Give her another ten minutes at least.' The three women burst into rapturous laughter.

Alice hadn't felt awkward at all, and their humour reminded her of Pip and Tish.

Oh, how she missed them already.

'I've been hearing that you're a born natural.' Harry smiled, looking at Alice when all the men walked into the kitchen. They took a seat and helped themselves to a glass of lemonade to quench their thirst from the recent exertion.

'One of the mares, shall we say, is... a little temperamental,' said Bruno who Alice believed was around Alfie's age. To her, all the stockmen, with the exception of

Tank, did not vary too much regarding height and build and all wore checked shirts, dark trousers, sturdy boots and Akubras. 'We tried our best to offload before Ralph said you could do it without any bones being broken.'

'Yeah.' Joe smiled. 'We'd like to see it. She's ready for you when you've finished up here.'

Alice wasn't sure if they were pulling her leg or not but they all appeared to be genuine when she looked to and fro.

'Up for the challenge?' asked Jock, winking at her as if to say, *Come on, don't let the side down.*

'Prove to these big strapping lads that you can do it, Alice,' encouraged Arthur.

'Then what're we waiting for?' She winked back at Jock and walked out of the kitchen. The Nerra Creek men looked at each other for a few seconds before following her outside. A short time later and with no fuss, to everyone's amazement, she led the mare out of the truck and down the ramp like she was taking a puppy out for a morning stroll.

'Temperamental?' she questioned, smiling and shaking her head. 'Think you'll be alright to take it from here, Tank?' She handed the big man the reins to a chorus of laughter.

'Come, I'll show you around the property,' said Harry after the laughter had died down and the stockmen went back to their work.

At six o'clock the kitchen table was at capacity where it was a joyous occasion to have guests stay for dinner. There was plenty of mixed conversations and banter was rife, much to Alice's delight. She loved the atmosphere; she'd never been part of anything quite like it before.

'What do you think of it here?' asked Tank. His manner gave the impression that he was a gentle giant.

'It's a great place and I've never seen so many cows. They're huge, but as you've all proved today, they're also softies. I love all your horses too. I know the three we brought from Finch's will be happy here.'

'What about your future?' asked Harry. Everyone went quiet and listened to his pitch. 'We can see you have a real gift with horses as you worked with us today. And because you will all be moving on at first light, we're getting in quick. You're looking for work and we see great jillaroo potential in you. Here at Nerra Creek, you will get to work with the horses in all aspects of the station and to look after them. I'll let you choose which of the three horses you delivered, you can name them, and they will be yours whilst you are here.

'We'll train you up and pay you the going rate and you will have a room here in the homestead as opposed to roughing it out in the stockmen's quarters. It's a serious offer, Alice. Goodness knows that the boys here could do with bringing in line.' He grinned to whistles from the men who howled their opinions.

'Give it a shot and then, if you feel it isn't for you, we will totally respect your decision. If that happens, Marion and I will drive you to Opal Racecourse to pursue a position there and we'll stay for a couple of days to make sure you settle in alright.'

'What do you say?' asked Marion, crossing her fingers while Alice gazed in Jock's direction for his opinion.

Jock, alongside his sons, appreciated that Alice was

faced with a pleasant dilemma, knowing that she didn't need rescuing otherwise they would have stepped in a while ago from what could have been an awkward situation. The Oatleys had presented a grand opportunity and if Jock were in Alice's shoes, he would've bitten the boss' hand off before he had finished his spiel.

'It's a good offer, lass,' he reassured and that was enough for Alice, who looked at Harry, and nodded her acceptance.

When the cheers simmered down, she said, 'Thank you, Harry. I think I'd best choose the *temperamental* one as none of your staff can obviously handle her.'

'Ouch,' said Ray. 'That hurt!'

'What'll you call her?' Bill laughed. 'Something tough and nasty that matches her personality?'

'Not at all.' Alice pondered for a moment. 'Lucy. She looks like a Lucy.'

'Lucy it is,' said Harry. 'Raise your glasses, everyone. Welcome to Nerra Creek Station, Alice and Lucy.'

'Alice and Lucy,' echoed throughout the homestead.

'What's a Lucy look like anyway?' questioned Bill as Ray shrugged.

'Dunno, mate, but Lucy will make us stockmen look like a bunch of galahs if we cannot get on. Think we'll have our work cut out with these two new women!' he joked.

*

After a hearty breakfast, Alice said her farewells to her road team and watched as they waved when driving through the yard destined for the racecourse. Despite having known the men for just a few days, she had felt like kin. They had all taught her so much, particularly Jock, with his patience in teaching her to drive. She was determined to practice her new skill and had already planned on asking Harry if she could drive some of the vehicles around the property.

The scenery with endless rolling hills were beautiful when she and Lucy rode with the stockmen through the pastures to check on the herd. The men were giving on the go training; it was hard work and the days were long but she had loved every minute and wasn't afraid to get her hands dirty. Alice felt alive, invigorated and totally in love with Lucy as they formed a special bond.

Oh, how she again enjoyed the swirling wind in her face and her hair billowing wildly around her. But, like today, when the wind was strong, she felt quite a strange almost scary sensation to be engulfed with oxygen yet feel that she could almost suffocate. It was exhilaratingly euphoric, particularly upon closing her eyes for a brief few seconds when the loss of one sense, together with the danger, heightened the others. Alice felt the heat from Lucy's powerful body galloping beneath her, pummelling through the lush rich grass. She heard Lucy's deep breaths and felt her mane whipping the back of her hands as she held onto the reins.

Freedom was a feeling like no other.

*

Three months had passed, and Alice was enjoying her time and work at Nerra Creek. 'That's very good, Tank,' she admired when sitting down and watching him put the final touches to a finely detailed drawing.

'Thanks, Alice, it's very relaxing,' he replied as her fascination hadn't waivered at seeing such huge hands control such a tiny pencil. It was almost lost within his palm. She could have watched him for hours.

'I've seen drawings around the place but wouldn't have...' She stopped and blushed.

'Didn't think that a big chap like myself could do such a dainty thing, eh?' He smiled, turning to look at her.

'Sorry, Tank, didn't mean to be rude. It's just that...'

'It's alright, you're not the first and you certainly won't be the last. It's a common reaction. Looks can be deceiving. Take Ray for instance. What's his hobby, would you say?'

'Don't tell me he's a ballerina?' And when they broke into laughter, the cows stopped chewing and ran in the opposite direction.

'Ah, sorry, Tank. There goes your subject.'

'No harm done. I'm just about finished anyway. Now, back to Ray. Even though he is slighter in build than the others and the youngest, his upper body strength is much stronger than I.'

Raising her eyebrows at him in surprise, she queried, 'Stronger than you? You're pulling my leg, right?'

'God's honest truth. We've some bricks in the outbuilding.' To demonstrate, Tank put his drawing down and outstretched his arms, like he was going to embrace someone. 'It's a trick of his. The bricks are stacked horizontal between his hands, not vertical. He can pick up and hold more bricks this way than I can. So, like I say, looks can be deceiving.'

'I've got to see that!'

'Alright and I'll see if I can better my score of fifteen.' He smiled. 'We'll do it after dinner tonight before it gets too dark.'

And that's exactly what happened. The Oatleys and staff gathered around in a semicircle inside the outbuilding that stored building materials and bales of hay where Ray started to gather the bricks together.

'We haven't done this in a while. You're in for a treat,' said Joe. 'Ray has held twenty bricks at his best, while old weakling Tank here, only managed fifteen.' Joe received a clip around the ear from Tank who then proceeded to hold him in a playful headlock.

'I'm nearly ready, Alice. I'll just gather some more,' Ray said, looking at her when he crouched down by a small stack, 'because I'm feeling confident and extra strong today and what Tank can't manage, I'll take on!'

Within a second the whole atmosphere changed when a flash of bright silver flew at Ray, just missing his hand when he blindly reached out for the two remaining bricks. Everyone looked in disbelief from Alice to the dead snake that bore her switch.

'How the hell did I miss that?' he said shakily when the adrenaline kicked in. Then he rushed over and swept Alice up into his arms and gave her a big kiss on the cheek while the other men ran over to the snake.

'How the...' Tank was speechless.

'That was lucky,' she said when Bruno handed her weapon back. Beginning to feel a little conspicuous, she wiped the blade on some straw, then wiped again with her handkerchief. It had become second nature to make sure the blade was clean and dry before detracting it and putting it back down her boot.

'Great trick, Alice!' said Harry to roaring cheers.

'One thing my father taught me,' she replied, shrugging her shoulders as if it were no big deal. 'I've been practising at hitting targets out in the meadow.'

'Well, I'm mighty thankful that you did,' said Ray.

After the excitement, Marion and Alice were back in the kitchen and clearing away the dinner things.

'I'll like to travel to Frances tomorrow morning,' said Marion, 'to stock up on supplies and such. It's a small town around a hundred miles away. There are a couple of smaller towns in between where we usually get our supplies as you know, but Frances is special to me due to an aunt who once lived there. It's a four-hour round trip. Fancy coming along?'

'I'd love to, thank you. Is there a post box there?' And when Marion nodded, Alice said, 'That's great. I have a few letters to send.'

'The last time I went to Frances, my mother came along. Oh, Alice, I love her dearly as you know but she gets my goat sometimes.'

Alice roared with laughter. 'I love goats and hope to have one someday. I'll call him Barry.'

'Well, that's grand, Alice, but in the meantime, you can

borrow my mother. She means well, bless her soul, but goodness can she talk the hind legs off a donkey!'

Trying her hardest to prevent laughter, Alice bit her lip at the irony because if Dot could talk the hind legs off a donkey, then Marion could do the same to the front legs. The poor donkey was now legless and Alice again fought to contain her giggles.

'Can I drive some of the way?' she recovered enough to ask.

'Of course, and I'd appreciate the company. We'll leave just after sunrise.'

The next morning, Alice entered the kitchen to find Harry cooking the breakfast who said that Dot had been unwell during the night, so the trip to Frances had been put on hold. Knowing the men would soon be arriving, Alice stepped in to assist him. While she would go and see Dot later if she were up to visitors, her instincts told her that there was more to it.

CHAPTER TWENTY

After almost nineteen months, Alice was beginning to feel restless.

There was something missing. But damn if she could put her finger on what it was exactly. She felt drawn to... well, she wasn't quite sure what she was drawn to, but the feeling remained strong and wouldn't go away.

Things seemed almost too comfortable.

Everything at Nerra Creek Station was fine. The people were all great and she enjoyed looking after the herds and Lucy and it was a beautiful place to work. She found herself at a crossroads and had been thinking more about her original plan of seeking a position at Opal Racecourse. Perhaps that was the answer? She wasn't sure, but it would be a start and she could almost hear Aunt Vera encouraging her to move forward.

Lucy was the problem.

Alice loved everyone but it would break her heart to leave Lucy behind. People would understand, but how could she explain to this beautiful, amazing creature, who may think that she had done something wrong, for her to simply walk away?

Time and time again, Alice played the scenario over and over, visualising the anguished look on Lucy's face, believing she had been abandoned. But her mind was also pulling her in another unclear direction. It got to the point where she had planned on discussing her thoughts and idea with Harry and Marion, but as the right time approached, Dot had been taken seriously ill. It was a very stressful time at the Station where everyone pulled together a little more to allow Marion to spend as much time with her mother as possible.

Deciding to wait for a better time, Alice took Lucy out for a ride before she was due back at the homestead. It was a beautiful sunny afternoon and after a while, she took the opportunity to dismount and take in the breathtaking scenery around her. She sat underneath an old Elm tree and placed her packed lunch and a flask of tea on the ground while Lucy stayed close by munching on the lush grass.

'Goodness, Lucy,' Alice remarked, as Lucy's ears turned towards her while still chomping. 'If I made a noise like that eating, I'd be disgraced!'

Lucy snorted on cue and Alice laughed unwrapping her tomato sandwich and after taking a bite she leaned back against the tree trunk. 'What was that you said?' She playfully continued her one-sided conversation. '"I love you, Alice." Why, thank you very much, Lucy, I love you too.' She then poured herself some tea into a tin cup where the many dents and scratches told her that it had been a part of many outside smokos.

Taking a deep satisfying breath and closing her eyes, she relaxed back against the tree, letting the warm breeze engulf her.

It was very pleasant, although the sunlight was on the cusp of being too bright upon her eyelids. Apart from the odd fly here and there and Lucy's chomping, all was serene to the point where she was drifting off to sleep.

Lucy suddenly squealed in alarm, snapping Alice out of her drowsiness. In her haste to stand up, she booted the flask and heard the inner cylinder shatter into tiny pieces clanging against a tsunami of tea.

'OH, SHIIIIT!' Alice sprinted and in one fair swoop, she leapt up into the saddle as Lucy, who by the grace of God hadn't bolted, began galloping toward the paddock fence as their lives depended on it.

After all the dangers that she had encountered in her young life, Alice wasn't as petrified as she was now where the headwind caused her tears to channel across her cheeks and flow into her ears from the speed in which they were travelling.

Holding onto the reins and pommel for dear life, the paddock fence thankfully drew nearer. But as it grew nearer, it seemed to grow impossibly high, and she feared they weren't going to clear it, sensing that the charging bull was rapidly gaining ground. Not daring a backward glance, she feared losing her grip and being trampled to death beneath powerful pounding hooves. She could almost feel the vibration as the raging beast pulverised the earth. Her somewhat waterlogged ears seemed to only hear its thunderous snorts and Alice swore she could smell its pungent odour from sweat-worked muscles. With intensified imagination enlightening her that the beast was within a hairy whisker of bringing them down, she urged Lucy to run faster.

Leaning forward, as she had seen jockeys do hundreds of times when they approached fences, she held a deep breath and prayed that Lucy would clear it and land safely on the other side. Forcing herself to keep her eyes open, preferring to see her fate if this was to be the last thing she ever saw, as Lucy lunged high with all her might.

Oh, how she had wanted to scream, but she didn't want to spook Lucy any more than she already was. Through gritted teeth, Alice became rigid, waiting for a clipping sound and feeling a jolt if Lucy's hind legs collided with the fencing.

They seemed to be static in a mid-air arc like they had jumped in slow motion. But past the arc, she was powerless to stop the descending approach as she sat at an alarmingly precarious angle, fearing that she would be flung high over Lucy's head.

Mercifully, Lucy made a perfect landing, where it took all of Alice's strength to stay in the saddle. But in the anxious few seconds before she had had time to turn around, Alice braced herself in expectation of the fence shattering into numerous shards. The biggest fear now was that the beast would plough through it like butter and Lucy would not be able to maintain the pace. But when she turned around, the ferocious bull had pulled up just short of the fence, looking somehow more sinister than her perception had been when a plume of dust almost engulfed him.

Streaming strands of disgusting mucus hung from his wet nostrils that were flaring from the exertion and short buffs of steam jutted from his powerful shoulders. Alice, not wanting to provoke the beast any further, broke eye contact and tapped Lucy's belly with her boot to move on. When they were far from the bull's territory, she dismounted and flung her arms around Lucy's neck who whinnied and seemed to hug her back.

'Thank you, Lucy. You saved my life when I put us both in danger. I'm so sorry.' She kissed Lucy's nose and hugged her once more. Alice's legs became trembly and it took her a few wobbly attempts to climb back into the saddle. 'That's more than enough adventure for one day. Come on, we'll get back to the stables and I'll give you lots of extra carrots. You deserve it.'

To an intense degree, Alice reprimanded herself over and over for putting them both in danger by forgetting that the bull was loose in that particular paddock. Wiping away her tears and taking advantage of the ride ahead to fully compose herself, Alice decided not to tell anyone about the encounter. Not only because there was enough going on at the homestead as it was, but also for her utter foolishness, stupidity and embarrassment.

In a way, the incident had highlighted that life was too short and that, to be true to herself, she had to tell Harry and Marion that she would be moving on. And, knowing it would be very hard, she had to say her goodbyes to Lucy, which seemed extra cruel given Lucy's bravery today. Putting things into perspective, Alice reminded herself that Lucy was not her horse and knew that the Oatley's and staff would look after her just as well.

*

Now that is strange, thought Vera when she returned from an overnight visit to see Pip and Tish. She placed her bag of overnight things on the floor and walked over to the hearth and stared at her ornate clock on the mantelpiece. Or to be more precise, she was staring at the small stack of letters behind the clock leaning against the wall. They were not in the order in which she had left them.

With eyes of a hawk, Vera scanned the room. Nothing else had been touched.

Knowing that someone had read the letters was puzzling to say the least. She had found no other evidence in her bedroom, kitchen or parlour that had been disturbed or that any valuables had been taken, which had heightened her curiosity.

For the time being, she decided to monitor things just a little more. *Or*, she thought, *was it simply that I had placed the letters back incorrectly?*

*

During a hearty breakfast a couple of weeks later, the mood had transpired through a mix of happy reminisce, banter and sadness when the team at Nerra Creek gathered to bid their jillaroo a fond farewell.

'You're going to be missed around here,' said Joe. 'And yes, for the hundredth time'—he smiled upon seeing her worried look—'we'll take good care of Lucy. She sure has calmed down a lot since you took her on and I'm relieved to say that she no longer poses a threat to us stockmen!'

'Thank you, Joe. I'm going to miss you all too. Not as much as Lucy, but I'll still miss you.' The men laughed. 'I said goodbye to Lucy at first light. She knows, she just knows, I'm sure of it...'

'Don't feel bad. We'll all look out for her. She's smart and she'll want you to do well,' Bruno reassured and she noticed Tank getting up from the table and leaving the kitchen.

'You gotta do what you gotta do and follow your heart,' said Bill, topping up her teacup.

'Thanks, Bill, that's nice of you.'

'Come on, don't be fooled gentlemen,' joked Ray, looking around the table. 'What short memories you've all got. Remember how we lost valuable possessions not too long ago through Alice's other trick...' He winked at her, patting down his pockets, feigning for missing items to the roar of laughter.

'The look on all your faces was a picture.' She beamed, looking at the group who were the most kind and loving people.

'Talking of pictures, this is for you,' said Tank, returning to the kitchen and placing before her a stunning pencil drawing of her standing beside Lucy. He had perfectly captured their likeness and characters. It was almost like a real photograph and was one of the most beautiful pictures that she had ever seen. She sprang up from the table and ran into his arms where she seemed to disappear into his large frame.

'Thank you, Tank. I will treasure it always.'

'That's a relief, for a moment there I thought you didn't like it,' he joked.

'Ready, Alice?' asked Marion, popping her head around the door. Alice nodded then followed Marion toward Dot's room.

'Thanks for everything, Dot,' she said, trying to be cheery. 'It's been a pleasure getting to know you, and everyone. I hope you continue to get better. I'll write and let you know how I get on.' She embraced the old lady, thinking how lucky she was to have had so many wonderful women in her life.

'Don't worry about me, Alice. I'm as strong as an ox and will be up and about getting those unruly fellows in line before you know it.'

'Well, someone has to, Mother.' Marion laughed for Alice's benefit and peace of mind, where mother and daughter glanced at one another knowing otherwise.

'Time to get going, Alice,' said Harry. She nodded and blew Dot a kiss before following Harry and everyone outside. She gave everyone a quick final hug then she climbed up into the back of the truck's trailer and Marion sat beside Harry who drove out of the yard heading in the direction of Opal Racecourse.

The solitude in the back of the trailer would give her ample thinking time for the journey ahead. But for now, she contemplated how quick the nineteen months that she had worked at Nerra Creek Station had flown while she waved frantically to the team until they grew small in the distance.

Her heartstrings were tugged upon hearing Lucy's distinctive whinnies getting softer and softer until she couldn't hear them anymore. Then after a while, as a cruel twist of fate, she happened to glance over at the far paddock where that brute of a bull was at the fence in an almost mock farewell. He was seemingly making long-distance eye contact, or was it just her imagination? *You bloody bugger,* she thought.

The journey became bumpier the more they travelled away from Nerra Creek. Even though Harry had shouted out of the window offering to stop and let her into the cab, where there was plenty of room, she had declined. Despite being bounced around in the trailer, she was enjoying the scenery from the opposite perspective to moving forwards in the cab. It was strange and riveting to see everything unfold backwards and it reminded her when she had travelled on the train to the Blue Mountains which seemed years ago now.

Even though it wouldn't be a long journey, they nonetheless took two short breaks along the way. Marion had packed tea, sandwiches and slices of fruit cake.

'More tea, Alice?' she offered and refilled accordingly. 'It's a puzzle – do you know that I couldn't find that other flask? You haven't seen it, have you?'

Alice spluttered, while holding up her hand to assure that she was alright.

'It seems to have completely vanished.'

Together with her splutter and flushed cheeks, Alice was convinced that they knew it was her. Believing that it would be pointless to tell them of her and Lucy's encounter with the bull, she made the decision to let it lie.

'Sorry, Marion, I haven't,' she said, shaking her head. 'May I have a piece of your delicious fruit cake?'

'We're making good time,' said Harry. 'Should be there by mid to late afternoon. We'll book into a bed and breakfast, then take a stroll. It'll be nice to see the city as we haven't been there in years. Is that still alright with you, Alice?'

'That sounds perfect, thank you. I know I've said this before...'

'Hold it right there, young lady. We've covered this ground. There's no way that we will leave you there and immediately drive back to Nerra. Marion and I want to do this. We're on an adventure here; we don't get out and about much and taking in the city. It'll be fun.'

'Absolutely,' agreed Marion. 'We'll stick to our plan and will drop you off at the racecourse in the morning. With your references from Finch's Equestrian and from us, together with your natural ability and skills, we have every faith that you'll get the job you want. They will be lucky to have you.'

'Thank you both. I appreciate it.' She beamed.

'You're welcome.' Marion smiled. 'Now, we'd better finish up here and make tracks. Would you like to drive the rest of the way?'

She nodded and made her way to the driver's seat.

*

It was somewhat strange being back in a city since she made her hasty retreat from Sydney nearly two years ago.

While she did enjoy the hustle and bustle, her opinions had changed, much preferring to live out in the country. It was also a little unnerving, not having had the opportunity before to drive among so many vehicles. She had declined Harry's offer to take over the wheel, although it was a relief when she parked outside the bed and breakfast.

Harry checked them into two rooms and wouldn't accept any payment from Alice but gave into her insistence to pay for dinner. It was the absolute least that she could do, particularly as they had been kind enough to drive her all this way.

'Nervous?' he asked, pulling into the grounds of the racecourse the following morning.

'A little,' she replied, trying to sound confident, knowing that it was a complete understatement. Her mouth was bone dry and in the pit of her stomach there were butterflies in abundance causing an absolute ruckus. She wasn't sure if it was hunger or nausea but she was grateful that she had eaten some toast as per Marion's firm persistence.

It was ironic feeling that she had lost her nerve just by entering a racecourse legitimately and she almost laughed aloud. The thing was, that if today was a big race meeting and she was here to pickpockets and work her way among the crowd, she wouldn't have been nervous at all. Working at the stables in Randwick had been different because that had been a separate entrance.

Despite having not pickpocketed for two years, she had the ability to continue where she had left off and that had frightened her. Alice pushed the thought away; there was no time to think about it right now.

That part of her life was over.

Being nervous right now was a huge problem, particularly as she had wanted to work here for so long. Alice took a deep breath and held it before slowly exhaling in the hope of calming her nerves.

The very idea of travelling all this way for nothing by failing to secure a position would be devastating. *What on Earth would I do then?* She had no idea. The Oatleys would insist on taking her back with them to Nerra Creek and as much as she loved and respected them, she knew deep down that it wasn't an option. Again, she heard Vera's voice, *You cannot move forwards by staying still, love.*

'Where would we find Mr Stokes?' Harry asked the man wearing a long white cotton coat standing at the car park gate, snapping Alice out of her thoughts.

'Park at the far end then head towards the stables on the left, you can't miss 'im. Someone there will tell you where he is.'

Harry was just about to respond when the man dismissed him by shouting, 'NEXT!' to the car behind them, prompting Harry to drive through the gateway.

'Thanks, Harry,' said Alice, stepping out of the truck and stretching her legs. 'I can see the stabling from here. I'll see you later and thanks for saying that you will wait.'

'Right you are, Alice. Marion and I will have a walk around and we will be back at the truck in an hour. Take your time, it doesn't matter how long you'll be. All the best.'

'Best of luck.' Marion hugged her. 'We'll be thinking of you.'

'Thank you both, see you soon.' Alice walked toward the stables. It was good to be back to familiarity where she also felt at her happiest breathing in a good lungful of manure and straw with a hint of beeswax. There was nothing quite like it. Her nerves began to subside, and she felt a whole lot better.

A man who appeared to be in his thirties walked towards her leading a beautiful chestnut mare. 'Excuse me, I'm looking for Mr Stokes, the manager. Do you know where I can find him?' She smiled.

Without stopping, the man looked her up and down and shook his head. When he bypassed her, he glanced back and said rather rudely. 'If I were you, I wouldn't bother, love. Do yourself a favour and go home.'

Alice was left stunned by his manner.

'You've been most helpful. Thank you so much!' she called back sarcastically, while thinking, *Arse*, as she kept on walking.

'If you can't get the job done, YOU'RE FIRED!' bellowed an angry voice followed by a girl of similar age to Alice, running out of the stable and crying from the harsh words. 'Do me a favour and quit,' his booming voice continued. 'You'll earn more money on your back,' he added as a passing shot.

Alice couldn't believe what she had just heard and watched the petite brunette rush into another stable. She pondered whether to follow her to see if she was alright. But instead, she headed to find the source of the angry voice whereupon she was amazed that the stable she entered was in fact an office within a converted stable.

'What do YOU want? We're not hiring!' snapped the middle-aged weasel-like man, flicking his weathered hand as if to swat Alice away while continuing to work. 'And even if we were, they're enough females here as it is. It's a man's game, sweetheart. Turn around and go back the way you came and stop wasting my time. I've work to do.'

'I take it you're Stokes?' Alice couldn't bring herself to address him as mister. She ignored his vulgarity and stood her ground by looking him in the eye when he gazed up from his paperwork. She had had enough of cowardly bullies and at this moment her dream of working here plummeted in her priorities.

It prompted her to remember the gentle warning that Ralph from the Finch's Equestrian team had told her that Stokes was slimy and rude to females. She even felt a little shameful for being sarcastic to the man who was just walking the chestnut mare and for thinking he was an arse.

Stokes leaned back in his battered swivel chair which caused the spring to creak loudly in protest from his stout frame. It was not the start she had envisioned but she implored the spring to snap so that he would tumble backwards for being so offensive.

He was taken aback by the girl's abrupt manner, tone and boldness but he didn't show it. She was feisty and he liked that. It was quite... interesting.

'I'm Mr Stokes, what of it?'

'My name is Alice Johnson and here are my references to work at the stables.' She placed the letters from Finch's

Equestrian and Nerra Creek onto the battered desk beside his overflowing ashtray, a bottle of whisky and a dirty glass that bore multiple greasy fingerprints.

'I've enough females here to contend with...'

'Do you always make it so unpleasant that they quit? The way you spoke to that girl was disgusting.'

'If you want a job, you're sure going the wrong way about it. Show some respect to your elders, girl. And I'll speak to whomever the way I choose.'

'Just because you're older doesn't mean you deserve respect.' Alice held his stare.

It was quite a standoff where the silence lasted for quite a few seconds before he spoke. 'Two-week trial. And, because we've gotten off to such a good start, it'll be unpaid. Take it or leave it. Go and find cry baby and she'll show you the ropes. By the way, when's your birthday?'

What an odd question, she thought before answering, 'It was last Friday, first of July, why?' she lied, when it was really at the beginning of October.

'No reason. Now bugger off, I've work to do.' He poured out another shot of whisky. Alice picked up her letters and put them back into her shirt pocket and left him to it.

Stokes hadn't read a single word of the letters and from that, she believed a bumpy ride was heading her way. But she could handle it. He said he wasn't hiring so she deduced that he saw a great opportunity in obtaining two weeks' free labour before taking gleeful pleasure in sacking her for being insolent. Alice knew she would prove him wrong but in the meantime, she was joyous just to be able to work with all the horses and that would get her by. Also, without a shadow of a doubt, if it came to it, she would recoup her unpaid wages and that it would come from Stokes' own wallet and not from the racecourse coffers.

Two could play at that game.

'Hello. I'm Alice. Are you alright?' she asked the girl who was grooming a handsome grey stallion.

'Hello, Alice. I'm Maisy. Sorry about before when I ran past you. I'm fine. He gets a bit vocal at times.' She tilted her head toward Stokes' office. 'Are you here about a job? Could sure use some support around here.'

'Yes, two weeks unpaid for talking back. But it'll be worth it just to work with the horses.' The girls smiled at each other in silent solidarity. As well as having dark brown eyes and long lashes, Alice noticed that her impressive cheekbones sported a dash of freckles that added to her beauty.

'There are a few empty beds in the girl's dorm and the top bunk is free where I am. It's a quick turnaround for us girls so I'll appreciate the company.' Maisy finished up and patted the horse. 'Come with me and I'll show you around.'

'Yes, but first can you come with me and meet Harry and Marion? They drove me here and are waiting in the car park. I need to say goodbye and get my things from the truck. I'll tell you all about it later.'

'Sure, but we shouldn't be too long...'

'We won't and it will be fine, Maisy. We will get the work done and give Stokes nothing to complain about. I have known bullies like him. Deep down, he's just a bitter man who barks to display his authority. Take that away and he's nothing.'

Harry and Marion were delighted for Alice and enjoyed meeting Maisy. Their minds were at rest knowing that she had met up with a girl her own age. Harry lifted out her bags and Alice delved into a pocket and brought out two letters.

'Can you please post these for me?' she asked, handing them to Marion. 'One for Aunt Vera and Pip and Tish. I wanted to be sure I got the job before I let them know where I am.'

'Of course, Alice. We will post them for you on our way home,' she said.

Seeing that she was happy, they bade a sad farewell to the daughter they never had and reluctantly drove out of the car park, heading for home. Alice was mindful that she had farewelled a lot of people since leaving the Blue Mountains and would always look back at her time at Nerra Creek with fondness. She would miss them all, especially Lucy.

CHAPTER TWENTY-ONE

It was almost like her time at Randwick. If Alice could have transported Mr Wyatt here, then all would have been perfect. She knew Mr Wyatt would never approve of Stokes' manner and treatment of the stable girls. It was as if he had some kind of leverage over the key staff who seemed to turn a blind eye to his appalling treatment.

Purposely keeping out of Stokes' way, she was determined not to give him reason or an excuse to be displeased therefore terminating her trial. Alice was competent in all her duties and was building a rapport with the jockeys and trainers alike while being conscious that this probably annoyed him. At the end of the fortnight, Stokes took her on and while it irked him that she wasn't afraid of him, he knew that by biding his time, she would pay for her insolence.

He already had a plan in place.

For the first time, Alice was living in an open environment where she hadn't known everyone, thus, keeping her cash secure and assessable was a huge concern. Pip and Tish had put her money in their safe and at Nerra Creek she had rolled the bundle as tightly as she could with a piece of string and wrapped it in a handkerchief. She then stuffed it down the toe end of a thick sock and placed it in the bottom of her bag hidden in her room. But now, at the racecourse and sharing the female dormitory with Maisy and two others, it was a little unnerving as to where to keep it hidden. This was problematic because the dorm did not have a lock where anyone could come and go freely and there was no provision to lock personal valuables away.

Temporarily having the money secured about her person was not ideal. Six hundred pounds was not only bulky, but an excessive amount to carry around. It would be reckless, particularly with manual work because it could jolt loose. From her previous life, Alice knew anyone could be killed for just a small percentage of her nest egg. It made perfect sense to stash it away and keep her switch concealed in her boot for protection.

Ever since making up her mind to leave Nerra Creek, she had begun to think of ways to conceal her money in plain sight. However, it wasn't until Maisy started to show her around the tack room that the answer presented itself. The room was much larger than the one at Randwick and was full of every conceivable piece of equestrian equipment from saddles, bridles, saddle soap, buckets and tins of oil and the like. It was risky – but *what was the alternative?* she reasoned.

As luck would have it, Maisy was instantly occupied by re-stacking some buckets that had toppled over toward the back of the room. Alice seized the opportunity and spotted the perfect vessel. She quickly walked over to the rows of shelving affixed to the left wall near the doorway that supported a vast selection of tins and plucked the one she wanted. It had felt slightly rattly, indicating that the contents had shrivelled up allowing for the perfect receptacle. Another tell-tale sign, along with its neighbours, was the absence of finger marks on the lid, therefore discarded due to the accumulation of dust and grime that had built up over a period of time. Knowing it would be perfect, Alice prised the lid with her switch and glanced at Maisy who was now clearing up a spillage caused by one of the fallen buckets. Making sure no one was near the entrance, she retrieved her bundle of notes from her boot and stuffed it inside the tin, mindful of not disturbing the grime. After securing the lid, she nicked the underside with the blade for easy detection if it were to be moved for any reason and replaced it just as Maisy approached.

'Sorry about that, Alice.'

'That's alright. Sorry too – I should have helped but I was intrigued by the room in having a look around. Much larger than the one I used to work at. Who uses it specifically?'

'Usually just us stable hands as we're responsible for cleaning all the equipment. Some jockeys may stop by and Mr Stokes pops his head in from time to time.'

Alice wasn't worried about Stokes. From the untidiness of his office, he wasn't capable of cleaning out his ashtray, let alone tack room equipment. He would see that as beneath him.

'We don't have to clean the saddles in here, though,' continued Maisy, re-tying her ponytail. 'If it's warm, we can do this outside in the yard. I think it's because Mr Stokes can just peer outside his office to check on us. Come on, I will show you more of the stables.'

Alice smiled with relief when she casually looked back over her shoulder upon leaving knowing that if she approached the tack room from the right side then she would be able to spot her tin from the doorway without entering.

'I've been meaning to ask you, Maisy. What did you do to cause Stokes to shout at you?'

'It was my own fault...'

'What was?'

'I got behind with my duties because the trainer was an hour late in getting back. So, to not miss the vet's routine appointment, I skipped grooming and was going to do it afterwards. But even then, I was too late as the vet had left early without telling Mr Stokes, who was even less happy that I failed to groom.'

'That wasn't your fault. You did explain about the trainer being so late?'

'Yes, I tried, but he wouldn't listen to anything I had to say. He saw it as a good excuse to have a go at me. I need this job and he knows it.'

'Try and stay away from him. Apart from being a creep, I sense something dangerous about him.'

'Me too, but I feel safer with you around.'

*

With plans afoot, Stokes had decided to keep the blonde girl on after her two-week unpaid trial and had reluctantly put her on the payroll. Alice had not felt as joyous by obtaining the position as she should have because of him.

'Good morning,' greeted a friendly voice as a solid and shifty looking man who appeared to be in his thirties stepped into the stable. 'Such a handsome fellow,' he said, approaching and patting the black gelding that Alice was grooming.

'Morning,' she replied, noting his posh suit and shoes so shiny that they reflected the underside of the gelding's belly. 'Yes, he sure is. Can I help you, are you lost?' She hadn't seen him around before. His strong aftershave vied with the hay and manure and he was too smartly dressed to be working. *Perhaps he is an owner?* she thought, although he looked far too young for that, so she deduced that as it was a race day, he had to be a punter.

'No, not lost. Stockbury's the name. Pleased to meet you...' He raised his eyebrows in question and tilted his head.

'Alice.'

'Alice,' he echoed, lowering his eyebrows and shaking her hand. 'Been here long?' He inched nearer to her on the pretence of ruffling the gelding's silky ears.

'No, not long. Can I help you?' she repeated.

He whispered in a conspiring tone, 'Well, it's a little delicate, Alice, but I believe we can help each other...' He winked, letting his words linger while she stiffened and moved discretely toward the horse's flank while continuing to groom. She remained silent, so he had no choice but to resume.

'A sure-fire plan to make us both rich.' He smiled, stepping much closer making Alice almost lost in the shadow between the horse and the stable door.

'What business are you in?' she asked, looking up and locking eyes to show that she wasn't in the least bit intimidated. He reminded her of the thugs that her father had often collaborated with.

'Inside information regarding The Opal Cup. We could make a lot of money,' he replied, ignoring her question. He was also a little disappointed that she did not appear to be afraid despite him deliberately towering above her and invading her space.

'Not interested, Stockbury. I bid you good day. Now, if you'll excuse me.' She extended her arm, moving the brush between him and the horse and not shying away as she stepped sideways, therefore nudging him out of her way as opposed to moving around him.

He had to change tactic and fast with no choice but to step out of her way. 'Pardon me. We seemed to have gotten off to a bad start. Let me explain. I'm not sure if you know about betting at all?' he said quite condescendingly as Alice thought, *You have no bloody idea.* 'But if we partner up, I can make us both a small fortune. All you have to do is feed me snippets of information and the like so I can place the bet to win huge.'

'What's the cut?'

He was almost lost for words. 'You don't hold back on negotiating, do you, Alice?' He tried to laugh but it came out false and irritated and they both knew it. 'Seventy-thirty to me.'

She stopped grooming and laughed for real. 'You expect me to risk my job and possible jail on a thirty? Ha! See yourself out.'

'I'm taking a huge risk too. But I'm encouraged that you are in.' He hoped the little fish hadn't escaped the baited hook.

'Just seeing how serious you are.'

'Sixty-forty. *Final* offer. And I mean, final.' His heart was pounding. He needed to win this bet so much and time was running out. 'It's only fair seeing as I will be putting up all the funds.' He produced a wad of notes from his breast pocket, noting that she hadn't reacted as expected. In fact, she hadn't reacted at all. Alice had looked a pushover but he was now beginning to think that he had mistargeted and should have focused on the brunette girl instead.

Alice estimated the wad of notes and did the math for the high-stakes bet, rapidly calculating her sixty-forty share. It would certainly boost her funds in the right direction. She was tempted to give him the information to make quick and easy money.

She played down her excitement.

This was, after all, illegal and against the racecourse's policy. Staff were forbidden to place bets, although she knew many did. Stokes included. It would be dangerous but she decided that she would do it. Always being able to spot a policeman, she had dismissed Stockbury as the law from the moment he entered the stable.

Stockbury could hardly contain himself. He knew she was weighing it all up. He found the charade intoxicating knowing that the odds were irrelevant. His biggest payday to date was in grabbing distance as the sixty-forty would turn out to be a phenomenal one hundred per cent in his favour.

'Fifty-fifty,' she counter-offered, hoping it would wipe the smug look from his face. 'You need me, otherwise there will be no profit at all for you. Fifty-fifty is better than zero.'

Oh, how stupid you are, she thought. *You're messing with the wrong girl.*

'What can I say, Alice? You have me cornered. I'll go fifty-fifty but *only* if the information is good enough.'

'What horse are you betting on?'

'Shallow Bubble,' he replied, aware that she was now leading the conversation and he became flummoxed when she shook her head in a patronising manner as if to say, *You stupid man.*

'Not Shallow Bubble? She's a winner.'

It was the *way* in which the girl had dismissed that he put aside his ego and began to take her seriously. 'If not, then who?' He was caught off kilter.

'Cold Hearted Jackie,' she answered. 'Trust me.'

'Her form isn't trustworthy. She's a lazy mare.'

'She's had a good week and the ground is in our favour. You asked me and now it's up to you. But if you wish to lose your money...' Alice shrugged her shoulders.

'Alright, I'll trust you on this. Cold Hearted Jackie it is, but if you dare...' He pointed a threatening finger at her.

'But. If. I. Dare. What?' Alice challenged and held his stare.

'I'm trusting you. Don't take me for a fool.'

'Likewise. I'll see you later with the winnings, then we can discuss the following race.' Alice turned her back and carried on grooming. She had to ensure that he came back for more. He was smug and arrogant and instinct told her that he would take off with the lot.

Her double standards fought heavily with her morals. *Isn't this why I wanted to leave home to start a new life?* she thought. Alice reasoned with herself that illegal betting was far better than pickpocketing, although she wouldn't be so sure that Mr Wyatt would agree with her. For now, needs must. It didn't solve her inner good-and-bad demon conflict but for now it would have to suffice.

At two-thirty that afternoon, Stockbury had amassed a fortune. Despite winning the most he had ever won on a single race, his priority now was to find Alice for her recommendation on the final two races to increase his wealth further.

'How much did I win?' Alice asked, knowing full well what it was when he followed her into the stable so she could saddle up and lead out her next horse. Holding out her hand awaiting her cut, she recognised his greedy look, which was not surprising as she had seen it often enough in her father. Deep down she had known that Stockbury was selfish and greedy, and he had proved her right.

The situation had to be handled with care.

'You know your stuff. I'm impressed. Here is your share.' He counted the notes and spread them out like a fan in his hand and waved it in front of her face before whipping them back within the wad. 'But, for now,' he said, 'I'll hold onto it for safekeeping and use it for the next race. We're on a winning streak. You give me the winners of the next two races then I'll pay up at the end of the day.' Before adding as an afterthought, 'I promise,' that lacked assurance.

Battling to hide her fury that was bubbling to the brink of erupting, she thought, *Yes, it is my father all over again*! She knew it was crucial to play nice. Stockbury was untrustworthy and she had to think of something to tempt him back otherwise she could kiss goodbye her share of the winnings.

She sided up to him.

'Going on form and conditions, I say it'll be Her True Colours and Easy Life. We'll win big on these and you will win even bigger if you come here at nine this evening to give me my winnings where I'll give you something worthwhile and special in return, Mr Stockbury...' Smiling coyly, Alice made her intention clear.

He knew what Alice was implying. *What a day this is turning out to be,* he thought. 'I'll be seeing you later then.' He smiled, tilted his hat and bolted out the door to make it to the bookie on time.

Usually, race days were enjoyable. The yards were a hive of activity and there was always an aura of excitement in the air. But today, Alice was on tenterhooks and tried to force herself to remain calm and not draw attention. She felt guilty and perceived that the whole world knew what she had illegally undertaken.

'Maisy!' she shouted, running over toward her friend. 'Been looking for you. I don't fancy the drinks get-together tonight – feel like a quiet night so I'll work your evening shift.'

'You, fancy a quiet night?' Maisy questioned. 'You always like to go. Come on, how about you help me, so we'll finish quicker and go together?'

'Just don't fancy it that's all. Bit of a headache, but I'm fine. Honestly.'

'Well, if you're sure. Thanks, Alice. Sorry, I've got to go otherwise Mr Stokes will be on my tail. I owe you.'

CHAPTER TWENTY-TWO

The scene was set.

At nine o'clock sharp, Stockbury walked into the stable, looking extremely pleased with himself. The girl had come up trumps and his wallet was busting at the seams.

'That was the easiest hundred pounds I've earnt.' She smiled at him holding out her hand.

'Not so fast, Alice. Not so fast. Aren't you going to give me a kiss first? I've been waiting around since late afternoon.' He smelled like a brewery.

'Surprised that you haven't been mugged if you've been flashing the cash.'

'Don't lecture me.' He took offence. 'I can do as I please. You promised me some... comfort.'

'Show me my winnings. You withheld it once.'

'You promised me sex and now you want payment. Are you some kind of whore who wants money up front?' he slurred.

Alice was appalled. This wasn't going well.

'My winnings, Stockbury. That I won fair and square where you also won a vast fortune. If hadn't it been for me...'

'Alice, Alice, Alice.' He shook his head and leant up against the stable wall to support himself while he rummaged for his wallet. 'I don't know what you are talking about. You lured me here on a promise and if you don't oblige then I'll get you fired for approaching me for sex and to illegally bet for you.'

'I'm sorry, Stockbury. You are right. You keep the money and I'll keep my job. But at least give me the chance to see the hundred pounds as I've never seen such a vast amount before.'

'Ah, glad you have come to your senses.' Concentrating to count the money, he then returned the wallet to his inside jacket pocket and tried to arrange the notes into a fan as before.

Quick as lightning, Alice made a grab for the money, catching him off guard. A brief scuffle ensued where his main aim was to keep hold of the money while managing to push Alice away.

'What the hell are you doing?' He was beginning to sober up.

'You never had any intention of paying up, did you?' Her eyes blazed with anger as she walked toward the corner of the stable. 'What is it with you greedy grubby men? You just don't know when to stop, do you?'

Stockbury was too stunned to reply and stood in the middle of the empty stable, clutching the hundred pounds with a vice-like grip and watched her walk back carrying a bucket. And when she slammed it on the ground, some of the contents slopped over the side.

Due to intoxication, it took longer than normal for his brain to catch up with his eyes when Alice precariously dangled his very expensive pocket watch over the bucket of pre-mixed manure. Being used to the fresh smell, she had to admit that when it was mixed with putrid water it did bring out another level of pungency. It was almost eye-watering to the brink where she could taste the smell at the back of her throat.

Stockbury slammed his empty palm against his pocket, baffled as to how his precious watch had come to be in her possession.

'Don't do it. Please don't do it. Here, take it, take it,' he begged, throwing the notes to his right side hoping that she would charge toward it. 'I was only playing. The money was always going to be yours...'

Alice knew differently and without taking her eyes off him, she took great delight by letting the gold chain slip between her thumb and forefinger. When she reached the end of the chain, she held it briefly to torment then let it go. The watch plummeted into the slop, making quite a pleasing plonk as it disappeared into the stinking abyss.

His expression was priceless. He never contemplated even for a second that she would do it, particularly as he had given her the money. He wanted to speak but words were not forthcoming. He again attempted to voice but all that came out were stuttered unfathomable noises. After a few seconds, they came rushing with venom.

'Why, you little bitch...' he shouted. 'You won't be able to walk out of here once I've finished with you. I'm going to give you the biggest hiding of your life then take what you promised.' He neared menacingly closer.

The key was to remain calm and not give him the satisfaction to show that she was scared. 'You want the watch that much, Stockbury? Well, here, you have it.' She picked up the stenchful bucket and stepped closer with her arms outstretched and threw the contents then stepped rapidly back. Clumps and runny manure, straw and putrid water splashed with force against his chest and streamed down his posh suit down to his once-shiny shoes.

When he looked up, Alice saw that some of the liquid had ricocheted up to his face and was now running down one side of his nose and into the corner of his mouth. And that was the point he knew the tables had turned because her eyes blazed empowerment. Alice backed up her advantage by producing and activating her switchblade.

'You come anywhere near me and you'll bleed out.'

It was the way in which she worked and handled the blade without even looking at it that told him that she was practised and competent to carry out the threat. 'You'll keep,' he snapped. Spitting on the floor, he then wiped his mouth with a clean handkerchief retrieved from his inner jacket pocket then used it to pick up his precious pocket watch before fleeing the stable, leaving a very unpleasant waft in the air. Alice retrieved the hundred pounds from the ground and placed it back within Stockbury's wallet. *Not bad for a day's work*, she thought, noting that the money was void of splashes as planned when she had stepped nearer to aim the contents.

Being far from stupid, she knew that Stockbury would return as his kind never gave up. She would need to watch her back; she smiled at the pun then began to clean up the mess before she turned in for the night.

*

Stokes was the sole reason why Alice wasn't enjoying her role as she had hoped. He had many loyal eyes and ears to the ground where it was almost impossible to do anything in the yards without negative exaggerated word getting back to him. The incidences were harmless and uneventful, but often they grew tenfold in accusation resulting in public reprisals. He bullied female staff for the sheer hell and fun of it while most of the men laughed along with him.

The three months that Alice had worked at the racecourse seemed more like years. Her dream job was turning out to be a nightmare and she tossed and turned, wondering if it was time to move on again. Nerra Creek had been different because it had been her decision to leave but now, someone else was making the decision for her and she hated it.

She was, nonetheless, restless but where would she go? As much as she had loved Nerra Creek, the Blue Mountains and their occupants, she wouldn't go back because she yearned to find somewhere of her own and someone to share it with.

Despite her young age, Alice knew in her heart that the love of her life was out there waiting for her. The pull was quite overwhelming.

'Can't sleep?' Maisy whispered up toward the overhead bunk aware of the other girls sleeping in the dormitory.

'If you toss and turn once more, you'll wear out the mattress.'

'Sorry to wake you,' Alice whispered back, leaning down over the side while they spoke in pitch darkness. 'Just thinking about things... What about this afternoon?' And instantly they both tried to scale down their quiet bursts of laughter. 'Although it didn't end too well.'

'The look on Mr Stokes' face was a picture. Still cannot believe what you said to him,' Maisy whisper-laughed.

'It just came out!' Then Alice blew a raspberry and heard her friend dive under the covers, gleefully kicking her feet up and down, roaring with laughter and thought, *Why did it always make hilarious situations more hilarious when you had to laugh but knew you shouldn't?*

'Stop it, Alice. Otherwise, I'll have to get up and pee!'

'Sorry, but he asked for it and how unnecessarily strict to be told to stop laughing when you are working. We weren't doing any harm at all. It wasn't like we were slacking or anything. It was the horse's fault for farting in the first place...'

'It wasn't the horse's fault at all. It was when you looked at him and mocked accusingly, "Mr Stokes!" that he took offence to. He went bright red before he blew a gasket. Did you notice?'

'Notice? I felt the heat from it...' They burst into laughter once more.

'Not so funny afterwards though when he dragged you out into the yard and verbally ripped you to pieces. Goodness, us girls thought he was going to strike you at one point. He was very near to it.'

'No, that wasn't funny. It's all he knows. Just like my father.'

'You never talk about your family. Why's that?'

'Nothing to tell. We'd better get to sleep, another early start tomorrow. Nighty night.'

'Night.' Maisy hadn't expected anything different because her friend always changed the subject whenever it came to her family.

*

During the following week, Alice had kept her head down trying her utmost to avoid Stokes. But it wasn't always possible. He took pleasure in swearing at her for no reason or making disgusting demeaning remarks. Oh, how she wanted him to get his well-deserved comeuppance and began to think of ways in which to make that happen.

Little did she know that a solution would soon reveal itself.

It was near the end of September 1938 and Alice's eighteenth birthday was approaching and as much as she had wanted to tell Maisy and the other girls, it was better to remain silent. It wasn't that she distrusted her friends, more that with so many spies around she did not wish to take the risk from an innocent slip of the tongue. She had seen how female members of staff had been appallingly treated on their birthdays. Often, she had thanked her nous and quick thinking regarding when she had lied to Stokes when he asked her on her first day.

It had only been her third week at the racecourse when

Agatha had been led out into the yard and forcefully submerged into the water trough. If that wasn't bad enough, Stokes had then supervised three men who threw buckets of manure all over her when she climbed out.

Maisy had purposely gripped hard onto Alice's arm, holding her back and warning her to keep quiet for fear of them all being punished. She had looked around and saw that most of the girls were in tears and unable to watch. It was wrong in many ways and had explained the high turnover of female staff who were powerless to do anything about it.

*

'I'll bring you some tea and something to eat in the morning.'

'Thanks Maisy, I'd appreciate that. Hopefully the night will be uneventful. I know horses, but this is too much responsibility.' Alice shook her head. 'I still do not understand why to be honest and the fact that it was rushed. There had been plenty of time during the day to get this sorted so why spring this on me in the last half an hour?'

'I don't understand either, but the vet will be by first thing and I'm sure that the foal won't be born tonight. You being there is just a precaution to raise the alarm if need be.' She tried her best to reassure her.

'I'll take your word on that. See you in the morning.' Scooping up her blanket and pillow, she made for the door.

'Not that I'll be of any help, but I am willing to come along.'

'Thank you but no need for both of us to worry and besides, it will be a little cramped in there with two sets of hay beds.'

Entering the stable, Alice placed three bales of hay together against the back wall of the stall and set down her pillow and blanket while the beautiful grey mare whinnied, perhaps thankful for the company. Having witnessed one birth previously where there had been vets in attendance, Alice felt jittery, but knowing she was only there to raise the alarm was slightly reducing her nerves. It did not stop her, however, from praying that the mare held on until first light, instantly feeling bad for wanting to prolong her labour.

Earlier, Stokes was not listening to her reasoning despite knowing her lack of qualification, and that the grey mare and unborn foal were valuable commodities. He had also dealt her a physically demanding day and try as she might, without meaning to, and as much as she fought not to, she fell asleep.

At the first high pitch whinny, she was wide awake, temporarily disorientated and instantly immobilised. A strong hand was pressing hard across her mouth and a heavy body sprang on top of her pinning her down. Alice could not move a muscle. She had known that repercussion was only a matter of time as she looked into Stockbury's eyes, just a couple of inches away from hers.

'We meet again. This is much cosier, don't you think?'

Alice was terrified and knew one thing with all her might: there was no way that she would be raped on her eighteenth birthday. This gave her the extra mental strength she needed in which to fight this disgusting man. It wasn't how she envisage her first time to be. Beyond the initial shock, she stopped struggling to comply, forcing herself to relax when he pawed at her breasts and roughly kissed her neck, feeling the roughness of his stubble.

'I've been waiting for this in more ways than one,' he hissed. 'No knife now to help you.' He glanced toward her boots that were placed just out of arm's reach. 'I want my money and my wallet. Now, I'm going to remove my hand and if you scream, I'll bury my fist so far down your throat that you won't be able to breathe. Understand?' She nodded. 'Good.' He released his hand and when he clenched his fist as a warning, Alice knew without a doubt that Stockbury and Stokes were associated.

'Now, before you take me to where you've stashed the money, we're going to have some fun.' He eased up, placing one hand on the side of the bale to support himself while raising his hips and fumbling to release his belt buckle. Even though Alice's arms were now free, she waited and despite feeling something she oughtn't press against her, she cupped his face and pulled him toward her and kissed him full on the mouth. Stockbury couldn't believe his luck and fully committed to the kiss. With his guard, and underwear, down, Alice slowly raised her right arm and activated her switch from underneath the pillow to drown out the sound then moved her arm over the side of the bale.

She broke away from his sloppy disgusting kiss, while thinking, *If they're all like that then I'll pass*, and said, 'You need to budge up a bit so I can remove my clothing.'

Stockbury obliged, raising his hips again, only to feel something sharp press nearly to the point of piercing one of his balls.

'I'd keep still if I were you unless you want to lose it completely.' Stockbury was dumbfounded yet again that she had tricked him. His nether region instantly lost the capability to proceed. 'Now get off me you parasite,' she hissed and moved the blade up a notch to show that she wasn't bluffing.

He had no option but to roll off sideways and landed with a thud onto the floor. He dressed, knowing what an utter fool he had been and swore that the third time, there would be no mistake.

Alice was shaky and counted her blessings, knowing that it could have easily turned out otherwise. Despite hating her father, she was nonetheless grateful again for his tuition.

*

It had been a rough tough week as Stokes assigned Alice all the hard and mucky jobs that he could find to force her into quitting. He could fire her but knew that she was strong and would take it much further. It made no sense to shoot himself in the foot by inviting busybodies to his door, so deduced that her quitting would be the best solution all round.

'You wanted to see me?' It was approaching dusk when Alice headed in the stable toward Stokes' desk.

'Think you're smart, do you?' Stockbury stepped out from behind the stable door and slammed it shut. Alice wasn't too worried.

Yet.

'You're outta here,' announced the boss, sitting back in his rickety chair with his fingers intertwined over his barrelled chest. 'Pack your stuff and be gone by breakfast.'

'On what grounds?'

'You're a criminal, a thief and a troublemaker.' He laughed smugly, unconsciously glancing at his desk drawer. 'I could make things difficult for you. Not only could you be prosecuted for giving inside information to a third party but also bribing Mr Stockbury to place your bets whereby you stole his cash in order to do so.'

'We all know that's ridiculous. Where's your proof?'

'I could call in a tram load of witnesses right here, right now...' He sat forward, heavily drumming his forefinger on the desk.

'Of course, you could,' she said, shaking her head and casting them both a disapproving glare. 'Look, carry on for all I care with your betting scams. Just leave me out of it.' Ignoring his threats, she turned to leave.

'Not so fast,' ordered Stokes. 'There's no scam here. That's slander...'

'Then call the police. I'm sure they would be interested to learn what goes on here.'

'YOU THREATENING ME, GIRL?' He slammed his clenched fist upon his desk with so much force that the ashtray jumped up in the air dispelling a cloud of ash that peppered the back of his hand.

'No. You're threatening me. Let it go. I've dealt with bullies like you before. Pathetic, the pair of you, and shame on you for intimidating your female staff, Stokes. And,' she addressed the younger man, 'you're just as bad as your uncle,

Stockbury.' She had taken a punt on uncle and from their looks, she had been right. Alice wiggled her little finger and pointed to the men who wore matching distinctive rings. 'Sloppy,' she said and left the office, leaving the men dumbfounded.

Having just one more night in which to unleash her revenge, Alice brought forward her getaway plan. It was just as well because the odds were not in her favour of evading Stockbury for a third time.

Unbeknown to anyone, apart from Mr Jenkins, Alice would be flying to Western Australia in the morning. Mr Jenkins was a young apprentice trainer and despite not knowing him too well, she trusted her judgment. Along with her peers, she had worked with him on several occasions and had built a rapport, as he had with all the stable hands. Mr Jenkins worked mostly in different circles at the racecourse, hence not a follower of Stokes or of his unscrupulous actions although the trainer had heard that he gave Alice a tough time, but not as to the extent.

Just three days prior, she had learned that Mr Jenkins was going home to attend a family wedding and it was at this point that she devised her plan. It was not only a plan, but a positive sign and a way to move forward. With all the unpleasantness at the stables and being forced out of a job that she loved, Alice knew this was a golden opportunity.

Feeling bad by lying *again*, although not a total lie, Mr Jenkins heard that her family from Fremantle had invited her to stay. She remembered that her own dear beloved mother had come from there as told by Aunt Vera. A pleasant rush of goosebumps accelerated from her scalp to her knees just thinking of them both.

*

Vera added Alice's latest letter to the stack behind her mantlepiece clock. But, this time, she had set a small trap as taught by her dearly beloved. 'If only you could tell me what's going on, Sid,' she addressed the urn, now containing his ashes after the porcelain vessel had previously concealed Rose's stash. She touched the lid and smiled at him before putting on her coat, picking up her bag and leaving the house for a brief stay in the Blue Mountains.

*

Later that evening, Alice told Maisy that she would be sleeping in the stables to care for one of the stallions who was recovering from surgery. In fact, the stallion only had minor surgery and would have been alright unsupervised overnight, but the ruse would give her the chance to creep about.

'Night, Alice. See you in the morning.' She yawned as her friend gathered her pillow and blanket. 'Think you'll be that cold?' She was puzzled that Alice was packing her bag with some extra layers of clothing.

'Does tend to get quite chilly in the early hours,' she replied before putting her things down and grasping Maisy tightly.

'What's that for?' She smiled, hugging her back.

'Just a whim. Can't go wrong with a whim hug.'

'Suppose not.'

Alice left the dormitory for the last time.

*

Barefooted, Alice crept towards Stokes' office that also doubled as his quarters and hoped that her old skills didn't fail her now. Earlier and discreetly that day, she had oiled up an old handkerchief and ran it down over the door hinges that otherwise would have given her away. Stokes was a thunderous snorer and farter; she had been listening to him for the past hour before she knew it was safe enough to enter.

It was three a.m. and apart from Stokes' bodily noises, it was eerily still and quiet. She edged open his top desk drawer, thanking him for unconsciously telling her where he kept his money. But there was nothing there, so she closed it and tried the middle drawer and that too was void of money.

Despondency seeped.

Stokes spluttered a snore from his bunk in the far corner followed by a disgusting liquidy throat gurgle, making her jump. She crouched down, wondering if the noises had awoken him, but he just turned over and fell back into his snoring rhythm. This was her last chance and grimaced at the high pitch squeak when the drawer moved over the dry wooden runner. Thankfully, he was in a deep sleep and never heard it. Lightly running her hand over the contents like she was reading braille, her eyes sprang wider in recognition and victory as she brought out a bundle of notes. A man like him would've had numerous hidey spots, but this wad would more than suffice.

There had never been the intention of taking it all. Just what she was owed fair and square plus disbursements. She counted off her original two weeks' wages that were unpaid. Plus, ample compensation for the sheer hell that he had put her through, plus her airfare money, plus compensation for all the girls and before she knew it, she was back in the stable with the recovering stallion.

Alice set about inserting each girl's share of the money into individual envelopes then placed them underneath the bale of hay by the far wall. She knew that Maisy would recover these the following morning upon discovering the note that she had placed in her boot explaining about the money. Alice emphasised that the girls should never speak of their good fortune for obvious reasons and that she was sorry for the way in which she had left and that she would never forget her dear friend.

Quickly packing the last of her possessions, together with her tin of money from the tack room, she left the stables in readiness to meet Mr Jenkins at their designated rendezvous at daybreak.

Alice began to relax and was looking forward to her very first ride on an aeroplane and wondered what her mother would have thought about her flying higher than a bird.

On conclusion of their journey, they wished each other well and shook hands when Alice alighted from the taxi in Fremantle that they had hailed from the airport. She assured Mr Jenkins that she would be fine as the taxi proceeded to take him to his destination.

CHAPTER TWENTY-THREE

What the hell do I do now? Alice tried hard not to look too conspicuous while her senses were on full alert aware of her surroundings. Carrying a concealed fortune within a medium-sized bag, she flung it over her shoulder and went in search for something to eat. This was what her father would have referred to as *easy pickings* as she downplayed her tell-tale signs and discreetly scanned the crowd, spotting a duo team of thieves.

'Looking for work?' enquired the man sitting on the stool beside her at the counter as Alice tucked into her meal.

'I am. Know of something?' she replied, looking at the old codger between bites.

'Might do,' he said, taking pity on the young beautiful girl with the most mesmerising light blue eyes and friendly face, then pushed his empty cup toward her with a nicotine-stained fingernail that looked stronger than steel.

'Miss?' Alice caught the waitress' attention. 'May we have two more refills please, on me.'

'Mighty kind of you.' He smiled. 'Twible's the name.'

'Alice.'

'A pretty name that is. Now, I know it isn't the place for women and all, but a job is a job, and they are scarce around these parts. Ever worked in a pub or know liquor? Mind you, you'd have to be tough to handle the punters.' He chuckled.

Trying not to laugh, 'I can handle it,' she assured and Twible nodded.

'I'm sure you can.' And when their refills arrived, he enlightened. 'The Arms down Miller Street is looking. Say Twible sent you and I might just see you in there sometime.'

'Thanks, Twible, appreciate that and your first whisky is on me if I get the job.' Alice finished up and left the money on the counter and bid the old codger a good day.

*

Alice stood for a moment across the street to assess the pub. It had the usual type of punters coming and going and it looked to be what she had been used to since she was a child. Visions of a frightened five-year-old, having been evicted and left by a father on the busy doorstep at a dangerous time of the evening with the task of making her own way home sprang to mind. She took a deep breath and pushed the image away while waiting for a break in the traffic then crossing the road and walking up to the door.

'Bit young for a drink, aren't you, girl?' commented a middle-aged man wearing a shirt that badly needed changing. He barged by her and stepped inside.

Come on, Alice, nothing to it, she told herself and opened the door where it seemed that all eyes fell upon her.

'Women round the side entrance!' ordered the old lady behind the bar who pointed to Alice's left.

'I've come about the job. Twible sent me.' Whereby everyone went back to how they were before. It was as if *Twible* was the magic word.

'Did he now? Why didn't you say? Come across.' She beckoned and lifted the counter to allow Alice to step through. 'Follow me.'

Smiling at the owner's quarters, which consisted of a kitchen and dining room all in one seemed quite familiar, Alice got a good feel for the place – it was not so unlike Aunt Vera's house.

'How come you know Twible? I'm Edna, by the way.' She thrust out her hand and pumped Alice's with a surprisingly powerful shake for such a slight person.

'Alice. Nice to meet you, Edna. I got talking to Twible when I went for something to eat and bought him tea and he told me about this place. Are you hiring?' she asked expectantly.

Edna threw her head back and roared with laughter where her upper set of teeth appeared a little loose. 'You'll never get rid of him now, girl. Buying him a drink whether it's tea or alcohol means that he's a friend for life. The old scoundrel. Yes, I'm hiring but I'm not sure you'll be up to it. No offence, mind you.' She looked Alice up and down, believing that she would not last an hour.

'None taken. Give me a couple of trial shifts and if it does not work out, then you don't have to pay me. I could start today. Well, perhaps tomorrow as I need to find somewhere around here to stay first...'

'Say no more. I agree to your terms. Top of the stairs, first on the right.' She indicated to the steep staircase in the corner of the room then flicked her hands over her floral apron that matched her dress to alleviate some creases. 'Stay here, it'll be company for me. Be nice to chat to another female. Get yourself settled in then come down and I'll show you around.'

'That's perfect – thank you, Edna!' Alice could not quite believe her luck. 'See you in a few minutes. I said that I'd buy Twible a whisky if I got the job. Does he come in here much?'

Her new boss roared again.

'You'll see the old goat soon enough.' Edna made her way back to the bar, before shouting back, 'The daft old bugger's my husband.'

*

Alice bought Twible a whisky and thanked her good fortune that she had been in the right place at the right time to secure a job and accommodation. She was confident that Edna would take her on because she was proving to be quite an asset in the pub and popular with the punters. They were good, hardworking and decent people and she was sure that they would've got along with Pip, Tish and Aunt Vera like a house on fire.

During the next few days, Alice took time to write letters to her aunt and the sisters in bringing them up to date with all her news. She had left out the unpleasantness regarding

Stokes, instead concentrating on Maisy and the horses. Just like when she had left Nerra Creek, she emphasised her need to move on even though she had only been at the racecourse for a few months.

Putting her feelings into words was proving to be difficult, particularly when she had trouble understanding what they were herself. She still felt restless but didn't know why. Somehow, she had believed that the answer would present itself when she stepped off the aeroplane and being in Western Australia, but she had been wrong. Appreciating that it was still early days, she temporarily put her letter writing aside hoping that the longer she was there, the more settled she would become.

Ever since she was a young girl, Alice had replayed the conversation with her mother the day they went to the movies followed by tea and cake. The memory of those precious few hours had proven to be priceless over the years. Alice always smiled, seeing her younger self clearly telling her mother that she had wanted to find a man that she could totally love and be loved back. That he would adore her completely and shower her with love and affection. Her smile always faded upon remembering, *As opposed to showering me with violence and fear.*

Above all, the frightening thing was that her mother had found her true love but he had turned out to be a bully and a monster.

Alice was petrified that she would make the same misjudgement.

On the positive side, she knew without a shadow of doubt

that the love of her life was out there waiting for her. And what encouraged her further was remembering Aunt Vera saying that things happened for a reason and sometimes you had to go through chaos in order to get to the other side. *Maybe being in Western Australia was meant to be,* she thought. *It is certainly the furthest I can get from my childhood in Sydney, so perhaps here will be my future.* Knowing that this could only be answered over time she was beginning to feel relaxed and closer to her ancestral origin and in the coming days she was able to finish her letters.

She also wrote to Mr and Mrs Wyatt and told them of the bullying at Opal Racecourse, knowing that they would never have condoned such behaviour. She still missed them and would always treasure the silver pendant they gave her at Christmas. The Wyatts played a huge part in her upbringing and she would always love them for that.

Since Nerra Creek, Alice hadn't stated a return address on her letters because she couldn't be sure if or when she would move on again. It was her intention, however, to telephone Pip and Tish very soon as they now had a telephone installed at Beech Cottage. It would be a great tonic just to hear their voices. Although telephone calls to Aunt Vera were far and few between, she would now alternate the calls between the ladies and her aunt and knew that they would relay the news to the other.

*

'Come on, Alice, we'll go for a walk and a tram ride. I would like to show you around,' said Twible. 'That's unless you have something else planned for your afternoon off?'

'No, no plans, Twible. That sounds great.' They said cheerio to Edna and made their way down the street.

'Lived in Fremantle long?' she asked.

'You could say that, although I've travelled a bit for work. But I've been here for decades.'

'Goodness, that's a long time. How old are you?'

Twible roared with laughter. 'Seventy-six and you don't mince your words, girl, do you!' They both laughed.

'This is Kings Park,' he said when they approached the entrance. 'I like to come and sit here often. Perhaps I'll bring Edna next time and you could man the pub for a while?'

'Glad to, Twible. It's beautiful here.' She admired the view and followed him to an old wooden bench that bore sweethearts' initials intertwined within hearts and arrows celebrating their everlasting love.

'So, you travelled for work. What did you do?'

'Ah, thought you'd never ask! I mined for opals...'

'Wow, that sounds interesting. Did you find many?'

'Look at the old man, Alice. From my attire, you could answer that for yourself.' They laughed again and Alice was transported back to the time when she had sat on a park bench with Alfie. She hoped that he was still around and well.

'It was very hard work, hardly any let up from dawn till dusk and after all your sweat and toil you could end up with a big fat zero to show for it. It was flaming frustrating at times, but you lived in hope, otherwise what else was there? You kept your ear to the ground for any mumblings for sites that were producing. It was often violent too as the prospectors protected their plot. Alcohol played a bit part because there wasn't much else to do on the little down time. You had to sleep with one eye open because there was always a scuffle of some kind going on.'

'Sounds tough. Did you find any valuable ones at all?' She nudged his side.

'One or two.' He winked. Then said proudly, 'Managed to buy the old girl the pub with one of them.' Her eyes widened with surprise. 'When it rewarded, it sure rewarded. But it also brought its own set of problems.'

'How so?' She was riveted.

'It was hard. You had to stop yourself from jumping up in the air shouting at the top of your lungs at your good fortune. It was like keeping the lid on a pressure valve. Oh, how you wanted to share your joy. But you knew that it would be short-lived if you did. I'd seen many a decent man robbed blind by so-called friends who would stab you in the back as soon as look at you. It was every man for himself.'

'Couldn't you take it straight to a bank?'

Twible nearly choked from spluttering and turned to face her. 'Gracious, girl. We were in the middle of bloody nowhere. It wasn't like you could just hop onto a tram to take you to civilisation. It was at least three days away from the city on horseback.'

The scale put things into perspective. 'Then how did you protect your find, Twible? You know, until you could get to wherever it was to sell it?'

'Ah, that's the thing.' He double-tapped the side of his nose. 'You've got to be smart, Alice. You've got to be smart.'

'Come on. Who am I going to tell?' She nudged him again. 'The deceased,' he whispered.

'The what?' Alice thought she had misheard. 'Pardon? What about the deceased?'

'That's right.' He lowered his voice a touch more. 'Bury your good fortune within the dearly departed and trust them to protect it. I hid the first one inside the deceased's pockets as it was a relatively fresh burial. The second time, the corpse was years old, so I found the skull and pushed the opal through the eye socket. And, do you know, I swear the bounder was smiling at me, but as I was so jumpy, I could've imagined anything. Most folk wouldn't dare to cross the line in disrespecting a corpse. But I found it was the perfect hiding place.

'I'd go in the dead of night.' He laughed at his own joke. 'And carefully chose a grave that showed no sign of rock interference and began to dislodge the stones to prevent them from tumbling. Out there, Alice, time was a factor and burials were swift. It was quicker to dig shallow graves and pile it back up with stones as opposed to digging deep. It was a convenient way of getting rid of the stones we unearthed. Think ya could've done that, Alice?' He looked at her, already knowing the answer.

Alice thought about it and answered honestly. 'Yes, Twible. I think I could.' He nodded his head in admiration.

*

'Hello, Pip. It's Alice.' She beamed from ear to ear standing excitedly in the telephone booth at the post office.

'Oh, Alice. It's so lovely to hear from you and glad you received our letter saying that we are now on the telephone. We had to do that knowing you could call us anytime. Just a moment please.'

Without warning, Alice's ear was then blasted by a sudden loud and explosive *T I S H!* when Pip yelled for her sister.

'How are you, love? What's been going on and are you looking after yourself? Hope you're eating well?'

Alice couldn't stop laughing. 'Everything's fine, Pip. How are you both keeping?'

'We're just the same and we talk about you often...'

'Alice!' exclaimed Tish as she came on the line. 'It's made our day to talk to you. How is the racecourse?'

'I'm in Fremantle.' She heard them both gasp with surprise. 'Ah, my last letter hasn't arrived yet. Rest assured that everything is alright.' Alice could hear the ladies getting comfortable with holding the receiver between them. 'It wasn't working out at the racecourse, so I grabbed an opportunity to leave with one of the workers there and took an aeroplane over to Western Australia. I remember Aunt Vera telling me that my mother came from here. So, here I am.'

'Sounds very exciting and an aeroplane as well. I am not sure I would like to go up in one of those. How it gets off of the ground is a complete mystery to me,' said Pip. Alice smiled, thinking that was very sweet.

'We are sorry that it didn't work out at the racecourse though,' said Tish. 'What are you doing now?'

'I'm working in a small pub run by an elderly couple,' she said and joined the ladies in their laughter. 'I know. Ironic, isn't it? But for the life of me, I cannot see your bottles on the shelf!' They all roared again. 'Have you heard from Aunt Vera? I hope she is well.'

'We spoke only last week and yes, she is keeping well and is planning on coming for a visit soon,' said Pip.

'Oh, that's good, please say hello from me and I will call her soon.'

'We will and it's so good to hear your voice,' said Tish.

'Likewise. I will write another letter soon and I will telephone whenever I can.'

'We will look forward to it and to your letters. Take care of yourself, Alice, bye for now.'

'Yes, bye, Alice. Remember we love you very much.'

'I love you both too,' she said and replaced the receiver and exited the booth with a huge smile on her face.

'Hey! Watch where you're going, love,' said the... well, Alice was not quite sure at first if the person was a man or a woman as they bumped heavily into one another.

'So sorry,' Alice apologised immediately, stepping back. She would have tripped over the person's ample belongings if it had not been for the strong hand that caught and supported her until she was stable.

'Thank you.' She was grateful, knowing that if she had fallen backwards and collided with the produce display, there would have been an almighty mess and the postmaster would have most likely presented her with a huge bill.

'No harm done,' said the friendly face.

'Are you alright, too? You look...' Alice said without thinking then found that she couldn't find the right words to dig herself back out of the hole that she now found herself in.

'Dusty, extremely dirty, probably a bit smelly, hungry and tired. Think that's a fair assumption,' the woman said, handing Alice an ample verbal rescue followed by an almighty bellow of a laugh.

The laugh was infectious and Alice was pleased that the woman had taken the bump and bad observation in good spirit.

'Sorry,' she apologised again with a smile.

'No need at all,' the woman held her hand up. 'I apologise to you as I should not have put my bags there in the first place. You looked very pleased with yourself when you came out of the booth.'

'Just spoke to family from New South Wales. It always brightens my day.'

'And hearing that has brightened my day too! Well, I'd better get my stamps before they close for the afternoon.' The women nodded and they went their separate ways.

*

It was bustling in the pub that evening. Alice and Edna were rushed off their feet keeping up with the punters downing their drinks. The weekend was on the horizon and they were eager to engage the young barmaid in conversation and banter.

'Attention please, Alice,' said Henly, siding up to the bar and beckoning her over.

'Quiet everyone,' shouted Twible, sensing that Henly had another rhyme to share.

Henly cleared his throat giving the punters time to quieten and began, 'I used to drink water, but my mates called me a sissy, so Alice, dear Alice pour me another whisky. Then line up the shots so I can get home briskly, to take the missus upstairs because by then I'll be too frisky!' Alice joined in the laughter as Henly took a well-deserved bow.

'You've too much time on your hands, Henly,' Alice said pouring him a whisky. 'On me.' She winked.

'Do men usually dedicate rhymes to you?' asked a friendly familiar voice when the woman approached the bar.

Alice smiled in recognition. 'We meet again.' She extended her hand. 'I'm Alice.'

'Pleased to meet you again, Alice. Everyone calls me Mrs Heppler. And after a fresh up, I'm as good as new and fancy a pint.'

'Coming right up. But shouldn't you be...' Alice blushed and glanced behind her toward the ladies' section at the back of the pub then turned to pour the pint and placed it on the bar.

'It's fine.' Edna smiled on her way to the pumps and when she passed Alice, she double-tapped her on the shoulder, indicating that this lady was an exception to the rule. Alice was puzzled but accepted without question. 'Good to see you, Mrs Heppler.'

'Likewise, Edna. And I appreciate your hospitality.' The landlady smiled before being ushered away to replenish empty glasses.

'Do you live around here?' Alice was intrigued by this woman.

'No, just getting supplies. I come into town every few months or so, or when needs must. Goodness, that tastes good. The first one never touches the sides. Has been a long day. But this is my local whenever I'm in town. I'll have another please, and rest assured, three is my limit!' she said, placing the money on the bar.

'Where's home?' Alice asked, feeling an instant rapport with the woman who looked like she had an interesting story to tell, and surmised that she lived quite a way away to warrant a visit every few months. Her face was kind but slightly weathered from working outside and she appeared to be in her late thirties, perhaps a bit younger. At five feet four herself, Alice deemed Mrs Heppler to be slightly shorter. Overall, she was, what her aunt Vera would say, *a good sort.*

'I live on McKinnley Sheep Station, which is about six hundred miles away give or take.'

'Goodness, that's such a long way!' Alice couldn't quite believe it. 'To come all this way for supplies? Must take you days.'

'About three. It's roughly a day's drive back to Burston from here. It's a small town and the nearest to McKinnley Station. I go there more often. From Burston back to the Station, it's around two days drive. It can be done a lot quicker, but I prefer to look after the vehicle and especially when travelling back with so many supplies. You would be surprised how heavy that can be.'

'Sounds like hard work. But don't get me wrong, there is nothing wrong with hard work. I don't mind digging in and getting my hands dirty.'

'That's very interesting.' An idea popped into Mrs Heppler's head.

Alice was thankful that the rush had died down giving her the chance to stay and speak some more. 'Is it a big station?'

'Not compared to some. We're about one thousand square miles with around thirty-five thousand Merino sheep give or take.'

'You must have quite a few staff to cover that ground and stock.'

'There are ten of us and we're certainly kept busy.' Mrs Heppler put her glass on the bar and used her fingers to count the staff. 'There's Mr McKinnley, he's the grazier and oversees all aspects of the Station. Mrs McKinnley works in the kitchen and also undertakes general homestead chores including the laundry and caretaking of the gardens just like Elsa and me. Then there's Mr Price who is the manager and shares the office work with Mr McKinnley. Next, there is the head stockman – his name is Wallace, nice chap. Then there's Joe and Ronnie – they are the stockmen. Just a word about Ronnie, he's a nice enough fellow but he has no sense of humour at all. Sometimes though, he's more entertaining than whatever is going on because you have to explain stuff to him. He's very smart but all so funny.' She took another sip. 'And finally, there's Squeak, our station hand and Ross, our Jackaroo.'

'Squeak?' Alice laughed.

'When he first joined us, he was breaking in new boots and one of them had an annoying squeak with every step he took. The name just stuck.' They both laughed. 'So that's ten staff plus three children.'

'Ah, I would've liked to have had little brothers and sisters. What are their ages?'

'Let me see. Jack is seven and his sister, Sylvia is five. They belong to Mr and Mrs McKinnley, and Emily is two and belongs to me,' Mrs Heppler said, smiling.

While Alice didn't want to pry too much, she had to ask. 'And your husband? Or was he included in the team you just told me?'

'Just me and Emily,' she said in a manner that was neither rude nor forthcoming and Alice knew that the subject was closed.

'Hearing all about the Station?' enquired Edna when she walked past Alice on her way to get a bottle of whisky.

'Yes, it's very interesting. The station and family sound quite like where I worked at Nerra Creek Cattle Station in Adelaide. They trained me up as a jillaroo. I was there for about a year and a half.'

Mrs Heppler's eyes lit up like a beacon. 'What are your future plans?' she asked with bated breath and Edna knew what was coming.

'Haven't really thought about it, to be honest. Edna and Twible have been very good to me, but I do miss the horses and know that I'll end up working with them again one day. It's like a pull I've got. Can't explain it any better than that. Does that make any sense at all?' She looked at the women.

'You've got to go where your heart desires. My mother told me that many, many years ago,' said Edna. 'But despite all that, here I am with Twible.' They roared at the joke.

'I like that,' said Alice. 'There is something else and don't laugh. You may think that I am too young, but the love of my life is out there somewhere waiting for me and I'm sure as damn hell going to find him.' She nodded. 'I just know it.'

'I'll drink to that!' said Mrs Heppler, raising her glass. 'That's as good as a future plan any day of the week.'

'Yes, I think so too! And to find him and work with horses would be a dream come true... My mother would be proud.' Her voice waivered.

Even though Mrs Heppler caught the underlying sadness she knew that would be a conversation for another day. 'Look, Alice. I know we've only just met, but I have a good feeling about this. I'll be leaving the day after tomorrow to head back to the station. We could sure use a set of skilled hands like yours, particularly with lambing starting any day now and the family would agree.

'How about you bring forward some of those plans of yours and come with me? There's a stable full of stockhorses waiting for you and hundreds of cute lambs...' Mrs Heppler wiggled her eyebrows.

Instantly, Alice's heart skipped several beats in delightful apprehension and smiled. It was like she had been pleasantly winded. On the spur of the moment, she called out to Twible and beckoned him over. Alice placed some money onto the bar before pouring four whiskies and handing them out. 'Thank you for everything and so sorry for the short notice'— she put her arm around Edna and Twible—'but I've decided to join Mrs Heppler at McKinnley Station.'

'Knew you'd up sticks soon enough, Alice. We wish you all the very best,' said Twible and Edna nodded her agreement.

'You have been a delight and an enormous help these past few weeks, and we could not be more pleased for you. Besides, you don't want to stay here with us oldies. Get out in the world and do what you love to do.' Edna gave Alice a hug then they all clinked their glasses.

'Well, that's just grand.' Mrs Heppler could not resist. 'Tell me... It was my amazing personality that swung it, wasn't it?' They all laughed and clinked glasses once more.

CHAPTER TWENTY-FOUR

'All set?' asked Mrs Heppler, putting the truck in first gear and releasing the handbrake ready for the off at first light.

'As I'll ever be,' Alice replied, leaning out the window and waving goodbye to Edna and Twible. She sat back, fully aware that this was her third employment move in as many years where the durations in stay were getting shorter and shorter. *If I keep going at this rate, there'll be no more of Australia left,* she thought and bit her lip from sharing this snippet because it did not convey her reliability at all.

The drive was delightful. Alice saw parts of Fremantle that she had not seen before and tried to imagine what it would be like living in the outback. It would be different from the lush hills of Nerra Creek, that was for sure. She was also hoping that she would not live to regret her rash decision in moving somewhere so drastically remote.

'Penny for them?'

'I hope I'll get on with everyone.' Stokes sprang to mind – she never wanted to get into another similar situation.

'And also putting things into perspective that it will take us around three days to get there. Sounds like the Station is cut off from the rest of the world.'

Mrs Heppler sympathised with the young woman. 'I can feel it in my water that you'll be just fine, Alice. I trust my gut and the McKinnley's trust me. But rest assured because I understand that outback life isn't for everyone. If it comes to it and you don't want to travel back by truck, we have a mail plane that stops every few weeks where you can catch a ride back into Burston and be back in Fremantle the very next day.'

Alice nodded her understanding and accepted the reassurance. 'Thank you, that's good to know. It brought to mind when I saw all the supplies loaded up in the back of the truck. It made me realise the remoteness.'

'We like to keep well stocked up and the mail plane delivers emergency supplies too if we need it. We just radio through and schedule a drop-off. You'll adjust.

'Besides, there is plenty of room in the back for more. I've a good stacking system and you'll be surprised just how much more I can load up. The main provisions I buy in Burston. If all goes well, we should be there early this evening. We'll stay overnight in the bed and breakfast. I called ahead and booked another room for yourself, then we'll get the rest of the supplies at early light and make our way on the track back to the Station.

'Just so you know, you'll be thrown into the deep end.'

Alice looked at her in question.

'As I mentioned before, lambing is due to start any day.

It may well have already started, but you will be busy from the off. It'll be good experience and you'll learn a lot from the team.'

'I'm quite excited now and looking forward to my next adventure. I don't mind hard work. It's refreshing doing work that is good.'

Mrs Heppler thought the last statement was a little odd and decided to let it go. If there was something to it, then Alice would tell when she was ready, with that, she was sure.

'Your next adventure will be much sooner than you think, for tomorrow night we will camp out under the stars among deadly nasties.' Mrs Heppler emphasised in a dramatic way to pull Alice's leg as she stole a quick glance.

'Oh, it won't bother me. In all seriousness, I've encountered far worse two-legged ones...' Alice accomplished more than anyone had before by leaving Mrs Heppler temporarily speechless, wondering what on Earth the young woman had been subjected to?

*

The remote town of Burston wasn't quite what Alice had envisioned as she had pictured a multitude of tumbleweeds rolling down dirt tracks with wooden shacks and people dressed in attire from the last century. But she found that the small town, comprising of the usual stores, looked like any other that she had passed through from the Blue Mountains to Adelaide. Although, there was not as much greenery and the earth was a deep orange.

'Righto, Alice. Here we are.' Mrs Heppler parked

down a side road that adjoined their bed and breakfast accommodation. 'Now, where is he?' Alice followed her gaze. 'Ah, there.' She pointed as a young lad ran toward them trailed by a bedraggled brown dog.

'Thought you'd forgotten about me, young Ernie!' She smiled and handed him some money.

'Wouldn't do that, Mrs Heppler,' he replied and pocketed the money.

'Usual deal, Ern. You and ol' Sandy keep a watch out overnight and I'll pay you the rest in the morning. Now, I'm in the usual room just overhead and if you need me just holler like crazy and I'll be down. And...'

'No sleeping, yes I know!' Ernie smiled back.

'Good lad. See you just before first light,' she said before leading Alice into the small reception area to check in.

*

Mrs Heppler had been right when Alice saw how strategically she had packed and stacked the extra provisions. She was also grateful for the suggestion to buy sufficient stamps so she would be able to give her letters to the mail plane pilot to post when he flew back to town.

'Is it like this all the way?' questioned Alice after a while when they had been driving on the long outback track between Burston and McKinnley Station.

Mrs Heppler couldn't help but smile when she looked at Alice who was swaying with the truck while trying to stay seated in the same spot.

'Problem?' she asked. 'In all fairness, it isn't all bumpy.

We'll get to some flatter land soon and then you can have a go at driving. I know you've been itching to.'

'Yes, I have. Thank you and perhaps you can pull over at the next tree or rocks or whatever...'

'If you need to pee, I'll just pull over. There's just us out here and you can go on the other side of the truck. Just watch out where you are aiming first as we don't want any surprises now, do we?'

'I've been outside many a time. I'm used to it,' Alice assured and smiled when Mrs Heppler pulled up and put on the brake.

*

'Well, that's a relief. At least I know I'm not going completely mad,' Vera whispered to herself when noticing that her trap had worked.

It had been lovely to see Pip and Tish where her overnight stay had turned out to be extremely enlightening. Chuckling, she eyed her bag containing an unlabelled bottle of whisky. *Wonders never cease*, she thought.

Despite knowing that her girls had access to the parlour, for when they joined her every morning for tea when she received their earnings from the previous day, she trusted them. Upon first discovering the disarray of letters, she had listened more intently regarding their *guests* from that evening and took particular note of any first timers, of which there was only one.

From his description, he could have been any average man until Dulcie, her best girl, mentioned that he had a scar down the left side of his face.

That was when Vera's heart leapt into her throat.

She considered going to the police with her suspicions, but that was all they were, suspicions. And with no evidence, she would be a laughingstock and besides, having the police come knocking at her respectable *boarding house* would not be good for business.

Vera deduced that Alice had written nothing of value to anyone apart from herself and pondered whether to mention anything to Alice or Pip and Tish but she did not want to cause any unnecessary worry.

The simple solution was to hide the letters, but something told her to leave everything just the way it was.

*

The landscape was a complete contrast to Nerra Creek, the Blue Mountains and Sydney and Alice marvelled that one country could have so much diversity. Never in her wildest imagination did she believe that she would end up in the outback of Western Australia. And this prompted her to wish with all her heart that she had known more of her mother's background and the family she left behind.

Apart from Aunt Vera, Alice had no idea if she had any other living kin and it occurred to her that she may have inadvertently walked past a distant relation in Fremantle without either of them being aware. It was almost too sad for words so she steered these thoughts away knowing that it wouldn't do her any good to ponder on what she could never change.

Not wanting to bring attention to herself, Alice blinked

away prickling tears and looked out of the window toward the horizon. It was almost mesmerising. She had never seen so much space as far as the eye could see. Her mother would have liked it very much, but her father would have despised being out here all alone. This was not an ideal environment for a master pickpocket.

It was the very beginning of summer but already the heat and humidity were stifling. Alice's long hair seemed to add to the intensity making her feel more uncomfortable and itchier. Knowing it would help, she extended her plait above her head and wound it back down to her scalp, so it looked like a large bun on the top of her head while the Akubra that Mrs Heppler had given her held it firmly in place.

'You'll get used to it, love. Let's say we get some lunch going and stretch our legs?'

'That sounds good, Mrs Heppler. Thank you!'

*

Taking a turn at the wheel, Alice appreciated what it was like to drive out here. The truck was quite straightforward to operate, although it took her a while to judge the track by avoiding large potholes, rocks and medium-sized ant hills that were just below her line of sight.

'Do you always do this journey on your own?'

'Yes, but it doesn't bother me being all the way out here. It's a case of being sensible with the truck and not taking unnecessary risks, for instance, not stopping in time for nightfall. I have the rifles, as you've seen, and there's ample water, fuel and food.'

'What's the worst thing you've had to contend with?' Alice was absorbed in finding the woman's limitations and what she considered dangerous.

'That's a mighty interesting question. Now, let's see.' She pondered for a moment. 'There was the time that I had an unwelcome guest in the cab with me. I knew straight away when I felt it slither across my foot. I always have a quick look around before I get back into the cab for something such as this. But on this occasion, I missed it completely. Little blighter.

'Don't get me wrong, I don't mind snakes. We all have a place in this world. But when it's a brown snake that could kill almost instantly, it's never a good time to panic. I also had to keep my eyes on the track. Remember, the snake is moving all the time and at this point, it was over both feet. Therefore, I couldn't brake without moving my foot off the accelerator and had no choice but to keep going and pray that it kept moving.'

At this point, Alice had regretted asking the question and couldn't help but look toward the floor as Mrs Heppler continued. 'I must admit that I started to pray because the track was bumpy and it could've struck at any moment, thinking it was being threatened.

'The angels were looking over me that day. It slithered on to where your feet are.' She cackled when Alice's reflexes sprung her legs up off the floor. 'I stopped the truck and shot the bugger.' She pointed to the bullet hole at the bottom of the passenger door.

'Impressive,' acknowledged Alice, involuntarily shuddering despite the intense heat.

CHAPTER TWENTY-FIVE

Feeling a little more apprehensive with every passing mile and with so many thoughts popping into Alice's head, they finally drove under the McKinnley boundary sign where Mrs Heppler announced, 'One more hour and we'll be there. Don't worry, love. You'll be fine. How's your back now?'

'Much better, thanks. I'd forgotten what it's like sleeping on the ground. I'll get used to it again. The stars were amazingly bright though, almost blinding, but very beautiful.'

'It's incredible what you take for granted, isn't it?'

'It is. You must be missing Emily. I'm looking forward to meeting her.' To which Mrs Heppler pursed her lips and nodded, being a little too emotional to respond. The minutes ticked by when suddenly Mrs Heppler blasted the truck's horn, announcing their arrival. They rounded a corner and drove into the extensive yard, where today, everyone came out to greet their newest member as Mrs Heppler had radioed through beforehand.

The new jillaroo jumped down from the truck to a

very warm welcome where all her fears vanished and was surrounded by a pack of excited kelpies.

'Welcome to McKinnley Station, Alice. I'm Mr McKinnley and we look forward to you working with us.' He was taller than most of the men, average build and appeared to be in his late twenties. All the men wore Akubras, checked shirts and dark trousers, much like the staff at Nerra Creek. He shook hands and introduced the rest of the team where this time, she hoped to remember everyone's name. 'May I introduce my wife, Mrs McKinnley and I know Mrs Heppler is thorough and would have already explained who does what. So, briefly, here is Elsa, Mr Price, Wallace, Joe, Ronnie, Squcak and Ross.' Alice nodded and said her hellos to the team who also returned greetings.

'And us. Hello, Alice, it's nice to meet you,' said seven-year-old Jack, stepping forward and shaking her hand. He was a handsome child with dark brown hair and eyes, and he did not appear at all shy.

'Pleased to meet you, Jack.' She smiled and noted that his sister, Sylvia, looked quite disinterested as she disappeared back into the kitchen. But then, she reasoned, she was only five years old, and the thought reminded Alice of herself being in the courthouse all those years ago when she lifted P W's wallet and all the trouble began. Then, a toddler, with beautiful baby fine blond hair, who was obviously Mrs Heppler's daughter, ran and practically knocked her mother off her feet.

'Hello, love. I've missed you. Have you missed me?' Mrs Heppler said, kissing her daughter's cheeks and spinning her around with glee.

'Sounds quite a bunch, doesn't it?' said Mrs McKinnley. Alice liked her immediately. She was on par with her own height, slight in build and appeared a little older than her husband. Her light brown hair was loosely pinned up where the sunshine highlighted pleasing copper tones. Her eyes looked a little weary but that was understandable with having young children and a homestead to run. 'Come into the kitchen, Alice. Dinner will be ready shortly. Elsa will make you a cup of tea then I'll show you to your room where you can freshen up. Don't worry about the supplies, Squeak and Ronnie will take care of it.'

'Thank you both and that would be lovely.' Alice followed them into the kitchen, which was dominated by the biggest table that she had ever seen.

'We can fit thirty at a push and have on many occasions,' Mrs McKinnley enlightened her when she noted the girl's surprise. Alice already admired the homestead. The room was larger than the one at Nerra Creek, painted in white and was well-used and looked after. There were two range cookers that supported a multitude of steaming pots and pans, and the aromas were making her feel extremely hungry.

*

'So, Alice,' said Mr McKinnley, reaching for a bowl of steaming vegetables. 'What's your story?'

She felt the room hush to hear what she had to say.

'I am from Sydney and worked in the stables at Randwick Racecourse. After my parents died, I travelled to the Blue Mountains where I stayed with Pip and Tish who are two lovely and kind old ladies who introduced me to Finch's Equestrian. I love horses and ended up accompanying a relocation team down to Adelaide to deliver ten horses. Three of which were bound for Nerra Creek Cattle Station. They saw how I was with the horses, and they invited me to stay and trained me to be a jillaroo. I left after a year and a half, did a brief stint at Opal Racecourse before flying to Fremantle where I literally bumped into Mrs Heppler. So, here I am...'

The room erupted into cheers as everyone was impressed at what Alice had already achieved.

'It's good you have experience working on a Station, so you know it's hard work. Tell me your favourite and least favourite job about station life,' said Mr Price so he could get an indication for rostering purposes. Alice turned and addressed the manager who was in his early forties and therefore the elder of the family and staff. Now that she had spent a little time with everyone, she viewed all the men to be roughly the same height, with the exception of Mr McKinnley, and they were practically the same toned build from doing such manual work.

'I have worked with horses since I was a child back at the stables and love to be with them as much as I can. I only have jillaroo experience from working on a cattle station, so what I don't know about sheep, I am willing to learn fast. My least favourite is kitchen duty. No disrespect to the hard work of you ladies, but I much prefer to be out and about. I'll do my share of course; it all helps to the running of a station.'

Mr Price was happy with Alice's answers and nodded

throughout as did Mr McKinnley. 'Joe and Squeak will give you a quick guided tour tomorrow morning after breakfast.'

'Including the stables?' She beamed.

'Yes, including the stables.' Mr McKinnley laughed. 'Although, lambing is starting and it's our busiest time of the year after shearing.'

'Yes, Mrs Heppler mentioned that it would start soon and I am eager to learn.'

'That's good to hear. Mr Price will draw up a roster for you and he'll let you know every morning at breakfast what your daily chores will be.'

While they all finished their meal during which Alice was asked a multitude of questions, she felt at ease and at home. Just like it had been at Nerra Creek. When the men left the kitchen to do their final checks before nightfall, she was enjoying the women's company as she helped them to clear away the dinner things then she assisted Elsa in preparing the table for breakfast. Alice hadn't known many aboriginal people, except for some of Twible's friends who came to the pub now and then to which she had enjoyed listening to their stories. Alice believed that Elsa wasn't that much older than she. They were of the same height and her curvaceousness suited her. Her hair was pulled back so tightly that Alice thought that it must hurt and when she got to know her better, she would ask Elsa about her story, just as she had told hers earlier.

'Right, you three. It's way past your bedtime,' Mrs Heppler said to the children. 'They are usually tucked up well before now but today was a special occasion. We like to keep to a routine here,' she explained.

'Good night.' Alice waved to Jack and Emily and noted again that Sylvia had run off ahead. Emily doubled back and gave Alice a big hug. 'Oh, that's nice. Thank you, pickle.' Alice tickled the child who roared with laughter. 'You're a little sweetheart, aren't you? I'll see you in the morning, goodnight.'

'Don't know about you, Alice,' said Mrs Heppler, 'but I'm done in myself. I'll put these rascals to bed then I'm turning in. I know Mrs McKinnley will give you a brief tour of the homestead, so I'll see you in the morning.'

'Good night, Mrs Heppler, and thanks for everything.'

'You're welcome, love.'

'Just one more cup of tea,' said Mrs McKinnley. 'We'll let the children get to their rooms before we head off. Come, Elsa, and join us,' she said as the three women sat back down.

'Now before I show you around, just a few things that you need to know. In the cupboard over there'—Mrs McKinnley pointed to the far corner of the kitchen—'there's a first aid box. There's also one in the staff quarters and down at the stables and one is always taken out whenever the men go out on a muster. We are quite safety conscious here and all the boxes have the same supplies.'

Alice appreciated the information, taking it all in.

'Also,' said Elsa, 'just outside the kitchen door is a large bell and it can be heard for miles around. If there is any problem, just ring it and someone will come running. We hope that no one will ever need to use it but it's there just in case.'

'That's good to know.' Alice nodded.

'And lastly, as you can see,' continued Mrs McKinnley, pointing to a shelf by the far kitchen door, 'is a rifle. It's loaded and the safety is always on, and a box of bullets is beside it. The main gun cabinet is in the office and I'll show you that later.

'Do you know how to handle a rifle?'

Alice blushed, believing they could see right through her and into her past.

'Yes, I've handled rifles and shotguns when I was at Nerra Creek,' was the safest answer and it wasn't a lie.

'Good,' said Mrs McKinnley. 'That will save some time.'

'And the radio, too,' said Elsa. 'Everyone has to learn how to use the radio.'

'Yes, that's right,' agreed Mrs McKinnley. 'Mr Price will take care of that for you.'

'I will finish setting the table,' said Elsa, getting up, 'while you do the tour. Good night, Alice. Nice to meet you and I'll see you both in the morning.'

'Thank you, you too, Elsa,' said Alice, following Mrs McKinnley through the far kitchen door that led to a long corridor that ran the full length of the property.

'The corridor is the main walkway to all the other rooms in the homestead,' continued Mrs McKinnley. Alice seemed to walk through door after door and like the kitchen, the homestead was painted in white. There was a dining room that had an antique polished table where Alice counted twelve chairs. The room was tastefully decorated and had solid oak flooring, and she could not wait to see the view from the two sets of windows that Mrs McKinnley had described the garden as being quite spectacular.

Next, Mrs McKinnley guided Alice through the interior double doors through to the spacious lounge where it also had views of the garden and paddock beyond. There was an enormous sandstone fireplace and plenty of inviting seats with ample cushions.

Walking back to the corridor they next went into the library that was understandably smaller and had two comfortable chairs and floor to ceiling bookcases. Next to this was Mrs McKinnley's sewing room that she described as being her pride and joy.

Further on, Alice had a quick look in the office that had two oak desks and chairs, filing cabinets, a gun cabinet and the radio.

'Ah, one other thing, Alice. As you can see, we like a family atmosphere here where everyone is welcome to join us for meals. Although there are limited facilities over at the staff and shearers' quarters. Staff can opt in or out, but if you wish to join us for meals, all we ask is a modest housekeeping fee that is deducted from your weekly wage. Mr Price will be able to help you with that too when you next see him if you wish.'

'Yes, I'd like to do that, thank you for telling me. I like being part of a family atmosphere. It's very special.'

Mrs McKinnley deduced that there had been sadness in Alice's young life, but she was sure that she would enlighten in time. Instead, she pressed on. 'You'll be busy tomorrow and it's a pity I'm showing you these rooms when it's dark outside, but as I mentioned before, when you are in any of the rooms overlooking the garden, you will see how breathtaking they are.

'We have native trees and bushes, and we try and keep a decent lawn if we can, but as water is a precious commodity we try and limit it. And lastly'—they entered the corridor once more—'we have eight bedrooms here that are split with four at one end of the homestead and four down at the other end. There are two bedrooms either end on the kitchen side of the house and the other two are opposite overlooking the garden if that makes sense. Come, I'll show you.

'As you know, the dunny is on the left of the homestead as are the wash facilities.' Mrs McKinnley lowered her voice and continued. 'Try and go before it gets dark but if you need it after dark, take the old gas lamp near the kitchen door. Yes, I know.' She laughed. 'We're still a little behind out here but it works just fine. Or you can use the chamber pot under your bed but it's up to you to empty it in the morning. Just be mindful that if you venture outside at night-time to be aware of nasties out there. You'll get into a routine soon enough.

'And here,' she said, opening Alice's bedroom door, 'is your room. Do you like it?'

'Yes, I love it, Mrs McKinnley. I like that the whole homestead is painted white where the colours of your furnishings and cushions give a warm homely feel. Pip and Tish had similar taste. It's beautiful and I like the paintings here. They're very interesting.' She walked over to look at a painting on her wall.

'That's nice of you. I appreciate your compliments. Even though we live all the way out here, there's no excuse for lack of standard and not belonging to the rest of civilisation. Yes, these paintings are lovely. I just adore the colours. Elsa painted them in honour of her Aboriginal ancestors. Every picture depicts a dreamtime story, she said.'

'Thank you for telling me. I'll ask Elsa about them.'

'Well, you'd better get a good night's sleep, busy day tomorrow. Goodnight, Alice.'

'Good night, Mrs McKinnley. Thank you and see you in the morning.'

Alice slept like a log. Her room was one of the loveliest that she had stayed in, reminding her of her one in the Blue Mountains. The bed was very comfortable, unlike the urine-infested mattress she once had back at her family home.

CHAPTER TWENTY-SIX

'Ready, Alice for us to show you around?' asked Joe, when they walked out of the kitchen after breakfast.

'Thanks, Joe. You're a stockman, right?'

He nodded.

'And Squeak? There's a lot of new names to learn, but I'll get there,' she said with a hint of laughter in her voice.

'I'm the station hand,' he said. 'It's the word *Squeak*, isn't it?' He laughed back, shaking his head. 'Those damn boots have a lot to answer for although they haven't squeaked since I can't remember. Mrs Heppler told you?' When Alice nodded, he said, 'Well, at least you know that it isn't my real name, which is Peter by the way. But I'm stuck with Squeak.

'The station hand means that I do a little of everything. Right, the yard is as big as it is due to fire prevention and why the outbuildings are spread so far apart. It's so the embers don't fly up in the wind and catch the other outbuildings alight. Plus, it's a large space to turn all the vehicles around easily enough.'

'The stockmen and shearers' quarters are in that big building opposite the homestead,' continued Joe, 'with various outbuildings housing feed, machinery and the like.'

'And down this way,' said Squeak, when they walked further away from the homestead, 'is the water tower, one of our corrals and fire pit area where we hold roast spits from time to time and...'

'What you wanted to see more than anything'—Joe pointed—'are the stables. Want a look inside?' He smiled.

Alice liked Joe and Squeak. Joe was handsome and had a cheeky grin, she thought he was around his late twenties, and she felt comfortable with him. As too with Squeak who looked a little mischievous and appeared to be around his early twenties and she hoped that she would get over his name and soon. It wouldn't be kind to laugh every time someone called his name. But she could sure have fun with it!

'You really need to ask that?' she replied like an excited child. 'How many horses do you have here?' she asked when they approached the entrance.

'We have ten but there's room for fifteen,' said Squeak, 'although Ronnie, Wallace and Mr McKinnley are currently out with theirs.'

Alice was in her element and patted every one of the horses. 'They like you,' observed Joe.

'Of course, they do!' Alice could've cried from happiness. 'It's been a while – how I love them.'

'And this one Mr McKinnley believes would be suitable for you. His name is Finn.'

And when Alice followed the men into Finn's stall, she fell

in love with the chestnut stallion. She was speechless and patted his beautiful coat and lovingly reached up on tip toe to ruffle behind his ear. He had the most gorgeous eyelashes and kind eyes and gave her small whinnies and when he swished his tail Alice noted that he had a white tuft on the end. He was a very handsome boy.

'Hello, Finn. I'm Alice and I love you already,' she spoke softly as Squeak went to fetch a saddle.

'I can see you have a connection,' remarked Joe while Squeak placed the saddle onto Finn. 'Watch this carefully because we saddle up differently to what you may be used to. Although, working at the cattle station, they probably do it the same way.'

Alice paid close attention to what Joe was doing. He then took the saddle back off and handed it to her and indicated for her to repeat what he had just shown.

In a matter of minutes, the three rode out of the stables and headed down toward the shearing shed.

'We like to shear during the springtime, but it depends as well on booking the shearing teams as they work from station to station. Mr McKinnley and Mr Price have been working on various times during the spring and have even considered changing to late winter. They keep us informed of Station's decisions and we all have an input which is good. You've just missed shearing for this year, but you'll be an expert with the sheep come this time next year.'

'How many in the shearing team?'

'Around fifteen,' replied Joe. 'Ten shearers, four roustabouts and one wool classer.'

'I'll look forward to that.' They headed off down toward the outer paddock to check on some of the sheep. 'Smaller livestock to what I'm used to,' she joked, 'you only have Merinos on the station?'

'Yes, quite a change for you, although the bulls would've been interesting.' And that statement brought to mind that frightening encounter when Lucy had saved her life. *Now that's a story for another day*, she thought.

'They were, but the stockmen took care of them.'

The morning sun was getting hotter and Alice knew that in the height of summer it would be like working in a furnace out here. This made her think that she should find a small covering for her switch because the heat that generated from inside her boot would cause the casing to burn her skin. *Or perhaps I should leave it at the homestead completely?* she wondered.

Thinking about a possible future at McKinnley Station brought to mind Twible's advice and she wondered light-heartedly, where she could locate the deceased? In the meantime, she had hidden her money within the chest of drawers in her room knowing she would move it again soon to somewhere more permanent. No doubt, she would come across a small cemetery on the Station during her work and while she would never seriously contemplate Twible's idea anyway, a silly thought entered her head. *'Ahem, excuse me, Mr McKinnley, where is your cemetery because I want to bury my money within their remains...'* She let out a short chuckle.

'What's funny?' asked Joe.

Alice turned it into a cough. 'Nothing. Nothing at all. Are the sheep friendly?' It was a dumb stupid question, but the only thing that came to mind.

'They have their moments like everyone,' said Squeak to which Alice thought was a good retort and wondered, from what Mrs Heppler had said, how Ronnie would have answered it.

'The kelpies keep them in line.' Joe's high pitch whistle sent his kelpie off to round up a straggler. 'We're starting to get busy with the beginning of lambing.'

It took Alice a while to realise. 'So, lambing occurs *after* shearing? Don't know why, but I would've thought it would be the other way around. Doesn't it hurt the ewe and lamb?'

'That's the general assumption,' said Joe. 'Here at McKinnley, lambing occurs around six weeks after shearing. As the pregnant ewes are bigger, they are more placid which makes it easier to get them into position. It also aids birthing and gives the lambs easier access to their mother's milk.'

'That makes sense. Thanks for the tour. Now what can I do to help? And don't let me stop you if you have to go.'

'I'll head off then,' said Joe. 'I need to help Ronnie and Wallace to do the rounds and re-check the fences. I suggest you go with Squeak to finish setting up the nursery.' Joe whistled for his kelpie then turned his horse and galloped toward the paddocks.

'The nursery?'

'Where we keep the lambs that have been rejected by their mother's. We bottle feed them and keep them warm in the outbuilding, so our job for today is putting down straw.'

'Oh, poor things. But I'm looking forward to bottle feeding them. Sounds like fun.'

*

For the next three weeks, Alice was thrown into the deep end by assisting the team. She was learning so much and had even delivered a few breech lambs under the expert guidance of the senior staff. The men liked having Alice around because she was keen to learn and didn't mind getting her hands dirty or her leg pulled. Mr McKinnley and Mr Price were also pleased because Alice was their first jillaroo at McKinnley Station, much to the delight of Mrs McKinnley, Mrs Heppler and Elsa.

'Pity that I missed the shearing by only a few weeks,' she said to Wallace, the head stockman, when they were checking in on the nursery.

'It'll come round soon enough. You young'uns are so impatient!' He laughed.

'He who is just thirty years old!'

'You got me there.' He smiled. Although Alice thought that Wallace was handsome with his short, dark wavy hair and blue eyes, she was not attracted to him romantically and rather looked upon him as being the older brother she never had.

'Have you been here long?'

'Almost five years, now. I was a shearer for nearly ten years and became fed up with moving around. At the end of my last season, I mentioned this to Mr McKinnley who offered me a job where I have worked my way up to head stockman. It's a good place with good people and I still see my old shearing mates now and again when they come here and sometimes at the rodeos.'

'I'm looking forward to the rodeo. Should be fun. So, do you become part of the shearing team when they are here?'

'It's damn hard work but I enjoy it as a temporary thing. I try and keep up with the shearers but I cannot shear one fifty a day like I used to.'

'One fifty? Goodness, that's a lot!'

'Yes, it is but some of them do much more. We'll get you to have a go and show those old boys how it's done!'

'I'm up for the challenge. Perhaps I'll have a go for the Station at the rodeo next year? Sounds very enjoyable from what the ladies have been telling me.'

'Don't be fooled.' His eyes twinkled. 'The rodeo is a scary place. I'd rather sleep in a snake pit as opposed to being among the female staff, not to mention the grazier's wives. Mrs McKinnley's the exception there, mind you. Very competitive they are particularly when it comes to the cake judging. I wouldn't want that job for all the vast fortunes out there!'

Alice laughed with him. 'Wallace, you big coward!'

'I can live with that and you'll see for yourself, come March. Now, from what we can hear'—he laughed—'these lambs are very hungry.' They climbed into the pen and selected a lamb each then climbed back out and started to bottle feed while the remaining lambs bleated loudly for their turn.

*

The days were long and hot, and the mornings came around too quickly when everyone piled into the kitchen before first light to fuel up on the McKinnley Station's legendary breakfasts. In the beginning, Alice used to have tea and toast but before too long, she needed to pack away a little more to keep her strength up and joined the men with eggs, bacon, sausages and steak with fresh bread washed down with endless cups of tea.

Alice had been so engrossed in her work that she only realised that Christmas was a few days away when Mrs McKinnley said, 'As you know, Christmas Day is on Sunday and Mrs Heppler, Elsa and I will be serving a special dinner in the evening,' followed by loud cheers as the men roared with delight.

'Then, depending on the weather, we'll have a spit roast on Boxing Day.'

'The ladies cook an exceptional Christmas dinner, Alice,' said Mr McKinnley, 'and you will enjoy the spit roast down near the paddock and stables. Squeak and Ross, perhaps you can clear up the area so the ladies can set up down there?' The men nodded.

'I like the sound of that, it all sounds like fun!'

'It is. What do you normally do at Christmas?' asked Ross, the jackaroo.

Alice could only conjure up one magical Christmas and that was with Pip, Tish and Aunt Vera in the Blue Mountains. Despite just losing her mother, the ladies had been compassionate and subtle with their celebrations. She also thought about Nerra Creek where they had been just as busy as here but they did have a lovely Christmas dinner and they sang songs in the evening. Then there was that special moment when Mr and Mrs Wyatt had given Alice the silver four-leaf clover pendant. It had not been on Christmas Day but golly, it had surely felt like it!

'I've usually been working,' she replied. 'But this will be my first in the outback. I cannot wait.'

Mrs McKinnley was delighted. 'We pull out the stops with the dinner and have a traditional pudding. Sometimes, if everyone is up for it, we may have a sing song and some of the boys play the banjo and I dabble with the piano. But it does depend how everyone is, particularly with coming to the end of lambing.'

'Yes, I can understand that and I'm more than happy to lend a hand in the kitchen.'

'Thank you, Alice. That will be most welcome,' said Mrs Heppler.

*

Alice loved being part of Christmas at the Station. After all the chores had been done, everyone went to change into their Sunday best, then they sat at the table for the McKinnley traditional Christmas feast. This had given Alice an opportunity to wear her pastel blue summer dress that Aunt Vera had bought for her.

Elsa had created wonders with the table by using Mrs McKinnley's best crockery and glassware while the ladies drank homemade lemonade and the men drank glasses of beer.

Mrs Heppler, Elsa, Mrs McKinnley and Alice delighted everyone when they laid out steaming hot dishes of chicken, goose and yearling mutton. And this was followed by plentiful crispy roast potatoes and a varied selection of fresh vegetables. Lastly, Mrs Heppler and Alice placed several jugs of steaming thick gravy on the table so everyone could help themselves.

The aroma was so mouth-watering that it was enough to make everyone salivate in anticipation of the oozing flavours to come. Feeling grateful to be among so many wonderful people, Alice was humble to the point of crying with happiness for being part of something so lovely. Mr McKinnley raised his glass in the air. 'Happy Christmas everyone!' and all followed suit, repeating the toast while the clinking of glasses reverberated around the room.

'Tuck in, everyone,' ordered Mrs McKinnley. 'Don't let it get cold.'

Instantly, many pairs of hands reached out for a bowl or pan of food and took their share before passing along to their neighbour, all the while chatting away until everyone had a plateful. In near synchronisation, empty bowls and pans were returned to the centre of the table then all that could be heard was the tinkling of cutlery and appreciation of a delicious meal.

Jack and Sylvia were enjoying their Christmas dinner despite doing their utmost to avoid the vegetables. And when Sylvia wasn't looking, Jack discreetly added a fork full of peas to Sylvia's plate. As usual, Mrs Heppler had cut up Emily's meal in small bite-sized pieces and was amused by constantly wiping Emily's chin from a stream of gravy. She was also like a coiled spring, ready to intercept the child's fingers from plunging into her dinner and ploughing them through her beautiful blonde hair at any moment.

'Ladies, that was beyond delicious,' said Ronnie in appreciation and raising his glass to them.

'Hear, hear,' agreed Mr McKinnley.

'Thank you all,' said Mrs McKinnley. 'It was magnificent and we enjoyed preparing it for you.'

'First outback Christmas, Alice,' remarked Ronnie, turning to her. 'What are you making of it so far?'

Since the beginning, Alice had been impressed that Ronnie always managed to look dapper, regardless of duty, and now, she had been a little taken aback because out of everyone, Ronnie spoke the least. She found him to be very reserved who acted much older than his twenty-five years. 'It's different but nonetheless wonderful, Ronnie. I know I've only been here a short while but I am enjoying my time and you all have been very kind. My first outback Christmas, how about that! Cheers everyone.'

They all responded by raising their glasses in the air.

Joe quickly patted his fingers on the edge of the table like he was pounding a drum. The room hushed. 'Tradition!' he announced and stood up, greeted by the roars and applause from his peers. 'I'll start. What do you call a sheep that goes crazy after shearing?'

Immediately everyone laughed, apart from Ronnie.

'Why is that funny?' he asked and looked at everyone around the table, shaking his head in bewilderment.

'It's the start of the joke,' said Ross.

'I know that, but nothing is funny yet...' he said, followed by a multitude of 'shhhh's all around.

Joe wasn't annoyed as such, but the momentum had gone, so he repeated, 'What do you call a sheep that goes crazy after shearing...? Shear madness!'

This was followed by raucous laughter. Alice looked at the puzzled look on Ronnie's face and went into a fit of giggles as Ronnie just shrugged his shoulders and took another sip of beer.

'Another!' shouted Squeak.

Wallace stood up. 'I saw a sheep tumbling down a hill... it was a lamb slide!'

Again, everyone roared with laughter for a few seconds before simultaneously peering at Ronnie who they knew would state the obvious and he didn't disappoint. 'But it's flat out here...'

Elsa, Mrs McKinnley and Alice made a start in clearing the table to make room for the pudding as Squeak took his turn. 'What do you call a sheep with no legs?'

'I know this one, I know this one,' shouted Ross enthusiastically. 'A cloud.'

Again, the room filled with laughter.

'You're thinking why a sheep would have no legs?' Squeak looked at Ronnie.

'Thank you, Squeak! Yes, I am.'

'You're smiling, Ronnie,' observed Mr McKinnley.

Ronnie couldn't keep up the pretence and broke into fits of laughter. 'Sorry, I couldn't keep that going for much longer!'

he said, to which he received a barrage of harmless heckling.

'You had us all fooled there for a moment, Ronnie,' said Mrs Heppler with relief that Emily had escaped unscathed by gravy. But she had been here before and was not out of the woods just yet knowing that custard would be her next challenge.

'Pudding anyone?' asked Mrs McKinnley who served up the portions to Alice who handed them around the table.

*

When the men returned from their nightly rounds, they gathered on the verandah to watch the sunset with a beer. Alice had helped the ladies to clear away then they also joined the men as Mrs McKinnley poured them a small sherry. Elsa arrived just in time to see the sunset after putting the children to bed.

As there was only limited seating on the verandah, Mr Price had brought out some of the kitchen chairs for the men while the ladies sat on the two-seater swing seat and armchairs.

'It's been a lovely day,' said Mrs McKinnley, taking a sip of sherry.

'Yes, it has,' replied Mrs Heppler, 'and the children had a grand time.'

'They're out like a light,' said Elsa.

Christmas night spent chatting with newfound family and friends was absolutely bliss to Alice and she enjoyed their reminisce of the year on McKinnley Station. Her mind wandered too, thinking about Aunt Vera, Pip and Tish and she wished she could also be with them this night. All too soon, everyone bade their goodnights and thanks for a good day.

*

Given that she had sipped two sherries' during the evening, it had been enough to give Mrs McKinnley the extra courage she needed to pursue the matter further. 'But why, Ben?' she asked her husband when they were alone on the verandah.

'Not today, Judith. Please.'

'I'm trying again to make amends. How many times do I have to say I am sorry? You know that I needed a lot of time after Sylvia was born. I had a rough time with it and then I was always so tired with the children and running the homestead...'

'Judith, this is old grounds. We don't have to torture ourselves over what is no more.'

'I cannot understand why you won't let me make it right? Sylvia is five years old now and that's how long it's been since we...'

'I'm not totally at fault here,' he said, looking at his wife. 'You continually pushed me away and wanted your own room. Yes, I understand that you couldn't cope, but too much time has gone by. We've moved on...'

'You're still screwing Elsa though, aren't you? I'm not stupid, I can tell.' She winced and regretted her coarse words. 'I am sorry, Ben, that was crude and unfair.'

'It was and I am sorry too, but we've been over this and you said that you were fine with the arrangement. Nothing has changed and no one will ever know – it's just how it is. I still love you, Judith, but that side of our lives is over and in the past. You have made that perfectly clear often enough.'

Judith knew that he was right but the strangest and most bizarre thing of all was that she liked and respected Elsa and considered her a good friend despite her having an affair with her husband. The women never spoke of the arrangement and no one suspected anything untoward going on, which was just as well because Judith could not live with the shame.

'You're right.' She smiled as he returned her brief embrace. 'I won't mention it ever again. Goodnight, Ben.' She left her husband to finish his beer and went back to her room.

CHAPTER TWENTY-SEVEN

Alice could not contain her enthusiasm. It was March 1939 and the District Rodeo had finally arrived. This year, Petersons Sheep Station would be hosting the annual event. The staff packed up the trucks, trailers and horseboxes, ready for the bumpy journey. The Peterson's station bordered the McKinnley's, so their journey of just over one hundred miles would be considerably shorter than anyone else's Mr Price had told her.

He also informed that he, Ronnie and Squeak would be staying behind at McKinnley because the Station could not be left unattended for the two-day event. They waved the convoy goodbye, watching as it left the yard, kicking up a dust cloud that enveloped the excited kelpies, then Alice smiled upon hearing Mr Price yell out, 'Bring home the cup, Alice!'

This had been the furthest that Alice had travelled since she had arrived at McKinnley Station. After hearing numerous stories about the rodeos, she was looking forward to meeting new people and to participate in some of the events.

There was one in particular that she had set her heart on.

Despite jackaroos far outnumbering jillaroos throughout the district, Alice had set her heart on winning the *Jillaroo 'A-jill-ity'* Course Cup. Wallace, Joe and Mr Price had built a mini assault course down near the corral and for the past month they had been training Alice and Finn. The whole team were confident that they had a fair chance in winning the event.

The Petersons had directed all their guests to the parking and camping zones where the McKinnley staff were allocated their own ample space. The ladies and Joe set up the camp and prepared the campfire in readiness for cooking while Mr McKinnley, Wallace and Ross had driven to another paddock to offload and settle in the horses. As with every rodeo, the men took it in shifts to stay with the horses including overnight. After a while they met up in a cleared paddock, known for the rodeo duration as the arena, before the scheduled events started.

'Come on, Alice, quick or you'll miss it,' urged Mrs Heppler when she sided up to her to watch the set of children's races. Sylvia was in the first lineup and there were ten riders in the four to six age range. 'COME ON, SYLVIA!' the McKinnley team encouraged.

Sylvia hated having to perform on-demand, wishing that she was back home. She didn't like the pony she had been allocated as basically this had caused a mammoth strop since they arrived. Mrs McKinnley was on alert, believing that her daughter would either storm off or would apply below minimum effort. She had been right, and the latter had conquered as her pony moseyed over the finish line in last place oblivious that it was meant to be a race. Sylvia had cheered up somewhat, knowing that she had won a private victory and took great pleasure in giving her mother a carefree smirk that spoke volumes.

Next, it was Jack's age group in the seven to nine years and he was fired up and ready to go. There were twelve riders, Jack being one of the youngest, but he gave it his all, getting off to a great start.

'JACK, JACK, JACK!' stormed the McKinnley team, urging him all the way down the half furlong stretch.

Alice could tell that the youngster was in a good position when he breezed by them. Knowing races as she did, she admired his natural ability and stance and wasn't at all surprised when he flew over the finish line much to the delight of all. *How different the siblings are*, she thought, joining in the congratulations.

There was nothing quite like being back in the thick of a bustling crowd, but for all the right reasons. Alice joined the throng, walking toward the enclosure, awaiting the main event of the evening. She guessed that there were a couple of hundred people who were beginning to spread out evenly to get a good view of the first bull rider.

'So sorry!' Alice apologised when she accidentally bumped shoulders with a woman who was aiming for the same free spot at the enclosure.

'You will be.' She spat. Alice summed up the feral woman, who appeared to be slightly older than she, knowing that she was no threat. Alice decided to ignore her while they waited for the event to start.

'Trouble?' whispered a handsome cowboy, leaning in close to Alice on her other side just as more people gathered around them to watch the event.

'Nah.' Alice shook her head while the woman took great offence and elbowed her, to which she again ignored, much to the woman's irritation and Alice knew it.

When the cowboy asked if she wanted to swap places, Alice looked up into gorgeous light blue eyes and her heart fluttered. 'I'm Dixon,' he said and despite standing next to this beautiful girl in the confined space, he did not have enough room to bring his hand up and successfully shake hands without the slightest risk of an innocent inappropriate touch. In order to complete the introduction, he had no other option but to extend his arm forward through the bar of the fence then bring it back round to meet hers.

'Alice.' She laughed. 'Nice to meet you...'

Before she had a chance to say that she was fine where she was, the feral woman spoke over her. 'Yes, you come on over here, darling.'

Alice and Dixon exchanged glances that said this could get quite awkward.

Just then another woman brusquely squeezed her way through to Dixon's other side. Alice fought the urge to laugh, knowing that the awkward situation may now ignite because the women were obviously sisters.

'Aren't you a pack of fine muscle?' She purred, taking the liberty of squeezing Dixon's biceps. 'Wanna have some fun after the event? We could sure give you a good time.'

'How tempting is that?' mocked Alice.

'Stay out of it, bitch—'

'Enough!' he said. 'Alice, would you care to join me and watch from somewhere else?' And when he stepped back, Alice was sandwiched between the sisters.

'Yes, I'd like that,' she said and took the opportunity to swap a gold bracelet from one sister to the other. When she joined Dixon, she looked back and pointed to the first feral sister. 'I like your bracelet...'

In total disbelief, the woman held up her wrist, turning it from side to side in amazement. Her mouth was agape and her sister's eyes fumed like the dark depths of hell. 'Why you little...' she started before her sister led her away by the hair and the gap they vacated was closed by spectators ignoring the feral family feud.

'What happened there?' Dixon asked, looking puzzled.

'I have no idea. Come on or we'll miss the start.' When Alice looked back at the sisters, she allowed herself a smug smile.

Just then the first bull rider was catapulted into the enclosure where the crowd's cheers surged in volume. Alice had never seen anything quite like it. The bucking bull spun around so fast like he was an explosive tornado in which to dispose the unwanted rider. It was exhilarating and she wanted to see much more. This was one of the most exciting things that she had ever seen as the rider was flung high into the air but managed to land upright and thankfully sustained no injury.

'How many more of these tonight?' she asked with delight.

'Another twenty-four. I've been to many of these. Quite exciting, isn't it?'

'Absolutely. I love it! Those guys are entertaining too.' She pointed to two men who were on the ground inside the enclosure dressed in bright colours.

'They are very important and do the most dangerous job of all. Their job is to distract the bull when the rider falls, to prevent him from getting trampled or killed.'

Her smile disappeared, remembering the frightening image of when that bull had almost bought her and Lucy down. She shuddered. It was too close for comfort.

'Are you alright?' he asked with concern. 'You seemed to have gone a little pale.'

'Yes, fine, thank you. I had no idea. That's terrifying.' She viewed the remaining rides much differently and found herself watching the clowns more as opposed to the actual bull rider. She observed how skilful they were and lightning fast with their reactions to interpret and intercept the bull's next move.

*

Feeling comfortable in her swag, Alice was enjoying camping out under the stars around the campfire alongside the men and Mrs Heppler while Mrs McKinnley, Elsa and the children slept in the tent. It had taken her quite a while to fall asleep because she couldn't stop thinking about Dixon. His smile, his laugh and his wit just wouldn't allow her to drift off as she wondered what it would be like to be wrapped in his embrace with his strong arms around her.

They had spent a great evening together watching the bull riders. He was excellent company, very attentive and had made her laugh. The butterflies in her stomach seemed to grow tenfold whenever she thought about the peck on the cheek when he said goodnight. He was handsome and strong, and his light blue eyes and blonde hair matched her own.

Dixon told her that he was travelling with the rodeo. He was part of a team who drove ahead to help the host station set up the enclosures. They had to ensure that the grounds and facilities were ready in time for when the crowds descended.

Despite little sleep, Alice arose feeling very refreshed. Elsa handed out hot tea and damper while the team got themselves ready for the morning's events. Alice, through a pleasant distraction, felt a little ashamed by almost forgetting about her upcoming jillaroo event.

'All set, Alice?' asked Mr McKinnley when he helped her to saddle up Finn.

'Yes, we're set. Aren't we, Finn?' she said, patting his neck as Finn bobbed his head, excitedly it seemed, perhaps sensing the importance of the day.

'That's good. I know you've both put in a lot of hard work, but the main thing is to just go out there and enjoy it... and bring back the cup to McKinnley!' he added for good measure.

'Will do, Mr McKinnley! See you later, everyone.' She mounted and led Finn toward the holding area while they waited their turn.

'Good luck, Alice!' They all chanted. Her heart fluttered when she saw Dixon wave to her. She bowed her head, acknowledging all their good wishes before her smile vanished. *This will be interesting*, she thought.

'My, my,' said the feral sister. 'It'll be a pleasure to thrash you, sweetheart.' Alice noticed her black eye. 'I'm set to win my third consecutive cup...'

Alice hadn't wanted to be nasty but reasoned that the sisters had started the fight, so she didn't feel too bad by retorting. 'I'm surprised that you know such a long word...'

The woman exploded with rage.

Before she recovered enough to respond, the gorgeous handsome cowboy that she had set her eye on the day before stepped up to Finn and hoisted Alice down, giving her a huge hug.

'Good luck, darling.' Dixon emphasised, placing a fleeting kiss on her lips and when he broke away, he winked and Alice knew exactly what was going on.

Although the kiss had been fleeting, it was no less powerful. The effects ploughed through her whole body. 'Hope you don't miss me too much, darling.' She played along and remounted, guiding Finn to the other side of the holding area where the fuming feral sister followed.

The competition was hard and the leading time to beat seemed nigh impossible when Finn stood on the starting line.

All the while Alice was reassuring, stroking Finn's neck and speaking softly to him. She focused on the starting pistol, trying to intercept it to the millisecond. Finn responded like lightning when it sounded. He easily cleared the first few jumps over bales of hay that varied in height as Alice guided him through the obstacles in number order.

Concentrating, horse and rider blocked out cheers, roars and encouragement as they sprinted between the two barrels located at opposite ends of the arena where Finn's skilful sharp turns saved precious seconds from their time score. Then it was down to Alice's balance and agility to steer and perfect the high and low flag praying that there wouldn't be a sudden breeze to lift them just beyond her grasp. In preparation for the high flag, she had raised the stirrups up a notch so she could stand up higher. This enabled her to stretch with all her might and snatch it then return to the saddle before quickly reaching down to collect the low flag positioned at Finn's belly height as he thundered past.

Much to Alice's joy and delight, she managed to secure both flags, which was something that she had only achieved once before and hoped she kept her nerve steady upon approaching the final obstacle. The fence looked impossibly high, bringing flashbacks to when Lucy had catapulted through the air to save them as Finn leapt with all his might, clearing the top panel with ease and sprinting over the finish line. They made a perfect round in the fastest time. The crowd roared and her supporters yearned that she kept onto the lead.

'Well done, Alice!' She and Finn were surrounded by Dixon and the McKinnley team when they ran over to her.

'Whatever happens, you made an excellent round. It was

just perfect. We're all so proud of you both,' said Mr McKinnley.

'Thank you all so much. Finn did very well, didn't you, boy?' Alice patted her hero. 'Goodness, that was great fun and I can't believe that I managed to keep hold of those flags and the reins! Oh, I'd like to introduce you all to Dixon...'

Everyone had been so caught up that they forgot to watch the final competitor.

'And the winner is Alice and Finn from McKinnley Station.'

The crowd went wild to honour the new jillaroo champion.

'Come on over, Alice, and collect the Cup.'

In her proudest moment ever, Alice walked up onto the stage to collect the silver cup from Mr Peterson. 'Congratulations, Alice. That was a perfect round and a great time. Please accept this cup to take back to McKinnley where it will be kept for one year until it's presented to next year's winner. But this,' he said, handing Alice a silver belt buckle, 'is yours to keep. Congratulations again.'

Alice was euphoric. She had never won anything before in her life and the feeling was indescribable. She kept looking at the cup and buckle. It was ironic that she immediately thought of her parents, knowing that her mother would have been so very proud while her father would immediately sum up the value and take them to the nearest pawn shop.

The McKinnley team couldn't congratulate her enough and it was as if Alice was floating on air. She felt privileged to be among kind and caring people. It was a very humble feeling.

'Dixon, eh! Where is he and what do you know about him?' Mrs Heppler asked, looking around before setting her eyes back on Alice. She smiled and raised her eyebrows at the same time, hoping for some more information as the women headed to the ladies' tent for some light refreshment ahead of the cake tasting competition.

'He had to go and help set up for the next event. He's twenty and works for the rodeo where he also goes ahead with a team to help set up the site before everyone arrives.'

'That sounds interesting. How did you meet?' encouraged Mrs McKinnley with interested delight.

'We started chatting last night and just got on, he said working at the rodeo was just a stop gap...'

'How about he comes to work with us?' said Mrs McKinnley. 'We could always use another pair of hands. He looks strong enough.'

'I'm not sure what he wants to do, Mrs McKinnley.' Considering that they had only just met, Alice felt a bit awkward.

'There's a simple answer to that,' Mrs Heppler said. 'Let's go ask him and while we're about it, I'd avoid last year's champion if I were you. To say she has been looking daggers at you is an understatement!'

CHAPTER TWENTY-EIGHT

Soon enough the team arrived back at McKinnley Station and were greeted by Mr Price, Ronnie and Squeak who came out to lend a hand.

'Good to see you back,' Mr Price addressed the ladies. 'We can't thank you all enough for leaving us the lovely meals. Because between us we couldn't even boil water without burning it!'

'Nice to know we've been missed,' said Mrs McKinnley. 'I'll put the kettle on.'

'Well?' asked Mr Price as he, Ronnie and Squeak looked at Alice expectantly.

'Ta-da!' Alice produced the cup and the buckle.

'Well done, lass. Congratulations!' said Mr Price.

'Knew you'd do it,' said Squeak. 'We've been thinking of you.'

'Never had a doubt.' Ronnie smiled. 'You're the jillaroo champion for the whole district. And the first at McKinnley. Now that's a great achievement. Well done.'

'Thank you all.' And before she could make introductions,

Mr McKinnley beat her to it.

'Gentlemen, this is Dixon and he will be joining us as another station hand. Dixon, this is Mr Price, our station manager. Squeak, our other station hand and Ronnie, our stockman.'

The men all shook hands.

'Nice to meet you all and to be here. I won't let you down.'

'You are more than welcome,' said Mr McKinnley. 'Squeak, could you please show Dixon the quarters and give a general tour?'

'Sure thing, Mr McKinnley.'

'And this evening,' said Mrs McKinnley, 'we'll celebrate Alice's win and an overall success at the rodeo with a spit roast down by the corral.'

And with that, the men went about their business and the women settled back into their station duties.

Mrs Heppler and Elsa prepared the slaughtered pig and placed the metal rod through the carcass to which Ronnie and Ross carried it down to the fire pit. They positioned the ends of the rod into the hooks of the metal stands suspending the meat over what would become a controlled fire where it would take a few hours to cook from mid-afternoon. This was Mrs Heppler's domain and a job that she took extremely seriously. She stayed down at the spit and regularly turned it, in between reading her favourite book, so it cooked evenly over the fire. And as always, to show absolute commitment to the role, she taste-tested toward the end of the afternoon to check that it was cooking as it should. This ensured that come the time, the meat would fall onto the plate with its oozing juices. The carcass would provide sufficient portions to keep everyone well-fed for a few days and served with a varied menu to delight everyone's palate.

As cooking progressed, the waft intensified to the point of mouth-watering when it travelled among the light breeze, finding eager noses whether they were in the homestead or down at the stables. And as the hours passed, tastebuds were tantalised while waiting for the magic words that it was ready to be served.

There was much chatter regarding recent events at the rodeo. McKinnley Station had many reasons to celebrate because not only did Alice and Finn win the Jillaroo Cup and Dixon became the newest member of the team but Mrs McKinnley had also come a respectable third in the cake competition.

'So, what do you make of it so far, Dixon?' asked Mr McKinnley.

'I like it. You're a friendly bunch and I'm looking forward to being in one place for a while.'

'You must've travelled around quite a bit?' commented Wallace.

'Yes, a fair bit. This is good, Mrs Heppler,' Dixon said and everyone voiced their agreeance.

'Thank you muchly! What about you young'uns?'

'Good, Mrs Heppler,' said Jack while Emily nodded, chomping away, and Sylvia didn't acknowledge her at all.

'You go for a stroll, Alice,' Mrs McKinnley whispered. 'Mrs Heppler, Elsa and I will clear up. Now go,' she prompted and they watched Alice and Dixon walk down near the shearing shed as twilight approached.

Wallace considered himself to be like a big brother to Alice and while he couldn't quite put his finger on it, he wasn't too sure about Dixon as he also watched the pair walk away.

'Who would have thought that only a few days ago we hadn't met and now I've moved here and started a new job?'

'It's crazy, isn't it? If those *charming* sisters hadn't started anything, then we wouldn't have met at all.'

'Yes, we would.' Dixon turned to look at her. 'I had my eyes on you before you even knew it. Hmm, that doesn't sound as good as it should, does it?' He laughed. 'I wanted to meet you, Alice. There was something about you and I also liked the way you were with the sisters, and from what I saw you had that under control.'

'I can take care of myself.' Her heart skipped a beat upon looking into his mesmerising eyes.

'I see that. I've also met lots like them – they're harmless.'

'I bet you get a lot of attention.'

'No, not much. I think they had a bit to drink. Can I kiss you, Alice?'

'You never asked the last time.' She smiled.

'That's true. But it was wrong of me as it was a spur-of-the-moment thing to wind the sister up. Perhaps not my best idea. Unlike my question.'

Alice stood on her tiptoe and kissed him.

This was Alice's first proper kiss because she would never acknowledge the one with Stockbury, thus it did not count. That had been a necessary decoy, while this time she wanted to savour the kiss and when Dixon wrapped his arms around her, it caused her senses to soar to the moon and back. His kiss was soft and gentle, making her feel all gooey on the inside. When his lips parted, she matched him and when their tongues lightly touched, it caused a surge of electricity between them as their kiss deepened. After a while, Alice fought the urge to smile, caused by a pleasant sharp pin sensation from his stubble and a few precious moments later they broke away.

'That was amazing, Alice,' he said quite breathlessly. 'Were you laughing?' He smiled.

Alice roared with giggles. 'Your stubble tickled.'

*

Over the coming months, Alice and Dixon's desire increased. Station life was hard work, and the days were long, but they tried to spend as much time together as possible.

'Come with me,' he said, leading her over to the staff accommodation. 'All the men are out on a muster, apart from Mr Price, who will be in the office with Mr McKinnley for the best part of the evening. We have the place to ourselves and I thought that you deserved a treat.'

'Where are we going?' She giggled when they neared the quarters and walked around the other side of the building.

Before her was one of the most beautiful and picturesque romantic settings that she had ever seen and with the sun close to descent they had a perfect view of the endless rugged outback. Alice was gobsmacked. Dixon had filled the old tin bath, that he strategically positioned, so they would have the best view of the sunset.

'How?' She indicated, pointing to the bubbles.

'Courtesy of Mrs Heppler. She gave me some a while ago, still not sure why she thought I needed them, because I prefer the shower.' He shrugged and sniffed his armpits. 'And don't worry, no one knows where we are or what we're doing.' He lit a small lantern and placed it behind them. 'What do you think?'

'Oh, Dixon. I love it. Thank you for doing this.'

'I'm pleased you love it. Been planning this for a couple of days now.' He lifted her into his arms and kissed her passionately.

Alice was in heaven. 'Your kisses make me go all tingly.'

They smiled, not taking their eyes off of each other.

'This is amazing, Dixon.'

He placed her back on the ground and she dipped her fingers into the water. 'It's warm. I didn't expect that!'

'Don't sound so shocked. I have another bucket heating up.'

'Then what are we waiting for?' They kicked off their boots before quickly liberating each other of their clothing. Alice couldn't stop laughing when they stepped in. 'So, what's the seating arrangement?'

'Good question.' They laughed again while standing naked within the soapy bubbles in the middle of the tin bath out in the open air. 'Ah, if we shuffle around a bit then I'll sit at the top end and you sit in front of me so we can watch the sunset together,' he suggested.

Soon they were sitting comfortably, without losing too much precious water in the process. Alice leaned back against him, enjoying the whole scene while Dixon scooped the warm water and bubbles up onto her breasts. She turned her head toward him and they kissed again. It was just perfect.

'One other thing.'

'Don't tell me you have a brass band who'll be appearing around the side of the quarters at any moment?'

'Damn, I missed an opportunity there! I don't, but I do have this.' He reached down and lifted two glasses then picked up the bottle of whisky and poured them a shot. 'Here's to you, Alice.' They clinked glasses and savoured the liquid that left an extra inner warmth.

For quite a few moments, they cherished the ambience of the outback and its spectacular sunset with the faint glow of the lantern behind them. After a little while, the water became tepid, which only added to their comfort in alleviating the humidity of the evening.

'Happy?' he asked.

'Very. I shall remember this moment always.'

'Trying to do things a little different in order to tempt you back to my bunk.'

'Who said I need tempting?' Alice stood up and stepped out of the bath, taking time to dab her feet with her shirt before putting her boots on.

'Glad to hear that, Miss Johnson. And this may not be as romantic, but you will be pleased to know that I have fixed the rusty springs.'

They broke into rapturous laughter and headed to the quarters, enjoying the flirtatious night air embracing their nakedness.

CHAPTER TWENTY-NINE

It was now July, and the station was as busy as ever. 'Hey pickle, aren't you extra beautiful today? What are you wearing?' asked Alice when Emily walked into the kitchen with her mother.

'My new dress.' Emily twirled much to the delight of the ladies.

'It's the best dress I've ever seen. Did you make it?' Alice enjoyed playing with Emily who squealed with delight and shook her head.

'Mish Inley.' To which all the ladies smiled endearingly whenever Emily tried to pronounce Mrs McKinnley.

'Well, she has done a grand job, Pickle. You look like a princess. I will call you Princess Pickle.'

Emily squealed with delight. 'It's for my birthday.'

'Your mother told me that you will be three!'

Emily nodded.

'You're a big girl now.' And Alice hugged the little girl whom she so adored.

'We just came in to show you all. Now, Emily, we've got to go and get changed before we feed the chooks. Come on,' said Mrs Heppler, leading Emily back through to her room.

'Aww that's so sweet. She has grown so much since I have been here, hasn't she? Well, all the children have. Your Jack is getting more handsome by the day, Mrs McKinnley. And Sylvia is... growing up fast too.' Alice hoped that the minute pause hadn't highlighted that she found it difficult to find something positive to say.

Mrs McKinnley had detected the pause but she didn't hold it against Alice. It was true. Even she had found Sylvia quite challenging at times. Elsa had more to do with the children, so she wasn't all that surprised. Mrs McKinnley loved her children; however, she accepted that she wasn't a natural mother, unlike Elsa. With no children of her own, Elsa was more of a mother to Jack and Sylvia than she would ever be.

The following evening, Alice was quieter than her usual chatterbox self and it was noticed.

'You alright, love?' queried Mrs Heppler with concern.

'Cat gotcha tongue?' joked Squeak. 'You were moping down at the stables today and that's not like you at all.'

'Just a bit tired. Probably have an early night after I check on Finn.' The others may have been convinced but Mrs Heppler wasn't.

'Everything alright?' Mrs Heppler prodded Dixon after Alice had left the table and when he nodded that it was, she said, 'Well, don't just sit there. Go after her, you big galah.'

Dixon found her in Finn's stall settling him in for the

night. 'Have I done something to upset you, Alice?' he asked gently, approaching Finn and patting his neck.

'I'm late, Dixon.' She turned to face him.

It wasn't until he saw the expression on her face that the penny dropped. Alice may not have heard it but from his immediate reaction, she knew his heart had shattered and with it, hers also. Despite the shock, she gave him the benefit of the doubt because she had known for nearly a week.

After an uncomfortable silence, she prompted, 'Are you going to say something?'

'I'm not sure what to say, in all honesty.' He ran his fingers through his hair as all kinds of thoughts stampeded through his head. How could he say that he wasn't ready to be a father – that he was only twenty and didn't want to settle down? But then again, Alice was only eighteen and it was probably the same for her. He decided not to say anything, not that he had anything that he could say to her. He was angry with himself. How careless they had been. He thought they had been careful; how could this happen? Why did it happen? What should he do?

He was so confused.

Alice wanted a hug. She wanted to know that everything would be alright. She wanted reassurance, support but most of all, she wanted not to be pregnant. She wanted children but not right now. How could she continue to do her job? Would the McKinnley's sack her and turn her out? They would be so ashamed and she couldn't blame them for that.

She was so confused.

For what seemed an eternity, Alice and Dixon held their

silence and embraced in the middle of Finn's stall, each lost within their own thoughts.

*

The next morning during breakfast, Elsa walked around with a pot of tea and filled any cup that was held out and enquired. 'Where's Dixon?'

'He's gone,' replied Ronnie without much concern. Alice sat bolt upright.

'Left for work already? He's keen,' remarked Wallace.

'Not work. Gone,' Ronnie repeated. 'Doesn't anyone listen?'

The colour drained from Alice's cheeks, believing that Dixon had skipped breakfast to avoid her. She turned to Ronnie. 'What did you say?'

'Elsa, what have you put in the tea this morning?' Then he looked over at Alice. 'Didn't he tell you?'

'That's absurd,' remarked Mrs McKinnley, shaking her head. 'He couldn't have just gone. Not without saying anything.'

Mrs Heppler glanced at Alice who was looking bewildered and decided to have a chat with her alone.

'The damn truck has gone!' fumed Mr McKinnley, walking in from the yard.

'Dixon's gone and left,' said Mr Price.

'Why the hell would he do that and take the truck?' He sat down with an annoying thump and looked at Alice. 'Did he say anything to you at all?' Then added more calmly upon seeing the devastation on her face, 'Look, if you have had a row, then he'll calm down and will be back. One of those things, you'll see.'

'We did have a row.' It was quiet for a few moments before it all became too much with all eyes upon her. Leaving the table and plucking her Akubra from the rack, she left to go and check on Finn.

Wallace beat Mrs Heppler to it. 'Hey, Alice, wait,' he shouted and when he caught up with her, he said, 'I am sorry he's gone. He's an idiot.'

It broke his heart when she turned to him with tears streaming down her face and melted into his arms for the hug she so desperately needed.

The following day, Mr Peterson radioed through to inform them that Dixon had turned up at their station and he was going to travel back to Burston on the mail plane later that day. Mr Peterson said that the truck would be safe at his property for whenever it was convenient for the McKinnleys to collect it.

Wallace and Ross offered to drive to the Peterson's to collect the truck, but Mr McKinnley denied the request, knowing full well that Wallace would give Dixon more than a piece of his mind. Instead, he told them to go in a few days; while he understood how they felt, it wouldn't do anyone any good if Wallace got himself arrested.

*

A few days later, Alice awoke to her monthly bleed causing a swarm of emotions. If it was at all possible, she had felt simultaneous relief, sadness, happiness and anger for Dixon's utter cowardice in abandoning her in such a cruel way. *If only I had waited a little longer, then he would still be here,* she reasoned but then she wouldn't have been enlightened to his true colours.

Alice's selfish thoughts surpassed her guilt, although she knew that her mother would be deeply appalled and disappointed that she had been with a man before being married. She had ignored the immorality of what they were doing simply because they just couldn't help themselves.

Trusting him with all her being, she had given Dixon her heart and he had shredded it to smithereens. She had looked up to him for strength, remembering how he had stood up for her at the rodeo, where deep down he had been nothing but a cold-hearted coward and therefore just like her father. This was probably too harsh but at this moment in time, that was how his betrayal dominated her state of mind. He was heartless. They were all heartless. She cried anguished tears into her pillow.

During the following week, Alice tried to regain her old strength and persona to when she had left Sydney when she had been tougher, guarded and reserved. But it was difficult. She was now a different person due to living with Pip and Tish and everyone in between. They were all good people and her stance had changed for the better. And while she had embraced the change, her defences had weakened.

But no more.

Seeing Dixon for what he was, her heart not only began to mend, but she made sure it reinforced itself with steel. Believing a corner was turning, Alice ploughed head-on into her work.

The McKinnley team understood her heartbreak and

gave her the time and space that she needed while keeping an unobtrusive eye on her. Mrs Heppler tried her utmost to cheer her up.

'Fancy a ride down to the lower paddock to check on the fences?' she asked.

'Sorry, Mrs Heppler. Mr Price has me rostered out with Ronnie this afternoon...'

'Now, don't you worry about that I will sort it with Mr Price. Go and get yourself ready. I'll pack us a little snack and we'll get down to the stables.'

*

Alice was at her happiest whenever she was out riding Finn and for a winter's day, it was very pleasantly warm.

'It's beautiful out here,' she commented, loving the rugged scenery and ochre ground.

'It sure is,' replied Mrs Heppler. 'This is just grand. I don't get out and about on horseback as much as I'd like, you know, with working in the kitchen, homestead and garden, and Emily of course. This is quite a treat for me as well, I can tell you.'

Alice appreciated what Mrs Heppler was saying and doing. And what better way than being out in the open with no one around in such a serene environment? 'I am alright, Mrs Heppler. Honestly.'

'Well, I know that, love. Just wanted to spend some time with you. You can always talk to me, you know that, right? Look at me as your big, big sister or something like that!' They laughed. 'I know you're hurting and we both agree that he was a swine for upping sticks in the way in which he did, all because of an argument. You have got to take the rough with the smooth. But you're both young and first love can be hard to get over...'

Alice bowed her head and began to cry.

How she hated herself for it when believing that she had shed every single tear. 'Sorry,' she managed as Finn pulled to a stop as if he understood that his special person was upset.

Mrs Heppler flinched for bringing it up but knowing that it had to be said in order to move on. 'It's alright, love. There's just us, let it all out. Scream if you have to. No one will hear you out here. Let's get to that tree over there, dismount and give the horses some water and I'll get our flask of tea and we'll take a moment. Come on.'

It was a good idea and she wanted nothing more than to scream, 'You bastarrrrd,' at the top of her lungs but knowing it would spook the horses. Instead, she added it to the thousands of others she had shouted from within.

By the time they sat against the tree in the shade, Alice had composed herself and when they started to drink their tea, she gave a brief laugh.

'This reminds me of when I was at Nerra Creek. I was out with my horse, Lucy. Goodness, I miss her. Anyway, Lucy was grazing and I was sitting like we are now enjoying a flask of tea when she suddenly whinnied in alarm. It turned out that we were in the paddock with the fiercest bull that you'd ever see. It was a very close thing, and I was so fortunate that Lucy hadn't bolted leaving me behind. With seconds to spare, Lucy made it to the boundary fence where she thankfully jumped it.'

'That sounds bloody frightening. You've given me shivers just by listening to it. I won't sleep now. What a nightmare that was.'

'Not the worst,' Alice said without thinking as Mrs Heppler's eyebrows raised in question like they always did when she latched onto something she wasn't prepared to let go of.

'My start in life was tough.' Alice was unsure where all this was coming from, but now seemed like as good a time as any. 'To cut a very long story short, my father was not a person that you'd want to meet down a dark alley. When I was little, he and his associate dumped a dead body in my room in the middle of the night. I still have nightmares from time to time, recalling when I had to get out of bed and step around it in the dark. In my nightmares, his hand shoots out and grabs my ankle and I trip over and end up staring into his dead eyes... but I don't want to talk about that anymore.'

Mrs Heppler's eyebrows raised a little higher, possibly reaching their limit. She had so many questions and it was clear that this poor child had experienced much tragedy and misfortune in her young life. And now there was Dixon, to boot.

'I don't know where to begin...' She looked at the young woman with compassion.

'It's alright, Mrs Heppler. I don't expect you to. It is a part of my life that I don't wish to dwell on. It just came out; sorry, I shouldn't have told you that. Yes, I've been through some tough times, but my life has changed for the better. I know that. Meeting you in Fremantle was meant to be. But I'd rather you not tell anyone about the dead body.'

'You have my word and yes, I was meant to bump into you.' They both laughed at the opportune pun.

'I have spoken to Mrs McKinnley and told her the barest of my childhood; she knows it wasn't a happy time for me and that I ran away but not much else.'

'I won't tell anyone. I may be a gruff old bird at times, but my word is sacred. And you can trust me with anything you wish to say. Anytime. Alright?'

'Alright.' They toasted their tin cups of tea.

'You're pregnant, aren't you?' And by the look on her face, Mrs Heppler knew that to be true. 'That explains why he scuppered. The bastard.'

Upon Alice saying, 'I was,' she felt a whole lot better that someone else knew. Particularly Mrs Heppler whom she respected knowing that it wouldn't go any further.

'And by his sudden departure, I take it he doesn't know that you're not?'

'Correct. The night before he left, I told him that I was late, and I am never late. I truly believed that I was pregnant but my usual bleed came a few days later. It was a huge shock for him, I understand that and appreciate we're both young, but...'

'Doesn't excuse for what he did though. I can see you are getting back to your old self and as I've said before, if you ever want to talk about it, I will always listen. Now, we'll better finish up here and make tracks back as I'm meant to be helping with the dinner.'

'Thank you, Mrs Heppler. You're a real tonic.'

'Even better when it's served with alcohol!'

The women were enjoying the pleasant ride back and the horses were content being fed and watered and were approaching the paddocks near the stables. Alice was marvelling at the peace and quiet and Mrs Heppler's thoughts were buzzing with every conceivable scenario as to what the young woman had endured during her childhood. But for now, all she could do was to reassure that she was there for her whenever she needed...

In an instant, she snapped to the present when Finn reared up without warning. Alice was also taken off guard, losing her grip on the reins, pommel and stirrups and tumbled over Finn's rump to land with a hard thump to the ground.

'ALICE!' shouted Mrs Heppler before instantaneously pulling her pistol and blowing the head off the snake before it had a chance to strike again. Finn bolted then after a few moments he seemed to stumble before falling heavily to the ground on his side.

Alice's ears were ringing from the close range shot and fought to regain her feet, having sustained no serious injury. Although winded, it did not stop her sheer determination in running as fast as she could over to Finn as Mrs Heppler's horse overtook her. Finn was now her main priority, knowing it was a blessing that the gunshot would've been heard back at the homestead and the alarm raised.

She jumped down from her horse and ran over to Finn who was obviously distressed. As well as being bitten, she saw that his front right leg was broken, caused when he stumbled down a shallow crevice. She had no option but to pull out her pistol one more time.

'NOOOOOO,' screamed Alice, seeing what Mrs Heppler was about to do as she skidded to a halt on her knees beside Finn cradling his head.

His cries were heartbreaking and when she looked at his leg and then into his eyes, she knew that Mrs Heppler was right. Tears streamed down her face as she kissed Finn's nose for the final time. She arose, taking off her jacket and covering his head before holding out her hand to Mrs Heppler who handed her the pistol.

Taking a deep breath, Alice put Finn out of his misery and the shot echoed all around them.

*

The golden rule on McKinnley Station was to always inform staff of the planned location before a journey was undertaken. They were also realistic knowing that shots were rarely fired unless there was an emergency of some kind. For situations such as this Joe, Ross and Squeak had arrived, carrying a first aid kit and necessary tools to cover whatever crisis they encountered.

After much deliberation, Mrs Heppler had managed to persuade Alice to leave Finn and to ride back with her to the homestead. The men reassured her that they would take good care of Finn as they waited for a while until the women were a suitable distance away before they started to dig the grave. When they arrived back and dismounted,

Mrs Heppler led her horse into the stable and told Wallace what had happened, leaving it to him to organise what was needed in which to bury Finn. Then Mrs Heppler guided her friend up to the homestead.

Alice had been numb and declined all offers of company, comfort and food, opting for solitude as she retired to her room. Her heart was yet again broken. The family and staff had sat down at the kitchen table and listened to what Mrs Heppler had told them about the tragedy where she had been right about the shots being heard at the homestead.

The following couple of days were hard and just when Alice thought that she hadn't any tears left, another wave would flow. She was up and about, although quieter than usual but avoided going down to the stables. Mr McKinnley and Mr Price were considerate regarding her duties and Elsa tried to involve Alice more in the entertainment of the children to which she seemed to enjoy.

'I am responsible,' Mrs Heppler admitted to Elsa and Mrs McKinnley after breakfast a few days later. 'Can't help but stew over it.'

'Come. Sit down,' prompted Mrs McKinnley. 'You too, Elsa.' She carried three teacups over to the table and Elsa poured out the tea.

'It's one of those tragic things,' Elsa began. 'Alice knows that.'

'She's right,' said Mrs McKinnley. 'And deep down you know that too.' The women slowly sipped their tea.

'Poor child. First Dixon then Finn – how much more can she take?' Mrs Heppler shook her head.

'We must do something positive,' Mrs McKinnley announced as the ladies looked to her for an answer. 'Open to suggestions, of course, but something like a memorial of some kind. Somewhere for Finn to be remembered or a cross with his name by his grave. Something like that...'

'I think that's a lovely idea.' The ladies turned to see Alice enter the kitchen. 'Don't feel responsible, Mrs Heppler.'

Her heart skipped a beat and she blushed, which was unheard of.

'You've all been so kind. Perhaps we can have a roast spit down by the corral and stables sometime in honour of Finn?'

'Consider it done. Good timing as well. Sorry, I did not mean it quite like that. Purely because no one is rostered out on a muster. We'll do it tomorrow evening as the dinner is already underway for tonight.'

'Thank you, Mrs McKinnley.' Alice picked up a teacup and joined them at the table.

Later that day, unbeknown to anyone, she entered the stables and sat in Finn's stall. 'I'm so sorry, Finn, for what happened to you. You were truly a great horse and I loved you so very much.' She turned around on the bale and brought her knees up, wrapping her arms around them as she tried to imagine him standing there and talking to her as he always did whenever she groomed him. His short burst of whinnies always seemed perfectly timed whenever she spoke to him.

Standing up, Alice retrieved her switchblade from her boot and walked to the far wall of his stall.

It took only a few minutes to carve 'RIP Finn. Alice 1939'

then she stood back and looked at her tribute to a great horse who would never be forgotten. And as an apt finishing touch, she wedged the silver belt buckle that they had won together at the rodeo, next to the carving between the wall and a supporting beam.

CHAPTER THIRTY

On Friday, 1 September 1939, McKinnley Station heard the devasting news via radio that World War II had begun in Europe. During the coming days, Mr McKinnley kept everyone informed when he announced that Great Britain and France had declared war on Germany on 3 September.

Born in Australia of German descent, Mrs Heppler was very concerned for her family. But she knew without doubt that the war hadn't or wouldn't affect anyone's opinion of her and likewise it was the same for her as everyone hoped and prayed that the war would soon be over.

In the meantime, it was business as usual as the Station prepared for the upcoming shearing season. At the start of the year, Mr McKinnley and Mr Price had planned the whole process to bring shearing forward a fortnight earlier than the year before. This meant that the shearing team would arrive at the end of the first week in October for their four weeks stay, concluding that shearing and lambing would be complete before Christmas.

Hopefully!

Alice had been looking forward to the shearing season because it would complete the Station's annual events since she had started last December. During discussions over dinner, she had listened when Mr Price listed the tasks in preparation for bringing in the sheep.

'But first,' he said. 'We need to get the shearing sheds up and working and all facilities, including the shearing quarters ready. I've drawn up a roster where you will see that I move you around a lot. This will give you time and experience in all areas and I'm sure the team will be helpful. If not, let me know.'

'Thanks, Mr Price. I'm ready to go.' She smiled. 'What's the plan for tomorrow?'

'Don't be too keen, Alice.' Ross laughed, finishing his meal.

'Nah, doesn't pay you to be too keen,' chirped in Squeak.

'Makes the rest of us look bad.' Joe smiled.

'That doesn't take much!' joked Wallace.

'I feel I should say something here.' Everyone looked at Ronnie expectantly. 'But...' A pin drop would have been deafening at this point. He just shrugged his shoulders and carried on eating.

'Bloody hell. Ronnie!' exclaimed Joe.

'Language, Joseph!' admonished Mrs McKinnley, much to everyone's glee, apart from Ronnie.

'Sorry, Mrs McKinnley,' he said, feeling like a naughty child just as Squeak and Ross swiftly kicked him under the table and snickered.

*

Alice declined Joe's offer to step back when the men went into the sheds to dispose of the nasties that had taken up residence.

'I need to do this, Joe,' she said. 'Teach me what I need to do and I'll do it.' The men admired her guts and have-a-go-spirit.

She bunched up her golden plait and stuffed it under her Akubra and followed Wallace, Joe, Ronnie, Squeak and Ross into the scorching shearing shed where the air was thick, musty and stale. The men carried hessian sacks and arm-length sticks, chosen due to their small protrusion-like prongs on the end in which to capture the snake heads.

'The idea is to get the snake safely into the hessian,' said Squeak. 'If you watch you'll see that the boys do it differently. There are a number of ways, but it's finding the one that best works for you. Ronnie and I, we prefer to pin the snakes head by the prong directly onto the ground then grip the tail and lift it into the sack headfirst. While the others lift the snakes head off the ground first via the prong they then grasp the tail and place it into the sack, also headfirst.'

Alice was trying to fathom out which way she would be comfortable with...

'Over here,' beckoned Wallace. She walked over to him. 'See? Under the bench there, it's a brown snake.'

Following his gaze, she had to admit that the creature didn't look too scary, while understanding that one bite would mean imminent death and that bought a wave of emotion remembering when Finn had reared up and bolted.

Concentrating on the present, she watched Wallace

approach the juvenile with caution while maintaining a safe distance and crouching down. The snake did not appear agitated when he slowly moved the prong closer. In fact, it obliged by slithering up onto the forked hook where he lifted the stick a few inches off of the ground and moved it out from under the bench while grasping the tail. He stood back up and lowered the stick while keeping the tail upright. Even though the snake was now upside down it was strong enough to double back on itself. To prevent this, Wallace kept its head within the crook of the prong and at arm's distance he moved toward Alice who held the sack open for him to place inside. He then took it from her, clenching the top closed in one hand while spinning the sack around with the other to secure the opening.

Alice's heart was beating wildly. Wallace smiled at her, admiring her mettle. 'You alright?'

'Yes. That was scary. What do you do with them now?'

'We release them back into the wild.' And he laughed reading her expression. 'Yes, I know we're already in the wild but we take them much further out.'

All in all, the team collected eight snakes from the shearing shed before gathering around for further instruction from Wallace. 'Not bad for an hour's work,' he praised.

'Are you sure you have them all?'

'Pretty much, Alice. But always be alert as you can never be one hundred per cent sure,' Ross said.

'Yes, that's true. I almost saw someone put his hand on one once, until I...' She stopped but it was too late.

The men looked at her questionably. 'Until you what?' asked Ronnie.

'I stabbed it,' she said before adding, 'It was a lucky throw.'

'A distance throw? Those blighters don't hang around if they feel threatened,' said Ross.

'There's more to this.' Squeak looked at Alice admiringly. 'Ross is right – it was a distance throw, wasn't it?'

'Therefore, your reflexes were superfast and controlled,' continued Ross.

'So, after all this time we're learning you're good with a knife?' said Wallace. They all stared at her.

'You mean like this one?' Alice felt comfortable with showing her switchblade to the men she now considered family. A few moments ago, she was cross with herself by inadvertently admitting to what she had done but now she was fine with it.

Wallace, Joe, Ronnie, Squeak and Ross all gathered around, admiring the blade and some of them let out whistles when she released the safety.

'That's quite a piece, Alice,' said Ross. 'Can you still handle it?'

She threw it past them, the blade digging deep into the far wooden wall of the shed.

'I guess so!' he exclaimed.

'A lucky throw.' She retrieved her blade.

'Can feel a contest coming on, boys,' said Joe. 'Fancy your chances, Alice?' He smiled.

'Better than yours, Joe.' She laughed with them all.

'Set up the target, Ronnie,' instructed Wallace.

Ronnie walked over to the far wall and studied it for a moment before pointing out a knot in the wood.

'That's your target,' he announced to the men's dismay.

'Come on, Ronnie. That's not a target, it's a damn ant...'

'Too hard for you, Wallace?' she challenged, winking at him. 'I'd hate for you to be upstaged in front of your fellow workers, but I'm happy to give it a go. If it makes you feel better, you can stand closer to the target.'

The men looked with scepticism, not sure if she was bluffing or not.

'No bluff,' she responded and scored a line on the floor with the heel of her boot around fifteen feet away from the target. 'Do you all wish to have a practice throw first like I did?'

The men realised that they had already lost before they had even begun but proceeded anyway to take one throw apiece in quick succession before retrieving their knives together.

'Just to make it more interesting,' she said. 'How about the one nearest the target misses their next turn in emptying the dunnies. Deal?'

'Deal,' said Wallace, accepting for everyone when he stepped up to the mark and got himself comfortable by limbering his shoulders before sending his blade on its way to the sound of *ooooh* as he was way off the mark. 'Bloody hell!'

'Me next,' said Joe who also missed the target. 'The target's too damn small, Ronnie,' he complained.

'Is that so,' said Ronnie, lining up and throwing where he was the furthest away yet. 'Yep, you were right, Joe.'

He wasn't too bothered. It was just nice to be included.

Squeak took his time but couldn't decide where to stand. He shuffled left, then he shuffled back to the right before he was happy then everyone's eyes followed his blade where it landed quite close. 'Yesssssss,' he roared. 'Beat that, Ross and Alice – oh, yes!'

'Smart arse.' Wallace laughed.

'Alice, do you want to go next or last?' asked Ross whereby Alice gestured with her arm in a sweeping motion toward the line. Ross stepped up and was just about to take aim when Ronnie said...

'No pressure, Ross. Take it slowly...'

Ronnie caught a barrage of abuse for his trouble.

Ross took aim and the blade went wide. 'He put me off. He put me off. Can I have another go?' he said, pointing to Ronnie where his plea fell onto deaf ears.

Alice stepped up to the mark in profound silence. They had wondered where her blade was until she produced and activated it in one fluid movement, sending it smack bang to rest in the middle of the notch. The silence lingered for a few more seconds. In disbelief, each man looked from the target back to Alice then they erupted into joyous shouts and praise when she retrieved her blade.

'You amateurs...'

'You'll have to do that one evening when the shearers are here, we could win a fortune!'

'Hey, Squeak, that's not a bad idea. What do you think, Alice?'

'Oh, so now you all want to be on my team then, Wallace?'

They all roared again.

'Good one, Alice. Alright, back to work everyone before Mr Price deducts our wages.'

That evening, she was surprised when Mrs McKinnley placed a birthday cake on the table in front of her. 'Happy nineteenth birthday, Alice!' she said and the whole room erupted with cheers, whistles and a multitude of happy birthdays and congratulations.

'Thank you! This is so lovely of you all.' She held up her lemonade and clinked glasses with everyone around the table. 'But how?' And as soon as she asked, she knew that Mrs Heppler had informed. 'That was a secret!'

Mrs Heppler feigned innocence extremely well. 'I don't remember you saying that it was a secret, at all!' She blew the birthday girl a kiss.

'Ah, what's this?' Emily ran up to Alice and gave her a picture.

'I did this for you,' she said, giving her a big hug.

'Oh, Pickle! I love it. It's the most beautiful birthday present. I'll treasure it always.'

CHAPTER THIRTY-ONE

The second that Alice saw her glorious sunshine approaching the homestead, she knew.

He was the one. There was no mistake.

None.

Her attraction was instant and powerful. She became quite breathless as her whole body tingled and her heart raced knowing that her search was over.

Shocked by her rapid response, particularly as it hadn't been long since Dixon had betrayed her, she knew that it was too soon to get involved with someone else. And then it dawned on her that the shearer may not even like her – her heart jumped a beat with the possibility.

Trying to put all this aside, she joined the staff in welcoming the team that would be staying at McKinnley for the next month.

More than anything, Alice prayed that she wouldn't stumble her words when Mr McKinnley made the introduction.

She was that nervous.

'Alice, this is Cameron...'

'Cam,' the man gently corrected. He removed his Akubra and looked down into her eyes and gave her the most beautiful smile that she had ever seen. He had dark brown hair and those eyes... they were the most rich and luxurious brown that she had ever seen. Even though he had only said one word, she had loved his voice already.

Her heart was lost.

Within a matter of seconds, she not only took in every detail of his physique but assessed that the attraction was mutual. When he shook her hand, his touch catapulted her senses to the stars and again she felt breathless. Not being able to help it, she ever so slightly reprimanded herself for wondering what he would look like shearing without his shirt on...

Her heart was then truly lost.

'Cam, yes, sorry,' apologised Mr McKinnley. 'Welcome back to McKinnley and welcome everyone.' He addressed the remainder of the team. 'Nothing's changed since last year, everything's still in the same place, so go and get yourselves sorted in the quarters and we'll meet for smoko in the kitchen in half an hour.'

The team acknowledged and dispersed.

'It's nice to meet you, Alice. We'll catch up later.'

'Yes, likewise, Cam.' She watched him fling his bag over his muscled shoulders, running to catch up with the others.

'Bushfires are dangerous out here,' whispered Mrs Heppler. 'You'll have to be careful with that spark.' She linked her arm through Alice's to lead her back to the kitchen.

'Mrs Heppler, really!'

'Oh, yes. I know the signs. You're blushing and you've gone all girly!' She couldn't help but laugh. 'Right, suppose we'd all better get smoko going otherwise we'll have a riot on our hands before we've even started.'

In no time at all Mrs McKinnley, Mrs Heppler, Elsa and Elsa's cousins, who worked at the station during busy periods, had gotten into a comfortable routine to cater for the McKinnley and shearing teams. It was hard work and it seemed that there was minimal gap between when one meal ended and the next one started. As well as kitchen duties, the women also managed the laundry and for a modest fee, the shearers could have their laundry done as well as cooked meals.

The station owned two mangles that were kept outside against the end of the homestead alongside large wooden tubs big enough to handle the bedsheets. The women used various brushes from soft to hard bristles and wash boards to get their washing clean. Once the laundry passed through the mangles to disperse the water, it was hung wherever there was ample space among the six rows of washing line and left to billow in the warm breeze.

The shearers had their own routine down at the sheds. Alice was enjoying the hustle and bustle as the place came alive with the sound of clippers, banter and the constant baaing and bleating of sheep. She was relishing the overall experience and as promised, Mr Price rotated her through the various stages so that she could get a feel for how the whole process was undertaken.

Mr Price had explained that the sheep were sorted into grouped pens and that they had been fasted beforehand to prevent a muck covered floor to which she deduced made a lot of sense.

One of her jobs was to assist the roustabouts by picking up the shorn fleeces, some of which were quite heavy, and taking them over to the wool table for classing followed by sweeping up to keep the boards as clear as possible. Alice was fascinated as Bernard, the wool classer, sorted the fleeces by length, thickness, quality and cleanliness. He was also teaching Reg, one of the roustabouts, on how to become a wool classer. This only added to her admiration of the shearers skill in producing complete quality fleeces in no time at all.

Alice also helped the roustabouts to ensure that the shearers received a constant flow of sheep and now understood why there were various pens and ramps leading in and out of the sheds including pens directly underneath where the men worked. She was enjoying the task and learned how timing was important to productivity in keeping the sheep moving up from the pens and ramps to the boards for shearing and back down to the pens afterwards. This was when she became grateful to have had almost a year's experience under her belt where she was more competent in handling the sheep and therefore a greater assistance to the team.

The shearers were a friendly bunch who didn't mind when she asked a lot of questions and she never felt uncomfortable considering that she was outnumbered. The banter and leg pulling was a complete contrast to the treatment that she had encountered at Opal Racecourse.

She and the McKinnley staff blended in like any good team should by putting in hour after hour. It was tough going and Alice tired quickly but as the second week approached, she was getting used to the backbreaking work upon discovering muscles she didn't know she had.

Mrs Heppler could see that Cam was smitten with Alice and it warmed her heart to see them talking and sitting near one another at smoko and other mealtimes. Mrs Heppler, Elsa and Mrs McKinnley were not only putting two and two together but were also looking out for Alice knowing that her heart was fragile, and woe be told the next man to put a step out of line.

It wasn't just the women either. Wallace also observed the attraction from afar and if it came to it, he would deal with Cam. He was still spitting feathers from missing out on *talking* to Dixon, whereas head stockman, he saw it as his duty to protect his staff.

In no time at all, Alice and Cam's heart seemed to beat as one, feeling that they had known each other for years. Despite reminding herself of the hurt that Dixon had left behind, she was unsuccessful in keeping her feelings under control. Her heart was ruling her head and deep down she had no doubt that this time it was different.

Alice's heart was beginning to soften toward this wonderful, caring, loving and beautiful man.

They enjoyed deep conversations in getting to know

one another and took many strolls together whenever time allowed during this busy period. 'Tell me more about the Northern Territory, Cam,' she said.

'Well, let's see. For generations, my family have owned a small cattle station. My father and brother, Vincent, still run the station and hire casual help from time to time. Mother died when Vincent and I were young.'

Alice squeezed his arm gently in response as they had spoken at length regarding the loss of their mothers.

'One summer, Father took us to a rodeo and I never forgot it. Ever since then I only wanted to get into bull riding. It was amazing, even magical. My heart was pounding and I'd never seen anything quite like it and knew it was what I wanted to do. Well, I was just a kid.' He laughed.

'Sounds quite thrilling being brought up on a cattle station. I went to my first rodeo back in March. I was mesmerised watching the bull riders and the clowns. It was scary exciting; they are all very brave. So, from what you just said, did you follow your dream and become a bull rider?'

'All but briefly. When we got home, my father built me a contraption so I could practice bull riding. He suspended an old oil drum with rope from the beams in the barn and fixed a saddle to it. When I sat in the saddle, my feet were about a foot from the ground, so when he swung and jolted the drum and I fell off, I didn't have far to land. Vincent padded the ground with straw and used to count so I would know my score. They were good times.' He smiled, reminiscing.

'Despite having plenty of bulls on the station, he wouldn't let me near them as I was still very young. I understand that now, but I didn't back then. Damn big brutes they are,' he said, to which Alice shuddered and nodded. 'I got pretty good too so, when I was seventeen, he relented, and I managed to get a job with a rodeo that travelled around the circuit in the Northern Territory.

'The old boys took me under their wing and literally showed me the ropes. I say old boys, but they weren't that much older than me. There was nothing like the feeling when I first sat on a bull in the holding pen. Even though we were in the practice area, they gave me the most docile bull they had. Temper Tantrum, his name was, but that was just a ploy. He was more like a placid pony but it was good experience and it prepared me for what was about to come.

'My dream was fulfilled and it felt so good. I had a few good events after Temper Tantrum, and it was amazing being that close to a powerful beast where one hesitation or bad judgment error could mean the difference between sweet success, serious injury or death. It was like a potent drug that I couldn't get enough of. The adrenaline rush was nothing like I've experienced before. I was enjoying every second...'

Alice detected a hint of sorrow. 'What happened?' she asked softly.

'Lady luck moved onto someone else but I had a good innings. It still sounds unbelievable to me to say that I retired at the tender age of twenty. I took a bad fall and sustained a few injuries along with a dislocated knee, which still gives me some hassle from time to time but not too disastrous for an old boy of twenty-five.'

'My, my. That is old,' she playfully taunted.

'You still sure it doesn't bother you that I'm six years older than you, Alice?'

'No, it doesn't. I'd like to say that I could learn from your great wisdom, but I'm yet to find some!'

He laughed and tugged her ponytail while they stood at the corral fence by the stables.

'So, what have you been doing since you left the rodeo? Did you go back home?'

'No, I didn't go back. I got talking to some shearers who were at the rodeo and they got me interested in shearing. It took some time and my knee doesn't fare too bad. I worked my way down to Western Australia, joining various teams travelling from one station to the next. It's a good way to meet interesting new people, although I haven't met any yet!'

'Hey!'

'Are you going to tell me more about your family now?' he asked, aware that Alice had avoided the subject on previous conversations. 'Although you don't have to if you don't want to.'

The time had come to tell him some more as it was only fair seeing as he had told her about his family. 'I'm originally from New South Wales and as you know, I ran away from home when I was fifteen when my mother died. My childhood was challenging, shall we say. My father was a good-for-nothing brute, and please don't look shocked because he was, but that's a story for another day, Cam, when I feel more comfortable. No offence to you, it's me who is uncomfortable with it. My mother didn't deserve how she was treated and didn't have an easy time.

'When they died, I went to stay with Pip and Tish. They are elderly sisters whom I adore so much. I lived with them for a while in the Blue Mountains before a great opportunity involving horses took me to Adelaide. You fell in love with bull riding, and I did the same with horses. In Adelaide I worked on a cattle station.' His eyes widened at the similarity. 'From there I got a job briefly at a racecourse but it didn't work out and so I took a flight to Fremantle and somehow ended up here talking to you.'

'I can see we have lots more to talk about. It is very refreshing getting to know you. We're two like-minded spirits.' He smiled and Alice's heart melted. 'But, for now, time is moving, and Mrs Heppler will have my guts for garters if you are back late...'

Spontaneity overcame Alice when she stood on tiptop and reached up to cup his stubbly face in which to bring him closer to kiss him. It was a kiss of all first kisses that she would replay over in her mind time and time again, sending the butterflies in her stomach into rapturous flutters.

Cam's strong arms enveloped her while refraining to cross the thin, almost transparent line between a sensual kiss escalating into the overwhelming underlying raw passion between them.

CHAPTER THIRTY-TWO

Feeling somewhat anxious as the days rolled by, Alice was all too aware that shearing was coming to an end. Her heart was falling for Cam in a big way and while she didn't want him to go, she wouldn't hold him back either. The last few nights had been spent tossing and turning, wondering what she should do.

Working at McKinnley Station and being a jillaroo was her dream job and one that she did not want to leave just yet, believing there was so much more for her to achieve.

Dixon had bruised her soul, but never in her wildest dreams did she expect someone to walk into her life so soon after. Deep down, Alice didn't want Cam to slip through her fingers, knowing that they could have such a great future together. She reasoned that it had only been one month, but she knew that it was right.

He was the one.

Compared to Dixon, Cam was different in so many ways. Good ways. From the first few days, she had yearned to take things further with this gorgeous man as her instinct told her to trust him. And from this, she could almost hear her mother tut-tutting at the prospect of her daughter having slept with two men before she was married.

The following night when they took their usual evening stroll down by the corral, Cam had listened without interruption as this beautiful woman to whom he cherished poured her heart out. He remained calm and listened to what she had told him about Dixon and the reason why he had left and the way in which he had left. She felt it was only fair that he knew that she had been in a serious relationship with somebody else. And in return, she had listened to Cam talk about his past.

In all honesty, Alice found it difficult hearing that Cam had had a few casual flings. Reasoning prevailed that he was older and that his job took him from town to town where there wasn't the opportunity to form a special lasting relationship. There was no denying that he was extremely handsome and charming and a gentleman to boot, so it was no wonder that he was popular with women.

Immediately, Alice questioned herself when her father's spiteful voice entered her head that she was just a girl and what right did she have to enjoy happiness with Cam who was too good for her. Feeling out of her depth, her confidence plummeted with the possibility that she was in Cam's casual category.

He read her thoughts and did his utmost to reassure her unequivocally that what they had and what they would become was true. Despite both being aware of the short time they had been together, there was an unmistakable powerful bond between them.

'Cam, my father was gentle and kind and loving in the beginning, then he turned very bad. I've already had a man promise me the moon where he upped and abandoned me. I need someone I can rely on, a soulmate...'

'From what you have told me, I am nothing like your father or Dixon,' he said, looking into her beautiful eyes sparkling in the moonlight. 'I have been with a few women and have been honest with you about it, but I cannot change the past. The only way is to move forward and I want us to do that together. I'll never let you down or leave you, however tough things may be.

'We have a future together and we both know and feel it. That's why I am going to speak to Mr McKinnley to ask if they could do with an extra pair of hands about the place.'

Alice's instant smile made his heart soar to the skies as they embraced.

'We've both been honest with each other. I'd rather it be this way. To know you are sure before we fall head over heels, or head over boots.' They laughed then Cam cupped Alice's face and looked at her deeply.

'I'm the one you've been searching for, Alice. You've found me.' He pulled her into his arms and kissed her, knowing that she would be his until their final breath.

*

By changing tactics, the man's luck had considerably improved when he *bumped* into the girl he'd slept with at

Vera's brothel a while back where he had found out some very interesting information.

At last, within the next few days, vast fortune would be within touching distance.

*

'May I have a word, Cam?' Mr McKinnley asked after smoko the following morning. But it wasn't discreet enough as Mrs Heppler caught Elsa's eye when the men walked through the far kitchen door.

'Sure, Mr McKinnley, I was going to ask you the same. Is everything alright?' he said, following the grazier down the corridor and through to the office.

'Fine. Just fine, please take a seat. How are you liking it at McKinnley?'

'It's good here. I enjoy the work and the ladies look after us well, much better than some of the places that we've worked for. It's a nice atmosphere and everyone gets along. Then there's Alice...' He smiled.

'Ah, yes. Alice. She's a nice girl and has been here for almost a year now. Actually, it's Alice that I would like to talk to you about.'

Cam almost laughed aloud because Mr McKinnley was, going by his guess, only four or so years older than he, and was going to give him the *father* talk.

But he was wrong.

'Please take this the right way. It's plain for everyone to see how much you mean to one another. I wanted to ask you on your own, without any of your team's influence, as to how you would feel about staying on at McKinnley as a full-time stockman? We could sure use your expertise and you would be a welcome member to our team.'

Cam was too taken aback by the coincidence that he didn't answer as quickly as he should, therefore, Mr McKinnley assumed that he had no intention of being with Alice after shearing was over. He nodded and was just about to end the conversation when the younger man spoke.

'You took me off guard there.' He smiled and shook Mr McKinnley's hand. 'That was exactly what I wanted to talk to you about. I accept, and I appreciate the way in which you did it.'

'That's great news. It was meant to be. Welcome to the team! And as today is the last day of shearing, I'll make the announcement at the celebration roast spit down by the corral this evening.'

Mrs Heppler was buzzing with excitement and was enjoying planning the evening's meal. Because the shearing was just ahead of schedule, she was able to rope in Squeak and Ross to do the necessary checks for nasties and the setting up of the fire pit.

Elsa and her cousins had taken the children for an afternoon stroll and Mrs McKinnley spent a well-earned afternoon in her sewing room as encouraged by Mrs Heppler who was also enjoying her afternoon pottering in the kitchen.

Mrs Heppler loved nothing more than a good potter about and was happy as a pig in muck as she prepared the pork spit roast, which she granted wasn't the best analogy. She was also elated that Mrs McKinnley had advised her that Cam would be staying on, making her swear to secrecy. Although Mr McKinnley had made his wife promise the same.

Having finished preparing the pork, Mrs Heppler was just about to call upon Ross and Squeak to take the spit down to the fire pit when Alice breezed into the kitchen and whispered, 'Cam is staying on as a stockman, isn't it great news! Please, do not say anything, it's a secret. Mr McKinnley will be announcing it this evening.' She gave Mrs Heppler a quick kiss on the cheek then she ran outside. Mrs Heppler muted the sound of her raucous laughter within a tea towel. It seemed to be the worst kept secret all round.

'Are you alright, Mrs Heppler?' asked Mr Price, walking into the kitchen from the office wondering why her head was buried.

'Yes, just fine, thank you, Mr Price. Can I get you a refill?' she asked and hoped that her sides wouldn't split from containing such thrilling news. Cam was a likeable fellow and she could tell that he was different from Dixon. He got on with all the staff at the station and equally, everyone had enjoyed his stories of his family's cattle station in the Northern Territory.

Mr Price returned to the office with his cup of tea and was a little perplexed by Mrs Heppler's unusual behaviour. And now that she was on her own, she started to sing her favourite song in her head, leading to untuneful bursts aloud when she got to the chorus. She put the final touches to the roast potatoes and was very pleased by all the preparations. As usual, she had eaten a little less at lunch to save some room for when she taste tested the spit roast, which already conjured up pleasant and tantalising aromas to come.

Also, due to the extra catering for the shearing team, she was now adding the final items to her list for her next scheduled visit to Burston in a couple of days to stock up on provisions. Alice had accompanied her on previous journeys but now that Cam was stopping at McKinnley, she wanted to stay with him. Mrs Heppler smiled. *They are such a well-matched young couple,* she thought.

It was a pleasant evening where the humidity wasn't too unbearable. There were just over thirty people who gathered down by the corral sitting on huge gum logs surrounding the fire pit. The atmosphere was jolly and jovial. The men compared their tallies for the season and dished out banter as they awaited Mrs Heppler's go-ahead for when the roast was ready.

'Quiet, please,' shouted Mr McKinnley, banging a wooden spoon against a saucepan to gain attention. 'Quiet. Thank you.' When the chatter subsided, he said, 'Thank you to all for your hard work this shearing season. You have sheared a massive thirty-five thousand, five hundred and twenty during your stay,' much to the delight of everyone who cheered and raised their bottles of beer.

'On behalf of both teams, I extend huge gratitude to all the ladies for looking after us so well with all the cooking and laundry.' The group burst into enthusiastic applause and whistles and when the cheering died down, Mr McKinnley continued. 'As always, the team at

McKinnley appreciate your help and we hope to see you all next season.' He held up his glass of beer and saluted the shearing team.

'And finally. I am delighted to say that Cam has decided to stay on at McKinnley and will be joining the team as a stockman. Welcome, Cam!'

Everyone cheered him and wished him well for the future while the atmosphere was engulfed by the most delicious aroma of the roast and the crackle of the fire as dusk descended.

'Ready, Mrs Heppler?' Mr McKinnley asked.

'Ready!' she announced, inviting the men to line up and receive a plateful of the most delicious spit roast pork that practically fell onto their plates. Then they moved along to the table where Mrs McKinnley, Elsa and her cousins served roast potatoes and vegetables. The ladies were delighted when an almost hush engulfed the group as everyone tucked in enjoying their meal.

*

'How were your few days away, Dulcie?' enquired Vera when the young woman popped her head round the parlour door to say she was back.

'It was very enjoyable, thanks.' She turned to leave, then an afterthought. 'Oh, while I was walking to the train station on Tuesday, I spoke to the man who came here once. You know, the one with the scar?' And when she ran her index finger down the left side of her face, Vera's rosy cheeks drained of colour.

'Well, he actually bumped right into me. He apologised and we got talking and he mentioned that he knew you and Alice, and enquired if she visited you. I said not and told him where she lives. Hope you don't mind. See you later.'

Vera sat with a heavy thump into her chair and cussed profusely under her breath. She had been so careful by destroying Alice's letter that stated her new address and now he had acquired it anyway! After a few moments, the penny dropped in realising that Dulcie had spoken to him three days ago, giving him plenty of time to... she could not bring herself to even think it.

Her mind was racing; her suspicions were now proven and she knew it was time to call the police when she stopped.

Alice was due to arrive with Mrs Heppler in Burston today and she always telephoned her. Vera decided that it made sense to wait and warn her directly. But first, she poured herself a stiff drink.

*

'Excuse me,' the man said to Mrs Perri, the postmistress. 'I am hoping you can help. I have business with McKinnley Sheep Station. Can you direct me?'

'Good morning,' she said. 'It's four hundred miles away or so and it will take you time to get a...' She trailed off when she noticed his eyes widen at the sheer scale of distance and knew that he wasn't from around these parts.

'But if you hurry'—she looked up at the clock on the wall— 'Ernest, the mail plane pilot, is due to leave soon for a couple of drop-offs around the district and McKinnley is usually the first stop.' She pointed to the front of the shop. 'Turn left at the door then left down the next road and it'll lead to the air strip, but you'll have to be quick...'

Around an hour later, Mrs Heppler stepped into the post office. 'Afternoon, Mrs Perri. How are you?'

'Very well, Mrs Heppler. Didn't expect to see you for a few more hours at least. No Alice today – thought she was joining you this time?'

'Good news, Cam is staying on at the station, so Alice wanted to stay and be with him. But she did ask me to call her aunt to tell her the exciting news. May I?' She indicated to the telephone near the counter. 'I haven't spoken to Vera for a while, so it will be good to have a chat.'

'Be my guest,' Mrs Perri said as Mrs Heppler placed some money on the counter and picked up the receiver.

'Good afternoon, Vera, it's Mrs Heppler...'

After a couple of minutes, Vera had informed her of the whole saga, believing that Alice was in danger.

Mrs Heppler tried to remain calm as she spoke, but it wasn't easy. 'Please try not to worry too much, Vera. We will make sure Alice is safe. In case he turns up here, what does he look like?'

Mrs Perri was intrigued and could not help in overhearing the one-sided conversation. Her ears pricked up when Mrs Heppler relayed back to Vera about a scar.

The urgency in which Mrs Perri grabbed Mrs Heppler's arm and thus detaching the receiver from her ear caused her to instantly stop talking. 'That gentleman with a scar was here – he said he had business with McKinnley Station and got a ride with Ernest just over an hour ago...'

Vera heard every word.

'Vera,' said Mrs Heppler, recovering from the shock, 'call the police and tell them to liaise with the police here. I am going to call Ernest on the radio now. We will speak soon.' She replaced the handset.

Mrs Perri pulled back the counter, allowing Mrs Heppler to go through to the radio in the back office, but Ernest was not answering. 'Damn, he must have landed already. I'll try McKinnley and hope Mr Price is in the office.' After a while, there was again, no answer. It was hopeless.

'Please, can you keep trying the Station, Mrs Perri? Someone has to answer soon. After that, can you go to the police office and tell them what has happened if the New South Wales police have not got through yet? I will make tracks back and it'll be the fastest that I've ever driven...'

She had gone before Mrs Perri had chance to respond.

*

Ernest and Alice's uncle had received a warm welcome as they sat at the kitchen table while Elsa made them a cup of tea.

'Alice won't be long; she is mucking out the stables...' said Mrs McKinnley.

'Always liked horses, that one,' he remarked. 'It's been a while since I have seen her. Would you mind if I made my way there on my own if that is alright? I want it to be a surprise.' He gave one of his best smiles.

'Of course,' Mrs McKinnley accompanied him to the door and pointed in the direction of the stables.

P W Jones had waited a lifetime, it seemed, to have come this far.

He knew when she did a runner around three years ago that she would've taken Shiv's vast hoard with her because the girl wasn't stupid enough to leave it behind. He scanned his surroundings, believing that it was hidden around here somewhere. The vast fortune was his by rights and he was determined to get it one way or another.

There was also a score to settle as she had not only stolen his precious wallet when she had been a snivelling child but years later had left him for dead in that alleyway.

But with recent knowledge, there was also an added urgency.

Noticing that one of the hefty stable doors was open, P W edged nearer and listened for voices. After a few moments when he was positive that the girl was alone, he stepped inside. He heard the familiar rustling of a pitchfork gathering soiled straw from a stall up ahead and saw that there were three horses in their independent stalls and knew that his quest was nearly over.

Spotting an iron pole leaning against the wall gave him an idea. Not wanting to leave anything to chance, he began to close the other door as quickly as he could without making too much noise.

The anticipation was intoxicating as he secured the pole through the handles to prevent the possibility of being interrupted.

The diminished sunlight was enough to rouse Alice's sharpened senses that heightened upon noticing the closed door, knowing that something was wrong.

P W was pleased by her reaction and then confusion as he edged closer.

'But you're dead.' She shook her head in disbelief but was not too shocked to activate her switch. 'It was so dark in that alley that I thought you were dead...' was all she could say. And that was when he knew that she had not purposely left him to die. It was something but it wouldn't help her.

'Thanks to your father, I nearly was. It took every ounce of energy that I possessed in which to drag myself out, whereas thankfully one of my associates spotted me, patched me up and took care of me until the wound healed. He also dropped Shiv's precious journal into the police station, anonymously of course, although that was prior to learning that he was dead, more's the pity. I would have liked to have seen him rot in jail.'

'But I raised your eyelid...' Alice was still stunned.

'Ah'—he gave a brief laugh—'thought I had dreamt that.' Then his eyes turned cold. 'It's taken me a while to find you.'

'Why would you want to find me? What are you doing here? I don't understand.'

'I was recently informed that the police have apparently found new incriminating evidence and want to question me regarding Shiv's murder. Having not caught anyone, I believe that they want to pin it on me.

'He was shot through the head at close range, but you know that I only stabbed him as you witnessed him coming out of that alley where I was *already dead* and couldn't have possibly done it. I want you to tell them.'

Alice hid her shock that the police wanted him for

questioning because she knew that it was Alfie who shot her father. But if the police ended up convicting her father's rival, then who was she to enlighten them? Because she sure as hell wasn't going to vindicate P W.

But most of all, if he were charged, Alfie would be off the hook!

'What's the real reason you wanted to find me?' She wanted to swerve the conversation away from the police but also knew that there was more to this visit.

'You're definitely your father's daughter.' He smiled because it was a genuine compliment. 'I won't harm you if you hand over all of his hoard. He amassed a fortune and we both know you have it.' All the while, he took frequent glances at the switch, knowing how competent she was.

'There is no money, there is no anything,' she said, shaking her head in bewilderment. 'When I left his journal with you, I knew the consequences and I knew that he would be arrested and most of all, I knew that my mother and I had to get away, and fast.'

'Nice touch with the journal. Knowing it would be enough to send him to prison. But what kind of a daughter incriminates her own father?

'That is...' He scratched his chin to find the right words. 'Immoral and unethical.' He looked at her in disgust, like he had just stepped into something unpleasant.

'*That's* immoral and unethical?' Alice returned his disgusted look. 'How many people have you murdered, P W?'

'Tell me where the money is NOW!' he ordered, bored with small talk.

Alice's pent-up anguish built to a raging torrent and she looked at the man with repulsion who bore the scar from her father's blade.

'There wasn't any time to think, let alone hunt for any money. If you believe we were privy to anything of value that he may have had, then you are completely delusional. That's why I rushed home to warn my mother. We had to leave because until he was caught, that was the most dangerous time for us. Can't you see that? He knew he would go to prison; hence he had nothing to lose by killing us as opposed to us living beyond his control.

'Not only that but also before all the reprobate vultures, like you, found us wanting the same non-existent fortune.'

'Then why don't I believe you?' He stepped closer and aimed his pistol. 'Tell me.'

'How dare you!' Her eyes seethed with contempt as she ignored the weapon. 'My mother and I left with nothing. Haven't you heard a single word I have just said? Like you, he was an arrogant, greedy and selfish bastard.

'He never provided for us when he was alive, so what makes you think he would in death?'

P W put the safety back on his pistol and returned it to his jacket pocket, then he slow-clapped mockingly. 'You are as good a liar as you are a thief, Miss Johnson.'

*

It was when Mr Price came rushing into the kitchen, noting Ernest and asking him if he had brought a passenger that Mrs McKinnley answered for him.

'Yes, Alice's uncle. He's with her down at the stables.'

'HE'S NOT HER UNCLE...' He sprinted outside, closely followed by Ernest, Mrs McKinnley and Elsa and beckoned wildly to Cam and Wallace who were walking back from the stockmen's quarters.

Alice was relieved to hear shouts of *ALICE!* as Cam's voice approached the stables, but her relief was short-lived when she then focused on P W who was again pointing the pistol at her.

'They might be busy for a while,' he said as she could see the doors being jolted and rocked, as the iron pole was preventing entry. 'Enough time to tell me where you have kept the money and I will then leave you alone. I promise.'

Unbeknown to P W and Alice, Cam and Wallace crept in via a side door halfway along the stables, while the others continually pulled and pushed the stable door.

Without warning, one of the horses reared up when Wallace gently threw a stone at his rump, causing the brief diversion Alice needed when P W flinched. She charged forward, dropping to the ground and swiping his legs out from under him as Cam and Wallace were upon him in no time, disarming and apprehending before the rest of the McKinnley team arrived through the side door.

*

Later that evening, Alice was sitting with everyone at the kitchen table having recovered from the shock, relieved that P W had gone. Mr McKinnley returned from the office and enlightened on the latest news.

'I have just spoken to the police in Burston. They met the mail plane and said we had done a grand job in tying up Mr Jones securely for the flight. They queried as to his cuts and bruises, but both Ernest and I were unable to throw any light as to how they were sustained. They said that through Mrs Perri's help in warning us, and Mrs Peabody's assistance, that they were able to arrest him.' He looked at Alice. 'Mr Jones will be transported back to Sydney where it is highly likely he will be charged with the murder of your father. We know he died but we're all sorry regarding the circumstances.'

'Thank you, Mr McKinnley. They were enemies and as bad as each other...'

'I will never let you out of my sight again,' said Cam as Alice smiled and leaned into him.

'A whisky all round, I believe,' said Mrs McKinnley. 'It's been a long night and it's late, but it will do us all good, especially you, Alice!'

'Make mine a double,' said Mrs Heppler whose distress melted upon seeing Alice safe as she ran into her arms while blasting her with a barrage of questions, 'Are you alright? Did Mrs Perri get through in time? Was he here? Where is he now?'

'I'm fine. Yes, Mrs Perri did a grand job. Yes, he was here and is now with the police under arrest, thanks to everyone, and I am sorry for you as well because you have gone through a greater ordeal than I have.'

'I doubt that, love. My mind was thinking of all sorts on the journey. I've never wanted to drive the dirt tracks during nightfall as it's very dangerous but all I kept thinking was that he had done you harm. I'm so happy you're alright. But damn hell, I'm totally on my last legs.

'Now where's that bloody double whiskey?

'And, I inform you all that the supplies are more than a little shaken, as am I.'

CHAPTER THIRTY-THREE

After two years, Alice and Cam's romance continued to blossom, while they spent many romantic walks and picnics in the garden and enjoyed sitting on the verandah at the end of the day just watching the sunset.

'It's just beautiful here.' Alice sighed, snuggling up to him on the verandah's swing seat.

'But not as beautiful as you,' he replied.

'You say all the right things.' She laughed, then more seriously, she said, 'I will miss you.'

'I will miss you too, but it's only a five-day muster. Apart from leaving you behind, I'm quite looking forward to it. Mr McKinnley, Wallace, Ronnie and Joe are great, and we all get along very well, so it should be good. Hard work, but good. It's Mr Price, Squeak and Ross that I feel sorry for...'

'How so?'

'Being left behind with all you women,' he joked and before Alice could reply, he embraced her and kissed her passionately. 'So, you don't forget me.'

'No chance of that, my gorgeous stockman. I'll have another one of those please.' Alice was in heaven; his aftershave was sending alluring tingles all over her body.

'Ahem,' announced Mrs Heppler's foresight before she rounded the corner of the verandah. 'Come on, Alice, put the poor man down. He's got an early start tomorrow, come on.' She shepherded the amused couple back through the homestead and bade Cam goodnight as she playfully shoved him out the door.

*

'Look who I found,' announced Mr Price when he walked in through the kitchen door with Ernest, the mail plane pilot, followed by Dixon who ambled in sheepishly.

Mrs Heppler's heart pounded with rage and it took all her willpower from escorting Dixon off the premises by his ear.

'Dixon!' exclaimed Mrs McKinnley. 'It's nice to see you. You too, Ernest. Come and have a cup of tea and some tucker.'

'Thanks, Mrs McKinnley,' replied Ernest, taking a seat at the table with Mr Price.

'But what are you doing here?' Mrs McKinnley addressed Dixon who had only taken a few steps inside.

'Hello, everyone, wasn't too sure if I'd be welcome...' He tested the water while Mrs Heppler shook her head thinking that he was either stupid or convinced that he could win Alice back. *You have absolutely no bloody idea,* she almost said aloud.

'Sorry to run out on you like I did, but I'd like to make

amends to you all, particularly Alice. Is she around? Ernest said she still worked here.'

'She's busy at the moment.'

He picked up on Mrs Heppler's offish tone, as did Mrs McKinnley who looked at her in question. Mrs Heppler forced herself to smile, indicating for him to join Mr Price and Ernest at the table. 'Could you take the cups over, Elsa? Now, where have you been, Dixon?' she said.

'I've been working in Burston and took the opportunity to catch a ride out with Ernest. I know I owe you all an explanation. Is Mr McKinnley around at all? I wanted to apologise about taking the truck.'

'He's out with the stockmen on a muster but they are due back early this evening,' answered Mrs McKinnley, thinking that she was missing something.

'I said to Dixon that we'd talk to Mr McKinnley about him reprising his old role as a station hand,' said Mr Price. 'Although he knows that we weren't impressed by the way he left and taking the truck.'

There was so much that Mrs Heppler wanted to say, but Mr Price was the manager, and it was his and Mr McKinnley's decision to make, so she remained quiet.

'Elsa, would you mind finishing up here? There's something I need to do.' Mrs Heppler picked up the vegetable basket as a rouse and walked outside to which she placed the basket beside the vegetable garden and high-tailed it down to the stables to warn Alice.

'He's what?' Alice couldn't believe it as she sat with a plonk on a bale of hay as Mrs Heppler repeated what had just happened. 'Of all the damn nerve.' Alice had gotten over the shock and was now just as angry as her friend. 'What the hell does he think he's doing after all this time? And... oh no. Surely not...'

'What is it, love? You've gone a little pale.'

'It's been two years. He doesn't know. Perhaps he's come to see...' She looked at Mrs Heppler with wide eyes.

'His child,' Mrs Heppler said before she added. 'Do you think? He did ask to see you.'

'I love Cam. You know that. But this has thrown me coming out of the blue like this. The last time I saw Dixon, I told him I was late, believing I was pregnant. But what if I never was? What if he's been thinking all this time that he was a father and now he's ready to be one?'

Mrs Heppler thought about that for a few moments. 'Despite what we think of him running out on you like that, you may have a point. I even feel a little sorry for him now, to be honest. But we'll never know until you speak to him. Coming here after two years; perhaps you should listen to what he has to say?'

'I know you're right. I told Cam everything back at the beginning and it's just as well that he isn't here. I'll talk to Dixon. Would you mind asking if Ernest can stay a little longer so he can go back with him? But what if Mr Price gives him his old job back?'

'I don't believe he will as Mr McKinnley was mighty angry that he just upped and left taking the truck with him. That's a good idea though regarding Ernest. I'll have a discreet word with him just in case.'

*

'Hello, Alice. It's great to see you again. How are you?' Her heart skipped a beat. He looked even more handsome than she had remembered.

'Hello, Dixon, shall we take a walk?' Alice indicated and he followed her around to the verandah, aware that every set of eyes were still fixed on the doorway.

His heart skipped a beat. She was just as beautiful, in fact, she looked more beautiful with her sun kissed skin and her long golden hair and baby blue eyes. 'You're looking good, Alice...'

'What are you doing here?'

'I felt so bad leaving you like I did. I am sorry. It was wrong. I was confused, scared and young. I know I have a lot of making up to do to make it right if you could find it in your heart to give me another chance. To give us another chance.'

They sat in silence for a while before Alice looked at the man she once loved. 'I won't lie to you, Dixon, it not only broke my heart when you left but the way in which you did it was also cruel. We should have talked it through. I know I had a little more time than you but after everything that we went through, you should've stayed.'

'Yes, you're right. I should've. I panicked and I have regretted it ever since.'

Her voice softened when she enlightened, 'There is no baby. I found out shortly after you abandoned me...' Alice felt tears prickling and was surprised that he could still affect her after all this time.

'I know,' he replied. 'Recently, I bumped into Ernest and he said that you still worked here and from all the news he told me about the station; I gathered there was no baby. After handing in my notice, Ernest agreed to bring me out here and I have strong hope that Mr McKinnley will give me my old job back. There is nothing I want more than for us to give it another go, Alice. Please. At least consider that we could have a future together.'

'Then if Ernest has brought you fully up to date, you will know that I am with someone.'

'Yes, he mentioned it, but I still persuaded him to bring me...'

'Excuse me?'

'I did wrong by you, Alice, but I am here now. You knew me well enough to know that I would be back...' He was starting to look stressed, agitated and troubled that everything was slipping away from him.

'Dixon, I love Cam. We've been together for two years...'

He raised his voice. 'Well, you certainly didn't waste any time getting over me, did you?'

Alice stood up and started to head back around the verandah toward the kitchen. 'I do not owe you an ounce of explanation. It's best that you go back with Ernest.'

Dixon followed her, 'Alice! Wait. Please. I'm sorry I raised my voice. Please, let's talk.'

'Why now? After all this time, why now?'

'I felt bad by my actions. I knew it was wrong from the first minute but I just couldn't stop myself by taking the truck. Then it seemed impossible to come back. I stewed for ages.'

'You stewed? How about me? I did more than stew.' Alice was a few steps from the doorway.

Dixon's tone increased, highlighting his desperation. 'Let me prove to you that you should be with me and not him. He's no good for you. I can give you a better life – I love you. I have always loved you. Come away with me. Today, we'll leave together...' Alice walked through the kitchen door with Dixon close behind.

'And why would she do that, pal?' Cam folded his arms, blocking the entrance, preventing Dixon from following Alice.

'Cam!' she exclaimed, totally thrown as the men weren't expected back until the evening.

Mrs Heppler put her arm around Alice's shoulders as the Mr McKinnley team kept quiet knowing Cam was handling the situation.

'You were saying?' Cam said with dominance.

'Get out of my way,' Dixon shouted at his opponent. 'Alice, please. Let's talk this through,' he pleaded.

'Ah, so *now* you want to talk. Not going to happen. You ready to go, Ernest?' he asked over his shoulder then he stepped closer, looking Dixon in the eye, and said, 'I suggest that you go back to Burston and stay there. Alice is with me now. We're getting married.'

Dixon's face dropped, knowing that Alice was lost to him, perhaps forever.

'Don't do it, Alice!' He tried to push past but Cam forcefully shoved him backwards and when Cam stepped closer again and stared at him with brunt intensity, Dixon knew it was all over. He retrieved his Akubra from the ground and walked despondently toward the airstrip as Ernest offered his congratulations before running after his passenger.

Considering that the kitchen was packed, it had never been as silent as it was during the last few seconds before Cam swept Alice up into his arms and kissed her passionately while the room exploded with cheers and salutations.

As soon as the congratulations subsided, Alice announced, 'We can't get married.'

There was a unified audible gasp.

'Why's that?' asked Emily, tugging on Alice's sleeve.

'Well, Pickle. Cam hasn't actually asked me yet!'

When he had stopped laughing, he placed Alice back down and motioned with his hands for quiet then he got down on one knee and took Alice's hand and gazed up into her eyes. 'This isn't quite the way in which I imagined it, as I'm sweaty and dirty from the muster, but Miss Alice Johnson, would you do me the utmost honour of becoming my wife?'

'I love you, Cam. Sweat and all and yes, I'll marry you!'

The room erupted again and Mr McKinnley gave everyone a whisky to toast the happy couple.

CHAPTER THIRTY-FOUR

A month later, Alice and Cam were dressed in their finest for their wedding day. The ladies and children had been in their element decorating the barn and had arranged the bales of hay for seating. Elsa and Mrs Heppler had cooked up a good old country wedding feast and the stockmen had been polishing up their musical talents while Mrs McKinnley would lead on the piano.

A few of the McKinnley's friends had flown in courtesy of Ernest alongside the minister. Ernest had also brought Cam and Alice letters, wedding cards and gifts from Pip, Tish and Aunt Vera. Alice was also delighted that Mr and Mrs Wyatt and the team at Nerra Creek had sent cards and gifts as well.

But most of all, Alice had been puzzled to find an envelope addressed to her in unfamiliar writing. Moments later, her eyes watered in astonishment.

'Alfie!' she whispered upon opening the letter and read how he had learned of her wedding via her aunt and had wished her and Cam every happiness for the future. She was pleased to hear that he was keeping well and due to the lack of address, she assumed that he was still keeping a low profile.

How she wished all these lovely people could be here today, although they were always in her heart.

While Alice understood that it was too far to travel for Pip, Tish and her Aunt, she had been beyond excited when they had radioed through the previous evening from Finch's Equestrian. She was delighted that Aunt Vera would be staying with the sisters for a while and that they had planned their own celebration tea in the garden which conjured up special memories of her sixteenth five years ago.

The trio from the Blue Mountains had been extra excited to have had the opportunity to finally speak with Cam who had the ladies eating out of his hand and when the talk steered toward the wedding dress, Alice had banished Cam from the office so she could talk freely. Weddings stirred many emotions and as well as thinking about her mother, Alice had enjoyed telling the ladies that she had accompanied Mrs Heppler into Fremantle where despite it being during wartime, she had found her perfect gown.

The ladies listened as the bride-to-be proceeded to describe her floor-length white satin gown and train that would flow elegantly behind her. She took particular joy in depicting how the bodice, with its long sleeves, had a V-neck collar with twelve satin buttons leading down to the waist, and added that these were just for show and that the real buttons ran down the back. And to set off the classic look, Alice said she had chosen a simple floor length veil that appeared almost transparent, therefore, not detracting from the gown itself when she walked down the aisle. The ladies were delighted to learn that Mrs McKinnley would be lending Alice her wedding tiara to hold the veil in place. Pip, Tish and Vera could picture the whole dress and had shed a few tears of happiness knowing how beautiful Alice would be.

Shortly after the radio call, Cam and Alice had then spoken to Cam's father and brother where, due to commitments at the station, they were unable to leave the property to attend the wedding but were very much looking forward to meeting Alice in the not-too-distant future.

Deciding not to mention anything to his bride-to-be, Cam had picked up an undertone during the conversation and planned to radio back within the following week to find out more. He knew they were hiding something from him, deducing that they hadn't wanted to bother them so close to the wedding.

*

'I've never seen you boys look so smart,' commented the bridegroom, looking at the impressive line-up when they stood in the barn awaiting Alice's arrival.

'You're not looking so ugly yourself,' joked Wallace. 'We scrub up pretty well, apart from you, Ronnie,' he added and the men burst out laughing as Ronnie looked quite perplexed then he smiled.

'I can't help looking better than all of you put together.

I'm a peacock compared to you bunch of sardines.' The men roared with laughter, trying to explain that galahs would have been a better choice before the minister coughed subtly. They all silenced just in time for when Mrs McKinnley played the first note announcing that the bride had arrived.

Cam's heart was fit to bursting when he saw Mr McKinnley accompany Alice down the aisle. She took his breath away in her beautiful gown and knew that her pink rose bouquet was a tribute to her mother. Alice usually wore her hair up when working, but today her hair was styled in loose curls that cascaded over her shoulders.

They were followed by Pickle in her new dress, feeling like a princess as she held a small posy of roses that her mother had rid of thorns. Sylvia was also meant to walk beside Pickle, but she had thrown a hissy fit preferring to spend the afternoon in the chook house. Jack had declined to walk with the girls, opting to stand up front with Cam and the men.

After the ceremony, Mr and Mrs Cameron Judge were congratulated by one and all.

'What's so funny, wife? You may have tried to disguise a laugh, but I heard you when the minister said congratulations Mrs Judge!'

Alice quickly blurted, 'Oh, my goodness, I can't believe it and I never thought about it until now. How ironic that my father would at this very moment be turning in his grave to hear that I am now a Judge when he spent most of his life trying to avoid them!'

He laughed alongside his wife, knowing all about his despicable father-in-law.

'Where are you going?' he asked when she turned to leave.

'I need to find Sylvia. Mrs McKinnley said she stormed off before the wedding and went to the chook house. She should be here; I won't be a moment.'

*

'An amazing day!' Cam said contentedly. 'Went in a blink of an eye, didn't it? You look beautiful, Alice. You always look beautiful, even when you are up to your armpits in sheep sh... dirt.'

'What a romantic I married.' Oh, how she loved this man. He scooped her up in his arms and carried her to their room in the homestead.

'I love you, Alice.'

'I love you too, Cam. From the first second I saw you, I was smitten.'

He kicked the door shut with the back of his heel and sat her down on the bed.

'All this material looks quite complicated, but I'm up for the challenge.' He winked at her, crouching down, and removed her satin shoes and placed them on the floor by the foot of the bed. He held her hands helping her up and kissed her tenderly while becoming a little puzzled when one of her front buttons would not undo.

'Just for show, try the ones down the back.' She guided and continued to kiss her husband, which quickly turned into tender laughing kisses while he resumed locating the buttons.

Wrapping his arms around her waist in between her dress and veil, he slid his hands up towards the back of her neck and slowly started to undo the tiny buttons. Alice was quite impressed that for big stockman hands he was quite dexterous and felt the buttons release one by glorious one and questioned why on Earth that she had picked a dress with so many. For a split second, she pondered whether to give him her switch so he could have undone the whole lot in one quick fair swoop but thought better of it. It was tantalising good and the suspense was pleasantly killing her.

They had made love many times with immense passion and tenderness but this was different. They were now married, and their love and yearning for one another had deepened to another level and while they desperately desired each other they knew that what they had was best savoured. Slowly. Thoroughly and entirely.

Alice reached up and undid his shirt, admiring his powerful chest and arms and intertwined her fingers through his chest hair before moving her fingers up to his shoulders and flicking his shirt over his back where he aided it to the floor.

Cam caressed her neck with tender butterfly kisses while his fingers glided her dress over her shoulders, but it slipped only so far, blocked by the sleeves, revealing a tantalising peek at the top of her breasts that yearned to be free. Breathing hard from the erotic tease their desire turned again to laughter when he tried to edge the sleeves further down but due to the humidity, it was easier said than done. Alice looked at him with such love and desire and in a mischievous way that said, *Brace yourself, boy.* She eased her arms out of the sleeves where the whole dress plummeted to the floor.

She undid his belt and slowly unbuttoned his fly then Cam kicked off his shoes and threw his trousers across to the chair. Being tidy had long gone out the window. He admired his beautiful new wife who stood almost naked before him and while looking into her eyes, he started to remove her underwear. Alice was in sensual heaven whenever his slightly coarse hands caught on her silk stockings while he slid the remaining garment all the way down before discarding. His bride laid back onto the bed, bringing her veil around and seductively placed it across her breasts while he removed his remaining clothing and joined her, trying to keep the slowness intact.

Savouring the moment, Cam couldn't take his eyes off the way in which her erect nipples were protruding teasingly beneath the almost transparent veil, crying out to be touched, kissed and licked, and that was exactly what he did, sending her adrift with pleasure. Their passion escalated and they kissed fervently, their intense hunger for each other built to when they could hold back no longer to become one in their love.

*

The newlyweds declined to take a few days honeymoon in Burston due to the Station's heavy workload. So, as another excuse for a celebration, the ladies decided to prepare a special meal and serve it down at the corral that evening.

The following day, Alice entered the kitchen. 'Hello, you two. I don't usually see you both together. My, you've grown up so much since I've been here.' Alice looked at ten-year-old Jack and Sylvia who was eight. 'What have you there?' She smiled and joined them at the table.

'Grown-ups always say how much children have grown. It's annoying,' Sylvia said huffily.

'Ignore her,' said Jack. 'We're writing to Maggie in England, or rather I am. Father and Mr Dwyer from England are cousins. Mr Dwyer lives in a country village and runs the post office and Maggie is a little girl who lives in the village. Mr Dwyer said in one of his letters that Maggie took quite a liking to the Australian four-penny stamp on the envelope. It was a picture of a koala and she had never seen one...'

'We live here and we haven't seen one either,' chirped his sister.

'Shut up, Sylvia. Anyway,' he continued, 'I thought it would be nice to write back. Sylvia doesn't want to. Do you want to say something, Alice?'

'I've never written to anyone in England before. I'd love to but what should I say?'

'It doesn't matter, whatever you want. She's only five, so she wouldn't mind what you said, I suppose.'

'Do you think she likes horses?'

'I guess she would. She lives on a farm, so she probably knows horses.' Jack handed the letter and pencil over to Alice.

'Dear Maggie,' Alice read aloud what she was writing as Mrs McKinnley, Mrs Heppler and Elsa brought her a cup of tea and sat at the table to listen to what she had to say.

'My name is Alice and it is nice to write to you in England. I work at McKinnley Station and me and my horse, Finn, won a belt buckle in a rodeo. Love from Alice.' She then returned the pencil and paper back to Jack.

'I know it was a while ago and that beautiful Finn died not long after, so it's best not to say that. Do you think that is alright?' she asked Jack who beamed.

'I am sure she will love that. Thanks, Alice.' He took the letter and went to the office in search of a stamp while Sylvia ran outside to play.

'Awww, that's sweet of you,' said Mrs McKinnley and poured the ladies another cup of tea.

'England. Goodness, so far away and from what we have been hearing on the radio, we hope that the war ends very soon. When you consider that Maggie is only five and what she may be seeing...' Alice thought back to when she was Maggie's age and pickpocketing in the courthouse when her father ruled his family with a rod of iron.

'Amen to that,' agreed Mrs Heppler. 'Are you alright?'

'Yes, I'm fine, thank you. Can I help by getting some vegetables for dinner?'

'Thank you, love. That'll be grand. Then if you can spare a moment, we could do with a hand down at the corral for this evening's soiree...'

'That's rather posh, Mrs Heppler.' Mrs McKinnley smiled, pulling her leg.

'I'm not all rough around the edges, Mrs McKinnley. I can do posh on the odd occasion.' She laughed, enjoying the banter.

Just then, there was a commotion at the kitchen door. Squeak and Ross flanked Joe by supporting and guiding him into the homestead where they plonked him down on a chair. Joe looked rather uncomfortable and was wincing in pain.

'Stupid man,' grumbled Mr Price who followed the men inside before the ladies had a chance to ask what was going on. 'How many times, man? How many bloody times?'

'I know, I know.' Joe nodded his head, rocking back and forth.

'Will somebody tell us what happened!' snapped Mrs Heppler, looking at the men. 'Elsa, quick, get the first aid kit.' She and Mrs McKinnley then looked for an injury.

'Oh, it hurts, it hurts,' puffed Joe, holding his foot and when Mrs Heppler and Mrs McKinnley saw Squeak and Ross stifle a laugh, they knew what had occurred.

'Elsa,' said Mrs McKinnley and when she turned and saw Mrs McKinnley shake her head and smile, she also knew and placed the first aid kit back on the shelf. Alice was confused. She couldn't understand why she saw giggles when Joe was in serious pain.

'Would a whisky help the pain, Joe?' asked Mrs McKinnley, unconcerned.

'Yes!' he said gratefully. 'It would.' And soon after he gulped the spirit, he felt somewhat better as the pain was subsiding. 'That ram was a massive bugger. I couldn't get out of the way in time...'

'What happened?' asked Alice, going crazy by not knowing.

'It stepped on my toes...'

Alice threw her head back and let out a piercing laugh. 'Oh, Joe, I thought it was something serious!'

Joe looked at her as if to say, *You'd think again if they were your toes.*

*

'I'll never tire of eating down at the corral.' Alice beamed, watching everyone enjoy their dinner around the fire pit that evening as again the ladies dished up an exquisitely cooked meal. 'This is really good, Mrs McKinnley.' Everyone nodded in agreement.

'Thank you, we do our best,' she acknowledged on the ladies' behalf.

Afterwards when the plates had been cleared away, it was a time for stories and banter by the firelight. The night sky was crystal clear and the stars shone brightly, adding to the ambiance. They could hear the distant baaing from the paddocks and the occasional whinny coming from the stables.

All was serene.

While everyone stood gathering around the table to get a drink, Alice thought she would have some fun. When Joe picked up his drink and started to walk away, she said, 'I hope your toes are much better. Sorry for laughing. Is this yours?' She held out his pocket watch.

'Much better and thanks, Alice. It is.' He took the watch without thinking about it and moved out of the way so Ross could also get a drink.

'Lovely night, Ross,' she commented.

'It surely is.'

'Oh, is this yours?' she asked, swaying his wallet.

'Yes. Thanks, Alice.'

'Drink, Squeak?' She poured and passed it to him.

'Cheers, Alice...' Then he looked perplexed when she produced his wallet.

'Hang on a minute.' Wallace smiled. 'What's going on?'

A hush descended.

'Nothing, Wallace. Nothing at all. Oh, by the way, is this yours?' She dangled his pocket watch before him.

'How'd you do that?' He was baffled and placed it back in his shirt pocket.

'Do what?' She smiled and as Ronnie closed in to get his drink, she said, 'Hold up there, Ronnie.' And they watched as she reached out and plucked Wallace's pocket watch from behind his ear much to their amusement.

'Another party piece, Alice?' Wallace smiled and again took back his pocket watch.

'Pardon, what?' she asked then Cam walked up and stood beside her.

'How'd you do that?' he asked in amazement and when they all looked from Cam back to Alice, she laughed where yet again she produced Wallace's pocket watch much to his and everyone's astonishment.

'What?' He couldn't believe it. This time everyone watched her more closely when she passed it back to him.

'I never even saw her take it!' Mrs Heppler addressed the group. 'Did anyone see her take it?' They looked at her, shaking their heads. Mrs Heppler stood next to Wallace transfixed.

'Didn't feel a thing,' he said, still puzzled.

'Not even then?' Alice asked, holding it up for a fourth time to a barrage of applause. 'No more, I promise you all, just for fun. Oh, except...' They looked at her in expectation. 'You may have something on your person that doesn't belong to you.' Alice stood back, watching hands dive into pockets as each one brought out a possession that belonged to someone else and took great delight in the entertainment, trying to find their rightful owners.

'Couldn't resist. That was definitely the last time. I promise. For real this time. Now, how about a sing-song? Mrs Heppler, you start us off.'

CHAPTER THIRTY-FIVE

January 1942 began with a life-changing decision overshadowed by a bittersweet life-changing opportunity.

Alice and Cam had been married for a couple of months and were making plans for their future in discussing the possibility of him going back to bull riding. He understood his wife's concern regarding his past injuries and she had seen for herself just how dangerous the sport could be. But she also saw the passion in his eyes whenever he spoke of the old times and when it came to it, she couldn't deny him his dream.

After numerous conversations, they decided to leave McKinnley Station and join the rodeo circuit before they had a family of their own. Having no commitments, apart from working at the Station, it was the perfect time as they were still very young. All they had to do now was to bite the bullet and break the good news.

But fate had intervened.

The following day, Mr Price had taken the radio call from

Cam's brother, Vincent, when Cam was working with the other stockmen in one of the outer paddocks to inform that their father had passed away.

On his return, Cam radioed his brother as they tried to come to terms with their loss. His heartstrings made him feel selfish and guilty for not returning home when he should have many years ago but reasoned that he always had his father's support and blessing while he travelled with his work.

During the radio call, Vincent enlightened him of the struggles that they had faced in order to keep the station afloat. The brothers knew that their father was a proud man, and because of this, Cam understood that he hadn't wanted him to know and return to the station out of duty.

Sitting by her husband's side, Alice thought that Vincent sounded down to Earth just like his brother who wasn't in any way malicious toward his sibling while he spoke gently in bringing Cam up to date. Cam learned that during the last couple of years, their father had declined in health and that the station became too much for the men to manage by themselves. The market had been slow and they couldn't afford to hire manpower, so they had moved what cattle they had left to within a more manageable area.

Alice felt their pain as the brothers discussed their father's funeral arrangements. Then Vincent surprised them by saying that he wanted to get on with his life and move away from the station and asked if Cam wanted to buy his share. Needing time to discuss while everything sank in, Cam said that he and Alice would talk to him more when they travelled up for the funeral the following week.

As by chance, Ernest was scheduled to make a mail delivery at McKinnley Station in three days. This enabled the newlyweds to arrange a return flight back with him to Burston as they would then travel to Fremantle then on to the Northern Territory. They were very grateful when Ernest said that he would reschedule his itinerary so that he could fly them direct to Fremantle to save them time.

It was within these precious three days that prompted Cam and Alice to have a more in-depth discussion about their future. It became apparent that they both felt the same to stay on permanently after the funeral and to make a go of it in the Northern Territory. While Cam knew it was the right thing to do, he still couldn't rid his guilt that it took an awful tragedy to make him realise where he should be. Although, in saying that, he also knew that if he hadn't followed his rodeo dream then he wouldn't be here at McKinnley Station and married to the most beautiful woman in the world.

Not wanting to wait until they had arrived, Cam had spoken a few more times with Vincent who was pleased that his brother and sister-in-law would return to the family property. During this period, he had obtained a valuation on the property and livestock so Cam and Alice knew the total they needed. Together with Cam's bull-riding money and wages and Alice's wages combined with her past winnings and her mother's money, they would have enough to buy Vincent's share and still have plenty over in which to invest in building up the livestock.

Their minds were set, but Alice still had to know for certain because it was only recently that they had discussed moving to the rodeo circuit.

'Yes, I am sure, Alice,' he had reassured. 'So much has happened this week that it's been a whirlwind. We are still young and our priorities have changed. This is a golden opportunity for us to own our own station and to build it up together. I will still have the chance to bull-ride when the rodeo comes to the district. We'll have the best of both worlds...'

'Then we're literally taking the bull by the horns!'

'Absolutely! And with you by my side, I can do anything. I love you so much.'

'And I love you, Cam. We were meant to be.'

All in all, since the initial radio call, it had been a very emotional week for everyone and a quick about-turn in Alice and Cam's lives as they packed up ready to farewell everyone at McKinnley Station to begin their next big adventure.

Just like when Alice had left Pip and Tish, she wanted a quick and swift goodbye. But the McKinnley team had persuaded her that they at least should have a special dinner for everyone the evening before they were due to leave. Alice had relented, knowing that it was as much for the team as it was for her and Cam. The evening had been part fun and banter with an underlying sadness where the mood carried through to breakfast as the couple said their final farewells.

Mrs Heppler ushered Alice out of the kitchen to head down to the corral fence. 'I'm really going to miss you around here...'

'Oh, Mrs Heppler, I am missing you all so much already. You have been a dear friend and confidant and I will cherish all our chats.' Alice began to laugh. 'Remembering when we first met...'

'Literally bumped into one another, how could I ever forget!'

'In all honesty, I was taken aback by your, how shall I say, unkempt appearance but now I understand. It gets extremely dusty and dirty out here.'

'That it does. I knew from the look on your face that you were weighing up what sex I was and don't worry, I get that a lot.' She laughed at Alice's expression that proved she was right.

'That is embarrassing. Sorry!' They hugged, cherishing their last moment that appeared to have come full circle.

'Remember, the world isn't as big anymore. Radio from time to time and we can catch up on news. And write too, Alice. Your days will be long and tiring but write a paragraph now and then, it will soon build up. We would all love to hear how you are going.'

'Will do. Thank you, Mrs Heppler. For everything.'

The McKinnley team approached and they waved them farewell when Squeak drove them down to the airstrip where Ernest was ready to fly them into Fremantle. Cam had held Alice throughout the journey. She had been emotional as yet again she farewelled lovely and kind people who had been family to her these past four years.

*

Vincent had greeted them at the airport and while they were driving to the Station, it warmed Alice's heart to hear the brothers reminisce their childhood memories. And it seemed they had gotten up to quite a few antics during that time. She was sad that she would never get to meet her father-in-law while the brothers recollected all the wonderful things that he had done for them in between discussing Station business and the handover details. Cam and Alice would be hitting the ground running, so it was good to be prepared for what they needed to do.

They had changed into their mourning attire at the airport in readiness for arriving at the Station for the funeral scheduled early that afternoon. Aware that Vincent would be leaving soon after the graveside service to be given by the district's minister, it turned out to be an extra solemn occasion. The attendees drove in convoy out to the small cemetery, around a mile from the homestead, where Cam introduced his wife to the minister and the owners of the two neighbouring stations who had come to pay their respects.

Vincent had prepared light refreshments back at the homestead and the graziers' wives had helped Alice in the kitchen. After an hour, the minister and neighbours said their goodbyes and wished them all the best for the future. Vincent walked one more time around the homestead then bade his farewell to his brother and new sister-in-law.

For him, the Station had been a place of sorrow these last few years and now he wanted to get on with the rest of his life. He planned on travelling around Australia until he found a place to settle. He was still a young man, but unlike Cam, he hadn't had the opportunity to venture away from the Station until now, so he was looking forward to making his own way in the world. His belongings were in the back of the truck, and he was ready to roll as he waved them goodbye.

Alice had fallen in love with the Station immediately.

The day had been crammed with a powerful gamut of emotions. From leaving everyone at McKinnley Station, to meeting her new brother-in-law, the funeral and now realising, that at twenty-two years of age, she finally had a home that she could call her own.

Without being deemed heartless or selfish, Alice felt happy. Her contentedness was overwhelming. She was married to a man whom she loved more than anything in the world and they now had their own home. Alice knew she belonged to this place. And more importantly, this was where they would raise their children.

Ever since Alice could walk, her father had exploited and exposed her to danger and she grew up believing she was worthless. But no more. She was finally free. She smiled with a vision of her mother jumping up and down clapping with glee that they were rid of him.

Suddenly overcome, she burst into tears as Cam rushed up and embraced his wife. They were in tune and he knew what she was feeling and held her.

'We're home, Alice. Please don't dwell on the past. We have a wonderful future to look forward to,' he assured. 'Come on, let's have a look around.'

Taking a deep breath, Alice nodded, blew her nose and put

her father out of her mind where he belonged. They walked up the wrap-around verandah steps while she was thinking that the rocking chairs would be the perfect place to watch the sunset after a long hard day. Then she laughed with glee when he scooped her up into his arms and carried her over the threshold.

The kitchen, like any homestead, was the heart of the station. 'I know you've already been in here and that you're keen to explore.' He was delighted and nodded to the far door. 'It's pretty much the same layout as the McKinnley homestead but a bit smaller. We have a living room, dining room, office, three bedrooms and as you know, the dunny is outside. Perhaps we will build one inside in the future, but for now we'll do a quick tour then you can take your time.'

Cam knew from her silence that she was overwhelmed by having her own home. His heart burst with pride as his wife ran her hands over the tops of the furniture as they went from room to room almost as if she were introducing herself. Each room had been kept clean and tidy and the quality wooden furniture matched throughout the property. She liked that the homestead was painted in white and knew that she would add coloured cushions like Mrs McKinnley had done where she changed the tones according to the season.

Their bedroom was larger than the others and the double iron bedstead was positioned facing the garden. There was a tall wardrobe, chest of drawers and two bedside tables. Vincent had thoughtfully placed a set of clean sheets on the mattress next to a blanket and pillows while Alice noticed some sheets billowing on the line at the end of the garden.

While the garden needed a little attention, it would be a great place to potter and she smiled when Mrs Heppler sprang to mind.

Coming back into the kitchen Alice once again admired the large sturdy table that had five chairs on either side and noted that the range cooker was plenty big enough to cater for the same. There was plenty of cupboards and workspace and in her mind, she was already planning on making matching curtains throughout. *Mrs McKinnley would be proud*, she thought.

The double dresser displayed beautiful blue and white crockery and she nodded, very much liking the theme. It gave a clean fresh feeling and complimented the white walls and she knew where she would place the picture that Tank from Nerra Creek had drawn of her and Lucy.

The pleasant reality was sinking in.

Yes, she was home.

Beyond the homestead were two outbuildings and, like McKinnley Station, they were built a good distance away from the homestead for fire prevention. Cam said they housed feed, straw, grain and machinery and when Alice spotted the small stable, she was smitten to see Fred and Ginger who were waiting patiently in their stalls. During the journey to the homestead, Vincent had told them that he had fed and watered the horses before he had left for the airport.

Fred and Ginger bobbed their heads, greeting their new owners, then while Alice was patting them, Cam brought the saddles and minutes later they went on a brief ride before dusk approached. They headed to the area where Cam knew the cattle were kept. Along the way, he noticed that the fencing was in good condition and again felt guilty that for all the years he had been away, it had taken the death of his father to bring him back home. All around was evidence of the sheer hard work that his father and brother had put into the place in order to keep their heads afloat. While he was determined not to dwell on what was impossible to change, he had pledged to work hard and to make Alice happy as they built up the business.

They had already discussed investing in two trained kelpies and had listened to Mr McKinnley's expert advice because he had bred and trained many successful litters.

'I still remember you telling me about when you first started at Nerra Creek.' Cam mocked a few evenings later over dinner. 'The relief you felt when you found out...'

'That the thousands of cattle didn't need milking! Yes, how green was I?' They laughed. 'Coming from the city, I thought that every cow needed milking. It wasn't until Harry told me that the cattle they had were for producing meat only, just like we have here. I didn't realise that for cows to produce milk they had to have given birth first. It was such a relief!'

'City people.' He winked at her. 'You're extremely lovable, Alice, but also very funny.'

CHAPTER THIRTY-SIX

'Do I still look pretty?' Alice asked when she dismounted and dusted herself down, knowing full well that she looked an utter mess. She was hot and bothered and could feel that her hair was weighed down with dust and grime as it felt cloggy and dirty to touch. She was also aware that she had accumulated dust in other places that just didn't belong. Above the need for food, she wanted a bath, clean hair and sleep.

'You'll always look beautiful to me.' He smiled and helped her unsaddle Ginger, who neighed in readiness for her feed while Dudley, Alice's kelpie, barked around them.

'Liar.' She smiled at the man she loved more than life itself. He took her into his arms and hugged her tightly. Then they fed and watered the animals.

'I've missed you today, you scruffy, dirty and smelly woman.'

'Hey, that's hurtful.'

'It's what you call me when I return from rounding up the cattle.'

'I never called you a woman!'

They both broke into raucous laughter.

'Come this way, I've a surprise for you.' He led her out of the stables and down to the outbuilding that housed the machinery.

'What are we doing down this way, Cam? I'm tired and dirty and as you pointed out, very smelly. I just want a bath and sleep.'

'Your wish is my command, dear lady.' And as they neared the side of the building, Alice was greeted by a campfire and the heavenly smell coming from a pan that was cooking something mouth-wateringly delicious.

'I don't believe it!' she marvelled, then eyed the old bathtub that they hadn't used before, just down from the fire. It looked almost full and appeared to have lather on the top. Also scattered around the bath on upturned logs of different heights were lit candles in jars.

'Cam, this is wonderful, I should go out more often! But wait, we've not used this area much in the last six months – what about snakes?'

'Taken care of. Come on, Alice, I'm a stockman – I do this for a living, you know. Don't worry,' he said reassuringly while she began to unbutton her shirt.

'Here,' he said, prompting her to sit in the chair by the water pump. 'Let me wash your hair for you first – you'll feel a lot better for it and the water won't get so dirty.'

'You think of everything.' She sat and leant her head backwards over the top of the old chair and felt pure joy when the first pump of tepid water soaked her head and soothed her scalp. 'Oh, my goodness that feels soooo good,' she purred as he then lathered up and washed and rinsed her hair. He then lathered up again and took his time to massage her scalp then eased his fingers through her long blonde locks. Alice was in heaven and his rhythmic fingers sent shivers, tingles and sensual sensations all over her body.

Cam was pleased that she was enjoying the treatment and again rinsed through. 'How was that?'

Alice was in a pleasant trance and didn't want to move and lose the sensation. 'That was amazing, total bliss. Thank you.'

'You are very welcome.' He handed her a towel and she wrapped up her hair. 'Your bath awaits,' he said, finishing unbuttoning her shirt then led her towards the bath where she fully undressed.

She took his hand while she stepped up and in and discovered that the water was the same perfect temperature as the pump and sat down. Cam took a few steps backwards, not taking his eyes off of her for a moment and bit his lip to stop himself from smiling from sheer anticipation as opposed to appreciating her beautiful body.

A split-second later, Alice shot up and was out of the bath, staring daggers at him who burst into laughter.

'You're a total shit, Cam!' she shouted. 'I cannot believe you even thought to do that.' She reached into the bottom of the bath and brought out the snake. 'I'll get you back for this, you'll see. You scared me out of my wits!' Alice started laughing and threw the dead snake in his direction.

'One I found earlier. Knew that would wake you up.'

He grinned, then he picked up his wife and gently placed her back into the tub.

'Don't know how I put up with you, you rat.' She reached up to kiss him then pulled him into the tub giving him a thorough soaking as a big wave of water splashed over the sides.

'I love you, but you're still a shit,' she said and kissed him deeply.

*

Alice and Cam had put in long hard days and were building up the business and in nearly two years, they had almost doubled their livestock to three thousand head of cattle. They also had five kelpies, a henhouse full of chooks and roosters and Alice's pride and joy, her beloved goat, Barry.

There was no denying that Barry was quite a character and Cam was puzzled as he often watched him follow his wife around the station like a puppy. Barry also liked to roam around the homestead, particularly around the kitchen, hoping for any tasty morsel that would come his way. He also knew Alice's routine when she secured him in the loafing shed's enclosure for the night, also referred by her as the goatery.

*

It was early.

Too early in fact.

All was quiet when Cam stirred. He had been in a deep sleep and his senses were coming to the surface. He could feel it was humid but before he even opened his eyes, his nostrils twitched detecting the non-mistakable aroma of Barry the goat. Cam tried to ignore it, hoping it would go away, but every couple of seconds, he could feel his breath on his face and the sharp prong of a protruding chin hair on his cheek whenever Barry moved his head.

Cam opened one eye. A large nose was just a couple of inches away and as if on cue Barry moved his lips upwards almost in a smile displaying his large teeth and uttered a little good morning bleat. Cam reached out and gently pushed him away and swung his legs over the side of the bed starting the day with a cuss. Barry bleated another welcome and Alice opened her eyes and giggled when her husband again cursed the wretched goat.

'Why aren't you in the goatery?' he asked and he received a *maaah* in response. 'Is goatery even a word?'

'I don't know and I don't care. It's cute and Barry's very clever, he lets himself out of the enclosure. Cup of tea?'

'Is that right, Barry, you let yourself out?'

Barry drew back his lips again and left the room. 'Can't believe I'm talking to a goat.'

He laughed.

Cam and Alice had been discussing the fact that they would soon need an extra pair of hands, particularly now that they were expecting their first child. Everyone at McKinnley was so delighted to hear their good news and before they all knew it, with Mr McKinnley's permission, Squeak had travelled to the Northern Territory to help them out while Alice took a break from jillaroo duties.

'Come on, Squeak. Help me out here.' Alice then turned to Cam. 'It'll be fun and you know I've always wanted another goat.'

'Yes, I know. You already have Barry, isn't that enough?' He lifted his eyebrows. 'What kind of a name is that for a goat anyway?'

'It'll be fun, no kidding.' She laughed. 'Get it? Kidding! I said we'd meet Mr Jarvis from the next station; he's got some for sale.'

'Some? Alice, you said some?'

'Barry will need a few friends, won't he? I'd said we'd meet Mr Jarvis on Wednesday. Plenty of time to extend the goatery...'

Squeak couldn't stop laughing. 'Is that even a word?' he asked and Cam nodded and pointed out to Squeak that he had asked the same.

'Probably not, but you knew what I meant, Squeak. Come on, Cam. You know you want to...'

'If it keeps you happy, my love, who am I to say otherwise.' They all laughed and finished their dinner.

*

Alice never took her home for granted and had loved and enjoyed every minute caring for it and making it her own. Her only regret was not knowing Cam's parents as their photographs took pride of place on the sideboard. It was only right because they were a huge part of the station's history. She also loved to see the photographs of Cam and Vincent when they were children.

Regularly, Alice picked up a small glass trinket dish that held the silver four-leafed clover pendant given by Mr and Mrs Wyatt all those years ago and alongside the dish was her mother's locket. She had kept the locket open to display the only picture that she had of her mother and grandparents.

Never would she forget all the wonderful people that had helped and loved her during her journey. She had kept in constant touch via the radio with Harry and Marion and the team from Nerra Creek alongside everyone at McKinnley Station, in particular Mrs Heppler, Mrs McKinnley and Elsa. Pip, Tish and her Aunt Vera did not have a radio so Alice telephoned them whenever she could when she was in town and they also corresponded via letter.

She always hoped that Pip, Tish and Aunt Vera would visit the homestead in the not-too-distant future but knew, deep down, that it wasn't a possibility. No matter how remote they lived, communication and comforting familiar voices were just a radio or telephone call away. And that was great for her soul and peace of mind.

*

The scream brought Alice out of a nightmare.

'Another one?' he asked, already knowing the answer. He felt so much for his wife, knowing that her past still troubled her and they had both worried wondering if the baby would be affected. It had torn his heart out trying to imagine what she had endured.

He would never forget how alarmed and angry he had been when she first told him about her recurring nightmares.

She described in horrifying detail as a child when her father and Alfie had dumped a dead body in her room in the middle of the night.

Cam knew Alice's history and that his father-in-law was a pickpocket, a crook and a murderer who ruled the house with fear. He vowed that if ever he would see him in another life, he would take great delight in showing him how he truly felt.

From the beginning, he had reasoned with Alice that her beginning was not her fault. That she wasn't responsible for the environment in which she had been born into. He told her that she was a good decent person and that she had turned her life around by her own doing and sheer hard work. She was tough, she was strong and a far better person than her father could ever have hoped to be.

More than anything, Cam understood. They had found and had belonged to each other.

'It's alright, Cam. At least the nightmares are not as frequent nowadays.'

He held her while they talked in the darkness.

'Throughout my childhood in my bleakest moments of despair, I always knew that you were out there waiting for me. You were my sunshine to disperse the dark clouds and deemed you as my...'

'Glorious sunshine awaits.' He finished her saying and kissed her forehead.

Alice smiled. How she loved this man.

CHAPTER THIRTY-SEVEN

During the summer of 1944, Alice gave birth to a son who they named Patrick Anthony, after Cam's father, then during the next five years they welcomed Rose Phillipa and Vera Patricia.

Squeak had stayed on at Beech Station, as renamed by Alice after Pip and Tish's house in the Blue Mountains. Squeak had married Madeline, a lovely girl that he had met during the district rodeo a couple of years back. They both lived on the Station in their own house that Cam had helped them build and were awaiting the arrival of their first child.

Cam's love of bull riding continued and he participated every year at the district rodeo. It was also a great opportunity to catch up with their neighbouring stations and to talk about new methods and machinery.

*

It was during the rodeo of 1961 when they were walking toward the arena for Cam to prepare for the next event when

Alice heard someone call their names.

'Alice? Cam?' asked a young man who was perhaps in his early thirties.

They both looked at him for a few seconds before there was a slight hint of recognition and when he said his name they responded with glee, 'Jack McKinnley! It is you. My goodness, how are you?'

They hugged.

'I'm well, thank you. It's so good to see you. May I introduce my wife, Maggie and our dear friends, Emily and Mellow.'

'Alice and Cam worked on our Station way back, I must've been about eight years old when Alice arrived...'

'Eight. Crickey, time flies, doesn't it?' she said.

'Oh, my goodness!' Maggie was astonished as everyone looked at her. 'I can't believe it. You're Alice? *The Alice?*' Maggie embraced the woman. 'You wrote to me in England, years back and you told me that you won a buckle in a rodeo...'

'Maggie from England! Yes, I remember. And now you're here and married to Jack. That's amazing how things turn out isn't it?' she said.

'Yes, it is. I have something for you,' said Maggie as she unclasped her belt and started to take it off much to the bewilderment of the others. Maggie began to slide off the buckle and said with joy, 'This is yours, Alice. You should have it back.' She placed the buckle into Alice's hand.

Alice turned it over and over and studied it before looking up at Maggie in astonishment. She nodded her head as Alice then beamed with delight as they hugged again.

'From the stables, remember, Jack?' said Maggie as she explained to Emily, Mellow and Cam. 'When I first arrived, I spotted the buckle in the stables with the carving on the wall. "RIP Finn".'

'Finn was my horse when I worked at McKinnley. Goodness, I haven't thought of him in years,' said Alice fondly. 'He was a beautiful boy but broke his front leg in a horrid fall and had to be put down.'

'That's awful,' said Emily.

'Yes, it was,' said Alice.

'The stables burnt down a while back,' continued Maggie. 'And I found the buckle in the ashes, so I polished it back up and kept it safe. And now it's reunited with its rightful owner. It couldn't be more perfect.'

'Thank you, Maggie, that is so kind of you, but no need. You should keep it.'

'Please, Alice. It is yours I wouldn't have it any other way.'

She smiled. 'Thank you again, Maggie. Sorry all, but we need to dash. I'll see you at the main event a little later.'

'I'm the bull rider,' said Cam. 'Perhaps we can all catch up afterwards for a beer and talk over old times?'

'We'll look forward to it, Cam, and good luck,' said Jack.

A short while later, Alice made her way over to the stands and caught up with Jack, Maggie, Emily and Mellow. 'Hi all. Cam should be on soon. Do you know'—Alice made her way over to Emily and embraced her tightly—'the penny dropped that you're *Pickle*. For the life of me before, I didn't associate Emily with Pickle. Remembering back, I knew your name was Emily, but still had the name Pickle in my mind, so sorry!'

Emily couldn't stop laughing. 'Yes, I am! It's been a while and it just occurred to me as well. I was so young when you left that I didn't realise it was you when we saw you earlier.'

'It's a small world. How's your mother? Oh, how I love Mrs Heppler. I know we talk on the radio but it's been a while. Time goes so fast.'

'She's very well and she will be over the moon that I have met up with you.'

Alice sat between Maggie and Emily, feeling a bond with the young women. The crowd started to cheer when they saw that the first bull rider was preparing himself in the bucking chute before being catapulted into the arena hoping to hold on for the most dangerous eight seconds of his life.

The rider was successful and gained valuable points where he acknowledged the crowd and Alice saw that Cam was next to go. Alice gained a huge respect for the sport and knew what it entailed and what the riders and bullfighters, or rodeo clowns, went through by putting their lives on the line.

Maggie and Emily felt Alice stiffen when the bucking chute opened and Cam was spun wildly into the arena by the powerful rearing beast. The women put their arms around Alice and the eight seconds felt like eight hours as they then all joined the crowd by springing to their feet and applauded a perfect round. Alice said a silent prayer of thanks that he was safe when he bowed to the crowd, seeking out Alice as he always did, and blew her a kiss to which she always returned.

'That was awesome, Cam,' said Jack, slapping him on the back.

'Thanks, Jack. How about we all go and get a beer to celebrate catching up with dear friends?'

*

Alice was content and exceptionally happy with her beautiful family, home and business and often counted her blessings that she had such a loving and supportive husband. They often took a little quiet time at the end of the day to sit on the gate to the paddock to admire the vivid sunset over the horizon.

'I had the best time this afternoon.' Alice beamed.

'Ah, you spoke to Pip, Tish and your aunt. How are they?'

'As always, they were on top form. I'm so pleased that they now have had a radio installed. It means I can talk to them more often!' She smiled. 'Aunt Vera is still buzzing from living with Pip and Tish in the Blue Mountains. I was so pleased when she sold her *guest house.*' They both laughed as Cam knew the whole story. 'They get along famously and look out for one another. Do you know that they still travel to the distillery now and again? I used to get worried about them, but even though they are all practically in their nineties, I know that they are capable.'

'They sound like great characters and it won't be long until our visit. After all that you have told me, I am looking forward to getting to meet them all.'

'They will love you, Cam.'

'And I will love them too as I have a lot to thank them for.

We're very fortunate, Alice,' he said, putting his arm around her. She nodded and placed her head on his shoulder. 'We have each other and our noisy, lively and crazy family.' They laughed. 'And this amazing place. Who could want for more?'

'No one could want for more. Absolutely no one. I love you.'

'Not as much as I love you. You're my world, you're our children's world and beyond all that, you're the most amazing woman. You're beautiful inside and out, kind and forever funny. But more importantly, you are your own person and never, as you once believed, just a pickpocket's daughter.'

Looking up at her husband she was warmed by his praise and moving words and loved him more than she thought possible. They kissed for just a few moments before they were interrupted...

'Ma!' shouted their youngest daughter. 'Barry's loose. You'll never guess what he's gone and done now...'

ACKNOWLEDGEMENTS

I wish to extend endless thanks to my supportive family and friends in Australia and England as you have all played a valued role in bringing this book to completion. I appreciate your uplifting encouragement and asking how my writing is going where it is always a 'made my day' moment.

To my husband, Wayne, I have only achieved my third book because of your selfless dedication and hard work in keeping everything ticking over while also keeping our lively pups entertained, allowing me to write. Now that's a lot of love and belief as I spent time with my 'other' family. Thank you xx

Special thanks to you, Kelly, because not only have you been an absolute gem with helping your old mum on her author journey, but you also found the time to get married this year! Dad and I wish you both every happiness.

Immense gratitude, Matt, for all your technical support, advice and gifting me the best tools of the trade. Not forgetting all those mochachoccalattes!

To my A1 Dad. Although this book completes my promised trio, I will keep going because I am loving the dream. Your endless support means the world and I hope that you will love Barry the goat – I couldn't resist.

Thank you, Debbie and Kelly, for your valued input as we struggled with the elusive title!

To Jim, huge thanks for every book sale. I very much appreciate your continued support and that of your customers.

My heartfelt gratitude to Bradley Shaw and the Shawline team. Thank you for believing in my story and giving me the opportunity to be a proud member of your author family. My heart is still smiling.

To Melinda for your awesome cover design, I absolutely love it! And to Alana, for being the most fabulous 'go to'. Also, a special shout-out to my editor, Katrina. Thank you for your guidance and feedback and for gently nudging me toward my creative conflict limit, you're the best!

And to my valued readers, I hope that you will love Alice as much as I do and that she will remain in your heart long after you turn the final page.

Shawline Publishing Group Pty Ltd
www.shawlinepublishing.com.au

SHAWLINE
PUBLISHING
GROUP

More great Shawline titles can be found by scanning the QR code below.
New titles also available through Books@Home Pty Ltd.
Subscribe today at www.booksathome.com.au or scan the QR code below.

Milton Keynes UK
Ingram Content Group UK Ltd.
UKHW022244270923
429475UK00015B/476